A WINTER KISS

on Rochester Mews

Annie Darling lives in London in a tiny flat, which is bursting at the seams with teetering piles of books.

Her two greatest passions in life are romance novels and Mr Mackenzie, her British Shorthair cat.

Also by Annie Darling:

The Little Bookshop of Lonely Hearts
True Love at the Lonely Hearts Bookshop
Crazy in Love at the Lonely Hearts Bookshop

A WINTER KISS
on Rochester Mews

ANNIE DARLING

HarperCollins*Publishers*

HarperCollins*Publishers* Ltd
1 London Bridge Street
London SE1 9GF

www.harpercollins.co.uk

Published by HarperCollins*Publishers* 2018
1

A catalogue record for this book
is available from the British Library

ISBN: 978-0-00-827567-9

This novel is entirely a work of fiction.
The names, characters and incidents portrayed in it are
the work of the author's imagination. Any resemblance to
actual persons, living or dead, events or localities is
entirely coincidental.

Typeset in Bembo by Palimpsest Book Production Ltd, Falkirk, Stirlingshire

Printed and bound in Great Britain by
CPI Group (UK) Ltd, Croydon CR0 4YY

MIX
Paper from
responsible sources
FSC™ C007454

This book is produced from independently certified FSC™ paper
to ensure responsible forest management.

For more information visit: www.harpercollins.co.uk/green

Dedicated to Mr Mackenzie,
the most splendid specimen of felinity in the world.

CHAPTER

1

30 days until Christmas

'Goodbye! Do come again!' With a bright smile, Matilda Smith ushered her last customer of the day out of the door of the Happy Ever After tearooms and hurried to lock it behind them. Her mobile phone, in the pocket of her apron, had been buzzing like a furious bee with incoming text messages for the last five minutes.

Mattie pulled out her still vibrating and flashing phone to read her messages; all of them from one person.

EMERGENCY MEETING!!!!!

The urgent capital letters left Mattie unmoved. She'd been on her feet since seven that morning and her feet were about to go on strike, so this so-called emergency meeting could do without her.

'I thought Beige Anorak would never go,' Mattie

remarked of their most frequent customer. 'I've a good mind to tell him that he can only hog a table of four for a maximum of one hour.'

'At least he shared the table this time,' Cuthbert pointed out as he slowly and lovingly wiped down Jezebel the coffee machine. Her old barista, Paloma, had left to go travelling and Mattie had despaired that she'd ever find someone who could handle the very temperamental Jezebel, until she'd met seventy-two-year-old Cuthbert Lewis.

Mattie's phone vibrated again. Another message from a person who really needed to stop using shouty capslock and, instead, get to the point.

THIS IS NOT A DRILL, THIS IS A GENUINE EMERGENCY!!!!!

'I bet it's not a genuine emergency,' Mattie exclaimed out loud.

'Trouble at t'mill?' Cuthbert asked.

'Just the usual flapping from next door.'

Cuthbert cocked his head in the direction of the set of glass-panelled double doors to the left of the counter. 'They are rather prone to flapping, it's true. Whereas you and I are of a calmer disposition.'

Now that Beige Anorak was finally gone, Mattie could get on with washing the floor. She plunged her mop into the bucket of soapy hot water that she'd filled earlier. 'We are a flap-free zone. Not like *them*.'

Mattie and Cuthbert were their own little fiefdom within the wider territory of Happy Ever After, the bookshop that lay beyond the glass-panelled double doors. The tearooms had their own traditions, their own way of doing things, their own set of rules, but they co-existed quite peacefully alongside the bookshop. They made sure that no customers brought books they hadn't already paid for into the tearooms to spill food and drink all over them. They checked daily that Strumpet, the portly, gluttonous cat who belonged to Verity, Happy Ever After's manager, was safely locked in the flat above the shop. There had been several incidents when Strumpet had staged a prison break and headed straight for the tearooms and the lap of anyone who had cake.

EMERGENCY MEETING IN THE MIDNIGHT BELL NOW!!!!!! WHY ARE YOU IGNORING MY TEXTS? HAVE I MENTIONED THIS IS AN EMERGENCY?

'Why she can't just toddle fifty metres and tell me in person, I don't know,' Mattie murmured, as she paused mopping to read yet another panic-stricken text message.

'A lady in her condition can't be toddling here and there,' Cuthbert noted as he gave Jezebel one last affectionate buffing.

Cuthbert was right. Cuthbert was usually right about all things.

Mattie swirled the mop in a hard-to-reach corner. 'Yes, but . . . but . . . she's managing to toddle all the way to The Midnight Bell for a so-called emergency meeting,' she said. 'Shall I make your apologies?'

'If you will. My Cynthia will already have my dinner on,' he said of the love of his life, his wife. 'Now you get your beauty sleep, my darling,' he ordered his sidechick,

3

draping a special cover over Jezebel. 'It's another busy day tomorrow, so you need your rest.'

It was so tempting to ask Cuthbert if he and Jezebel would like some privacy. Mattie shook her head, patted Cuthbert on the shoulder as she squeezed past him (it was a tight fit behind the counter) to empty the bucket and finish tidying away. 'I'll see you tomorrow then, Cuthbert.'

'Indeed you will,' Cuthbert agreed, shrugging on his coat and donning a nifty trilby hat for the five-minute walk home to a flat in the beautiful, Art Deco 1920s Housing Association estate just around the corner.

Mattie's phone trembled again.

DON'T IGNORE ME, MATTIE! WHY ARE YOU IGNORING ME?

It probably would be a good idea to reply to one of these so-called urgent text messages, Mattie decided.

I'm not ignoring you. I'm doing my next-day prep and I'll see you in The Midnight Bell when I'm done. I hope you'll have a large glass of white wine and a bowl of cheesy chips waiting for me. Mattie x

She didn't even need to take one full step to enter the tiny kitchen shielded from public view by a curtain adorned with little teapots. So tiny was the kitchen that if Mattie stretched out her arms she could touch the walls.

But she didn't stretch out her arms, instead she washed her hands, then set to work making the flaky pastry for tomorrow's viennoiserie: croissants, pains au chocolat, pains aux raisins and several other buttery, melt-in-the-mouth delights. The dough needed to chill overnight, which was why Mattie wasn't currently quaffing Chenin Blanc in the pub.

Before she took off her apron and retrieved her handbag from the one cupboard that she had room for in the kitchen, Mattie pulled out her compact to confirm what she already knew: her face – skin the colour of the lightest, most delicate caramel sauce with a smattering of freckles across the bridge of her nose – needed a generous dusting of matte powder to tone down the effects of slaving over a hot stove all day. Adding a slick of tawny-pink lipstick, a re-application of mascara and a quick check that the two flicks of liquid eyeliner from this morning were still in place, all she needed to do was make sure that there weren't any flour or grease stains on her black trousers and jumper, and Mattie was good to go.

It helped that she had a look and she stuck to it rigidly. Mattie had seen the film *Funny Face* at an impressionable age and even though she was now a very grown-up twenty-eight, she still wished that she was Audrey Hepburn, the bookshop clerk who jetted off to Paris with Fred Astaire and modelled for a fashion magazine when she wasn't dancing to freeform jazz in seedy bars.

Not only did Mattie now work *next door* to a bookshop, she'd also been to Paris. In fact, she'd lived in Paris for three whole years and had danced to freeform jazz in seedy bars on several occasions. But that was long in the past and Paris was now dead to her, yet she still dressed like Audrey Hepburn in *Funny Face*: long, dark-brown hair caught up in a ponytail with a blunt-cut thick fringe which was the perfect foil for her permanently arched eyebrows, above eyes which were the exact same shade as a mink coat her grandmother had once owned.

And like Audrey, Mattie always wore black. Before Paris and especially after Paris, she wore black. In summer, a black cotton shirt with the sleeves rolled up to her elbows and slim-fit black cropped cigarette pants, and the same pair of Birkenstocks she'd been wearing in summer for years. On winter days like today, she swapped the shirt for a jumper, the cropped trousers for a longer version and the Birks for a pair of black Chuck Taylors.

Wearing the same thing every day (Mattie had many black shirts, jumpers and trousers, both cropped and long – it wasn't like she wore the same two pieces every day until they crawled to the wash basket of their own accord) was practical and quick. No agonising over a wardrobe full of different colours and styles. Which was just as well, because as Mattie stepped out onto the cobblestones of Rochester Mews and locked the front door behind her, she'd be unlocking it again at seven thirty the next morning. Such was the lot of someone who had a hell of a lot of breakfast pastries to bake before the tearooms opened at 9 a.m.

Mattie's phone buzzed insistently.

WHERE ARE YOU? HOW LONG DOES IT TAKE TO CHUCK TOGETHER SOME FLAKY PASTRY?

But that was tomorrow. And Mattie wasn't going to think about tomorrow, especially the part where she had to get up at six, while it was still dark. She was going to think about the large glass of wine that she hoped was waiting for her.

Mattie wasn't disappointed. As soon as she hefted open the heavy door of the pub around the corner from Happy Ever After, swapping the waft of fish and chips from There's No Plaice Like Home opposite for the fug of beer, someone waved frantically at her.

'Mattie! Over here!' yelled Posy, the owner of Happy Ever After and sender of multiple, needlessly dramatic text messages, as if they hadn't bagged their usual corner table and banquettes and Mattie might not know where they were. 'Your wine is perfectly chilled.'

Mattie dropped gratefully onto an empty stool and picked up the glass of Chenin Blanc. 'Thank you,' she said fervently. 'And cheers.'

As they all clinked glasses, Mattie checked for panic in the eyes of her co-workers. Posy, who was fairly heavy with child and drinking elderflower cordial and soda, the glass resting on the top of her bump, looked serene. Verity, the manager of the bookshop, was nursing a gin and tonic and a faintly harried expression, but then Verity always looked faintly harried. And then there was Tom, and Mattie didn't really care what Tom's mental state was because Tom was on her list.

Mattie's list, as Tom well knew, was not a good list to be on, so she ignored him.

'How are you?' she asked Posy and Verity. 'How was the world of bookselling today?'

'Very, very busy,' Posy noted with a quiet satisfaction. She rubbed her bump and then very gently and delicately burped. 'Thank God for that. Have I mentioned that I have the worst indigestion?'

She had. Several times a day, ever since her three-month mark had passed and she was able to tell people that she was pregnant. Now she was almost at seven months and couldn't even look at a tomato any more, much less eat one.

'I read somewhere that if you have indigestion when you're pregnant, you'll give birth to a baby with a freakishly full head of hair,' Verity said, which did little to cheer Posy up.

'Sebastian has very thick hair, so it's obviously all his fault,' she said mournfully. 'I wish I'd fallen in love with a bald man instead.'

Fascinating though this was, it didn't really explain why Mattie had been summoned so urgently. 'What was with all the emergency text messages?' Mattie asked. 'Is Rochester Mews earmarked for demolition or something?'

'What? No! It's much more serious than that.' Posy gasped. She turned a suddenly anxious face to Mattie. 'Have you any idea what the date is?'

Was it some kind of trick question or was it pregnancy brain? Mattie glanced over at Verity, who shook her head as if to say that she'd already had a similar enquiry from Posy. And then Mattie managed to catch Tom's eye. She couldn't help but recoil and Tom's upper lip curled, which meant that he was about to make some dull observation, but before he could, Posy clapped her hands.

'It's the twenty-fifth of November,' she cried. 'The twenty-fifth? Do you know what that means, Mattie?'

'Is it one of those random national days that have been invented by advertisers or PRs? National Pie Day? No, I'd know about it if it were. National Hug A Puppy Day?'

'I think it must be National Humour Pregnant Ladies Day,' Tom murmured with the little smirk that someone needed to tell him was very unattractive.

'No! More like National Annoy Pregnant Ladies Day,' Posy snapped, digging Tom in the ribs with her elbow, which wiped the smirk off his face pretty sharpish. 'It's a month until Christmas! Worse! There are only thirty days in November so actually, it's thirty days until Christmas. Thirty days!'

Her panicked statement was met with blank looks.

'How is this news to you?' Tom ventured, adjusting his horn-rimmed glasses so he could peer sternly at Posy's flushed face. 'You can't turn on a TV without falling over some cloying, sentimental Christmas ad featuring woodland animals. The supermarkets have been flogging mince pies and stuffing balls since August.'

Tom had a point. 'Surely you noticed the streets of London are adorned with Christmas lights and decorations?' Mattie asked.

Posy placed a hand on either side of her bump. 'Forgive me for being a little preoccupied,' she said huffily.

'I have mentioned Christmas promotions and extended opening hours *several* times,' Verity said in a more concil-iatory tone. 'We had a whole conversation about getting new Christmas lights for the trees in the mews.'

'No. Nope, I have no memory of that,' Posy insisted, her voice starting to tremble, which meant that soon she would be crying. When she wasn't trying to burp, Posy was trying not to cry – pregnancy really didn't agree with her. 'And now I've had an email from the Rochester Street Traders' Association demanding that I pay my share for our joint Christmas decorations, and all the other shops are doing extended opening . . .'

'Yes, I did already mention this,' Verity murmured as Mattie shot her a sympathetic look. 'Quite a few times, as it goes.'

'You should have mentioned it more forcefully,' Posy said, shifting on the banquette to find a more comfortable position. 'There's so much to do. We haven't put up any tinsel or even done a display of books that would make wonderful Christmas presents.' She wrung her hands. 'Mattie! Why haven't you started selling mince pies? You're normally much more organised than this.'

Mattie prided herself on her organisational skills but she refused to rise to the bait. She was not going to flap. 'I already have my Christmas bakes planned, which will come into effect on December first and not a day before. Not everyone wants Christmas rammed down their throats as soon as the clocks go back.'

'Pret A Manger have been selling their Christmas sandwiches for weeks, M&S too,' Tom said, and he should know, because he *never* bought his lunch from the tearooms. If he had, he'd have found it particularly delicious and filling and he wouldn't have to hog the cheesy chips like he was currently doing.

Mattie firmed her lips. She wasn't going to flap. Nope. Even though Tom always made her want to flap and hiss like an angry cat.

'Well, Waterstones have had *their* Christmas promotions in place for *weeks*,' she countered. Tom lifted his glass of wine as if to say 'Touché' but it had a detrimental effect on Posy who moaned as if she was in pain and clutched her bump as if an alien were about to burst out of it.

'We need to have a Christmas brainstorm. NOW,' she proclaimed in a shrill voice.

'I thought this *was* a Christmas brainstorm?' Mattie said, because Posy loved a brainstorm almost as much as she loved Sebastian, tote bags with book quotes on them and romantic novels.

'It's more of a pre-Christmas-brainstorm brainstorm,' Tom explained helpfully as he refused to relinquish his grip on the bowl of cheesy chips, moving it out of Mattie's reach when she tried to make a grab for it. 'Oi, get your own.'

'December first is plenty of time to launch all our Christmas plans,' Verity said firmly, prying the bowl from Tom's hand and moving it back towards Mattie. 'And I hate to play the vicar's-daughter card, but technically you shouldn't put up Christmas decorations until Christmas Eve, and also *technically*, we shouldn't really have a Christmas brainstorm without Nina. Nina *loves* Christmas.'

'Oh, I miss Nina!' Posy exclaimed and the first tear began its slow descent down her right cheek.

'Everyone misses Nina,' Mattie said softly, because when

11

Posy was having a maudlin moment it was best not to make any loud noises. 'But she'll be back soon, right? She was only meant to have been gone six months, and she left in May, and it's almost the end of November.'

Nina was a dearly beloved but absent member of the Happy Ever After family because she was currently road-tripping across the United States with her boyfriend, Noah, while working on the shop's marketing remotely. She was the perfect, exuberant foil for quiet Verity, panicky Posy and Tom. Dour, sarcastic, up-himself Tom.

'Well, I hope she comes back before I give birth,' Posy lamented. 'I would like to go on maternity leave before I actually start my contractions. Ugh! Contractions! Honestly, this pregnancy lark is one catastrophe after another. Have I mentioned my swollen ankles? Anyway, what are we going to do about Christmas? There's so much to sort out and no time at all! We're screwed. So very screwed.'

'Not screwed. Christmas bakes are locked down and ready to go,' Mattie said a little desperately. She wasn't a big fan of Christmas and all these histrionics about the run-up to December twenty-fifth were giving her a leaden feeling in the pit of her stomach. 'Anyway, how long does it take to pin up a bit of tinsel?'

'We're going to have to do a bit more than pin up tinsel,' Posy said, the tears now a steady stream. Tom inched down the banquette to distance himself from a sobbing woman, a look of pure dread on his normally quite lofty-looking face.

'Help!' he mouthed at Mattie and Verity. Mattie shrugged and Verity sighed, then leaned forward.

'I was going to wait . . . But, well, no time like the present, and there doesn't seem any point in delaying the news, does there, not if we're about to start opening late every night, and it's not a big deal, really just a medium-sized deal.' Verity's ramble had stemmed Posy's tears and she was now looking quite stricken. Even Tom seemed to realise that this warranted putting down the bowl of cheesy chips.

'Oh my God, are you resigning?' he asked, which was what Posy had suspected too, if the devastated expression on her face was anything to go by.

'No! Don't be silly. Why would I resign?' Verity asked in bewilderment. 'What a weird conclusion to come to. Although . . . I suppose in a way I am resigning.'

'Please, Very, my blood pressure can't take many shocks,' Posy moaned.

'Christ, spit it out, Very, or kill me now,' Tom snapped and for once, Mattie found herself in agreement. Verity looked up to the heavens. 'I'm resigning . . .' She paused and there was a collective intake of breath which made Mattie suspect that Verity was enjoying this a little bit too much, '. . . from my tenancy of the flat above the shop. Though I do feel rather validated that you were all terrified I was leaving Happy Ever After. It's nice to know I'm wanted.'

'For one awful second I thought I'd have to do the VAT returns on my own and my whole life flashed before my eyes,' Mattie said and Posy reached across the table, with some difficulty, to clink her glass in solidarity.

'You and me both,' she said, then turned her woeful face to Verity. 'When are you moving out? The new year?'

'Well, a bit sooner than that. If we start extended opening hours, which will mean opening on a Sunday, then I guess it will have to be . . . well, the day after tomorrow, if that's OK,' Verity said apologetically. 'I could leave it until the new year, but Johnny has had one of those boiling-water taps installed so I can have instant tea, and he's had a new window seat put in my favourite reading nook, it's very comfy, and I spend all my time round his anyway . . . Oh! Yeah, I would be moving in with Johnny,' she added, as though there had been any question.

Johnny was Verity's beloved. A posh architect, who, much like Darcy in Verity's favourite book *Pride and Prejudice*, with his 'very fine grounds at Pemberley', had a five-bedroom house in Canonbury and no one to share it with. Until now.

'Oh! Very! Why didn't you say something earlier?' Posy exclaimed, grabbing Verity's hand. 'Let's look at the ring! Oh . . . no ring.'

'Because we're not actually engaged. Just living together.'

'Living in sin,' Tom intoned, his hands in the prayer position, now that he'd eaten every single last cheesy chip without any thought for anyone else. 'And you a vicar's daughter, too.'

'You know, Tom, that's Nina's line, you can't really pull

it off,' Verity said. 'And also, hello, welcome to the twenty-first century.'

Mattie was delighted for Verity, she really was. Even if living with a man was her idea of hell. She tried to smile happily and sincerely while she wondered what would be an acceptable period of time to pass before she could ask, plead, even beg Posy to be allowed to . . .

'Well, if Very's moving out, then I'll take her room,' Tom said calmly, as if his living rent-free in the flat above the shop was a done deal. 'That's fair, isn't it?'

'Wait, no, it's not at all fair!' Mattie exclaimed. 'I was about to ask if I could take the room.'

'Well, you should have been quicker,' Tom said in that patronising way of his that made Mattie want to bash him over the head with the nearest heavy object to hand. In this case, a fire extinguisher. 'Anyway, the flat is for book-shop staff.'

'The tearooms are very much a part of the bookshop,' Mattie said icily, never mind that she usually insisted that though they were very grateful for the footfall of the romantic-novel-buying public, she was running an auto-nomous business. 'Though thank you very much for making me feel part of the Happy Ever After family.'

'In case you'd forgotten, I've worked at Happy Ever After much longer than you've been at the tearooms,' Tom pointed out superciliously.

'You were part-time for ages,' Mattie said calmly, although on the inside she was raging. 'I bet if you add up all the hours I've spent in the tearooms, then it would be more

15

hours than you've clocked up on the shop floor. I'm in at seven thirty every morning, I don't leave much before eight most nights, and now you want to deprive me of the two hours of sleep I could snatch back.'

'You're completely overreacting,' said Tom sourly, even though he'd worked among women for the last four years and knew only too well that to tell a woman that she was overreacting when she was reacting *just enough* was practically a hate crime. 'Posy. It's your decision.'

Posy burped. 'My heartburn's back. You two have given me heartburn and I've a good mind not to let either of you have the flat.' She burped again. 'I'm not meant to be getting stressed out, so you can sort out who gets the flat between you. Tomorrow,' she added. 'Now one of you go and get me another elderflower and soda, because I need to burp like no woman has ever needed to burp before.'

'You've been burping on and off for the last hour,' Verity ventured because she was a much braver woman than Mattie was.

Posy sighed. Then burped again. 'Believe me, this is just the warm-up,' she said sadly. 'I've got an absolute ripper lodged somewhere in my midsection, which is yet to make its presence heard.'

29 days until Christmas

T he next morning, after the usual rush of customers desperate for one of Mattie's breakfast specials and the bespoke blend of coffee that she had sent over from Paris, she, Posy and Tom inspected the upstairs flat.

Mattie didn't want to get her hopes up, though she had an impassioned speech all ready as to why she should move into Verity's soon-to-be-vacated room. Her heart was racing as she walked through the several anterooms of the book-shop, past the counter in the main room, through a door and up a flight of stairs. If she lived here, she'd be home by now instead of having an hour-long commute to and from Hackney – longer, if the traffic was terrible.

'I've been meaning to say it for ages, Pose, but pregnancy really agrees with you,' Tom said earnestly as Posy unlocked the door.

He really was the lowest of the low: his attempts to curry favour with Posy were laughably transparent and there was no way that Posy was going to fall for them.

'That's so sweet,' Posy said with a watery smile and Mattie's racing heart raced a little faster. 'Nice try, Tom, but I'm a neutral observer in all this and also, I'm writing you up in the sexual harassment book.'

'You know as well as I do that the sexual harassment book doesn't even exist,' Tom muttered, standing aside to let Mattie into the flat first because he did have a modicum of good manners, she'd give him that. 'And if it did really exist, then I think you'd find that the only person who's sexually harassed in this workplace is me. By post-menopausal women who are alarmingly handsy, and then instead of getting support from my colleagues, I'm further abused.'

Mattie couldn't understand what the post-menopausal women saw in Tom. Objectively, he was all right looking, she'd have to admit if she was under oath. He was tall, made taller by his wheat-coloured hair, which was swept up in a quiff at the front and a short back and sides everywhere else. Mattie had never gazed into his eyes deeply enough to know what colour they were, but they were hidden behind old-fashioned horn-rimmed glasses that looked like they'd been given out free on the NHS in the 1950s, which somehow worked for him. He also had an OK build, though Mattie didn't spend much time speculating at what Tom looked like under his clothes. God forbid!

Tom's physical attributes might be passable but his clothes

were another issue entirely. A major issue. He wore trousers that looked like they'd started life as part of a suit belonging to a country curate or some other dull sort of man that had lived eighty years ago and had a fondness for sombre tweed. His shirts, always white, weren't too objectionable but the ties he wore, sometimes a jaunty polka-dot bow-tie and sometimes a *knitted* tie, and the cardigan with its leather patches on the elbows, all offended Mattie's eyes.

Then there was his personality. Mattie knew that he was bookish: he had spent the last four years working part-time in the shop while he also studied for a PhD in philosophy or late medieval literature or some other dusty, dry subject. He refused to go into the details so Mattie had always assumed that it was something very dull and boring, or else, why all the secrecy? Still, Tom never let anyone forget that he was big with the book smarts. He was always superior, always ready with a smart remark full of big-syllable words. It was a wonder he worked in a romantic fiction bookshop when his top lip curled at any mention of romantic fiction.

Mattie couldn't imagine why Posy had kept him around for as long as she could, even letting him become full-time when he finally completed his PhD. Or why Tom hadn't wanted to pursue an academic career. Probably because in academia, there were loads of tweedy, supercilious men and at least at Happy Ever After, he had novelty value.

Still, there was no way, no way in hell, Tom was taking this room out from under her, Mattie thought as she peered into the large living room with its original fireplace with beautiful tiled surround and, inevitably, fully stacked bookshelves on either side. There was also a quite hideous floral three-piece suite. 'It's much comfier than it looks,' Posy promised. 'And across the hall, this is the bathroom. We've just had a new shower installed.'

'Perfect, love what you've done with it,' Mattie murmured.

'So much better than perfect,' Tom insisted. 'It's very rare that I find a bath long enough that I can stretch out in it.'

'Not getting involved,' Posy said in a sing-song voice. She was in a much better mood this morning than she had been the evening before. Apparently she'd drunk a bottle of Gaviscon with her breakfast and her indigestion was temporarily abated. 'Then this room is Nina's. It is the bigger bedroom, but that's neither here nor there, as Nina will be back imminently, I hope.'

'She hasn't said then?' Mattie asked, as they all stared at the closed door of Nina's room.

Posy shook her head. 'No, she's been very diligent with the remote marketing malarkey, but every time I ask her when she's coming back, she ignores me. It's very annoying, especially when I'm very pregnant.'

'You're only seven months pregnant. I think you've still got a few weeks to go before you're very pregnant,' Tom said, moving away from the door so he couldn't see the daggers that Posy was shooting at him.

'How would you know?' she demanded. 'When was the last time you were very pregnant?'

This was going much better than Mattie had imagined. Tom was going to talk himself out of the room without any help from her. Still, a little nudge couldn't hurt.

'Men don't have periods either. Or the menopause. Or have to maintain ridiculous standards of grooming to conform to a patriarchal society's ideal of what a woman should be,' Mattie said with a sad sigh.

'Good points, Mattie, but I'm still neutral,' Posy said with a disapproving look. 'Do you want to see the kitchen before we get to the room? And take your hand away from the door, Tom. I'm not having you go in there and try to bags it and claim that bagsying it is legally binding, like you did that time when The Midnight Bell only had one bowl of cheesy chips left.'

'That was one time!' But he stepped away from the door of Verity's room and continued down the hall towards the kitchen, pausing in front of a strange bell-and-lever contraption fixed to the wall so he could give it a fond pat. 'God bless you, Lady Agatha.'

The first owner of the bookshop had been one Lady Agatha Drysdale, who'd been gifted the business by her parents to distract her from her suffragette activities, with only limited success: Lady Ag was as passionate about women's suffrage as she was about books.

'It's a butler's bell that Lady Agatha installed so she could summon her employees up from the shop,' Posy explained, giving it a fond pat herself. 'Apparently, the wiring disintegrated some time in the seventies, which was a real shame. It would have been great to be able to do some summoning when Sam and I lived here.'

Posy and her younger brother Sam had lived above the shop almost all their lives. Lavinia, Lady Agatha's daughter who'd by then inherited the shop and sounded as though she had been the most splendid woman, had employed Posy's father to manage the bookshop and her mother to run the tearooms, but they'd died in a car accident some ten years before. Lavinia had continued to let Posy and Sam live above the shop, and when she died, she'd left both shop and flat to Posy. It also seemed as if she'd left Sebastian, her wildly dashing yet incredibly obnoxious grandson, to Posy too, for they were now married and expecting, and living in Lavinia's house on the other side of Bloomsbury.

'Though of course, you could have just summoned by text message,' Mattie said, then she wished that she hadn't because it sounded as if she was pouring cold water on Lady Agatha, when she wasn't, she was just being practical. She also didn't feel as if it were her place to give the butler's bell a fond pat, so instead she dipped her head as she passed on her way to the kitchen.

'It's awfully small,' Tom said, as they took in the old-fashioned kitchen cabinets painted a sunny primrose yellow with blue trim and grey Formica worktop. The kitchen wasn't as small as the kitchen in the tearooms – there was even room for a small table, two chairs and a fridge-freezer – and Mattie wasn't going to let Tom undermine her.

'It's a beautiful kitchen and anyway, size has absolutely nothing to do with it. I once made a triple-layer cake on a camping stove.' So there, she wanted to add and stick her tongue out at Tom, but she resisted, though it took every ounce of strength that she had.

'So, the room,' Posy prompted, hands settling where her stomach used to be so she could rub soothing circles on her bump, which she did whenever she was agitated. 'It used to be my room. It's a nice size and the windows look out onto the mews.'

She squeezed past Mattie and Tom back the way she came, so she could open the door on a room. *The* room. The most perfect room. It was comfy and cosy but large enough for a double bed, a wardrobe, a chest of drawers and, of course, several bookcases. There were two picture windows and on this bright but chilly day, the weak winter sun streamed in.

'It's lovely,' Mattie said in all sincerity.

'I'll take it,' Tom said in a peremptory fashion, as if he dared Mattie to disagree, in which case he was doomed to disappointment. 'I have worked in the shop longer than even Verity and Nina, yet they were still given first dibs on the rooms, which was very unfair, even though I never brought it up at the time.' He tapped his chest. 'That wounded me, Posy.'

'Oh dear.' Posy pulled a face. 'It's just that Verity is the manager and I just assumed that it would be less awkward to have Verity and Nina take the flat, on account of them being, like, ladies. Two ladies.'

'When you assume, you make an ass out of you and me,' Tom said gravely.

Mattie saw her chance and seized it with both hands. 'Don't call Posy an ass,' she gasped in shocked tones. 'And her pregnant, too! You know, it would be awkward, wouldn't it, for Tom to share with Nina, Nina being a lady, but I'm a lady too, so that would be absolutely not awkward.'

'Nina is my dear, dear friend,' Tom said, his eyes flashing behind his glasses though his dear, dear friend Nina had once confided to Mattie that she suspected that Tom didn't even *need* glasses and just wore them to make himself look even more like a tweedy nerd than he already did. 'Also, it's the twenty-first century, and if you won't let me share a flat with a woman, then, I don't want to, but I would have a very good case to take to a sexual discrimination trial.'

'Yeah, nice try,' Mattie blustered, because she could feel the flat slipping through her fingers.

Tom nodded. 'Maybe even the European Court of Human Rights. It's your decision, Posy.'

'It's not my decision,' Posy said, backing out of the room. 'I'm not making any decisions that are likely to cause my blood pressure to rise. I'm stressed out enough about all this Christmas stuff. You'll have to decide between your-selves, like the sensible, grown-up, adult people that I know you both can be.'

Mattie hated to beg, but just because she hated something wasn't a good enough reason not to.

'No Posy, please, please, let me have the room. I have to be here by seven thirty, eight at the very latest. I get up at six every morning. Six o'clock! Then I have evening prep, which means I'm not home much before nine, so I have no social life and I'm living with my mother, and please, Tom. Come on, don't be a dick about this.'

'I'm not being a dick,' Tom said, though he was totally being a dick as far as Mattie was concerned. 'And my current living conditions are also far from ideal,' he added stiffly, then pressed his lips together as Mattie and Posy waited expectantly.

'Far from ideal, you say?' Posy prodded, stepping back into the room, her eyes gleaming at the prospect of finally learning something, anything, about Tom's private life.

'Yes,' Tom said evenly. 'That's what I said. You don't need to know my personal business.'

'Oh,' Mattie said, making her eyes especially wide. 'Oh. How odd!'

'What's odd?' Posy asked, lowering herself onto Verity's rather lovely blue velvet reading chair with some difficulty.

'Well, it's just that Tom doesn't want everyone knowing his personal business and yet he wants to move into the flat above the shop.' Mattie tried her best to look sorrowful, as if she'd just been told that her favourite French cooking chocolate was no longer available in the UK. 'I'm sorry, Tom, but I don't see how you're going to maintain that work-life balance that's so important to you if you take the room.'

'I will, because unlike the rest of you, I'm perfectly capable of compartmentalising and also fixing a padlock to my bedroom door,' Tom said in stern tones.

Posy snorted. 'Yeah, right. I've asked you to perform several minor acts of household repair in the past, and you couldn't do any of them.'

'Couldn't or wouldn't,' Tom said, and Posy looked furious,

but then she remembered that she was being neutral and sank back in the chair.

'You have to sort it out between you,' she repeated, and it was clear that Tom wasn't going to give an inch, and Mattie didn't see why she should, so there was only one thing for it.

'We'll toss a coin,' she said. 'I don't see any other way, do you?'

'I don't,' Tom agreed, already pulling out a handful of loose change. 'Heads or tails?'

'Heads,' Mattie said, her fingers crossed as Tom handed Posy a pound coin.

'You'd better do the honours,' he said with a Cheshire cat grin as if the flat was already his. 'Being a neutral third party.'

Posy flipped the coin, failed to catch it so it fell to the floor and bounced off the skirting board, and Mattie and Tom were a whisker close to bumping heads as they rushed to see what side up it had landed.

'Oh, tails,' Tom said, not even bothering to hide his glee. 'Bad luck, Mattie.'

'Yes, sorry,' Posy said with a weak flutter of her hands. Then she fluttered weakly again. 'Sorry, can you give me a hand getting out of this chair? Or hire a hoist.'

Tom and Mattie took an arm each and tugged Posy out of the blue velvet depths. There was nothing for it now but to head back to the tearooms and maybe if Mattie worked like a dog all day, then she might be able to leave a whole fifteen minutes earlier than she normally did.

'Are you all right, Mattie?' Posy asked as they stepped back into the hall. 'If past history is correct, Tom will soon be hooking up with someone and want to move in with them. Who would have thought that in the space of a year, Nina, Verity and I would all be in committed long-term relationships? I think Lavinia must have cast a spell on the shop before she died. Mattie! Mattie, I know you're upset but can you start moving? Work to be done and all that.'

Mattie was rooted to the spot and staring at a closed door behind which there could be . . . 'Is that a broom cupboard?' she asked, because if it was a large broom cupboard, then maybe . . .

'Oh, you don't want to see in there. It's nothing,' Posy said quickly, a hand on Mattie's back to push her along. 'Absolutely nothing.'

'I really don't want to be the one to say this, but didn't that used to be Sam's room?' Tom queried in a long-suffering voice.

'Room! Hardly a room,' Posy said, wriggling past Mattie so she could form a human, pregnant shield in front of the door. 'Anyway, there's stuff in there. So much stuff.'

'Again, I really don't want to say this either, but when you say "stuff", do you actually mean a copious amount of books that you (a) haven't got round to moving to your gigantic house in Bloomsbury, or (b) can't move because you told Sebastian quite categorically that was the very last of your books when you managed to fill two van-loads? Or is it (c) you actually killed Nina some months ago and that's where her decomposing body is wrapped in bin bags? I thought I could smell something funny.'

Posy gave Tom a feeble slap on the arm. 'Of course I haven't killed Nina. I think the smell is just Verity's newest meditation candle.'

'Which just leaves (a) and (b),' Mattie said, folding her arms and planting herself squarely so that Posy was hemmed in. 'Which is it?'

'OK, it's (a),' Posy admitted. 'Also, (b). It used to be Sam's room and now it's my overspill books room.' She pouted winsomely in a way that would have had Sebastian Thorndyke agreeing to build an extension to their already very big house just so that Posy could have more books. 'I've filled every last shelf and bookcase that we own and Sebastian made me promise on my first edition of *I Capture the Castle* that for every new book I brought into the house, a book had to leave. It was very unreasonable of him.'

Mattie would never understand what the deal was with the Happy Ever After staff and all their many, many, many books. 'Really, Posy, couldn't you just go digital? Have you any idea how many books you could put on an e-reader?'

Posy made a furious huffing noise.

'Best not to go there,' Tom advised as he reached over his huffing boss to open the door to her unofficial library. 'Anyway, look, there's no room to swing a cat. Not even a very small cat.'

Mattie peered around the door and for one moment she thought that, annoyingly, Tom was right. There were piles of books, books and yet more books, and it was a wonder that the floor joists hadn't given way. But when she tried to visualise the room without any books, it was . . . not spacious, but definitely bigger than a broom cupboard.

'You could get a single bed in there,' she decided, which was fortunate because she hadn't shared a bed with anyone since . . . Anyway, she had no plans to share her bed with anyone. Ever. 'And a clothes rail. Maybe even a shelf on the wall.'

'I suppose . . . I could mention to Sebastian that I'd overlooked some books?' Posy said, rubbing her bump. 'And I am carrying his child, which is a very useful thing to bring up when I want to win an argument. Besides, Sam managed perfectly well in this room for years.'

Mattie smiled aggressively at Tom, who looked quite taken aback and blinked uncertainly. 'Well, I guess we're both moving in, then.'

'I guess we are,' Tom said.

Mattie gestured at the room. 'And I'm sure you'll be comfortable in here. If it was good enough for Sam, then I'm sure it will be fine for you.'

'Why should I get stuck with this glorified cupboard?' Tom asked incredulously.

'Because you're a man,' Mattie said with a dismissive wave of her hand, as if Tom's so-called manliness was in question.

'That's reverse sexism,' Tom said.

'It's not. It means that I'm a woman, so obviously I have more things than you,' Mattie pointed out with a slight gritting of her teeth. 'Clothes and things.'

Tom swept his eyes over Mattie, then it was his turn to employ a dismissive wave of his hand. 'You can't have that many clothes. You wear the same thing every single day.'

'Not the exact same thing! I have multiple pieces. I'm not some dirty Gertie with poor personal hygiene.' Mattie had rarely been so offended, and also so paranoid that she wished she could give each of her armpits a surreptitious sniff.

'Still, I already won the coin toss for Very's old room so you'll have to make do with this one.' Tom was now smiling as if his superior intellectual prowess had once again triumphed.

'Not fair. We'll toss again,' Mattie demanded and she wanted to stamp her foot so much that her toes curled up in her Converse.

But in the end she lost the toss – though she wouldn't have put it past Tom to have a special double-tails pound coin solely so he could win coin tosses – and had no option but to smile thinly and say, 'Fine, I hope you'll be happy in your needlessly large room.'

'Thanks, I'm sure I will,' Tom said with another mocking smile, and it wasn't until she was finally back on her home turf that Mattie could give way to her true feelings.

'I hate him!' she exclaimed, to the surprise of Cuthbert and several customers.

'"Hate" is a very strong word,' Cuthbert admonished, putting his hands over a couple of Jezebel's levers as if he didn't want the coffee machine to hear any harsh words.

'It's not strong enough,' Mattie said as she stomped into the kitchen, which sadly had no door that she could slam.

CHAPTER 3

28 days until Christmas

The very next evening, the last they all had free until after Christmas, Verity moved out, Posy moved her books out and Tom and Mattie moved in.

The logistics were not ideal. In fact, the logistics were a nightmare. Mattie had come home from work yesterday and worked long into the night packing up all her worldly possessions while mainlining black coffee.

Then she'd squeezed a day's baking into a morning so that after the lunchtime rush, she could hightail it back to Hackney to finish her packing.

Meanwhile, to mark the auspicious occasion, Happy Ever After and the tearooms closed their doors at 3 p.m. so that the Afternoon of Moving Many Things could get underway. 'It won't take long to shift a few boxes of books,' Posy said blithely but Posy had lied.

Despite quite a few fraught text messages about timings, when Mattie turned up at four in her mother's car, Posy's books were *still* being carried out at the same time that Verity and Johnny were trying to get her blue velvet armchair down the narrow stairs without breaking it.

There wasn't much room to park in the mews, what with two vans being there already. Mattie was just about to reverse out when there was a furious hooting behind her and she was hemmed in by yet another van. She could just make out Tom's face in her rear-view mirror as he gestured frantically at her.

She was tempted to gesture back with her middle finger. 'Ugh, he has zero chill.'

Her brother Guy, who'd come to help, immediately swivelled around then squawked when Mattie dug him in the ribs. 'I know someone else who has zero chill,' he complained. 'I just wanted to see if he was cute.'

'Well, I saved you the bother,' Mattie said, inching the nippy little Nissan forward so she could park in the far corner of the mews, next to the derelict row of abandoned shops, which Sebastian kept talking about redeveloping. 'You've already met Tom so you should know that he's not cute. He's the anti-cute and I have plenty of chill, thank you very much.'

Guy exchanged a look with Mattie's friend, Pippa, who'd also come along to help. 'If you say so.'

'Come on,' Pippa admonished. 'I've told you this three times already, but it takes teamwork to make the dream work.'

Mattie tried not to roll her eyes. Pippa worked for Sebastian (it was how Mattie had come to hear of the then-vacant tearooms, and how Pippa had wangled a couple of hours off) as a special projects manager, which meant she had great organisational skills and was a big fan of a stirring pep talk stuffed full of inspirational quotes.

'I do say so,' Mattie said because she was chilled and also because she would rather die than let Guy have the last word. Besides, she could bicker with Guy, her older brother by all of two minutes, without so much as breaking a sweat. In fact she could do all sorts of things with minimum fuss. She could multi-task the lunchtime rush, a special last-minute order for a birthday cake and wrangling Jezebel because Cuthbert had slipped out for five minutes, without getting pink in the face or swearing or mucking up a customer's order for a macchiato with almond milk and no foam. There were only two men who brought out the unchill in her and Tom was one of them, which didn't make him special, it just made him really, really annoying.

The three of them got out of the car at the same time that Tom descended from his van, which was now blocking the entrance to the mews, because he might have a PhD but he had no common sense.

In honour of the Afternoon of Moving Many Things and the need for manual labour, Tom had ditched his bow-tie and cardigan and was wearing a moth-eaten jumper over his shirt in a very unattractive fawn colour. And he hadn't come alone . . . he'd brought some *people* with him.

Unlike their tweedy BFF, Tom's friends (were they really his friends, though?) favoured tight jeans and tight, plunging T-shirts revealing lots of muscled he-vage. They all seemed to have tribal armband tattoos and a lot of product in their hair. More product than any hair really needed. Mattie didn't want to stare but Guy was already striding over.

'Tom!' Guy and Tom had met several times before at various Happy Ever After events, including the opening of the tearooms. Now they shook hands and Guy grinned because he was having no truck with the blood of thine enemy etc. and also he could never resist trying to get one up on Mattie. 'Shall we help Very and Posy move stuff out so we can move in sometime before midnight?'

'I was just going to suggest the same thing,' Tom said, which Mattie sorely doubted. 'After all, the light's already fading. It'll be dark soon.'

'I'll make coffee,' Mattie decided, because what with Guy and Pippa, who was already consulting the spreadsheet she'd put together to achieve a favourable and time-effective outcome to moving all of Mattie's goods and chattels, and Tom and his three . . . *helpers*, nobody needed her to heft heavy boxes. Also, Mattie couldn't risk injuring her whisking hand.

'I'd rather have a tea,' Posy called out from one of the benches in the middle of the mews where she was best situated to supervise things. She was wearing a huge puffa coat and had a travel blanket tucked around her, though for a late-November afternoon, it was actually quite temperate.

'Why do you need tea? Are you cold? You should have said!' Sebastian Thorndyke was at his wife's side in an instant. 'I did say there was no need for you to come, Morland.'

'And *I* said that I wasn't going to give you an opportunity to cart my treasured collection of Chalet School books to the nearest charity shop,' Posy replied. 'And I don't want tea because I'm cold, I want tea because I'm thirsty.'

Sebastian dropped to his knees in front of his wife, uncaring that he was wearing a suit that probably cost more than Mattie earned in a month before tax. 'Are you dehydrated? Are your kidneys hurting? Is the baby pressing on your kidneys?'

Posy patted his hand fondly. 'I can be thirsty just because it's about an hour since my last cup of tea.'

'I'll go and put the kettle on,' Mattie said and though she found Sebastian quite overbearing, he did dote on Posy and seemed to make her ridiculously happy. He also wasn't even dressed remotely appropriately for the occasion. 'I wouldn't have thought a suit would be practical if you're lugging boxes of books about.'

Sebastian's haughty face looked even haughtier. 'I don't lug,' he said, as if Mattie had accused him of a little light breaking and entering. 'I pay people to lug. In this case, Sam and his young friend, the unfortunately named Pants.'

Right on cue, Sam and Pants emerged from the shop laden down with a big box each.

'They have a free lesson last thing on Wednesdays, so it's all worked out rather well. You're doing a great job, boys,' Posy called out encouragingly and Mattie hurried over to the tearooms to provide refreshment for the labouring masses.

By the time the last box of books was carried out, she'd made a second round of tea and a quick batch of chocolate chip and hazelnut cookies, which she brought out as Verity left the flat for one final time with her most prized possession. In a special carrier, mewling unhappily, was Strumpet, her immense British blue short-hair cat. He might be going to live in five-bedroom splendour in Canonbury with a massive back garden, but that couldn't even begin to compete with living round the corner from a fish and chip shop and a Swedish deli with its own smokehouse for curing salmon.

'You're an ingrate, Strumpo,' Verity said, as she struggled under the weight and heft of her enormous feline. Her boyfriend Johnny hurried over to relieve her of her precious burden.

'I'm sure he'll settle in once we get back to mine.' He paused. 'Not mine. Ours. When we get back to *our* house.'

Generally, it could be quite hard to read Verity unless she was going through the petty cash receipts, in which case it was clear that she was very stressed indeed and it was best to leave her well alone. But now she smiled up at Johnny, with his ridiculously chiselled good looks like he spent his spare time modelling for Burberry.

'Not our house,' she corrected him. 'Our *home*.'

It was all very lovely and heart-warming, Mattie thought, but her heart refused to be warmed. It stayed just where it was, beating out a steady rhythm, which in itself was miraculous, considering all the traumas she had endured.

'I hate to spoil the moment,' Pippa said bluntly, because there was only so long that Verity and Johnny could stand there making googly eyes at each other while everyone else was on a clock. 'But according to my spreadsheet, you two should have been out of here twenty-seven minutes ago.'

Of course, by this point Tom and his *friends* had all disappeared, leaving their van blocking the entrance to the mews, so Verity and Johnny and Posy and Sebastian couldn't get out. After several texts from Posy, he eventually reappeared with his little posse, all of them clutching breakfast paninis from the Italian café round the corner, even though it was now gone five on a Wednesday. Mattie clenched her fists.

'These are *amazing*,' one of them said and then they all doffed imaginary caps.

'Top marks to the professor!'

Mattie had no one to roll her eyes at because Pippa was glued to her spreadsheet and Guy had abandoned her for the delights of Rochester Street. Despite numerous texts, he eventually turned up twenty minutes later, once Mattie had carefully manoeuvred the car as close to the entrance of Happy Ever After as she could get, and after telling Tom in no uncertain terms to stop trying to box her in with his rent-a-van.

It very quickly became apparent that you couldn't have six people going up and down the narrow stairs, ferrying boxes and bin liners and laundry bags and suitcases, without bottlenecks and chaos. Pippa decided that Mattie should stay in the flat and have her stuff brought to her, and Mattie agreed profusely.

'That sounds like an excuse to get out of all the fetching and carrying,' Guy grumbled.

'If you stop whinging, I'll make you both dinner when you've finished fetching and carrying,' Mattie said tartly, which sped him on his way.

That still left all three of Tom's helpers getting in the way, giving her curious looks as if they'd never seen a real live woman before. Maybe they hadn't. Who was to know what Tom and his friends got up to?

'Are they your people?' Mattie asked Guy when he brought up the holdall with all her bathroom paraphernalia in it.

Guy raised one impeccable eyebrow in horror. 'With those T-shirts? God, no, they are nothing to do with us. Your gaydar is worse than useless.'

By now, one of Tom's friends was lingering in the kitchen where Mattie was unpacking a box of cooking utensils: it seemed that Verity had taken pretty much every last teaspoon with her.

Said friend was small and wiry and quite incapable of standing still, bouncing on the soles of his boxy trainers.

'I'm Phil or the Archbishop of Banterbury,' he said at last, holding out his hand.

Mattie shook the hand. 'I think I'll stick with Phil,' she said. 'I'm Matilda. Mattie.'

'A beautiful name for a beautiful lady,' Phil said and they heard a pointed cough from the hall.

'Don't even bother,' said Tom as he passed the doorway with a couple of tweedy suits over his arm. 'She's not interested and she's way out of your league.'

Mattie blinked. Was that Tom paying her an actual compliment? Surely not! Phil nodded in agreement. 'True that,' he said gallantly.

Over the course of the next fifteen minutes, Tom's other two friends introduced themselves. By their given names: Daquon and Mikey; and their respective preferred names: The Bantmeister and Bantdaddy.

'And what do you call Tom?' Mattie asked Daquon as he wiped down the little bookcase in the kitchen so she could arrange her cookbooks on it. All three of them had cracked on to her, but she was quite capable of batting them away and they were also very helpful. 'Bants-R-Us?'

'Haha! Tom has no banter. He's like a banter-free zone. The banter stops when it gets within fifty metres of him.' Daquon slapped his thighs at the very notion of Tom having good banter. 'These days we call him The Professor, on account of all the book-learning.'

'Right . . .' Mattie filed this piece of information away for later use. 'And where do you know Tom from?'

'Funny you should ask that, because The Professor you see before you today is very different from . . .'

'Shut up! Seriously, stop making sounds come out of your mouth.' Tom was in the kitchen doorway again. He'd even taken his glasses off, all the better to polish them furiously and glare, although Mattie wasn't sure if the glare was for her or The Bantmeister. Most likely, it was meant for both of them. 'We talked about this.'

'You talked about it,' Daquon muttered.

'Didn't stop talking about it all the way here,' said Mikey, coming up behind Tom. 'But what we didn't talk about is why you have the big room and the lovely lady here is stuck in a tiny cupboard like Harry Potter when he was living at the Dursleys'.'

'Mattie and I have already discussed that,' Tom said, and if he kept polishing his glasses with such vigour, there was every possibility that they might shatter.

'We didn't really discuss it.' Mattie sighed. 'He made me toss a coin and then he was very smug about the outcome.'

'Rude!' decided Mikey, with a shake of his head. 'You should let the girl have the biggest room on account of the fact that she'll have loads of girly stuff to put in it.'

'Handbags and shoes and pretty dresses,' said Phil dreamily because now he was at the kitchen doorway too. 'Probably Matilda really needs an extra room just for her shoes.'

'She doesn't have that many shoes,' piped up Guy, who was passing. 'Just several pairs of very ratty Converse.'

Fortunately, everyone ignored his contribution. 'Mattie should have the bigger room. It's just, like, basic good manners,' Phil said, bouncing on his feet again and working his jaw furiously. 'It's not like you even need a double bed.'

'Yeah! Like, who's going to want to pull your ugly mug?'

There were hoots of laughter and Tom's face was clenched so tight that it looked as if he had lockjaw. Mattie even felt a little bit sorry for him.

'It's all right,' she said and she sighed again. She knew that she looked quite forlorn in the dungarees and jumper that she'd worn for moving day, because her perennially chic mother had complained about her appearance before she left Hackney. '*Ma cherie*, you look like Little Orphan Annie.'

'Fine! She can have the larger room,' Tom snapped. 'Though I do need a double bed and I don't see how my one is going to fit in the smaller room.'

'Oh, it should do,' Mattie assured him sweetly. 'Mine does. Pity that there's not much room for anything else in there besides the bed, but you can't have that much stuff, can you? Being a man and everything.'

Tom did have lots of stuff. Or rather, he had boxes and boxes of books – he couldn't possibly have read them all, Mattie decided, as the contents of the two rooms were transferred, with Tom glowering silently in the background. Why would anyone surround themselves with books all day, then come home to yet more books?

Still, there was plenty of room on the shelves in the living room for Tom's library and she even offered to help him unpack, but he shooed her away with a tight 'I can manage perfectly well by myself, thank you.'

Tom was the only person that Mattie had ever met who could make 'Thank you' sound like 'Get out and never darken my doorstep again.'

So she got out and finished hanging up her quite sparse collection of clothes in the wardrobe in her new room. Unlike the other ladies that the Banter Boys knew, Mattie travelled light. All her clothes and shoes had fitted comfortably in one suitcase. And she didn't even possess a single solitary handbag – just a leather-strapped backpack that had seen much better days – because all her money went on kitchen equipment and fancy ingredients and the odd cookbook. Whereas Tom had so many tweedy suits and jumpers and probably a trunkful of bow-ties and ties in contrasting colours. Mattie realised that she was actually feeling quite guilty again . . .

Maybe they could put the bigger room on a six-month-rota basis, she decided as Phil, Daquon and Mikey took their leave, each of them lining up to kiss her hand, look deep into her eyes and express the desire to see her again very soon.

'It's weird, but normally that kind of chat from men makes me want to rip them a new one,' she remarked to Guy and Pippa as she set about making them dinner. 'But those boys are so obviously harmless that I didn't really mind.'

'Do you still hate *all* men?' asked Guy. It had been a little while since they'd last had a catch-up.

'Mattie is taking time out from relationships to work on herself,' Pippa said loyally. She knew exactly why Mattie had good reason to hate all men. Or one man in particular. 'Not that Mattie needs to do a lot of work on herself, but I think we can all benefit from an opportunity for personal growth.'

'Thanks, Pips. And I don't hate *all* men, Guy.' Mattie considered her brother's question as she grated extra-mature cheddar for the twice-baked cheese soufflés she was going to serve with a warm salad. 'I don't hate you and anyway, I haven't met *all* the men in the world yet, have I? There must be four or five that aren't hateful.'

'Do you hate Tom?' Guy asked in a whisper. 'You're certainly not very nice to him.'

'I am,' Mattie said, though all the evidence suggested otherwise. 'He's not very nice to me.'

'It's the chicken and egg, really. Who wasn't nice to whom first?' Guy stared at Mattie without blinking. Pippa tilted her head and looked at Mattie too, as if she was disappointed in her, so Mattie felt forced to put down her grater with a beleaguered air and flounce out of the kitchen to knock gently on the door of Tom's room.

'Do you want dinner?' she called out, while silently praying that he'd say no. 'I can easily make enough for four.'

There was silence and Mattie wondered if Tom had been crushed between the wall and his huge kingsize bed. 'I'm all right,' he called back finally. 'I had a very late breakfast panini.'

'Yeah, of course you did,' Mattie muttered under her breath, going back into the kitchen so she could stand there with her hands on her hips and demand, 'Happy now?'

'Deliriously,' Guy drawled back. 'I'd be even happier if I didn't have to drive Ma's car back so I could have another glass of wine.'

Although she begged them to stay, Guy and Pippa left as soon as they'd cleared the last smear of apple and black-berry crumble from their bowls. After she'd locked the shop door behind them, she very slowly and very unwillingly retraced her steps back to the flat.

Tom was in the kitchen with a tin of baked beans and a loaf of sliced white. 'I was just making dinner,' he said defensively as if Mattie had asked him what the hell he thought he was doing. Then he opened the tin of baked beans in a very passive-aggressive manner, sighing and shaking his head and generally acting as if both tin opener and tin had done him wrong.

'Well, you know where I am if you need me,' Mattie said, exiting the kitchen as fast as she could. But just before she shut the door of the room that they'd fought so bitterly about, she heard Tom say to himself in withering tones, 'What on earth would I need *you* for?'

CHAPTER
4

27 days until Christmas

Thankfully, when Mattie woke up at seven thirty the next morning, which pretty much constituted a long lie-in, Tom was nowhere to be seen.

Last night had been awkward enough; both of them confined to their rooms apart from the mortifying ten seconds when Mattie had tried to get into the bathroom, only to find it already occupied.

'Go away!' Tom had shouted rather than politely requesting that Mattie come back in a short while.

As it was, she'd left it for a good half an hour before she plucked up the courage to venture into the bathroom, terrified of what horrors might be lurking. But there were none. Just Tom's electric toothbrush (which seemed very cutting edge for Tom) and a few of his toiletries: shampoo, hair pomade, some fancy gloop that called itself a skin elasticiser rather than moisturiser. It struck Mattie, as she massaged her own moisturiser into her face then cleaned her teeth, that she hadn't given a moment's thought to how intimate it was to share a flat with someone.

Mattie had shared flats before. At university, she'd lived in a four-bedroom house with seven other girls, which had been chaotic and messy, but mostly fun. And of course, when she'd lived in Paris, she'd shared a tiny attic garret with . . . well, that hadn't ended up being fun, for reasons that had nothing to do with the actual living together.

But sharing a flat with Tom, wondering if he could hear her brushing her teeth, felt intensely intimate. Mattie made a solemn vow that she'd never leave her room unless she was fully dressed or had her dressing gown tightly belted over her pyjamas. Not that she thought that Tom would be overcome with lust at the sight of her – Tom wasn't the lustful sort at all – but she could picture his lip curling and he'd mutter something sarcastic under his breath. And the idea that she might bump into Tom wearing nothing but some very old-fashioned underpants, like those baggy shorts that men wore in old black-and-white films, had her choking on her toothpaste.

This Thursday morning Tom was still tucked up in bed and if he was snoring, then Mattie couldn't hear him through his bedroom door.

And for all the awkwardness and the intimacy that had been thrust upon them, that thirty-second commute down the stairs and through the shop was worth it. Mattie unlocked the front door of the tearooms just in time to surprise Kendra, who ran a dairy in East London.

'What are you doing here?' Kendra said, as she hefted in the crate of milk instead of leaving it outside, as she usually did. 'You must have been up almost as early as me.'

'Actually, I've only been up half an hour,' Mattie said a little apologetically. 'Moved in above the shop, haven't I?'

'All right for some! How's that working out for you?' Kendra asked a little enviously.

'Not without its challenges, but also kind of life-changing,' Mattie decided as she checked the cartons of eggs to make sure that none of them were broken.

Kendra left, the glass bottles on her milk float rattling as she carefully manoeuvred over the cobblestones, and then Mattie was alone. It was her favourite part of the day in her favourite place; early morning in her little kitchen at the back of the tearooms.

Mattie looked at her hideaway with a pleasure that was still undimmed after eighteen months of running the tearooms. The kitchen walls had beautiful Art Nouveau tiles, dating back to when the bookshop had first opened in 1912, in the suffragette colours of purple, green and white. They were partly obscured now by the shelves and hanging rails Mattie had installed so she could store her pots and pans, whisks and wooden spoons. Jars and tins of dry ingredients and little glass bottles of spices, essences and flavourings sat on the scant wooden worktop, where she whipped up cakes and cookies, tarts and turnovers, breads and bakes. The oven where all this magic happened was the only new piece of kit and had cost the same as a small hatchback.

Along the opposite wall was an old-fashioned butler's sink and tiled drainer, a tall, very skinny fridge and a door that led out into the back yard where there was an ancient privy for the hardiest and bravest of paying customers, especially on a chill winter's day like today.

You couldn't create culinary delights in a kitchen so miniscule without being very organised and very tidy, which Mattie was. 'A place for everything and everything in its place,' she said at least a dozen times a day when a dirty cup and saucer were left unattended for longer than thirty seconds. Or when Cuthbert left the milk out instead of putting it back in the fridge under the counter, because he was busy serenading a customer with a rousing chorus of 'They Drink an Awful Lot of Coffee in Brazil'.

As well as her usual bakes, which tended towards English classics with a French twist like her famous citron drizzle cake, Mattie also had both a sweet and a savoury daily special. Today, it was a cinder toffee and apple layer cake and individual stilton and leek tarts. With a quick glance at the right page in her handwritten recipe book to check quantities, Mattie started amassing the ingredients she needed.

By the time Cuthbert arrived at ten to nine, all the breakfast pastries were out of the oven and arranged on their cake stands and trays on the counter. And by the time Posy and Verity arrived to open up Happy Ever After just before ten, the tearooms had been open for almost an hour.

Half the tables were filled with customers lingering over a cup of coffee and a flaky buttery croissant, with others dashing out with a coffee to go (fifty pence cheaper if they brought their own cup) and something delicious in a paper bag.

At ten past ten, even though Happy Ever After opened at ten, Tom arrived with his breakfast panini purchased off the premises at the Italian café round the corner and his own mug, which proclaimed 'Academics Do It In A Mortarboard', so he could take advantage of free, freshly brewed coffee.

Mattie had never said anything about the actual blooming liberty of Tom expecting free coffee when he never once purchased anything from the tearooms, and after nearly eighteen months, it was too late to bring it up. That didn't stop her seething every time he did it, though.

And considering that they were now roomies, it wouldn't have killed Tom to say, 'Good morning,' rather than a sour, 'You might try and be a bit quieter first thing and not slam the door on your way out.'

'I'll be sure to remember that,' Mattie snapped, snatching Tom's mug of coffee from Cuthbert and slamming *that* down too. 'Anything you might like to *purchase* while you're here?'

Tom held up the bag that contained his sodding panini. 'No, I'm good. Thanks for the coffee, Cuthbert.'

Cuthbert, traitor that he was, touched his hand to his head in salute. 'Always a pleasure, young sir.'

'It's not a pleasure,' Mattie muttered as Tom wended his

49

way through her actual paying customers and slipped through the double doors that led to the shop. 'Never has been and never will be.'

'You'll end up with an ulcer with that kind of attitude,' Cuthbert said as he worked through the next set of orders. In the past, Mattie wouldn't have tolerated that level of backchat from her baristas, but then, Cuthbert was older than anyone else she'd interviewed by several decades and she'd been brought up to respect her elders. Cuthbert Lewis was seventy-two and had worked for the Post Office all his life until he'd retired two years ago. He'd spent two weeks being retired, decided that he didn't like it very much and had retrained as a barista. His granddaughter Little Sophie, who worked in the tearooms on Saturdays, had told him that Mattie had a job going, and the rest was history.

Now, come rain, come shine, come whatever inclement weather you could throw at him, Cuthbert turned up for work, always immaculately dressed in suit and tie, and charmed both the coffee machine and customers alike with his grace, mischievous twinkle and old-fashioned good manners. Although Mattie did wish that he wouldn't keep saying that operating Jezebel to her optimum potential was like bringing a beautiful woman who'd had her heart broken back to life, she still regularly thanked whatever deity (and Little Sophie) had brought Cuthbert into her life. Apart from when he was singing the praises of her arch nemesis.

'Young Tom is a perfect gentleman. He has a lovely smile. Lovely manners too.'

'I've never seen evidence of either,' Mattie said with a sniff, disappearing into the kitchen to prepare her lunchtime bakes, which always included a speciality jumbo sausage roll. This week she was trialling a pork belly and apple confit sausage roll.

Mattie was disturbed in her apple prep by the arrival of Posy, who brought her own stool with her: she was obviously planning to stay a while.

'I can't be on my feet for longer than a minute,' she said by way of a greeting.

'Swollen ankles still bothering you?' Mattie asked, attacking a mountain of peeled apples with one of her favourite knives.

'Honestly, Mattie, I'm happy about the baby, really I am, but being pregnant sucks,' Posy said with great feeling. 'I wouldn't recommend it.'

'I'm not planning on getting pregnant anytime soon,' Mattie said with a shudder, because when other girls had played 'Mother' she'd pretended that she was running her own Michelin-starred kitchen. 'I know that you feel lousy, but you look very well on it.'

It was true. Posy had always been pretty, but now her pink-and-white complexion had a rosy glow, her hair shone and had picked up an auburn tint and OK, yeah, her ankles did look quite swollen but she had a very pleasingly round bump.

'I don't, but it's sweet of you to say I do,' Posy said. 'I was up half the night worrying about the Christmas brainstorm. I really want to wait until Nina gets back, but she won't reply when I email to ask her for an ETA.'

'That's not like Nina,' Mattie noted with a frown, because usually Nina was so welded to her phone that she responded to messages within the minute. 'I hope something hasn't happened to her.'

'No, she's definitely still alive because she is sending me all sorts of other emails. For instance, how I feel about having life-sized reindeer in the shop,' Posy said unhappily.

That definitely warranted putting down her paring knife. 'Live reindeer in the shop?'

'Not live. Life-size. Though either way, I don't think it's a very good idea,' Posy said unhappily. She sighed and then her expression changed from harassed to something more speculative, if the narrowing of her eyes was anything to go by. 'So, Tom, then. I was very surprised when he showed up with those lads yesterday afternoon. Tom has friends, who knew?'

'Well, I suppose he had to have at least one friend,' Mattie said uncharitably. 'Some poor unfortunate who didn't know any better.'

'But there were *three* of them. Three!' Posy said wonderingly. 'Did they say where they knew Tom from? How long they'd been friends? Are they academics too? I mean, they didn't *look* like academics.'

'Well, Tom isn't an academic. He works in a bookshop,' Mattie said as she threw the now-cubed apples into the big pan on the hob.

'But he *was* an academic,' Posy said and she wasn't going to let this go. She was twitching with curiosity, so Mattie took pity on her and told her about the Banter Boys: they'd been quite nice, actually.

'Really? I thought you'd have shut them down in five seconds flat.'

'I don't shut down every man I meet.'

'Most men. So, you and Tom living together . . .'

'Are you going somewhere with this?' Mattie asked, turning to Posy, knife in her hand. 'Because Tom and I . . . in fact, there is no Tom and I. There is me having to share living space with Tom under sufferance, and neither of us is happy about it, *and* his friends insisted that he give up the big room, so he's much more unhappy about it than I am.'

'But if in the course of living with Tom, sorry, living in the same space as Tom, you were to find out some personal details about him, you will let me know, won't you?' Posy's eyes were gleaming with the prospect of finally having any nugget of information that might explain the enigma of Tom, her colleague of five years about whom she knew nothing.

'Posy, just listen to yourself! I'm not Tom's biggest fan, but you know as well as I do that there are rules about sharing living space with someone, and I'm not about to go rifling through Tom's underwear drawer or steaming open his post,' Mattie exclaimed as she grated nutmeg into her pork and apple mix. 'I, and you, have to respect his privacy.'

'Of course, of course,' Posy said quickly. 'Absolutely, but if you were to find out something, even if it seems quite mundane, like where he was living before, or if he has parents, then it would be perfectly all right to share that with a friend.'

'It would be information that was in the public domain, as it were,' Verity pointed out when she came calling to discuss the Christmas decoration budget for shop and tearooms, which turned out to be just a flimsy excuse. As was her not-at-all casual enquiry as to whether Mattie had chanced upon a stray pair of socks that Verity couldn't find. What Verity really wanted, like Posy before her, was intel on Tom. 'And if you don't have intel at the moment, you can still gather intel in the general course of day-to-day living with him. And then you could share that intel with me.'

'Isn't there a commandment about that?' Mattie asked. She sprinkled flaked almonds on her cherry frangipane loaf cakes that she was just about to put in the oven, because it was now after lunch and soon the afternoon tea crowd and the four o'clock energy slumpers would be in, wanting something sweet to get them through the rest of the day.

The reminder of Verity's father's calling worked like a charm, as ever. She huffed a little, said, 'Well, if those socks do turn up, I'd like them back, please,' then flounced back to her office.

After Mattie turned the tearoom sign to 'Closed' that evening, the machinations of her colleagues made her hesitate as she moved towards the stairs up to the flat. That flat that she shared with Tom. The flat where she would now have to spend the evening with Tom. What had seemed so straightforward was now giving her pause for thought, so it came as a huge relief when Tom came thundering down the stairs.

'I'm going out,' he said shortly. 'And when I do get in, I'll be quiet in much the same way that I hope you'll be quiet tomorrow morning.'

Mattie wasn't sure she'd ever known such sweet relief tempered with spitting indignation. 'It's not my fault that you're obviously such a light sleeper,' she said, but Tom was already gone, slamming the shop door behind him and leaving Mattie home alone.

After that, she wasn't even a little bit tempted to rifle through Tom's belongings. He hadn't made good his threat to put a padlock on his bedroom door – she'd be mortally offended if he had – but there was no way that Mattie was going to invade his territory. She liked to think that she had a strong moral code, even though life had taught her that very few people shared her sense of ethics. Anyway, the thought of Tom returning the favour and going into her bedroom when she wasn't there, made her go hot and cold.

Not that Mattie had anything to hide, but it was her space, her stuff. The idea that Tom or anyone might look through her underwear drawer was bad enough, but there were some things that were far more personal than under-wear.

Like her little collection of Paris snowglobes: the Eiffel Tower, the Arc de Triomphe, the Moulin Rouge windmill, all trapped in a winter wonderland under glass. They were neatly packed away in a box that had once stored the most delicious *sablés au beurre*, because Mattie could hardly bear to look at them.

Or her framed graduation certificate from L'Institut de Patisserie and the framed graduation snap of Mattie and her classmates, all of them in chef's whites and toques, smiling happily, while Mattie stood off to the side, her lips compressed thinly, a haunted look in her eyes. That was packed away too, along with all the other painful reminders of her other life, her Parisian life; the very idea that Tom would pick through them with a sarcastic inner monologue cut Mattie to the core.

She was sure that Tom didn't have the same souvenirs of heartbreak – she wasn't even sure that Tom had a heart to break – but if he did, then it would be just as agonising for him to have someone go through them with careless fingers.

So she wasn't even tempted to gather intel. Not even a little bit.

But as she had the whole building to herself for once, Mattie gave in to the temptation to wander around the empty shop. Usually the little series of anterooms on each side of the main shop were places Mattie passed through to get to the office to speak to Verity or for one of Posy's dreaded brainstorms, like the imminent Christmas show-down where they'd discuss the possibility of life-sized reindeer for *hours*. In fact, the anterooms on the right, on the opposite side of the shop to the tearooms, were uncharted territory.

At night, lit softly by the spots above the counter, Happy Ever After was full of shadows and ghosts. But they were kindly ghosts and the empty shop had a peaceful feeling.

The main room had floor-to-ceiling bookshelves on either side with an old-fashioned rolling ladder, and in the centre were three sagging sofas in varying stages of decay grouped around a display table. On the table was a selection of books: everything from Jilly Cooper's *Riders* to *Pride and Prejudice*, as well as ten or twelve other titles, ranging from familiar classics to books that Mattie had never heard of. There were also velvety-smooth, pale-pink roses in a chipped glass vase and a black-and-white photograph of a young man and woman standing behind the counter of the shop decades earlier. The woman was gazing up at the man with an adoring smile on her face and he was gazing down at her with tenderness in a way that Mattie could never imagine. But then, according to everyone who'd known them, Lavinia, the former owner of the shop, and her husband, Peregrine, had had eyes only for each other.

There was one other item on the table, a notice printed on fancy card:

In loving memory of Lavinia Thorndyke, a bookseller to her bones. On this table is a selection of Lavinia's favourite books; the ones that brought her the greatest joy, that were like old friends. We hope that you may find the same joy, the same friendship.

'If one cannot enjoy reading a book over and over again, there is no use in reading at all.' – Oscar Wilde

Though she kept it on the downlow (mainly because she'd never hear the end of it), Mattie's preferred books were cookery books. She'd tried once to explain to Posy that when she curled up in bed with *How To Eat A Peach* by Diana Henry or Nigel Slater's *Kitchen Diaries* or even her treasured copy of her own grandmother's handwritten recipe book, she was as transported as Posy was with one of the Regency romances that she could bolt through in an afternoon.

Mattie loved to imagine all those recipes, all those meals that she'd yet to eat; loved how they inspired her, were a springboard to creating new dishes of her own. With a cookery book open in front of her, Mattie had travelled the world. She'd visited Italy with Elizabeth David, India with Madhur Jaffrey and the Middle East with Yotam Ottolenghi. She'd found comfort in the recipes of Delia Smith and Julia Child, which echoed the food of her childhood, whether it was the English cakes and biscuits and puddings of her father's mother or the more fancy éclairs, flans and *financiers* of her French mother's mother.

But now, with the empty shop at her disposal and more free time than she knew what to do with, on the second night in her new abode, Mattie found herself drifting to the boxes of books in the back office behind the shop counter.

These books weren't for sale but were proofs, or advance copies, sent out by publishers to booksellers and reviewers. The staff were allowed to take anything that they fancied, which Cuthbert had really leaned into, taking armfuls of sassy office romances home to his beloved Cynthia.

'Even read a couple myself,' he'd confessed to Mattie, his

eyebrows waggling. 'Gave me quite a few new ideas, let me tell you.'

Mattie didn't need any new ideas and she certainly didn't want any romance in her life, much less to read about it, but that night she felt as if she'd read all her cookery books a thousand times over and, nestling on top of one of the boxes was a novel called *Passion and Patisserie at the Little Parisian Café*.

'I'll be the judge of that,' she muttered, picking it up and, half an hour later, she was tucked up in her bed reading about the heroine Lucy's adventures as she opened what was actually a *boulangerie* rather than a café and resisted the charms of a hunky French pastry chef called Pierre because she was wedded to her career.

Though Mattie didn't think much of the recipe for macarons in chapter two, she was nevertheless enjoying Lucy's exploits when she heard a noise outside.

Although the mews felt as if it was its own little oasis of calm away from all the hustle and bustle, it was still in the centre of London. It wasn't even eleven o'clock, so on Rochester Street, No Plaice Like Home would only have just finished serving, and The Midnight Bell and the fancy new bar in what used to be the undertakers would still be open. So there was no need for Mattie to stiffen just because she'd heard a noise outside.

After all, she used to live in Hackney, where she'd often been woken up by sirens or a police helicopter overhead. But this was a different kind of sound; a frantic squalling, like an animal in distress. And was that . . . was that a rattling of the electronic gate that Posy and Sebastian had installed at the entrance to the mews? It was left open all day but Tom would have closed it when he went out earlier and you needed a code to get through. Was someone trying to break in?

Mattie cowered for a second and then she remembered that she was made of much sterner stuff than that. She got out of bed and padded over to the window so she could open it and peer out into the darkened courtyard below.

'Is anyone there?' she called, but if someone were trying to break in, then they'd hardly reply with a 'Yoo hoo! Over here!'

Instead, the squalling noise got louder. Was it foxes having sex? Even in the centre of town, there were plenty of foxes who'd take their chances for the rich pickings outside restaurants and shops, or for discarded and half-eaten fast food. Mattie had once seen a rat on Rochester Street, bold as brass, proudly carrying a chicken drumstick in its mouth.

The gates rattled again, and the squalling got even louder.

The best thing to do was to go back to bed, maybe put in some earplugs and . . . wait to be murdered in her sleep.

CHAPTER 5

27 days until Christmas

But Mattie was far too sensible to allow herself to be murdered in her sleep. With a resigned sigh, she turned away from the window so she could dig out her Ugg boots. She shrugged her big puffa coat over her pyjamas and before she left the flat, she grabbed one of her really heavy cast-iron pans.

The empty shop was no longer a comforting, warm space but full of terrifying shadows, and Mattie felt like the cliché in a horror film as she unlocked the front door. Instead of staying inside, she was going out towards who knew what fresh hell?

As soon as the door was open and Mattie heard the noise again, it chilled her bones. Because now she recognised the sound, which was why she broke into a run towards the electronic gates where, oh God! There was Strumpet trapped between the railings and very unhappy about it.

'Strumpo! What on earth are you doing here?' Mattie exclaimed and poor Strumpet gave her side eye, as much as he could, and yowled again as if to say, 'What does it look like I'm doing, you foolish human?'

'What on earth are you doing?' echoed from the shadows beyond the gate, and Mattie tore her gaze away from the distraught cat to see Tom on the other side. Then he looked down too. 'Oh God, you idiot!'

'You are talking about Strumpet and not me?' Mattie clarified sharply.

'You're not the one who's trapped in the railings, are you?' Tom took off his glasses so he could scrutinise Strumpet (which also kind of proved that he didn't actually need glasses at all), who tried to turn his head to look back at Tom, but instead just meowed unhappily. 'How did he manage to get here, all the way from Canonbury, when the furthest afield he ever used to get was as far as Stefan's smokehouse?'

'I have no idea,' Mattie replied, crouching down so she could take stock of the situation. Strumpet had managed to get his head and his front paws through the railing of the gate on the right, but was stuck at his fattest part, his Buddha-like belly. 'How about you push and I pull?'

'Well, I haven't got any better ideas,' Tom admitted. Mattie gently took hold of Strumpet under his armpits and Tom grabbed hold of his hind legs but, despite their gentle wiggling, which Strumpet took in remarkably good grace, the cat was stuck fast.

'You stupid beast,' huffed Tom. 'My old cat could wriggle through the tiniest gaps, like she was boneless, but Strumpet has far too much blubber. Should I come over to you?'

'No! Don't! Stop!' Mattie screeched as Tom's index finger paused over the keypad. 'What if you electrocute him?'

'I don't see how,' Tom grumbled but he stood back. 'Well, what else could we try? Could we lubricate him? Have we got any butter?'

'Yes! Good thinking!' Mattie yelped. 'I always have spare butter. Wait here!'

'I'm hardly planning on going anywhere,' Tom shouted at her back as Mattie took off towards the shop because, even in the middle of a dire emergency, Tom couldn't resist having the last word.

But she was far more upset to realise that the only butter she had, ahead of tomorrow's delivery, was her precious unsalted butter from Normandy, which you couldn't even get in the UK. Every six months or so, Mattie and her mother made a trip across the Channel to stock up on all the French provisions that they couldn't live without, mainly butter in Mattie's case. And now she was going to have to donate it to a greater cause. She didn't even have any vegetable oil left, she thought sadly as she put the butter in the microwave for a few seconds just to warm it enough for optimum cat manhandling.

When she returned, Tom was squatting down, his hand reaching through the gate to scratch Strumpet behind his ears. 'I know that it seems like the end of the world right now, Strumpet, but I promise you one day we'll look back on this and laugh.' It was the nicest thing that Mattie had ever heard him say.

Then he saw Mattie standing there and he straightened up.

'Let's grease him up,' Mattie said unenthusiastically. 'And, you know, we don't have to use *all* the butter.'

But Tom had already taken a large handful and was smearing it around Strumpet's belly while Strumpet squirmed and wriggled and tried to eat the butter. Then Mattie and Tom tried the whole push/pull thing again but it was little use, not helped by Strumpet's now-frenzied licking. He'd clearly forgotten all about his current predicament and was in full-fat heaven. Verity had him on a strict calorie-controlled diet, so he was intent on slurping up all the very expensive butter he could reach.

'We're going to have to call the fire brigade,' Mattie said after ten futile minutes during which Strumpet had managed to eat a good half a stick of butter but was still stuck fast.

'I'll have to call Very. If she knows Strumpet has gone missing, she'll be frantic.' Tom being all nice again was most unsettling. Mattie glanced through the gate at him as he pulled an ancient-looking mobile phone from the inner breast pocket of his old tweedy coat.

He dealt with Verity while Mattie called 999 and requested a 'fire crew or someone that can rescue a very obese cat from the railings of an electronic gate. I swear this isn't a hoax call.'

'Honestly, Very, it's not something I'd joke about. I can't take photos on my phone but when Mattie's finished talking to the emergency services, I'll get her to send you a picture so you can appreciate the severity of the situation,' Tom was saying crossly as Mattie reeled off the address and Strumpet yelled his displeasure at having polished off all the butter he could reach around his tubby forequarters.

'I'll make us a hot drink,' Mattie decided when the phone calls were done: they would have at least a half-hour wait for a fire crew, supposing that no buildings went up in flames in the meantime. 'Tea? Coffee?'

'Tea, I suppose . . . though have you got any of the hot chocolate you served at that book launch a couple of weeks ago?' Tom asked hesitantly. 'If it's not too much trouble.'

It was like Tom had had a personality transplant – or maybe the crisis had brought out the best in him.

'I have,' Mattie confirmed. 'I could even put a little French brandy in it.'

'Sounds great. Thank you,' Tom added, and Mattie was about to pretend to faint but decided that she didn't want to ruin their little *entente cordiale*.

When she returned with two steaming mugs of spiked hot chocolate, they quickly realised that there wasn't enough room between the railings to slide the mug through. It was a wonder that Strumpet had even managed to get his fat head and barrel-like shoulders as far as he had.

'I could get you a straw?' Mattie suggested, but Tom shook his head.

'Stand back,' he ordered, and before she could say a word, he took a run at the gate, leapt in the air and vaulted clear over the top of it, landing next to Mattie, who almost dropped both mugs in shock and surprise. Later, she'd be sure that she imagined it – Tom clearing the six-foot gate like it was a little country stile. But right then she simply handed him one of the mugs and wished that she'd had the presence of mind to film it, because no one was ever going to believe her.

It would have been more comfortable to wait in the warmth of the shop but they couldn't leave Strumpet alone, so they stayed where they were, taking turns to scratch him behind his ears until they heard a distant siren. Then, a little later, there was the reflection of a flashing blue light as the fire engine negotiated the cobbles of Rochester Street and finally pulled up at the entrance to the mews.

Mattie had never known relief like it. 'We'll soon have you out of there and once again you'll be free to terrorise anyone with food,' she told Strumpet, who looked quite sceptical about this claim.

Tom was talking four firemen through the situation, all of them fully kitted out and ready to dash into burning buildings to rescue children. Though Mattie couldn't get a good look at them, she suddenly felt quite hot, even though it was a freezing November night. She might have sworn off all men and spat in the face of romance, but she wasn't dead. Aesthetically, she could still appreciate the physical charms of four very fit, very brave firemen, which was why she was crouched down on Strumpet's level with glazed eyes and her mouth hanging open.

'Is the cat friendly, ma'am?' one of the fireman asked. He came closer so Mattie could see that he looked about fifteen – it was probably time to stop swooning. Also he'd just called her ma'am, like she was somebody's grandma.

'Very friendly, but quite distressed by his ordeal,' she explained. 'Also we covered him in butter to try and slide him out, so he's very slippery to the touch.'

Strumpet was indeed quite distressed but he also loved nothing more than a man's touch, so whenever one of the firemen came over to assess the situation, he'd start purring like crazy and headbutting the gloved hand assessing him, which didn't really help matters.

When a white-faced Verity arrived with Johnny, the firemen had decided to disconnect the gate's electronics before they cut Strumpet free.

'We had a flat battery,' she said distractedly. 'Then it took us ages to find a cab. Oh, Strumpet! What have you done, you silly boy?'

Strumpet gave her quite a bit of backchat, and just as the electronics were disabled, (they made a group decision not to tell Posy until the morning, 'If we tell her now, she won't sleep and then she'll just be horrible tomorrow'), a taxi drew up alongside the fire engine.

'Maybe that's Posy now,' Mattie muttered. 'Her spooky pregnancy spidey-sense must have alerted her to the fact that the gate was about to be vandalised.'

But it wasn't Posy. Tumbling out of the back of the cab

was a woman with letterbox-red hair, a leopard-print faux fur and the kind of heels that weren't designed for walking on cobblestones.

'Hi guys,' called out Nina O'Kelly, back from her six-month sabbatical, ten days late. 'Thank you for arranging for four hunky firemen to welcome me home!'

CHAPTER 6

26 days until Christmas

Nina's sudden yet delayed arrival quite overshadowed Strumpet finally being cut free and stuffed into a pet carrier before he could abscond again.

'He's grounded for ever,' Verity said grimly as she waited for another taxi to take her home.

'And we're stopping his allowance,' Johnny added, which was quite funny, but not as funny as Nina stamping her foot.

'Guys! I've been gone for nearly seven months, pay attention to me!'

Though it was way past Mattie's bedtime, she had to stay up for another hour to listen to Nina's *double entendres* about the new living arrangements.

'Mattie and Tom,' Nina kept saying with lots of theatrical winks. 'Who'd have thought it? Just as well I'm here to chaperone you.'

'Why haven't you got jet lag?' Tom demanded, as he sat primly on the edge of one of the armchairs as if he was desperate to make a quick getaway too. 'Shouldn't you be sleeping, and by sleeping, I mean shutting up?'

'I slept on the plane, and rude!' Nina said as she sprawled on the sofa and gave no indication that she wanted to get to bed any time soon. 'How do you put up with him, Mattie?'

'We all have our crosses to bear,' Mattie said automatically, though she and Tom had just managed to bond over a stressful hostage situation. And the way he'd vaulted over the gate! Tom must have very impressive upper-body strength. 'Anyway, talking of crosses, I have to be up early tomorrow, so I'm going to bed.'

Even in bed, Mattie could still hear Nina talking and talking and talking some more while Tom answered in monosyllabic grunts. Mattie hadn't appreciated that the walls in the flat were paper thin. She rolled over, groped in the drawer of her bedside cabinet until she found the round plastic box with her earplugs in (her mother's boyfriend, Ian, snored like he was trying to rouse the dead) and finally settled into an uneasy sleep.

The next morning, the flat was silent when Mattie got up and it wasn't until eleven o'clock that she had a chance to visit the shop, armed with a plate of spiced buns to sweeten the shock, to see how Posy was coping with the desecration of her electronic gate.

'Tom was annoyingly vague about the specifics and Verity's not back from taking Strumpet to the vet,' Posy complained as she struggled to get comfortable on one of the sofas. 'These haven't got citrus in them, have they, Mattie? I can't even look at an orange without getting heartburn.'

'Completely citrus-free, but I might add them to my festive menu so they have all the Christmas spices,' Mattie promised, perching on the arm of the sofa.

'But you said you had your festive menu locked down!' Posy cried, pointing an accusing finger at Mattie.

'It is locked down, but I still reserve the right to add more delicious items to it as I see fit, which is a good thing,' Mattie reminded Posy, who settled back on the cushion with a mollified sigh. 'I'm sure you have plenty of other things you could be fretting about. Like the electronic gate, for example. Sorry about that, but it was the only way to free Strumpet.'

'Oh my God! I can't believe that none of us thought to film Strumpet's ordeal,' exclaimed Nina from the bottom of the stairs. She stuck her head round the door. 'We'd have been sure to go viral. Hey, Posy! God, you weren't joking about being pregnant, were you?'

Posy patted her bump and held a bun aloft. 'There's a bun-in-the-oven joke to be made but my pregnancy brain isn't providing a punchline, and I would get up to hug you but it's just taken me ten minutes to sit down.'

'I'll come and hug you,' Nina decided and she flung herself very gently at Posy. 'I can't believe you're going to have a little sproglet.'

'I can hardly believe it myself,' Posy said in a muffled voice as her face was smooshed against Nina's breasts.

'Though I'm very cross with you, Nina – you were meant to be back ten days ago.'

'Pffftttt! What are ten days between friends?' Nina scoffed. She straightened up, pinched a spiced bun and held it to her mouth at a very peculiar angle. 'So, notice anything different about me?'

Nina was wearing a vintage black fifties sundress, adorned with poppies, which were no match for the brightly coloured tattoos which covered her arms from wrist to shoulder, but if anything, she was looking quite toned down.

'Like the hair,' Mattie said, indicating Nina's bright-red hair, which matched her lipstick. 'Suits you.'

'Thank you, though I'm going to change it very soon because I realise now that I clash with Noah, and he absolutely refuses to dye his. Says he has first dibs on being a redhead,' Nina said, holding her hand to her face, so that Mattie wondered if she was hiding a very ill-advised facial tattoo. Though surely she'd have noticed last night. Although she had been very tired. 'Guess again.'

'Well, you're not wearing your official Happy Ever After T-shirt, though Tom will never wear his and I'm too pregnant to get into mine and Verity said that she wasn't going to be the only one wearing it, so I guess I can let you off,' Posy noted. She grinned. 'Were the firemen very good looking?'

'From a distance,' Mattie admitted. 'Then one of them turned out to be about twelve and another one of them was knocking on for fifty, but the two in the middle weren't bad.'

'Oooh! Did you have stirrings? I didn't think you were the sort to have stirrings,' Posy said.

'This is huge if true! Mattie, did you get a fluttering in your nethers?' Nina asked as Tom appeared stage right from the Classics anteroom.

'Good God,' he said in a truly appalled voice and disappeared stage right again. Mattie put a hand to her cheek to confirm that yes, it was hot and yes, she had just blushed.

'Why have you got *your* hand on your face?' Nina demanded. 'When I've had *my* hand on my face for ages!'

'Is there some law that only one person in a gathering can have their hand on their face at any one time?' Mattie asked tartly; this had to be the jet lag talking. Though she was just grateful that nobody was talking about stirrings and flutterings any more.

'LOOK AT MY HAND!' Nina shouted loud enough that three customers turned to look at her hand and Tom reappeared.

'Do you mind?' he began furiously. 'I'm trying to help a customer put together a list of feel-good romances for someone who's been recently bereaved.'

'FOR THE LOVE OF ALL THAT'S HOLY, WILL YOU LOOK AT MY SODDING HAND?' Nina shouted, thrusting her left hand forward so they could all get a good look at it.

'Your nail polish is chipped,' Tom said in a disapproving voice. He was very good at standing firm in the face of Nina being absolutely impossible, which was impressive of him, but he was also very unobservant.

'Is that . . .?' Posy stared down at Nina's hand. 'Is that what I think it is?'

'Yes, yes!' Nina prompted, dancing on the spot as if she were about to wet herself.

'Engagement ring and *wedding ring*!' Mattie said in disbelief. 'Did you get married?'

'GUYS, I GOT MARRIED!' Nina shouted again to a smattering of very half-hearted applause from the customers who hadn't been frightened away.

'Massive congratulations,' said Verity, who'd come through the door in time for the announcement. 'I think there's a family in Wigan who didn't quite catch your news.'

'Very, I got married,' Nina said and collapsed onto the nearest sofa so hard that poor Posy sitting next to her bounced. 'And can I just say, that you lot are rubbish at getting a clue. Anyway, that's why I was ten days late.'

'You could have got married any time in the six months that you were away,' Posy pointed out. Then she struck a pensive expression. 'Unless . . . it *is* Noah that you're married to?'

Noah was a business analyst and friend of Sebastian's who'd come in to help them transform from a quirky and inefficient niche bookshop to a fully digitised and relevant to the twenty-first century niche bookshop. Though it turned out he'd spent most of his time falling in love with Nina and vice versa. Mattie looked at Nina. Not at her ring, but at her face. Underneath the heavy retro glamour make-up and the jet lag, Nina's eyes sparkled and her usual knowing grin had been replaced by a beaming smile as she talked about their Vegas wedding.

'I decided that I was going to surprise him, not realising

that he'd decided to surprise me,' she recalled. 'It was very modern, a joint proposal. And we were going to just slope off and get married by an Elvis impersonator but our friends, Marianne and Claude, were coming out for our last few days anyway. Then Noah wanted his two sisters to fly out, if they could, and so we had to delay it for a bit, but it all worked out because then we could order more hula girls for the ceremony.'

'But you didn't invite any of us,' Posy said in a hurt little voice and then a big fat tear rolled down her cheek, rapidly joined by an equally large tear rolling down her other cheek.

'I thought about it,' Nina said quickly, taking hold of Posy's hand and linking their fingers. 'But it was originally meant to be just Noah and I, and probably only one of you would have been able to leave the shop to come to Vegas. So we decided that we'd keep it a surprise and then have a massive party when we got back. Hey! We're having a massive party and you're all invited. But after Christmas. I'm not having the birth of Jesus Christ overshadowing our celebration.'

'I invited you to my wedding,' Posy insisted tearfully. 'Though I do appreciate that my wedding was at St Pancras town hall, which was just a bus ride away, and you should know that everything makes me cry at the moment.'

'She cried reading the blurb on the back of a book,' Tom explained dryly. 'Just the blurb.'

'So, you're not mad at me?' Nina asked with a frown. 'Don't be mad at me! I'm back now, full of ideas for the Christmas season. Hey! You haven't had the Christmas brainstorm without me, have you?'

Verity pulled an agonised face. 'We're a little bit behind schedule on our Christmas planning, so we should have the Christmas brainstorm as soon as. In fact, let's do it tomorrow night. You'd like that, wouldn't you?' she added to a still-tearful Posy.

'Maybe.' Posy shrugged, determined not to be jollied out of her funk.

'We'll definitely need a flipchart,' Tom said with the tiniest of smiles. It was very unlike Tom to try to jolly anyone out of a funk, so his gentle teasing of Posy was unexpected and actually kind of *sweet*. 'You love using a flipchart almost as much as you love a tote bag.'

Tom's cunning use of the t-word worked like a charm. Posy perked up instantly. 'Oh! Maybe we could have a special Christmas tote bag!'

Mattie was no longer needed. She had sausage rolls that needed to come out of the oven, the lunchtime rush was imminent and also things tended to get quite heated when the topic of tote bags came up.

'I'm out of here,' she said quickly. 'Let me know about the Christmas brainstorm.' She tried not to shudder at the prospect of both the brainstorm and Christmas itself.

'I'm going to make everyone wear reindeer-antler headbands,' Nina threatened as Verity ixnayed the idea of a Christmas tote bag in no uncertain terms. 'And also, is this a good time to mention that I'm moving out of the flat? Don't want to start married life with Tom's underpants drying over the bath. No offence, Tom.'

'So much offence taken,' Tom huffed and Mattie couldn't

blame him. But still, she'd been desperate for Nina to come back and act as a buffer between her and Tom.

'You won't be moving out immediately?' Mattie lingered by the arch on the left. 'You'll wait until after Christmas.'

'Why would I do that when we're on our honeymoon?' Nina asked incredulously. 'No, I'll be moving out tomorrow night when Noah's back from his work trip. We can't keep our hands off each other at the moment. Mind you, there's no change there.'

Mattie caught Tom's eye and for one moment they were in perfect, exquisitely awkward accord, Tom's hand on his head like he was having a migraine and Mattie patting her burning cheeks.

'. . . can't have you two cramping our sexy style,' Nina continued. 'So, we're moving into Noah's old flat in Bermondsey. Apparently the tenants after him flooded the kitchen, and so it's just been done up, and the landlord knows Noah's a good 'un. Besides, you don't want an old married couple like us ruining your fun, if you know what I mean?'

And then Nina actually nudged Posy twice and treated them all to two theatrical winks. It was a good thing that Nina was moving out, otherwise Mattie would have had no choice but to kill her while she slept.

25 days until Christmas

The next day, November 30th, after the shop had closed at six, even though it was meant to be the start of their new extended opening hours, Mattie's presence was requested at the Happy Ever After Christmas brainstorm.

She was meant to be there by five past six sharp, but the final versions of her speciality Christmas savoury and sweet items had taken a bit longer to bake than she'd planned for. Not that Posy would mind. Mattie always turned up to a brainstorm with freshly baked provisions and anyway, it didn't sound as if Mattie had been missed.

She'd been able to hear the shouting all the way from the main room of the shop through the Classics, Regency, Historical and Paranormal anterooms, across the tearooms and into the back kitchen. Now, as she carried her precious cargo through, Posy's voice was pitched so high with excitement that Mattie feared for her glass cake tiers.

'I love it!' Posy squealed, writing something down on the inevitable flipchart as Mattie reached the main room. 'Love it so much. Very, you're a genius.'

Verity was perched on one of the sofas, hugging a cushion (being an introvert, the loud and raucous Happy Ever After brainstorms were quite the ordeal for her). 'I try,' she said modestly.

'What have I missed?' Mattie asked, putting down her tiered plates on one of the new-releases tables.

'So much Christmas book-related goodness,' Posy said. In the past few days, her bump had got even bigger and rounder – Nina had wondered aloud if it might be twins – but Sebastian had booked her a course of pregnancy massage sessions, which had restored her good cheer and done wonders for her swollen ankles. 'We're all coming in early tomorrow to Christmas-ify the shop. Crispin from the Rochester Street Traders' Association came by this afternoon and he had some quite harsh things to say about our complete lack of decorations. I wanted to strangle him with a length of tinsel by the time he left.'

'We've decided to go for a very tasteful, almost understated, look with the decorations though,' Verity said.

'No we haven't,' Nina insisted forcefully. 'Last year, we didn't really embrace Christmas, so this year I want it to look as if Christmas has vomited all over the shop.'

'Such a lovely and festive image,' Tom murmured, echoing

Mattie's own thoughts. 'The only idea that I actually like is Verity's suggestion that we have a selection of wrapped books under the Christmas tree—'

'You're having a Christmas tree?' Mattie asked. Last year there hadn't been a Christmas tree, just industrial amounts of tinsel and fake snow, which had got everywhere. She'd even found fake snow in her bra when she took it off each night.

'Of course we're having a Christmas tree. It's arriving tomorrow,' said Sam, Posy's sixteen-year-old brother, from behind his fringe. He helped out on Saturdays and in the school holidays, while Little Sophie (though they really had to stop calling her Little Sophie because she now towered over Verity and Posy) also worked on Saturdays but in the tearooms. 'We're going to move out two of the sofas.'

This was also news. Obviously they were anticipating a lot of foot traffic over the next month.

'So, tree, presents . . .' Mattie prompted, because the other notable thing about Happy Ever After brainstorms, apart from the noise levels, was how quickly they got off-topic.

'Yes! Presents,' Posy nodded. 'Customers can choose to pay for an extra book which we'll distribute to residents at the care home around the back of Coram Fields. Nina went in to see them yesterday.'

'Big fans of Regency smut,' Nina reported from her sofa, which she was sharing with Tom, who had barely glanced in Mattie's direction, though he was eyeing up her cake tiers avidly.

'Sounds good,' Mattie said. 'I'd have to look at costings,

but maybe if they donate a book then they can have a free cup of coffee. What else?'

'Well, that brings me nicely to my next idea,' Nina said, glancing down at her iPad. 'I was looking for a way to create a synergy between the bricks and mortar and the social media side of the business. Really grow our brand awareness and core message.'

'Eh?' Posy asked, and she spoke for all of them. Noah and his business analysing skills were obviously rubbing off on Nina if she was bandying about words like 'synergy' and 'brand awareness'.

'It's not just about driving customers to spend shedloads of money in Happy Ever After over the festive season,' Nina exclaimed.

'But it's a lot to do with that,' Verity said firmly. 'Last year we took twenty-three per cent of our annual profit just in December. So, let's make the spending of shedloads of money our top priority.'

'Yes, but we also want those customers to understand what Happy Ever After is and we want to give them an experience that delivers our brand message,' Nina insisted.

'It's like I don't even know you any more.' Sam directed a sad look at Nina. 'Could you please make a completely inappropriate and deeply personal remark?'

'I'm building up to something, guys,' Nina said.

Tom groaned and splayed out his legs like he was in mortal agony. 'Sometime before next Christmas would be great.'

There were murmurs of agreement at this. Mattie really

wished that she'd given it another half hour before she'd come through. She could have made her flaky pastry for tomorrow and had it chilling in the fridge.

'You are a tough crowd,' Nina said cheerfully. 'What I was building up to . . . can I at least get a drumroll?'

'Kill me now and the last beats of my heart can be your drumroll,' Tom said. He was in quite the snipey mood tonight, Mattie noted, as Little Sophie and Sam obligingly stamped their feet.

'I'm talking about a Mistletoe Photo Booth!' Nina said with a flourish. 'We're going to hire a special photo booth and people, only on receipt of a Happy Ever After purchase, can go into the booth with the one they love and take a picture smooching under the mistletoe. They'll also get a digital download of their picture, which they can upload to their social media accounts. How exciting!'

'A photo booth? Won't that take up a lot of space?' Posy wondered.

'Not if we're going to take out two of the sofas anyway. Besides, photo booths don't take up that much room.'

'Sounds expensive.' Verity looked pained at the prospect of extra expense.

'Not that expensive. I've already spoken to the guy who handles the account and given him all the Happy Ever After artwork, because the booth and the pictures will all be heavily branded. Anyway, you have to spend money to make money, so I said that you'd send him the deposit by tomorrow, Very,' Nina said briskly. 'Lots of people want one of these booths but we decided that it works best with the

Happy Ever After brand. Because mistletoe equals kissing and we're a romantic fiction bookshop. Come on! Let's get excited about this! Whoo!' Nina punched the air.

'Maybe whoo . . .' Posy tapped her chin with her magic marker as she thought about the possible benefits of the Mistletoe Booth. 'It's quite sweet, really, isn't it? We get all these men looking put upon as their partners browse our shelves, but they'd soon cheer up if they were pulled into a photo booth for a sudden kiss.'

As far as Mattie was concerned, the whole thing: mistletoe, public displays of affection, pulling people into a small dark enclosed space, was ghastly.

'You do know that kissing someone without their consent, even if there is mistletoe involved, technically counts as an assault?' she pointed out and watched in satisfaction as jaws dropped.

'Oh no, we can't have any assaults in the shop. Absolutely not,' Posy said, aghast.

'Unless . . . well, maybe we could get people to sign a consent form,' Verity suggested, but Nina was flapping her hands and screwing up her face in protest.

'Nobody likes a Scrooge, Mattie,' she said censoriously. 'Happy Ever After customers love romance, so obviously they're going to love a passionate smooch under the mistletoe. Jesus, don't be such a buzzkill.'

'Well, I hate to be another voice of dissent,' Tom said, though actually being the voice of dissent was one of his reasons for living. 'But if this monstrosity comes to pass, I'm not having anything to do with it. I don't want our older ladies getting ideas. You know, sometimes I think they ask me to climb up the rolling ladder to get books down from the top shelves solely so they can ogle me.'

Mattie couldn't help snorting. 'Ha! Who'd want to ogle *you*?' It came out much harsher than she intended, and all those present turned to give her a hard-eyed stare.

'We'll move on from the Mistletoe Booth for now,' Posy decided wisely. 'Verity will need to see a full breakdown of the figures and I need to know exactly how it's going to work, because it's all sounding a bit complicated to me. Now, Tom, I can't wait to hear about all the exciting things you have planned for the shop Twitter in the run-up to Christmas.'

'I've reworked the Twelve Days of Christmas with a romance theme and I'll tweet a line a day, starting on the thirteenth of December,' he said in a bored voice. 'Oh yes, there'll be all manner of festive hi-jinks. Our favourite Christmas romance novels, one of those stupid Twitter hashtag games where we replace a word in a book title to make it more Christmassy. Like, *Pride and Presents*, *To Thrill a Mockingbird*, *Me Before Yuletide*, blah blah blah, we can give the best ones a prize. Then obviously we'll have a new Twitter avatar, where the picture of the shop sign we currently have will be adorned with fat robins gaily cavorting. Et cetera and so on.' He finished up with his weariest sigh yet.

'Oh my God, Tom! That would all be fantastic,' Posy said, struggling to write all Tom's ideas down on her flip-chart. 'I don't know why you sound like you're being tortured beyond all measure.'

'Because the stench of rampant commercialisation makes me sick to my stomach,' Tom said, and Mattie could just tell that he was about to go into one of his rants about the dangers of capitalism or neo-liberalism or some other -ism that he didn't like. There'd also be lots of multi-syllable words that no one else understood.

'Dude, if you don't like rampant commercialisation then don't work in retail,' Nina drawled, but Tom wasn't to be put off.

'Christmas is just an excuse for people to spend money they don't have on presents for people who don't actually need them, all in the spurious name of Jesus,' he pontificated. 'And I think you'll find that *actually*, according to Aramaic texts, Jesus wasn't even born in December but on a date in the Hebrew calendar that *actually* corresponds to September. So, if we're going to be picky about it . . .'

'Oh yes, do let's be picky about it,' Little Sophie murmured to Sam, and they exchanged an eye roll so exaggerated and scathing that it could only have come from two sixteen-year-olds already tested way beyond their boredom threshold.

'. . . I mean, really, is one Christmas-themed tweet, in all its banality, going to sell books or is it simply going to be part of the problem . . . ?'

Mattie wriggled her right leg because her calf was cramping. Was anyone even listening to Tom? Judging from their glazed expressions, Nina scrutinising her fingernails for any signs of chipped polish, Posy shifting uncomfortably because she'd been on her feet for too long, Verity gazing into the middle distance, then no. Everyone had stopped listening. Had stopped caring. Had stopped having the will to live.

Someone needed to step up and rescue them and it looked like Mattie was going to be that person. 'Please, I'm sorry to interrupt,' she fibbed. 'It's just that I have some dough proving that I really need to get back to.'

'I wasn't finished,' Tom snapped, but Mattie had delicious festive-themed snacks so she was going to win.

'Anyway, let's talk about my Christmas bakes,' she said, leaning forward with her cake tiers aloft. It was quite gratifying the way that everyone perked up, except Tom, who shot her a look that was blacker than a coalmine in a power-cut. She held up the left-hand tier. 'These are my savouries. Vegan friendly, individual red cabbage and Brussels sprout tarts, turkey and cranberry Scotch eggs and, instead of my usual sausage roll, for Christmas I'm doing a pig-in-blanket roll. A pork and sage sausage wrapped in home-cured bacon and encased in puff pastry. Here, help yourselves!'

'Truly, we are living in miraculous times,' Nina mumbled around the end of a pig-in-blanket roll. 'This is one of the three best things I've ever put in my mouth.'

'These Scotch eggs, I don't care if they give me heartburn, it will all have been worth it,' Posy said and Mattie smiled modestly, though her smile became very thin when she saw Tom taking one of her vegan tartlets and giving it a suspicious look.

'Then for my sweet selection,' she held the right-hand tier aloft, 'I'm doing miniature salted caramel Yule logs, mince pies with a clementine-infused pastry and what look like little Christmas puddings but actually they're red velvet cake balls,' Mattie explained, sending her sweet treats round the sofas again. 'Then throughout December, I'll also have additional items. For instance, cranberry and orange flavoured shortbread and Christmas spiced buns.'

Again, there was lots of praise and moans of ecstasy and Verity declaring that she hated all mince pies except for Mattie's mince pies.

'Good, so glad was all sorted,' Mattie said, gathering up her empty tiers. 'We can get some shots up on the Happy Ever After insta and also, Verity, mulled wine, we don't need an alcohol license for that, do we?'

'We kind of do,' Verity said unhappily because she'd have to be the one to sort it out. Anyway, Mattie's contribution to the Christmas brainstorm was done.

She turned to leave but Posy's voice called her back.

'What about cupcakes?' she asked in an innocent voice, though she knew full well Mattie's feelings about cupcakes. 'Go on. One Christmas-themed cupcake. For me. Because I'm pregnant.'

'I don't do cupcakes,' Mattie reminded her, as she'd been reminding Posy at regular intervals ever since she'd first signed the lease on the tearooms. 'Cupcakes are a triumph of buttercream over bland sponge and they represent everything that is repugnant about a regressive represent-ation of femininity and God, Posy, I've given you a whole other selection of Christmas-themed goodies, so stop going on about bloody cupcakes.'

Posy wilted and rubbed her bump in a forlorn manner – Mattie was a terrible person who said mean things to pregnant ladies. 'I was only asking,' Posy said in a tiny voice.

'I know.' It was no use, Mattie's blood was up and all this talk about Christmas and now cupcakes was making the red mist descend in a way that it hadn't for ages. 'It's just, you know, I hate cupcakes and I really don't like Christmas either, so can we just drop it, please?'

'Consider it dropped,' Posy said, though she was sounding rather sulky now.

'Sorry,' Mattie offered weakly.

'You're such an Eeyore,' Verity said, her face red with the effort it took to confront someone. 'Honestly, Mattie, you seem to hate so many things, but I'm at a loss to know what you really love.'

'I love lots of things,' Mattie protested, though she couldn't think of a single one when she was put on the spot like this. 'Lots and lots of things.'

'Very's right,' Posy said, abandoning her flipchart to sink gratefully onto the sofa next to Verity. 'You're so negative about everything. You don't like romance, you don't like Paris, or Christmas, or cupcakes. What else is there in life but romance and Paris and Christmas and cupcakes?'

'I have my reasons,' Mattie said, because she did, and they were no business of anyone gathered on the sofas in front of her. Also, though she was proud to proclaim the tearooms as a sovereign state within the Happy Ever After continent, Mattie often felt like she was speaking a foreign language when she was dealing with the Happy Ever After staff. They always made her welcome, invited her along to the pub, but they'd all known each other for years, had a deep, complex, shared history and a love of romantic novels, so it was no wonder that Mattie sometimes felt as if she was on the outside looking in.

But at this precise moment in time she felt like an enemy alien. Misunderstood and mistrusted.

'Come on, people, let's not fight,' Nina said in a jolly, very un-Nina-like voice. 'It's meant to be the season of goodwill and all that, so let's not fall out over the fact that Mattie *hates* the season of goodwill.'

Tom had been silent, for which Mattie was grateful, if somewhat surprised that he wasn't chiming in with his own observations on how she was a Christmas killjoy who despised all that was good in the world. Now he stretched out his legs again. 'I think you'll find that I hated the season of goodwill first and Mattie is just jumping on my band-wagon.'

Was that . . . was Tom actually attempting to take Mattie out of the line of fire, or was he genuinely cross that Mattie's Christmas-hating was getting all the attention? As usual with Tom, it was impossible to tell.

'I have that dough proving,' Mattie said stiffly, though that mythical dough would have proved so much by now that it would have colonised most of the kitchen. 'And FYI, I like lots of things, including kneading dough.' Mostly because she could work out all her aggression about the many things she hated while she was kneading it.

There was nothing left to say and the atmosphere was

so deflated and awkward that Mattie couldn't wait to hurry back to the safe space of her kitchen. She was just stepping through from Classics to Regency when she heard Nina, who didn't possess an indoor voice, say, 'I don't know why you and Mattie are at each other's throats all the time, Tom, when you have so much in common.'

'We have nothing in common,' Tom said, though Mattie had to strain to hear him.

'You both hate Christmas and romantic novels,' Posy piped up.

'I don't hate romantic novels, I just never ever want to read one . . .'

'Tom and Mattie sitting in a tree, talking about how much they hate Christmas and K.I.S.S.I.N.G.,' Nina chanted, and there were giggles and snorts from the cheap seats.

Tom huffed with great disdain. 'The day I K.I.S.S. Mattie is the day that Satan goes to work on ice skates.'

CHAPTER 8

25 days until Christmas

With the brainstorm over, and Noah returned from his business trip, it was time to move Nina out. Noah arrived with a rent-a-van and a triumphant toot of its horn as soon as the brainstorm was over.

'Can't wait to get me on his own again,' Nina said with great satisfaction and another wink as Noah and her brother carried her mini bar shaped like a ship's prow down the stairs. With all the winking, it was a wonder that Nina hadn't irreparably damaged an eyelid.

With Nina moving out of the largest room, Tom moved in. To give him some credit, he asked Mattie if she wanted to toss a coin for it.

'I'm more than happy for you to have it because I never want to move my stuff again,' Mattie said, as she helped Nina pack up her staggering collection of skincare and beauty products. She even had an old-fashioned hood-dryer at the back of her wardrobe.

'If you're sure.' Tom didn't even bother to wait but was out of the room like a greyhound. 'We can use the box room for storage. The flat's not really big enough for three people, is it?'

Mattie thought back to her eight-woman, four-bedroom student house-share but now they had a truce over the room allocation, she couldn't bear to be at loggerheads again. Besides, they'd never be able to agree on a flatmate and more to the point, Mattie had a whole Le Creuset set, a collection of vintage enamelware, a slow cooker and a bread machine back in Hackney, which her mother kept threatening to donate to charity.

'Anyway, a third flatmate would just complicate things,' Nina insisted, as they all took a break from packing and moving and re-moving for a restorative cup of tea and a piece of the festive cranberry and orange shortbread. 'Whatever flavour, boy or girl, it's going to lead to sexual tension.'

'I don't see why it would,' Mattie said, giving Tom a flinty look, which he returned. 'If a girl moved in and she and Tom fell in love, then why would I care?'

Tom didn't blink. 'Exactly. If some man with the patience of a saint moved in and fell in love with Mattie and she felt the same way, I'd be amazed, astounded, but I wouldn't care.'

'You would when the shagging started,' Nina said imperturbably as everyone else choked on their shortbread.

'Believe me, you'll be able to hear everything and I mean *everything*. There was the time that Verity—'

Noah clapped a hand over his new bride's mouth even as Tom said, 'Stop! I'm begging you. Whatever you're about to say, I know that I'll never be able to look at Verity ever again if you get to the end of that sentence.'

'Anyway, we're not taking on a flatmate,' Mattie said quickly. 'We're going to use the box room for storage.'

Nina pulled a face as if using the box room for storage was a wasted opportunity when one of them could be having sex with an imaginary third flatmate in there. 'Your call,' she said then looked from Mattie to Tom and back again. 'I know you've taken a vow of chastity, Mattie . . .'

It was hard for Mattie to remember why she'd ever missed Nina because she certainly hadn't missed Nina's knack for inserting herself in other people's business. 'Not a vow of chastity. Just a vow that I'm not going to waste the best years of my life on *some worthless man* instead of reaching for my dreams.'

'Not all men are worthless,' Noah muttered, as Tom sighed wearily.

'And as for you, Tom, have you ever even been out on a date?' Nina asked, and Mattie leaned forward because she didn't want to miss a word of this or the discomfited look on Tom's face, as if the collar of his shirt had suddenly become three sizes too small. 'Are you into women? Or are you into men? Or are you into both? No judgement, but it's been four years and you've never once shown any interest in getting down and dirty.'

'Nina, Nina, Nina,' Noah said, shaking his head, but his expression was more indulgent than exasperated.

'You know, it's not too late to get a divorce,' Tom told him, his expression entirely exasperated. 'There's not a judge in the land who'd expect you to stay married in the face of such emotional cruelty.'

'Not emotionally cruel, just curious,' Nina said. 'But if neither of you are going to bring anyone home for fun sexy times, then at least you don't have to have a set of boring house rules. Like, don't come into a room if there's a sock over the door handle unless you want to get an eyeful of—'

'House rule! Neither of us are to ever bring anyone home for fun sexy times,' Mattie said desperately. 'All those in favour, say aye!'

Tom raised his hand. 'Aye! For the love of God, aye! And also, on the subject of house rules, can you make sure that you wash up after you've cooked. It's just that it's a small kitchen and . . .'

'I always wash up after myself,' Mattie snapped, stung at the accusation that she didn't. She prided herself on always running a neat and tidy kitchen. Then her eyes drifted towards the sink where everything she'd used to make her shortbread was piled up, waiting to be washed. 'Except when people are so desperate to eat that they don't give me a chance to do the washing up. You had four shortbread, Tom,' she added accusingly.

'Fine. I won't eat your baking if you don't leave the washing up not done,' Tom said as if it were something that he could easily forego.

It was pretty much the worst thing that anyone had ever said to Mattie, or at least in the top ten worst things.

'Fine,' she said herself.

'Fine,' said Tom again.

Nina grinned. 'Is anyone else feeling like maybe things aren't actually fine at all?' she wanted to know. Then her grin grew broader. 'I hope this isn't unresolved sexual tension and the reason you don't want a third flatmate is that you're going to be at it like rabbits as soon as we all leave?'

'I'm not even going to dignify that with a response,' Tom said icily, launching himself away from the kitchen doorway where he'd been leaning. 'If anyone needs me, I'll be in my room. Please knock before coming in.'

As soon as they heard the door shut, Nina turned to Mattie eagerly. 'I will pay you actual cash money for any dirt you get on Tom. Name your price!'

'She doesn't mean it,' Noah said, gently cuffing Nina's chin.

'I do,' Nina said, but Mattie folded her arms.

'I'm pretty sure that there's no dirt on Tom, because why would anyone in their right mind want to get dirty with him?' she said with a shudder at the thought of Tom having . . . ugh! Carnal relations! 'But even if he brought back the entire chorus line from *Anything Goes*, there's a flatmate code of conduct and I'd never spill. In much the same way that if I brought back the English rugby team, Tom would be sworn to secrecy.'

'I never would have thought that your type would be a rugger bugger,' Nina mused, and Mattie's type absolutely wasn't. In the past she'd gone for brooding, dark-haired men who'd looked good in chef's whites, but the thing about the past was that it wasn't the present and it definitely wasn't the future.

Not that Nina needed to know that – and the only way to deal with Nina was to beat her at her own game.

'Actually, talking of the English rugby team, they're coming over in about an hour so it would be really good if you were gone by then,' Mattie said calmly as Nina hooted in delight. 'We're going to need a lot of room for what I have planned.'

Nina was already on her feet, while Noah made his excuses and all but ran from the room. 'Say no more. It's always the quiet ones!' said Nina.

Once Nina and Noah had finally left, Tom stayed in his room the whole time Mattie cleaned the kitchen, leaving no crumb and not one butter smear unvanquished.

Then as soon as she went into her room, Tom was out of the flat door and down the stairs without a word. Which suited Mattie very well. Now she could have a bath without worrying that Tom would hear her splashing about (the thought of being naked with only a door separating them was quite the headtrip).

They'd been in the flat for three days now and this was the third night in a row that Tom had gone out. It was better that he was out than in, especially if she was in too, but where on earth did Tom go? Did he find a quiet corner of a quiet pub and read a book rather than stay in with Mattie? Did he go out with the Banter Boys? Or perhaps

Tom really did have a girlfriend who he preferred to spend his evenings with.

As Mattie ran her bath, pouring a generous dollop of her favourite fig-scented bubble bath into the water so that heavenly-scented steam clouds rose up, she decided that Tom couldn't have a girlfriend. If he had, then there would be no reason to be so secretive about her. And also, what woman in her right mind would ever want to date a shabbily dressed man with a superiority complex?

CHAPTER

9

24 days until Christmas

Generally speaking, Mattie had always found it easy to avoid Tom, even now they were living and working in the same general space.

She barely saw him in the tearooms apart from when he came in for his free coffee at 10.10 exactly, and when she popped into the shop to talk with Posy or Verity or present them with spare baked goods, Tom was usually lurking in one of the anterooms with a customer or sitting on one of the sofas, his head bent over his staff-issue iPad as he updated Happy Ever After's Twitter account. Usually, he gave no indication that he'd even registered Mattie's presence, unless she was carrying cake. And surprisingly, it was very easy to avoid Tom of an evening because he went out every night like some tweedy party animal.

But the night after Nina left, they finally came into close

contact on the stairs that led up to their flat. Mattie trudging upwards ready for nothing but bath, box set then bed, Tom descending with his ancient Nokia phone clamped to his ear.

They both immediately clung to opposite sides of the stair; Mattie pinned to the bannister as Tom pressed himself up against the wall so there'd be no chance of body contact. It was all Mattie could do not to shudder at the thought.

'I'll be there in ten minutes,' Tom said, as he inched past her down the stairs. 'I'm practically at the tube station.'

Liar, liar, pants on fire, Mattie thought to herself, then frowned, as she was once again thinking about Tom's pants. No! Not going there! As the door slammed, she shook her head to free her mind from the searing image of Tom clad in a pair of baggy old-fashioned underpants.

Mattie made a quick supper of an omelette that was more melted cheese than egg and studded with field mushrooms, then settled down in the living room with her plate, a large glass of red wine and Netflix. She wasn't really making the most of living in Central London – but all her non-bookshop friends were single and all they ever wanted to do was go to places where they could meet people who might make them less single. And Mattie was actually very happy alone. Deliriously happy that her heart was safely tucked in her chest where it couldn't be hurt or broken.

It was all very well making eyes with some stranger in a bar, letting him buy you a drink or vice versa, flirting, agreeing to a date, then another and another. But that led to welcoming someone into your life only for them to take it over, destroy it, ransack and belittle everything that you hold dear.

Added to that, the Christmas party season was well under way, so any strangers that Mattie might meet would be wearing questionable festive jumpers with snowmen, robins and other assorted festive miscreants on them. They'd also think that they could take all manner of liberties 'because it's Christmas!' So, Mattie would much rather spend a night staying in, trying not to let her now-unhappy train of thought derail the simple pleasures of good wine, melted cheese and a new episode of *The Crown*.

As she tried to concentrate on the latest adventures of Liz and Phil, her attention kept wandering. Not just with bad memories that she tried not to dwell on but because something about the living room was different.

It was quite empty without Nina's mini bar and coffee table and yet it didn't look empty. The shelves set into the alcoves on either side of the fireplace had been full of Verity and Nina's books. ('But not all our books,' they were both at pains to point out, as if not having enough books was a terrible crime.)

Since Nina had left, the shelves had been bare but now the ones on the left had books on them once more. Tom's books, obviously. They were bound to be dry, academic tomes that would hold absolutely no interest for Mattie, who had very little interest in books – although *Passion and Patisserie at the Little Parisian Café* had been quite enjoyable and she was deep into a proof of *The Little Cake Shop on Buttercup Lane.* She'd had no idea that there was a whole sub-genre of romantic fiction about young women running cake shops and, despite herself, Mattie was into it.

Surely there would be no romantic fiction nestling on Tom's shelf – but maybe it wouldn't hurt to check. When Mattie returned from a quick trip to the kitchen for afters (leftover bread and butter pudding from the tearooms that she'd made to use up yesterday's pains au chocolat) she wandered over to see what books floated Tom's boat.

Quelle surprise! There was all manner of wordy books by important wordy people. Everything that Sigmund Freud had ever written, by the looks of things. A lot of volumes about something called Critical Theory, which sounded like the complete opposite of fun, and actually a surprising number of feminist texts: *A Vindication of the Rights of Woman, The Dialectic of Sex, The Female Eunuch, Sexual Personae, The Beauty Myth, How to Be a Woman* by Caitlin Moran. Mattie picked the last one from the shelf, as it was the only book on display that she (a) had any interest in and (b) might be able to decipher.

Did all these books mean that Tom was a feminist? Could men even be feminists? Mattie thought that they probably could but Tom acted, dressed and spoke like he wished that it were still the 1930s, so she'd never expect him to be forward thinking. Although he did work in a romantic fiction bookshop surrounded by women. And then there were the Banter Boys . . .

Much as it pained her to admit it, Tom was an enigma. Mattie slotted *How to Be a Woman* back in its place. Even though he had displayed his books in a communal area of the flat, Mattie didn't want to snoop or feel forced to report back to Posy, Nina and Verity that Tom had a well-worn copy of a book called *Speculum of the Other Woman*. Ugh! Gross! It turned out to be a book about French feminist theory rather than a sexual health manual, but even so Mattie decided to leave Tom's books alone because she wasn't sure she could cope with any more discoveries about Tom's life away from Happy Ever After.

She really was going to return to the royals, but then one of the books jumped right out at her. A big leather-bound book with gold lettering on the spine.

Tom Greer.

Wait! WHAT! Tom had written a *book*! He'd kept that pretty bloody quiet, and Mattie wasn't going to snoop but neither was she a saint, and Tom had written a book! She yanked it from the shelf so she could get a proper look at the title on the cover.

No More Mr Nice Guy

The Role of the Alpha Male and the Effects of Feminism in Romantic Fiction

Tom Greer

'Oh, my days!' Mattie muttered to herself, because she'd just hit pay-dirt. The mother lode. If anyone wanted intel on Tom, then here it was; his much-speculated-upon but previously unknown PhD dissertation, *and it was all about romantic novels*.

Mattie flung herself back down on the sofa and turned to the first page with fingers that trembled with anticipation. Even the acknowledgements page was fascinating. Tom had parents, Jerry and Margot – who even knew?! He thanked his supervisor, the staff at the British Library and Senate House and dedicated the whole kit and caboodle to 'my mentor, employer, sounding board and, most importantly, friend, the late Lavinia Thorndyke.'

Not for the first time, Mattie wished that she'd known the late Lavinia, even though the former owner of Happy Ever After sounded like the sort of person who saw right through you and could instantly sum up what you were made of. Mattie didn't think she was made of anything that was particularly impressive.

Unlike Tom, who'd written a whole dissertation about romantic fiction! Tom always acted as if he'd never read any at all, though Nina always insisted that he did on the sly. And this wasn't just about romantic fiction; it was about alpha males, though Tom was distinctly *not* an alpha male. He wasn't even a beta male. He was, like . . . what was the last letter of the Greek alphabet? Mattie did a quick google on her phone. Yes, that was it. Tom was like an omega male.

This was going to be good, Mattie thought, turning the pages to get to the first chapter and settling down for a juicy read . . .

Fifteen minutes later she thrust the book away from her in frustration. She could hardly understand a single word of it and the words that she did understand tended to be the little ones: of, the, and; that sort of thing.

Tom used words that Mattie had never come across before. *Jouissance.* Poststructuralism. Epistemology. Though she was pretty sure that the last one was something gruesome that happened to women when they were in labour.

She picked up Tom's thesis again and turned to a random chapter. *The Pen is Mightier Than the Penis – the phallic symbol castrated.*

'The potent phallus is an enduring symbol of romantic literature. From the Regency novel, where the heroes have both thrusting wit and thrusting rapiers, to the corporate alpha male of the eighties bonkbuster in his skyscraper, a literal depiction of his manhood and virility . . .'

'. . . violent misogyny of the sexual act. When he takes her virginity, the author uses the metaphor of a conquering army. She is invaded, her rights and her autonomy stripped from her . . .'

'. . . but fifty years of feminism and the ever-evolving roles between the sexes have allowed for a softer alpha male. To win his lady, he must self-castrate, become soft, empathetic and yet not flaccid. He must be a seductive combination of soft and pliant, and yet rock hard so he can satisfy and satiate the needs of a partner who . . .'

Enough! Mattie jumped to her feet, face burning with the heat of a thousand fiery suns. She hurled herself at the old-fashioned sash window and with some difficulty managed to grapple with the lock, and heave it upwards. Then she stuck her hot, hot, hot face outside so the cold, crisp night air could offer her some relief. Though not the relief of a modern-day alpha male from a romantic novel who, according to Tom, regarded women as his intellectual equal even as he made mad, passionate love to them.

'Oh dear!' Mattie stuck her head out even further and only once her face had resumed its usual, regulated temperature, was she able to shut the window. Then she seized hold of Tom's dissertation and rammed it back in its gap on the shelf, and even that seemed like a metaphor for a sex scene in some tawdry bodice ripper written in the 1980s before, as Tom posited, the romantic novel got woke.

As for the bibliography! Mattie might not read romance novels – apart from her current flirtation with the little-baked-goods-emporium genre – but even she recognised the book titles Tom had listed. *Fifty Shades of Grey*, *Lace*, *Wuthering Heights*, *Bridget* bloody *Jones* and her diary.

Tom was a gigantic hypocrite with his lofty airs and graces, making out that he was above the whole romantic fiction thing and that he only worked in a romantic fiction bookshop because he had Posy wrapped around his little finger and was allowed to get away with murder. Well, not any more!

Posy, Verity and Nina had wanted gossip on Tom? Well, they were never going to believe this!

Mattie could hardly sleep that night in anticipation of how she was going to break the news to them. She was tempted to bake a cake and ice the words, *Tom has a doctorate in romantic fiction* on it, though it would have to be quite a big cake.

However, she was forced to admit to herself that her wakefulness might have something to do with thinking about Tom reading all the dirty bits in a lot of books and how he might have used that knowledge for something other than his dissertation. Around three in the morning, Mattie had to get out of bed and hoist open the window again . . .

23 days until Christmas

The next morning, as Mattie was shaping (what turned out to be some very phallic-looking) croissants and talking to her mother on speakerphone, she finally came to her senses.

'Have you thought about internet dating?' her mother asked, as she always did during their morning call. 'Or that HookUpp thing. Your aunt says that even Charlotte uses it and she much prefers horses to men.'

Mattie's cousin Charlotte liked horses and men in equal measure. She'd once told Mattie at their other cousin's hen do: 'I ride men for pleasure and horses for glory,' after far too many pornstar martinis.

'I'd only think about internet dating if I was thinking about dating, and I'm not. We've been through this,' Mattie said, staring in dismay at her phallic-looking croissants. 'Also, that dating app was created by Posy's husband, so I am keeping well clear of it.'

'So sad,' her mother sighed. 'My only daughter. Young, beautiful, pure of heart and yet she's given up on love.'

Mattie's mother, Sandrine, was French and had very strong opinions about love, personal grooming and that a woman was never fully dressed without dousing herself in Chanel no. 5.

'I tried love, it didn't work out,' Mattie said as she put her first tray of croissants in the oven. 'We've been through this a million times. I'm concentrating on my career and I'm perfectly happy.'

'Pfffttt! You're not happy. Guy agrees with me. There's a sadness in your eyes, *ma petite Mathilde*. Also, when a woman gets to your age, she should have sex at least once a day. It does wonderful things for the complexion.'

'I'm hanging up now,' Mattie said, sliding in the second tray. 'And my complexion is just fine, better than fine. I use an exfoliating mask twice a week.'

Her mother wasn't to be fobbed off. 'You can't let one bad man, one bad experience, put you off *l'amour*,' she said. 'Yes, he broke your heart but when you find the right man, he'll make your heart whole again.'

'My heart is whole, though it's actually beating quite fast because you're being annoying now, Mum,' Mattie said crossly.

'I'm going to come down to your little tearooms with this lovely boy who came around to cut one of the trees in the back garden. Couldn't see a thing out of the spareroom window. We'll sit on one of your tables ordering endless pots of tea until you agree to go on a date with him.'

'Bye, Mum. Have a great day and if you come within fifty metres of the shop, I'm getting a restraining order,' Mattie said, and she was barely joking.

Sandrine had only ever been allowed to enter Rochester Mews once for the official opening of the tearooms and she'd disgraced both herself and Mattie. She'd cried all the way through Mattie's speech, which had actually been quite touching, but then she'd cornered Posy and Sebastian, who were only just married, and asked Posy how she was managing with the cystitis. 'They call it the honeymoon disease,' she'd said as Posy's face had turned a painful shade of red and Sebastian had choked on one of the profiteroles from Mattie's croquembouche. 'I spent two weeks in bed with Mattie and Guy's father when we first got married and then when I did get up, I could barely walk. He was a marvellous lover even if he was a terrible husband.'

Mattie had dragged her mother away then – and hadn't been able to look at Posy, much less talk to her, for a good week after that – and now Sandrine was banned. She wouldn't mean to, because she wasn't at all malicious, but she'd end up filling everyone in on the whys and wherefores of Mattie's broken heart.

Mattie felt the hot rush of shame as she imagined Sandrine on one of the sofas explaining to Nina, Posy and Verity why Mattie spent her evenings making cakes rather than sweet, sweet love with a handsome young man, and reminded herself that everyone had a right to their privacy. To their secrets.

Even Tom. She didn't know why he was hiding his academic interests from his friends and colleagues but he was. So, Mattie had to respect that.

Though that wouldn't stop her from continuing her own investigations into the puzzle that was Tom Greer. He'd always been a thorn in her side, but now the irritation that he roused in her was less to do with his superior ways and the whole free coffee thing and more that Mattie couldn't begin to fathom him out.

Tom was like a recipe that just wouldn't behave itself. But just as she'd made thirty-three attempts to perfect her broken-hearted brownies (finally nailing them by adding some crushed pecan nuts to increase serotonin), so Mattie wouldn't rest until Tom was no longer a mystery.

With the impending doom of a rapidly approaching Christmas (much like that boulder in *Indiana Jones*), it very quickly transpired that Mattie had many other things to worry about than unlocking the enigma that was Tom. While she'd been shaping croissants and fending off Sandrine, the Happy Ever After staff had transformed the shop into a glittery, sparkly, tinselly, festivey wonderland. By the time Mattie ventured across the anterooms at ten, concerned that no one had been in for their coffee, it was to find that neither Nina nor Posy had stopped at just a bit of tinsel, or a few paper-chains, or even some Christmas cards from loyal customers strung up about the place. Oh, no. Christmas had come to town and made itself right at home in Happy Ever After.

There were Christmas gewgaws and paraphernalia everywhere she looked. A gigantic Christmas tree, which had to rival the one in Trafalgar Square for size, had been erected in the centre of the main room of the shop and decorated with some fairly tasteful pink and silver lights, baubles and tinsel, to echo the pink and grey colour scheme of the shop. 'The temptation to add more colour is bloody killing me,' Nina moaned because she was in full Xmas-zilla mode, but apparently Posy had put her swollen foot down.

As Mattie stood there with her coffee pot in one hand and a plate with her first official batch of clementine-infused mince pies in the other, Verity was telling Nina in no uncertain terms that she couldn't do a nativity-scene window display with books replacing the key figures. 'You can't have *Bridget Jones's Baby* as the infant Jesus,' Verity said aghast. 'It's quite offensive.'

'You're only saying that because you're a vicar's daughter,' Nina said, but Verity failed to rise to the usual bait.

'Actually, I'm saying that as a person with a modicum of taste. You agree with me, Mattie, don't you?'

'You know, some people don't even celebrate Christmas,' Mattie pointed out and Posy, who'd been about to grab a mince pie, grunted in annoyance.

'Christmas isn't really about the birth of the infant Jesus any more,' she said. 'It's about togetherness and family and something to look forward to in the bleak midwinter.'

'Sentimental twaddle,' Tom called out from behind the

counter where he was serving a customer and, unlike his three colleagues, was not wearing a pair of flashing reindeer antlers. As it was, Mattie could hardly bring herself to even glance in his direction, knowing what she now knew. 'Just be honest, Posy, and admit that the only reason that I'm inhaling fake snow with every breath I take, is because you want to increase your profit margins.'

'My profit margins pay your wages, buster,' Posy snapped, snatching up one of the mince pies.

'For some people, Christmas isn't about togetherness or family, it's just a harsh reminder of all the things that are missing in their life,' Mattie said with great feeling as she looked around the all-flashing, all-glittering Christmaspalooza that had once been an understated bookshop. 'Every Christmas advert, every Christmas card with a cosy fireside scene, every email with gift suggestions for their loved ones is like a little dagger in the heart. There are an awful lot of lonely people in the world and Christmas just makes them feel lonelier.'

'Hear hear!' said Tom, who was now halfway up the rolling ladder. 'Couldn't have put it better myself.'

It was the nicest thing that Tom had ever said to her. Mattie allowed herself a small, pleased smile. Posy looked at her, then looked at the mince pie she held in her hand, then she looked at Tom who was saying in a pained voice to Nina, 'Don't you think you've decked the halls with enough bloody holly by now?' then she put the mince pie back on the plate.

'You're ruining Christmas, you two! I hope you're happy!'

By mid-afternoon, the anterooms were adorned with pink and silver tinsel, pink and silver bunting swung gaily from the bookshelves, and pink and silver stars of varying sizes hung from the ceilings. Nina had also created a place-holder Christmas window display featuring piles of gift-wrapped books. She was planning a far more ambitious display featuring a Christmas tree made entirely out of books. But it would have to wait until after she had paid a visit to a special Christmas shop-fitting warehouse in Deptford where she could get her hands on yet more festive fixtures and fittings for the shop.

'And the tearooms,' she said, entering Mattie's domain with a boxful of Christmas decorations and a determined expression. 'Seeing as I'm not allowed to go full festive throttle in the shop, I thought I could really go to Tinsel Town in here.'

'Oh, did you?' Mattie tried to keep the challenge out of her voice. The key to dealing with Nina was to be vague. Not commit to any one thing, then deny it all at a later date. It only worked approximately thirty per cent of the time.

'Yes, yes I did,' Nina said, her eyes shining with a mission-ary-like zeal. 'Now what I was thinking – don't make that face, Mattie, like you just caught your finger in the door, hear me out – was that the tearooms could be, wait for it . . .'

'If my dodgy ticker doesn't kill me first, then the suspense definitely will,' Cuthbert whispered for Mattie's benefit, and she had to school her features into something impassive so she wouldn't laugh.

'. . . a reindeer refuelling station. Like, refuelling because you serve food and drinks, yeah?'

'Interesting,' Mattie said calmly, while her heart beat out a frantic rhythm. 'Very interesting.'

'I thought you could rewrite your whole menu with a reindeer theme. I mean, you've got Donner, Blitzen, Prancer, Dancer . . . there are more.' Nina snapped her fingers. 'Oh, it's on the tip of my tongue.' She waggled her tongue piercing, which always made Mattie feel a little sick.

'Rudolph?' Cuthbert offered as he sprinkled chocolate powder onto a freshly made cappuccino, using the Christmas-tree stencil that he'd bought of his own volition. Not even discussing it with Mattie first. He'd also brought in an ancient ghetto blaster and had been treating Mattie and the tearoom customers to a heavy rotation of Christmas hits on tape. Mattie hadn't had the heart to tell him that she was going to scream if she heard Boney M sing 'Mary's Boy Child' one more bleeding time.

'Well, you've certainly given us something to ponder,' Mattie said, smiling at a customer who'd come up to pay.

'I think there's another reindeer besides Rudolph,' Nina said, looking around the tearooms, then looking down at her iPad. 'Of course, you'll have to take out a couple of tables.'

Mattie and Cuthbert shared an agonised look – it turned out that even Cuthbert's love of Christmas had its limits. 'I'm not sure that's a great idea,' Cuthbert ventured.

'Well, how else are we going to have room for three life-sized reindeer?' Nina replied, although Mattie had been hoping that Nina had forgotten all about her plans for life-sized reindeer. 'Stop looking at me like that, Mattie. I said life-sized, I didn't say full-sized. One of them will be a little baby reindeer, then a mummy and daddy reindeer. It will be adorable! But the guy at the Christmas fittings place said we have to pick them up by six today, so we need to decide where they're going to go. Could we get rid of the two window tables?'

The time for being vague was gone. 'No, we absolutely can't,' Mattie said as firmly as she'd ever said anything. 'Even taking out one table would lose me five hundred pounds a week. Unless you're planning to reimburse me?'

'Five hundred quid? But I bet people come in and nurse a coffee for an hour, so I don't see how you get five hundred quid a week,' Nina argued, then she looked around the tearooms again. It was four on a Thursday afternoon and every seat at every table was taken. No one was eking out a cup of tea for as long as they could. Mattie would have been offended if they had – it would have meant they'd come up to the counter to order and been able to resist the tempting display of cakes, pastries and savouries. The people on the table in the corner alone had started with savouries and were now onto their second cake apiece, and they'd only been seated for half an hour.

'Also, three life-sized reindeer? An absolute Health and Safety hazard,' Mattie said in the same firm voice.

'Two reindeer?'

'No reindeer,' Mattie countered.

Nina tipped her head back and groaned. 'You're meant to agree to one reindeer.'

'All right then, one reindeer,' Mattie said magnanimously and Nina brightened.

'Really?'

Mattie nodded. 'A very tiny reindeer, no bigger than this.' She indicated five centimetres with a finger and thumb. 'It can sit on top of the display case on the counter. Isn't that great? Everyone's happy! Are you happy, Cuthbert?'

'Deliriously!' Cuthbert shouted over the hiss of Jezebel as he deftly dealt with half a dozen coffee orders with all the skill of a maestro conducting an orchestra. 'Though I have to say that a baby-sized reindeer would have been cute,' he mused and Mattie made a mental note to remind Cuthbert that they were a united front. 'Though some small child would be sure to climb up on it, fall off, split their head open, go into a coma and then die,' he added with some relish. 'And then we'd get sued.'

'Exactly,' Mattie said but Nina was having none of it.

'I'm getting Posy,' she said and five minutes later, she returned with a very long-suffering Posy, who immediately sat down on a just-vacated chair.

'Everything hurts,' she said by way of a greeting. If the Department of Health wanted to do something to combat the rise in teen pregnancy, they could just get Posy Morland-Thorndyke to tour the nation's schools and list all her pregnancy-related ailments. 'Nina's explained everything to me and I've said that there is no way that you're having three life-sized reindeer in here. Not even one!'

That was unexpected but very welcome news. 'Hallelujah!'

Mattie put her hands in the prayer position. 'Look, I know our Christmas decorations are a bit scant . . .'

'They're practically non-existent,' Nina pointed out, because the tearooms' Christmas decorations currently consisted of a forlorn piece of tinsel Blu-Tacked to the front of the counter by Cuthbert when Mattie had been in the kitchen and the Santa hat that Cuthbert insisted on wearing.

'I'm happy to have some tasteful decorations in the pink and silver you've used in the shop, but they have to be flameproof and I'm not having anything *on* the counter where we serve food,' Mattie said. 'But tasteful is the key word here.'

'I'm the very definition of tasteful,' Nina declared, when only that morning, she'd admitted that she didn't know where tacky ended and tasteful began. 'But yes, I will do some very basic, very boring Christmas decorations in here even though you people are always stifling my creativity.'

'More importantly, my new Christmas items are going down a storm so we can shoot them and stick them on the shop Instagram. Look! I've even drawn a couple of sprigs of holly on the blackboard,' Mattie continued, gesturing at the menu blackboard on the wall behind the counter. She wasn't negative about *everything*. She didn't mind a brief journey on the Christmas train, especially if it increased her profit margins too.

'Well, this was a lot easier than I thought it was going to be,' Posy said as she put a hand to the small of her back. 'While we're talking about Christmas and because I had to drag my aching carcass all the way here, will you please do a Christmas-themed cupcake? For me? Have I mentioned that I'm growing an actual human being inside me? That should get me a free pass and it should definitely get me one Christmas-themed cupcake.'

When Posy put it like that, Mattie felt like she could hardly refuse her. Only kicking kittens and punching puppies was worse than denying a woman suffering a very difficult pregnancy one measly Christmas-themed cupcake.

But.

It wouldn't be just the one Christmas-themed cupcake. Then it would be 'But you made a cupcake for Christmas, why can't you make one for Valentine's Day? And Easter? And Mother's Day? And because it's raining outside and because the whole bloody world loves cupcakes.'

'No, Posy! For the final time, no! I hate cupcakes,' Mattie insisted vehemently. 'I absolutely hate them and I hate Christmas and oh God, how I hate Paris!'

'What's Paris got to do with the price of eggs?' asked a male voice, and there was Tom.

For the last half hour, with all this talk of reindeer and cupcakes, at least Mattie had been spared from thoughts of Tom and his obsession with phallic imagery. Mattie looked down at the counter, so she wouldn't have to look at Tom, caught sight of the cucumber she'd been chopping up for sandwiches before all this Christmas nonsense, and blushed.

'Forget I said anything about Paris and let's just focus on the bit where I'm never, ever going to serve a cupcake on these premises,' Mattie said, and Posy's bottom lip trembled and she blinked rapidly, and how Mattie missed the days before Posy got pregnant, when she didn't burst into tears every time someone even looked at her funny. 'But I will make you a lovely raspberry-leaf tea to ease your backache, Posy, and I'll bring it through to the shop with a piece of cinder toffee and apple cake.'

'All right.' Posy sniffed and tucked her wobbly lip away as Tom hoisted her to her feet with a very ungentlemanly grunt.

'Can I have cake too?' Nina asked.

'No, you can't.' Tom fixed Nina with a disapproving look. 'We're meant to be on our way to that ghastly-sounding place with all the Christmas tat, or, as I prefer to think of it, my own personal ninth circle of hell.'

'You and Mattie, with your Christmas-hating vibes.' Nina shot them both an arch look. 'Maybe you should spend Christmas together.'

Mattie and Tom both winced at the idea, although Mattie also blushed to boot. Don't think about sausage plaits, or Yule logs, or any other Christmas phallic-shaped food, she told herself as she fanned her face with the laminated drinks menu.

'And maybe you should move your arse in the direction of the van you insisted on renting,' Tom said, making shooing motions with his hands at Nina, who stuck her pierced tongue out at him. But miracle of miracles, she moved away from the counter and, thank God, towards the glass doors that led back into Happy Ever After.

CHAPTER 11

23 days until Christmas

Mattie was just finishing her evening prep when she heard a tap at the tearooms' door and nearly sliced off the tip of her finger with her paring knife. It was after eight, the bookshop and tearooms were now closed, and Tom and Nina still hadn't returned. She poked her head round the kitchen door and saw a shadowy figure waving at her through the glass of the front door. It had to be a friend, because foes didn't have the code to the electronic gate (now recovered from its recent ordeal).

Probably Tom had forgotten his key, though he was somewhere between friend and foe, she decided as she hurried to unlock the door. But it wasn't Tom. Standing there with a cheesy smile was the Archbishop of Banterbury.

For the life of her, Mattie couldn't remember his real name.

'Hi,' she said, with a bright smile to disguise her embarrassment. 'Tom's not back yet.'

'Mattie, you're even more beautiful than when we first met,' he gushed, which wasn't true because Mattie had very recently had a mishap with a bag of icing sugar and looked as if she'd gone prematurely grey. 'Tom texted me. Said he was going to be late. He and the also very beautiful Nina were stopping at Beigel Bake.'

Why was it that Tom wanted to eat everyone else's baked goods but Mattie's? Although even she could admit, Beigel Bake did the best bagels in London and also rye bread, which was studded with caraway seeds and was perfect with smoked salmon and cream cheese. Mattie pulled her phone out of her apron pocket to text Nina with an order.

'So, Tom said I could wait upstairs for him, but,' he dropped the cheesy grin and banter in a flash, 'I . . . if it would be weird . . . 'cause you hardly know me . . . I'll go and find a pub, shall I?'

'You can wait upstairs, it's fine,' she said. 'In fact, I was just heading up there. Do you want a cup of tea . . . ?' She left a pause and he took the hint.

'That'd be lovely, thanks, and it's Philip, or Phil,' he said, as Mattie let him through the door.

Fifteen minutes later, Phil was sat at the little kitchen table in the flat upstairs and doing his best to crack on to Mattie, in between sips of tea so strong that it was practically black.

'Your dad must have been a drug dealer,' Phil said, looking

deep into Mattie's eyes as she sat opposite him. 'Because you're dope!'

Mattie couldn't help but snort.

Phil wasn't going to give up that easily. 'All right then, I bet your dad was a weapons dealer because . . . you're the bomb!'

Usually if a man was trying to chat her up in the face of absolutely zero encouragement, Mattie would bristle and take offence and say something cutting.

But she was more amused than furious. If you took away the overworked pecs and biceps and the really ill-advised low-cut top (it was December, after all, and he was going to catch his death), Phil wasn't bad looking. He had an open, friendly face and the most startling blue eyes, which compensated for the fact that his sandy-coloured hair was starting to recede and he was quite short.

'Actually, Phil, my dad ran off with our next-door neighbour when I was six and he's now on his fourth wife and they run a small bed and breakfast in St Ives,' she said calmly. She was quite fond of her father, despite his many failings, but it was definitely a case of absence making her heart fond, rather than anything that her father had actually done to get into her good books. 'So, do any of your chat-up lines ever work?'

Phil nodded vigorously. 'All the time. The ladies can't get enough of them. I'm fighting them off.'

Mattie pressed her lips together so she wouldn't laugh and got up from the table to fetch the tin of shortbread she'd brought up from the shop. 'Are you sure about that? And do you want a top-up?'

Another cup of tea and two of her cranberry and orange shortbread cookies, and Phil was bearing his soul to Mattie: her shortbread was like a truth serum.

'I'm going to be honest with you, Mattie,' he said, eyes fixed on her so she wasn't sure if he was about to spin her another yarn.

'OK . . .'

'You've got to admit, me and the boys: we've got all the moves and we've got all the chat. We've got, like, top bants. The ladies love the banter, right?'

'I'm not sure that the ladies do actually love . . .'

'But we just can't pull.' It seemed Phil didn't really want to hear what the ladies genuinely loved, and Mattie realised that this might be part of his pulling problem. 'We're talking a serious love drought. Drier than the Sahara. Drier than the Gobi. Drier than the . . . the . . .'

'I get it,' Mattie cut him off. 'I suppose you need to think about what you're doing wrong. Maybe if you scaled back the chat-up lines and had more of a friendly discussion, that might work better for you.'

'No! Because then you're friend-zoned before you've even had a chance to connect on a deeper, more spiritual level,' Phil said sadly. He looked mournfully at Mattie. 'Like, now you and me are in the friend-zone. Nothing's ever going to go down between us.'

'Oh well, worse things happen at sea,' Mattie said cheerfully and clinked her mug against Phil's. 'Here's to friendship.'

'Not that anything ever could happen,' Phil continued. 'Tom has warned us all off.'

Mattie bristled then, every tiny little hair on her body standing to attention. 'Oh, did he?' she queried tightly.

'Said it was bad form to crack on with his flatmate. That we were all punching far, far above our weight and even if you did fancy one of us, probably because you'd suffered a blow to the head, it would only end in tears and that he'd be the one to suffer the consequences.' Phil took a sip of tea. 'That's pretty much a direct quote.'

There was quite a lot to unpick from Phil's verbatim retelling. Surprisingly, none of it was that unflattering. Tom would probably have been well within his rights to tell his friends to steer clear of Mattie because she was a bad-tempered shrew who hated everything, but instead he'd inferred that Mattie was far too good for his friends. Which was rather decent of him and also sounded a bit too good to be true.

'What else did he say about me?' Mattie demanded because Tom must have had plenty of other things to say about her and none of them that good.

'Tom, Tom, Tom! Why is every girl I meet obsessed with Tom?' Phil put his head in his hands.

'I am *not* obsessed with Tom!'

'Like, every time one of us puts the moves on a lady and she tells us to sling our hook, then bloody Tom, though I love him like a brother, just slides right in there and within seconds he'll have her smiling and giggling and giving him her number.'

'Tom? Our Tom? No!' Mattie scoffed.

'Straight up!'

'Does he wear his bow-tie and that hideous cardigan with the leather patches on the elbows when he's out on the pull?' Mattie asked, and she wished that she were recording this conversation on her phone so she'd have later evidence that it wasn't part of some fever dream.

'He does, though sometimes he wears a tweedy jacket that looks like something my granddad used to wear when he was working on his allotment.'

Mattie pinched her arm hard because she still wasn't sure if this was all a dream. Now, more than anything else in the world, Mattie wanted to see Tom out on the pull, with her own eyes. She wanted it more than she wanted her own chain of little tearooms. She wanted it more than she wanted to have a cookbook published. More even, than she wanted Nigella Lawson to follow her back on Twitter.

'What on *earth* does he say to them?' she asked, but before Phil could answer, there was the sound of a tread on the stairs. 'Quickly, tell me!'

Phil grinned and leaned forward as they heard the front door open. 'I wish I knew, because if I did, then—'

'Philip!' Too late, Tom was there in the doorway and Mattie fancied that there was a panicked look on his face, to see one of his best buddies and his flatmate/thorn in his side all cosy with tea and biscuits. 'I thought you were going to wait in my room.'

'Mattie offered me tea and these amazing cookies,' Phil said. He grinned again. 'You know I can never refuse a beautiful lady.'

'You could at least try,' Tom said stiffly, though he didn't pour scorn on Phil for describing Mattie as a beautiful lady.

'Plenty of shortbread to go round,' she offered, holding up the plate. 'Do you want a cup of tea?'

Tom looked as if he'd rather undergo a little light torture. 'I won't, thanks.' He seemed to be holding himself very stiff as if he was tensing every muscle. Then he looked down and realised he was holding a thin carrier bag which bulged promisingly. 'Oh, for you. Rye bread and onion bagels, as requested.'

'Buying you presents? Think someone's got the hots for you.' Phil winked theatrically – he did love to wind Tom up.

Tom scowled. 'They're not from me. They're from Nina,' he said, coming into the kitchen so he could dump the bag on Mattie's lap. 'Shall we go?'

Phil made a great show of reluctantly draining his mug, then standing up. 'You coming, darling?'

Tom's scowl was now positively ferocious. 'Mattie doesn't like being called darling by strange men,' he said. 'Or any men, come to that.'

'Oh, I don't mind Phil calling me darling,' Mattie said. She could see why Phil kept teasing him – Tom reacted so beautifully. 'But, I won't come out with you. I'll let you two boys catch up.'

'Shame,' Phil said, as he pulled on his coat and a flat cap, which was going to be no barrier against the chill of the evening when his tight jeans stopped a good two inches above his ankles and he was wearing yacht shoes and no socks.

'Somehow, I think we'll get over such a tragedy,' Tom said, trying to herd his friend out of the kitchen, but Phil stood his ground.

'We're having a party on Thursday, me and the rest of the lads from the footie team, a Christmas bash: you should come,' he said to Mattie. 'Bring a friend. Or if all your friends are absolute stunners like you, and single, bring the whole lot of them. And if they want to dress up as sexy Santas, all the better!'

It was an automatic reflex to refuse any invite from a single man, so Mattie was just about to decline when she saw the discomfited look on Tom's face. A lesser woman would have taken pity on him, but Mattie was no lesser woman. Also, she wasn't going to turn down the opportunity to discover even more fascinating facets to Tom's character. 'I'd *love* to come. Email me the details,' she said, handing him a business card that she was suddenly grateful Nina had insisted she needed. 'And I'm sure I can rustle up at least one single friend. So, this football team – are you on it too, Tom?'

'We're going. Now,' Tom said, taking Phil by the collar of his coat and frogmarching him down the hall.

'Mattie! It's been a pleasure,' Phil called out in a choked voice. 'Let's do it again . . .'

THUD!

The door slammed shut, though Mattie could just make out a muffled, '. . . soon!'

Then Tom saying, 'Come on, dead man walking,' as they made their way down the stairs.

There was so much information to process that Mattie ended up taking a two-hour bath, periodically letting out the cooling water with one foot, then turning on the hot tap with her other. By the time she hauled herself out of the tub, she resembled a woman-shaped prune.

As she massaged in her night cream, she wondered what other secrets Tom might be hiding? Verity always insisted that he was a Russian sleeper agent deep under cover and just waiting for his handler in Moscow to activate him, while Nina had invented a wife and four kids that Tom had stashed away somewhere.

Knowing what she now knew about Tom, Mattie wouldn't be at all surprised if either theory were actually true.

As the last step in her skincare regime, she slathered her face in rosehip oil – slaving away in a hot kitchen always dried out her skin – then came bowling out of the bathroom clad in just her towel, at the exact same time that Tom came bowling in through the front door.

'Oh my God!'

'Jesus Christ!'

Mattie clutched her horribly skimpy towel tighter around her. Much, much tighter. 'What are you doing home?' she screeched. 'You're never home this early.'

She'd been lulled into a sense of false security by the fact that she was nearly always fast asleep when Tom came back from whatever he did every night. Playing football or chatting up really impressionable women or whatever. Occasionally Mattie would briefly wake when Tom came home. She'd check the time on her alarm clock – it was never before one o'clock – then go straight back to sleep. But now it wasn't even eleven and here he was.

Mattie stepped to her left as Tom stepped to his right, nearly bumping noses and other *things*. Then Mattie stepped to her right as Tom shuffled left, and they nearly collided all over again. It seemed safer to stand exactly where they were and not make any sudden movements.

'I wasn't aware that I needed to provide you with a timetable of my whereabouts,' Tom said, his gaze fixed firmly to the left of where Mattie stood, completely naked under a towel that she knew showed the upper curve of her breasts. Though if she tugged it up, then it would reveal far too much of her thighs. It was quite the dilemma. 'May I suggest a new house rule?'

'You may, but be quick about it,' Mattie snapped, her skin so red with the blush of mortification that she looked like she'd been parboiled.

'No walking about half naked,' Tom snapped back, his face flushing as red as Mattie's half-naked body. 'I mean, without any clothes on.' His glasses were completely steamed up from the residual heat from the bathroom, but Mattie still saw him shut his eyes because it was a very small hall. Hardly enough room for the two of them. 'In a state of undress.'

'Yes, I understood what you meant the first time you said it,' Mattie hissed, furious with herself because she never usually wandered about in just a towel. The one night that she forgot to take her pyjamas to the bathroom with her was the one night that Tom came home early. Of course it was! 'Message received. Copy that.'

'Good,' Tom swallowed hard. Mattie had never appreciated how tall Tom was. That he seemed to fill every inch of the small space and she could smell the cold night air on him and the clean, fresh scent that she always associated with Tom. Though by rights he should smell of mothballs, and the musty, fusty aroma of old clothes and old books. He suddenly caught her eye. 'Are you . . . are you *sniffing* me?'

'What? No! Oh God!' Mattie took a step back but there was nowhere to take a step back to and she was desperate to dive for the safety and sanctuary of her room, but Tom was in the way. 'Can I just . . . ?'

'Just what?'

It was hopeless. Both of them embarrassed and not able to spit out a full sentence.

'My room.' Mattie had both hands clutching the top of her towel and couldn't dare spare one to gesture at the doorway behind Tom. 'I should probably go in my room. Put some clothes on.'

'Yes! Of course. God, sorry.'

They performed the same routine again: Tom sidestepping to the left, at the same time that Mattie sidestepped to the right. Then back again. Then the other way. Like they were dancing.

'Stop,' Tom said and he put one hand on Mattie's shoulder,

her naked shoulder, his fingers setting off a thousand fires against her skin, so she gasped, and he snatched his hand back as if he'd burned himself. 'Sorry. I'm so sorry.'

'No. No harm.' Mattie could still feel the phantom tingling touch of Tom's hand; it wasn't an entirely unpleasant sensation. 'Look, I just want to get in my room.'

'I know,' Tom said desperately. 'Here, you stay where you are and I'll just step to the left like this . . .' He moved away from Mattie's door and the way was now clear to hurtle into her room and slam the troublesome door in his face, but she was still rooted to the spot. Tom gestured at the door, in case Mattie wasn't familiar with what it looked like. 'There you are. Sorry again.'

Mattie was free to go, but still she couldn't move. 'We're cool, right? And also tomorrow I'm going to buy the most voluminous dressing gown I can find.' Then she realised that she'd have to let go of the towel with one hand to get her door open. 'Could you get that for me?' She gestured with her elbow.

'Of course,' Tom stuck his arm out awkwardly to open Mattie's door but kept his gaze averted, which was quite gentlemanly of him, especially as there was a little pile of clothes on the floor that Mattie had stepped out of before heading for the bathroom. 'And I'll be getting a voluminous dressing gown too.'

'We'll match,' Mattie noted and finally, *finally!*, she was in her room so she could use the door to shield her body. 'Sorry this has been so hideously awkward.'

Tom was sidling down to the hall towards the safety of

his own room. 'We'll never talk of it again,' he said. 'Goodnight.'

'Night, Tom,' Mattie said. Then they both slammed shut their bedrooms doors in perfect harmony.

CHAPTER

12

20 days until Christmas

Phil had emailed Mattie details of the Christmas party first thing the next day. But if Mattie was labouring under any illusion that Phil's prompt invitation was because he was keen on her, he was quick to set the record straight.

Don't forget to bring at least one friend. A <u>FIT, SINGLE</u> friend. Also, female. So, a FIT, SINGLE, FEMALE FRIEND, or several FIT, SINGLE, FEMALE FRIENDS ready to fall in love with the Philmeister.

Mattie wasn't sure that 'the Philmeister' was an improvement on the Archbishop of Banterbury, but she mentally scrolled through her many female friends, all of them FIT, and quite a few of them SINGLE, and decided that of all of them Pippa would be able to handle the attentions of the Banter Boys without breaking a sweat.

'I find that toxic masculinity is usually a mask for insecurity and fear,' Pippa said, as Mattie described the treats that lay in store for her at the Christmas party they were attending on a Thursday night at the furthest reaches of the Piccadilly Line.

'But it is quite hilarious that they live in Cockfosters,' Mattie pointed out as the tube trundled through Holloway Road station. '*Cock*fosters, get it?'

'I do get it,' Pippa said. Mattie loved Pippa dearly but even Pippa would be the first to admit that she didn't have a sense of humour.

'Which is odd, really, because I'm a very happy, very positive person,' Pippa had once told Mattie. 'But the only thing that really makes me laugh is fart jokes.'

Mattie had met Pippa on a Eurocamp exchange summer holiday in Dusseldorf when they were both fifteen. Unlike their fellow Eurocampers, neither of them had any wish to drink cheap wine or get off with some boy with a mullet and acid-wash jeans from the Low Countries. Mattie had wished that she was in Paris so she could have a holiday romance with a Parisian boy, who would obviously wear all black and carry *Nausea* by Jean-Paul Sartre under his arm, and Pippa was furious that her parents had paid good money for her to improve her German when she'd have much preferred to spend her summer holidays in The OC.

On paper, Mattie and Pippa were complete opposites. Mattie was mercurial and flighty (after all, she'd decided to relocate to Paris to study at L'Institut de Patisserie with €200 in her pocket after a drunken game of truth and dares). She was very obviously the 50/50 DNA split of a father who'd made running away with only the money he had in his pocket a lifestyle choice, and a mother who took violently for or against people within ten seconds of meeting them and nothing would ever change her mind.

Pippa, on the other hand, was the product of two Yorkshire teachers and was as steady and as solid as the stone farmhouse on the outskirts of Halifax where she'd been brought up. She was reliable, robust and resolutely determined to see the best in people, which were very good qualities to have when you worked for Sebastian Thorndyke, who would try the patience of a whole cathedral full of saints.

That said, she'd also accepted Oprah Winfrey as her personal lord and saviour, and adding to that a year at a Californian business school meant that Pippa had swapped her bluff Yorkshire common sense for dense business-speak and inspirational quotes. Mattie had to steel herself every time a new picture from Pippa arrived on her Instagram feed, because it would usually feature a sunset and an on-brand message like 'Stop waiting for someone else to fix your life.'

And now as Mattie filled Pippa in on the latest goings-on in Happy Ever After land, Pippa's advice was blunt yet Oprah-approved.

'And so Posy, Verity and Nina think that I'm an absolute negative nelly, but I'm not.' Mattie had been trying to be upbeat and positive ever since then, which was exhausting. 'Am I a negative person?'

'Someone else's opinion of you is none of your business,'

Pippa said, as she checked her appearance in her pocket mirror, though Pippa's appearance was always on-point. She had the glossiest, shiniest, conkeriest brown hair of anyone Mattie had ever met, and Mattie was someone who'd once handed out drinks at a charity function attended by the Duchess of Cambridge.

Pippa also did Boxfit and yoga on alternate weekday mornings, practised reducetarianism, which meant she only ate meat once a week, and looked amazing in yoga pants, which were her non-work outfit of choice. Really, she and Mattie had nothing in common, but somehow they worked. And there was also the small matter that once Pippa decided that you were her people, she'd move heaven and earth for you. Quite literally.

It had been Pippa who'd driven her mother's Renault Clio all the way from London to Paris two days before Christmas to scoop up Mattie and all her worldly belongings and bring her home. That had been two years ago, and every week since then Mattie had baked a cake for Pippa (this week's was an apricot crumble cake) as an entirely inadequate way of saying thank you.

'But they *made* their opinion of me my business,' Mattie explained in an aggrieved voice as Pippa stroked clear gel over her already perfectly arched eyebrows. 'Verity called me an Eeyore.'

'Oh, I wouldn't say you were an Eeyore,' Pippa said. 'You're more of a Piglet.'

'I just have a very low tolerance for the things I have a low tolerance of.'

'But you get to choose your mood,' Pippa said. 'I choose to be happy, therefore I am happy. I find it helps to write ten things I'm grateful for in my gratitude journal every day.' She put down her compact mirror so she could fix Mattie with an even, non-judgemental look. 'Are you writing down ten things each morning that you're grateful for in the gratitude journal I got you last Christmas?'

'Yeah, kind of.' Mattie squirmed under Pippa's non-judge-mental look. It had been known to even defeat Sebastian. 'I've maybe ended up writing recipes in it, but then again, I'm always grateful for a new recipe.'

'And you're no longer writing down lists of your enemies and how you're going to exact revenge on them, so I think we can put a tick in the progress box,' Pippa said, and she took Mattie's hand so she could raise it in the air. 'Yay you! So, these guys that are throwing the party, are any of them viable?'

The last man Pippa had dated had been a holistic, vegan personal trainer who had done wonders for her abdominal muscles but 'left my emotional needs begging for a good workout.'

Mattie sighed. 'Unless you like top bants, and we both know that you don't, then I'd say that they're distinctly non-viable.'

Pippa's face fell a little. Mattie could see her struggling to choose happy. It took from Arnos Grove to Cockfosters before Pippa was able to produce a passable smile that showed off her even, white teeth. 'Well, it's always good to meet new people, and I did a Boxfit class this morning, so

I can consume lots of empty calories, by which I mean that I'm going to get quite drunk.'

'That's the spirit,' Mattie said as they got off the train and followed the exit signs. 'I didn't do any form of exercise this morning but I still intend to get quite drunk.'

If she wanted to catch Tom in action then she had to be stealthy and she also had to be unrecognisable. Tom didn't even know that she was coming to the party, as he'd left the flat a good hour before Mattie and hadn't said that he'd see her later. In fact, he said, 'I'll be back late unless I'm suddenly taken ill, so do please remember our new house rule. Voluminous dressing gowns at all times.'

Now Mattie pulled a black woolly hat and scarf from her bag and by the time she'd put them on and made the necessary adjustments, only her eyes were visible.

'Isn't this meant to be a house party? Aren't you going to be too hot?' Pippa asked as they came out of the station. 'All in black too. You know, we receive what we put out to the world. That's why I've worn something sparkly.' She unbuttoned her coat just enough to give Mattie a glimpse of something silvery and sequinned. 'Well, that and because it's a Christmas party.'

'I *always* wear black,' Mattie said, consulting Google Maps on her phone.

'You didn't *always* used to wear black.' Pippa gave Mattie a sideways look, which Mattie ignored. 'Before Paris, you sometimes wore all different colours.'

'I did a lot of things before Paris that I don't do now,' Mattie all but growled. 'We have to take this road on the left.'

'Remember, you choose your mood,' Pippa chirped. 'Anyway, how do you know these boys who are throwing this party?'

Mattie hadn't quite got round to explaining that. She decided to go for the simplest and vaguest of explanations. 'Oh, they're friends of Tom's.'

'Tom! You haven't said much about Tom, even though he's the first man you've lived with since—'

Mattie shook her head so wildly that the bobble on her woolly hat felt as if it were about to launch into space. 'I'm not *living* with Tom. I'm sharing living space with him. It's an entirely different vibe.'

'Tom has many layers,' Pippa said thoughtfully. 'Pretends not to be a team player – he's quite a challenge in a brainstorm – and yet I think secretly he'd lay down his life for Happy Ever After. You know what I always say, loyalty is royalty.'

'Yes, he does have many layers,' Mattie said. She was dying to tell someone that Tom had spent four years analysing romantic fiction. The enormity of her secret weighed heavy on her and Pippa was an impartial third party. If you told Pippa a secret, she'd take it to the grave with her. Mattie suspected that Pippa's principles were so strong that she'd even withstand waterboarding. She'd make a brilliant spy. But there was the small and not at all impartial fact that she worked for Posy's husband, so Mattie decided it was best not to share. 'More layers than a millefeuille.'

'Quite good looking too,' Pippa said matter-of-factly, as

if Tom's alleged good looks were a given and not up for debate. 'Is this the place?'

They were standing in front of a typical 1930s semi-detached house, like all the other 1930s semi-detached houses they'd passed on the walk from the station. But 23 Hazeldene Avenue wasn't in such pristine condition as its neighbours. Its privet hedge needed urgent trimming, there were no net curtains in the windows and with all the lights on, it was possible to see that said windows could do with a good clean. And whereas their neighbours had really embraced the festive season with Christmas trees twinkling behind aforementioned net curtains and flashing fairy lights strewn all over the exterior of their houses (number 27 even had a light-up Santa Claus and sleigh on their roof), the Banter Boys had made do with a straggly strand of tinsel hanging over the open front door.

So this was where Tom used to live? Another piece of the puzzle that didn't match any of the other pieces.

They squeezed through a clutch of people creating a bottleneck in the hall until they came to a kitchen, which was also full of people, and had last been kitted out some-time in the 1980s. 'Wow,' Pippa breathed. 'I never knew there were so many different shades of beige.'

Mattie cast a professional eye over the cooker, as she automatically did every time she was invited into someone else's home. 'That hob hasn't been cleaned since Queen Victoria was on the throne.'

'Victoria? I haven't seen her in ages,' said a woman in workout gear who was standing with her friend, also in workout gear, by a sink which also hadn't known the touch of a J-cloth and some Cif for decades, by the looks of it. 'How is she?'

'She's doing great,' Mattie said, because that was the easiest option. 'So, are you enjoying the party?'

'Not really. Be warned, there's sprigs of mistletoe where you least expect them, with some loser primed to jump out and try to kiss you, so we're going quite soon,' the woman said. 'To a singles' spinning class in Kings Cross.'

'I love spin classes,' Pippa said with all the fervour of someone who got off on high-impact cardio. 'I wondered why you were wearing workout gear. Are those Lululemon pants?'

'They're Sweaty Betty,' the second woman said. 'Very sculpting. They do amazing things to your arse.'

'They really do,' Pippa said admiringly. 'Though I like the Gap ones too.'

Pippa had found her people. If she didn't have such a strong moral code, Mattie suspected that Pippa would happily dump her in favour of going to this singles' spinning class. Mattie squeezed past the three of them with a vague smile, and investigated the huge pan of mulled wine simmering on the dirty hob.

Surely the heat and the alcohol would sterilise any germs? She helped herself to a mug and side-stepped a sprig of mistletoe hanging over the kitchen door as she went outside.

Mattie held her breath as she moved past the little coterie of smokers standing on the patio and ventured down the surprisingly long garden towards the end where most of

141

the partygoers were standing around a bonfire that was burning with great gusto. She took a cautious sip of her mulled wine and nearly spat it out. There was nothing mulled about it; no Christmas spices, not one lousy cinnamon clove. It was just cheap red wine heated up.

She surreptitiously poured the contents of her mug in a nearby and very overgrown flowerbed, then her nose twitched as she smelt the scent of sausages. As she got closer she could see two Banter Boys (possibly Bantdaddy and another one she didn't recognise) manning a gigantic grilling station and hurrah! A plastic bin full of ice and bottles of lager.

'Come on, girls, fancy a banger?' the unknown Banter Boy called out to three girls shivering in tiny sparkly dresses as Mattie swooped in, snatched a beer and then swooped away, opening the bottle with the aid of the right attachment on her chef's penknife. 'And then after that, you can have one of these bangers.' He held up a sausage on a long fork and the three girls groaned as one and moved away.

Mattie didn't blame them. But the poor things had barely gone three steps when they were greeted by Phil and another man Mattie didn't recognise.

'Ladies! Looking lovely as ever,' Phil said. 'I'm Phil, but my friends call me the Archbishop of Banterbury.'

The three girls all gave good side-eye to his T-shirt which said, 'When I Think About You I Touch My Elf' but Phil didn't seem to notice. 'And this is Costa. Like Costa Coffee.'

'It's why I like my women hot, dark and sweet,' Costa said. He was wearing a T-shirt which featured a cartoon of a drunken reindeer and said 'Brew-dolph' in flashing letters. Mattie snorted into her beer and then stepped back into the shadows so she couldn't be seen. She wished that Pippa wasn't still in the kitchen, no doubt still extolling the virtues of butt-enhancing work-out pants, because this needed witnesses.

'I only drink tea,' one of the girls said flatly and her two friends giggled.

'I take my tea like I take my women,' Phil said. Mattie willed him not to say any more, but he wasn't done. 'Um . . . strong and erm, strong . . .'

'You already said strong.' These girls were a tough crowd.

'Strong and er, brewed to perfection.'

Two of the girls rolled their eyes hard enough to detach their corneas while the girl who'd made the mistake of saying that she preferred tea, fixed Phil with a dead-eyed stare that made him visibly wilt.

'That doesn't even make sense,' she said. She gestured with her thumb in the direction of a dilapidated potting shed. 'Do one, mate!'

Mattie winced. Phil didn't deserve that. He was actually quite nice when you got to know him, but these girls were never going to get to know him because he disappeared as fast as his legs would carry him, Costa bringing up the rear.

'Lame.'

'So lame.'

'Who even was that?'

'I'm so sorry that you had to be the unwilling recipients

of the worst chat-up lines ever,' said a familiar voice and Tom was there, in the space so recently vacated by his good friend, the archbishop. Mattie shrank even further back, so she was practically inside the overgrown hedge and invisible in her all-black ensemble unless you were looking for a stealthy beer-drinking ninja.

'Right, and what hot drink do you like your women to resemble?' Tea Girl asked challengingly.

'Not really a big fan of hot drinks,' Tom said, which was a total lie, Mattie thought as she adjusted her scarf to ensure that most of her face stayed hidden in the shadows. 'And please don't confuse me with those *boys* you were just talking to.'

It was Tom's stern voice, the one that made his menopausal fanbase flush when he told them that he absolutely wasn't going to try on one of the Happy Ever After T-shirts so they could see what size they needed to get for their husbands.

It seemed to be having a similar effect on Tea Girl, now quite wide-eyed. 'No, you're really nothing like them,' she said in a breathy voice.

'Quite. They wouldn't know what to do with a woman if they lived to be a hundred,' Tom said in a husky voice, leaning closer to the girl, close enough that Mattie would bet his breath was tickling her earlobe. There was something about the timbre of Tom's dark, deep tones that caused Mattie to shiver slightly, even though it was quite mild for early December. Mattie wasn't the only one affected: as Tom took his leave of the three girls with an apologetic smile, touching his forehead in a farewell salute, all three girls swooned slightly.

'Who *was* that?' one of them asked in a dreamy voice.

'Only the man I'm going to marry.'

Mattie had heard quite enough and followed Tom at a distance. He walked down the garden, skirting around the bonfire so he could stand slightly to the side, while she skulked in the darkness just beyond the light of the fire. Daquon, in a T-shirt featuring devil horns and the proud proclamation, 'I'm On The Naughty List', was trying out some of his world class banter.

'And so I said, "Is that a rocket in your pocket or are you just pleased to see me?" No! Hang on. "Is that a rocket in . . ." Sorry! "Is that a rocket in *my* pocket or are you just pleased to see me?" Jesus! I mean, "am I just pleased to see you?" Shall I take it from the top?'

Tom clearly couldn't take it any longer. 'Please don't,' he said, stepping forward so that Daquon had to step to the side. 'I do apologise for this . . . well, "gentleman" doesn't seem the right word.'

'Man, you always do this,' Daquon muttered, shaking his head at Tom, but backing away, leaving Tom and a girl in a pink pussyhat alone.

'I can get rid of losers all by myself,' the girl said.

'I didn't do it for you,' Tom said with a friendly smile like he was a normal, friendly man. 'I did it for purely selfish reasons. I was actually going to die from shame if he'd tried another permutation of that clichéd chat-up line.'

The girl, who was sharply pretty, like she didn't suffer

fools gladly, allowed herself to smile. 'I was beginning to feel sorry for him.'

'I wouldn't,' Tom advised and now they were both smiling at each other, and Mattie had to run through a checklist to make sure that yes, this was Tom, wearing his glasses and a bow-tie and his most hairy tweed jacket. Because Tom kept smiling and a smile from Tom Greer was a lesser-spotted event; there were comets that appeared more frequently than the upper quirk of Tom's lips.

'I couldn't help but notice your hat,' Tom was saying now. 'Did you go on the Women's March last year?'

'Absolutely, and this year too. And I've been running a series of workshops on activism at my little sister's school. I'm Clea, by the way,' she said, holding out her hand.

'Tom.' They shook hands. 'I think it's so important to be an ally. I've realised that one of the most important contributions I can make to standing up for gender equality is to listen and support rather than thinking that my voice needs to be heard.'

'Wow. I thought men like you were rarer than unicorns,' the girl said, with an appreciative smile as she gave Tom a lingering look. Obviously she didn't find the bow-tie too much of a turn-off. 'The amount of men I've met who've tried to mansplain feminism to me.'

Tom held up his hands. 'I live in fear of being accused of mansplaining.'

'Well, if you promise not to do any, I'd really like to get together with you some other time when there's less open flame?' Pink Pussyhat said, twisting away from someone who brushed past her with a sparkler. 'I'm wearing a lot of manmade fibres.'

'Though given the gender divide of the majority of people working in the garment industry, they're probably womanmade fibres,' Tom said, and they both laughed, and if it wasn't for the smoke from the bonfire making her eyes water, Mattie would have been convinced that she was dreaming. She had to be, because Tom tapped his number into Pink Pussyhat's phone and she rang him to make sure he had her number.

'I'll call you,' she said very eagerly, waving goodbye as she left to find her friends.

Tom wasted no time, and swiftly moved to the other side of the bonfire where he quickly despatched poor Daquon again and, within five minutes, was shamelessly flirting with yet another girl. By this time, their corner of the garden was quite deserted so Mattie didn't dare sneak any closer and draw attention to herself.

Instead she had to watch Tom and his third victim smiling and laughing, there was also a lot of arm touching until the girl reached up to wipe at a spot on Tom's face. 'A smut from the bonfire,' Mattie heard her say, as Tom smiled. Then he and the girl, who now had a deathgrip on Tom's arm, walked back down the garden towards the house.

It was amazing, Mattie marvelled, that Tom could be all things to all people; the stern alpha male, the feminist ally, the shameless flirt. Yet all this time, he'd only shown one side of himself to her: the deeply annoying, buttoned-up pain in the arse side.

Would the real Tom Greer stand up? Mattie pondered this thorny question for a good five minutes until she realised that Tom was at her side, and it must have been the heat from the bonfire that was making her cheeks burn so brightly. Or maybe it was because she was trapped in a black-wool chokehold.

'I come bearing gifts,' Tom said and he held up another bottle of lager. 'So you won't have to drink what passes for mulled wine round here. And a sparkler.' He held up his other hand. 'Want to light my fire?'

Mattie had had enough. She pulled her scarf loose so that Tom could see her cross face. 'It's me,' she said. 'And I am immune to your . . . your wiles!'

Tom frowned from behind his glasses. 'Of course it's you. And what do you mean, my wiles? You sound like someone in one of those ghastly Regency romance novels Posy loves so much.'

'You'd know about that,' Mattie muttered, but she muttered it very quietly because she wasn't ready to have *that* conversation with Tom. She'd need much more than a bottle of lager before she felt emotionally fortified enough to bring up the topic of his PhD dissertation. 'I really should go and find Pippa.'

'She's busy supervising Mikey and Steve as they prepare to light the fireworks, because they know nothing about Health and Safety, or indeed the Fireworks Code. Anyway, she was the one who told me come and find you. Said you'd gone outside and to just search for the woman who looked like a member of the Baader-Meinhof gang.'

'Ha! I bet she didn't say that I looked like a member of the Baader-Meinhof gang,' Mattie said. If she didn't know who the Baader-Meinhof group were, then she was pretty sure that Pippa wouldn't either.

'They were a German terrorist organisation,' Tom explained, which was all the motivation that Mattie needed to tear off her hat, though she could tell it had done terrible things to her fringe. Still, it was only Tom, and even if every other woman at the party seemed to think that he was some sort of nascent sex god, Mattie certainly didn't.

Although, to be fair, he had brought her lager and a sparkler, but now he was trying to steer her towards the house, his hand on the small of her back. Mattie was about to take umbrage at the steering when Tom said, 'Probably best to watch the fireworks from a safe distance, especially if Mikey and Steve plan to light them so close to the bonfire.'

'Good idea,' Mattie said, scurrying for the haven of the patio. 'Also, why is there a bonfire and fireworks at a Christmas party?'

'They were meant to have a Guy Fawkes party in early November but they got very drunk the night before and were too hungover to go ahead with it,' Tom explained as he followed Mattie up the garden. 'It's taken them so long to reschedule that it had to be rebranded as a Christmas party.'

'Hence the mistletoe and the comedy Christmas T-shirts?'

Tom groaned. 'Posy must never know about the comedy Christmas T-shirts, it will only give her ideas. Agreed?'

149

Mattie couldn't help but shudder at the very idea. 'Agreed.'

They'd reached the safety of the patio, where Pippa had found Phil and was enthusing about the personal growth workshop she'd attended the week before. Pippa wasn't the type of person to worry about being left unattended at a party – she could always find someone to talk to, then make a connection with them on a deeper, more personal level. Or so she claimed, and Mattie wasn't one to doubt her.

'I think it's really good to give your self-esteem a regular health check,' she said while Phil nodded and stared at her in dumbstruck awe. 'Like, having a smear test or getting the oil changed in your car.'

'Right,' Phil said uncertainly. 'What's a smear test?'

'Nothing you need to worry about,' Tom said quickly because he'd met Pippa on a number of occasions and, like Mattie, he knew that she never shied away from the diffi-cult questions. On the contrary, she ran towards them.

'That's a very good question, Phil. I'm so glad you're showing an interest in women's health,' she said now and Mattie had no choice but to take her by the arm so she could whisper in her friend's ear, 'If you tell Phil what a smear test is, I'm withholding cake for the foreseeable future.'

'But women's reproductive health impacts everybody's health,' Pippa said, earnestly.

'Phil's not emotionally strong enough to be able to cope with you explaining speculums to him,' Mattie said a little desperately. 'And it's a party! Woo-hoo! Oh! Look! Fireworks!'

'Oooh! I love fireworks,' Pippa exclaimed.

Mattie found herself sandwiched between Tom and Pippa as they watched a slightly chaotic display, which contained all the crowd-pleasers. Catherine wheels and rockets and Roman candles which lit up the sky over Cockfosters with a colourful shower of sparks and bursts. Happily, someone in the next street was also having a late-in-the-season firework party with no expense spared, so they could happily 'oooh!' and 'aaaah!' their fireworks in the long pauses when Sean or Mikey would announce that there'd been a malfunction with a Roman candle and they were just going to check what had happened to it, accompanied by warning shouts of 'Leave it! Just *leave* it!'

After twenty minutes and a third bottle of lager, all that was left was Mattie's sparkler, which Tom lit so she and Pippa could pose for selfies.

'Come on, Tom!' Pippa said, pulling him in between the two of them. 'You have much longer arms than us, which makes for a much more flattering angle. And you too, Phil.'

Mattie instantly pulled her selfie face – face tilted to the right, chin down, eyes wide. Pippa opened her mouth wide in a silent joyous scream, Phil did a wacky thumbs up and Tom stood there like he was posing for his last photograph before being sent off to fight in the trenches of World War One.

'I do hope these pictures aren't going to appear on any form of social media,' Tom said gravely. That was an interesting point: he'd managed to never appear on the Happy Ever After Instagram, even though Nina constantly shoved her phone in people's faces as they were trying to work.

But it was a really good picture of Mattie. Far too good to waste. 'Sorry Tom, I'm putting it on my Instagram,' Mattie insisted, already scrolling through filters. 'I have hardly any followers, it's not a big deal.'

She actually had quite a lot of followers, nearly five thousand at the last count, who came for the daily cake shots.

'Except I just asked you not to,' Tom said, but Mattie was immune to Tom's stern voice.

'You shouldn't have agreed to be in the photo if you didn't want to be on social media,' Mattie said, as she now went hashtag happy with:

#fireworks #bonfire #sparklers

#christmasparty #bahhumbug

#justignoretherandomguywiththemardyexpression

'There's no law that says you have to put photos on social media,' Tom said in a manner that made Mattie instantly take offence at his self-righteous tone.

'But why would you bother taking a photo then?' Pippa asked, genuinely perplexed, because when she wasn't posting sunsets and inspirational quotes on her Instagram, she was posting #fitspo shots from her daily workouts or #ginoclock selfies from whatever fancy pop-up bar she'd read about on The Londonist. 'What would be the point?'

'Exactly, if you don't post pictures on social media then how can you even be sure that you've taken a picture?' Mattie said, because she'd had three bottles of lager in the space of an hour and apparently when she was tipsy it really brought out the urge to rile Tom, who was very tight of lip. But it was more than that. Much more than that. She'd sworn to herself that she would never *ever* let a man tell her what to do, ever again. It started off innocently enough, with them expressing a preference for a certain dress or a perfume and then one day you realised that your life wasn't your own any more because it had been completely taken over by someone else's preferences. 'Like a tree falling down in a forest and all that jazz.'

'I think the fact that the picture would be sitting there on your phone would be proof enough that it existed,' Tom said, peering over Mattie's shoulder as she tagged Pippa in the photo, which was very annoying. 'For goodness' sake, Mattie, can't you just respect my wishes?'

'I would if your wishes made any kind of sense,' Mattie said, looking up from her screen. 'Give me one good reason why I shouldn't click "Post"?'

Tom raised his eyebrows. 'Because I asked you not to.'

Oh, how that made Mattie want to click on 'Post' even more. But Phil was looking like he might cry (for a man who styled himself as the Archbishop of Banterbury, he didn't seem to like confrontations very much) and Pippa was doing her 'I'm not cross with you, I'm just disappointed in you because you're behaving like a bit of a dick' face. Pippa only pulled out that expression when she really had to.

'Fine,' Mattie capitulated with a sigh, holding out her phone so Tom could see her click on 'discard draft'. 'But this whole shunning the twenty-first century shtick of yours is deeply weird. Shady, even.'

'Mattie, we should go home now,' Pippa said decisively. 'I have a very early reformer Pilates class and, I'm not judging, but I think you've probably had enough to drink now.'

'Yes, you probably have,' Tom added as if anyone had asked him, and then he insisted on walking them back to the tube station because he said it was easy to get lost. Though Mattie, in a near-constant state of bristledom by now, felt that this was another dig about her alleged drunkenness, as if Tom suspected that she wasn't capable of working Google Maps.

'I might as well see you all the way home,' Tom decided. 'Just to make sure you don't end up at Heathrow.'

'As if I would,' Mattie hissed as she repeatedly slapped her Oyster card down on the card reader, only for the pesky orange light to appear. 'Why won't this stupid thing work?'

It wouldn't work because Mattie had run out of credit. She had to top up and eventually, she, Pippa and Tom were on a westbound train, Pippa valiantly keeping the ball of conversation in the air as she talked about her new initiative at work to ban all single-use plastic items.

But Pippa said goodbye at Finsbury Park, leaving Mattie and Tom sitting there side-by-side in silence. Mattie couldn't even think why Tom had wanted to see her actually-not-that-drunk-anymore self home when he could have carried on collecting phone numbers or – she could hardly form the thought – copped off and gone home with a girl.

'You . . . you're quite popular with the ladies, then?' she

heard herself say as if her brain was acting independently of her mouth.

Further down the carriage a group of middle-aged revellers, all in Santa hats, broke into a spirited rendition of 'God Rest Ye Merry Gentlemen'. Tom glanced at them in horror then pulled his gaze back to Mattie, who couldn't help but stare at him across the armrest that separated them. So tweedy and yet such a hit with the opposite sex. It made no sense.

'You know the rules,' he said stiffly. 'I never discuss my personal life.'

Mattie snorted. 'Much as it pains either of us to admit it, we're sharing a flat. That means that our personal lives are going to cross sometimes. I mean, we've just been to a party together!'

'We weren't together.' Tom shook his head as if he were trying to dislodge the notion that he and Mattie had been social with each other in public. 'You went to the party without my knowledge, consent and certainly against my better judgement.'

'You didn't want me to go to the party? Why? Because you hate me?' Mattie couldn't keep the hurt out of her voice, but she had downed three lagers in the space of an hour.

'I don't hate you,' Tom said in the manner of someone who was humouring a small fractious child who was up long past their bedtime.

Mattie dug him in the ribs with her elbow. 'Then you *like* me?'

Tom put a hand to his side and 'oof'ed as if Mattie had mortally wounded him. 'I don't know why it's so important that I like you when you hate *all* men.'

'Not all men!'

'So you keep saying, though I see precious little evidence of it,' Tom said with a sniff and when Mattie opened her mouth to argue the case, he startled her by placing his fingers very gently over her lips. 'This is the part where you start listing the very few men that you don't actively hate, but can we skip it just this once?'

Mattie smacked his hand away, though she could still feel her lips tingling where Tom had touched them. 'Any more out of you and I'm putting that picture on Instagram, only after I've zoomed in on your face.' Mattie smiled at Tom's pained expression, though that might have been because the Santa Hats at the other end of the carriage were now attacking 'Good King Wenceslas' with great gusto.

'You wouldn't dare,' he breathed.

'Not another word,' Mattie warned him, holding her phone aloft.

'Fine,' Tom sighed.

'Fine,' Mattie confirmed.

And they travelled the rest of the way to Russell Square in blissful quiet. Or it would have been blissful and it would have been quiet but for their fellow travellers doing 'Silent Night' in rounds.

CHAPTER 13

19 days until Christmas

The next morning relations between Mattie and Tom were still frosty.

When Mattie emerged from her room much later than she should on a working morning, wrapped in her new voluminous dressing gown and with a mild hangover, there was Tom up early and making scrambled eggs in the kitchen. Mattie knew a moment of fair-to-middling shame.

'So sorry about last night,' she said as she sidled kitchenwards. 'I was quite the brat and I will absolutely delete the photo from my phone if you want me to.'

'You don't have to do that.' There was a very long, very awkward pause. 'I trust you.' But this was said so stiffly as he peered down at the saucepan, it was clear that Tom didn't trust Mattie at all.

He was also wearing slim-fit trousers and shirt, hadn't

had time to add a bow-tie or a baggy cardigan yet, so Mattie could see there wasn't a spare ounce of flesh on him, despite his poor food choices. Talking of which . . .

'You're not having a panini this morning, then?' she asked, trying to keep the edge from her voice.

'Evidently not.' Tom was using a fork to stir his eggs in one of Mattie's non-stick pans and it was all she could do not to snatch the fork from him and demand that he stop his culinary crimes right that very minute.

'Right. You know, you really don't need to add that much milk to scrambled eggs.' She just couldn't help herself. 'I would just use butter. Everything tastes better with butter, and could you *not* use a fork in that pan, please? I have a wooden spat—'

'I might not have some fancy French qualification in pastry work but I am quite capable of making scrambled eggs,' Tom snapped. It was clear that he wasn't capable at all but Mattie felt so ashamed at her behaviour the night before that she had to let it go. Though she didn't know why her poor non-stick pan also had to suffer.

Worse was to come downstairs. While Mattie and Tom had been partying, but not together, Nina had worked until 11 p.m. on Thursday night to finish dressing the shop (a sacrifice which she said that she intended to stop talking about around next Easter) so that next morning Happy Ever After officially looked like Christmas had vomited all over it, just as Nina had promised it would.

Nina had also taken full advantage of the fact that Mattie was off the premises and had attacked the tearooms with what looked like a pink and silver glitter cannon. However, she managed to keep her creative efforts away from the counter where food and drinks were prepared, so Mattie didn't feel as if she could raise an objection.

'Those boring Health and Safety regulations stifled my creative flow,' Nina complained, though her creative flow really didn't appear to have been stifled one bit. Mattie followed Nina through to the shop, her journey through the anterooms hampered by yet more low-hanging pink and silver stars, which were going to have someone's eye out if they weren't careful. 'Anyway, behold my masterpiece!'

Nina proudly presented her *pièce de résistance*, a window display which featured the promised Christmas tree constructed entirely from green books. (Nina had had to borrow some of Verity's precious Virago Modern Classics with their dark-green spines, a sacrifice that Verity said was much worse than having to stay at work until eleven.) There were also pink and silver wrapped presents under the real Christmas tree, waiting to be donated by customers to grateful recipients in the nearby care home.

And there was the not-small matter of the life-sized baby reindeer that Nina claimed to have no knowledge of.

'What reindeer?' she asked with a quizzical expression, even as her elbow rested on its little head, when Posy said that she'd quite categorically forbidden Nina from bringing any life-sized reindeer into the shop. 'I can't see a reindeer. Tom, do you see a reindeer?'

'I'm having no part of this,' Tom sniffed, ducking under a *'Joyeux Noel'* banner that hung down from the arch that led to the Classics rooms. He brushed past Mattie, giving her a wary sidelong glance, and then disappeared into the depths of the Regency Romance room to shelve some books.

And even worse was to come. Lunchtime heralded the arrival of a BBC London TV crew who were there to film the unveiling of the infamous Mistletoe Booth, which, despite Nina's assurances, was taking up as much room as the gigantic Christmas tree and was completely obscuring the lower half of the new-releases shelves.

'Well, it's not like there's that many new releases in December,' Nina had countered cheerfully.

To Mattie's eyes, it looked like a bog standard photo booth, albeit one with Christmas decals and the words 'A Happy Ever After Christmas' stuck on it. Behind the curtain was a Christmas backdrop with snow and yet more reindeer; a big screen so you could see yourself posing; and a healthy sprig of mistletoe hung from the top, with a stool underneath for the kissers to sit on while they kissed.

'So, they kiss and then as well as their photo popping out of the little slot on the left, the photo is automatically uploaded to the Happy Ever After Instagram account, and they can regram it from there,' Posy explained to the TV crew as they had a quick run-through. Then she looked anxiously at Nina who'd spent the last hour coaching Posy. Nina gave Posy an encouraging thumbs up. 'And also our mistletoe is ethically sourced from an apple orchard in Kent.'

Waiting out of shot was a very telegenic customer and her embarrassed boyfriend who had been selected by the TV crew to be filmed as the first couple to test out the booth.

'Although, and I can't stress this enough,' Posy said, her face as red as the holly berries on the wreath attached to the shop door, 'anyone wanting to use the Mistletoe Booth has to purchase a book first. We can't just have people coming in off the street and expecting to have their picture taken.'

'Yeah, right, of course,' the cameraman said, as if they were going to cut that bit out. 'Can we get a shot of one of your colleagues sitting on the stool?'

'Not me!' Verity said from behind the counter. 'Nobody said anything about me having to be filmed and just . . . no!'

'Only if you can shoot me from the neck up?' Posy said. 'It's just when I sit down, if you catch me from the wrong angle, I look like I'm gestating sextuplets.'

Mattie needed to get back to the tearooms but, with Tom in the farthest reaches of Regency Romance, this was just the entertaining diversion she needed. Even though Sebastian Thorndyke had joined her and was surveying the scene with a faintly aggrieved huff.

'What's going on?' he asked. 'Why is there a gigantic photo booth blocking the new-release shelves?'

'It's not just any photo booth, it's a Mistletoe Booth,' Mattie said. 'It's the *pièce de résistance* of Nina's Christmas plans, apparently.'

Sebastian sniffed. 'I thought that was the gigantic Christmas tree and/or the fake tree made of books in the window and/or the life-sized reindeer.'

'Nina's Christmas plans have many *pièces de résistances*,'

called out Tom, from the Regency shelves. 'I don't think she actually understands what a *pièce de résistance* is.'

'Has someone told Tattoo Girl that most of her *pièces de résistances* are taking up valuable floorspace for actual paying customers?' Sebastian asked.

'We have tried,' Mattie said, glancing round to see that Sebastian's usual haughty expression was distinctly unhaughty, and instead rather soft and tender as he gazed at his wife, who was still insisting that she wasn't sitting in the Mistletoe Booth until she got a guarantee that she wasn't to be filmed from the neck down.

'They'd better not be upsetting my Morland,' Sebastian grumbled. 'If her blood pressure rises to unconscionable levels, then heads will roll. And anyway, this Mistletoe Booth thing; isn't there meant to be kissing under mistletoe? Morland isn't going to be kissing anyone, is she?'

'She's not *your* Morland, she's her own Morland,' Mattie said, because Posy wasn't Sebastian's possession, though it was quite *endearing* that The Rudest Man in London (as he was known by the *Guardian*) was so solicitous of his wife's wellbeing. 'And kissing is the whole point of the Mistletoe Booth. People buy a book and then they're allowed to take their partner into the booth to snap themselves kissing, though why they can't do that on their own phones, I don't know.'

But Mattie was talking to thin air because Sebastian had whirled round to grab a book from the nearest shelf. As the cameras started rolling, he strode into the shop and, in one fluid movement, sidestepped Posy so he could perch on the stool inside the booth. 'I fully intend to pay for this book, Morland,' he announced, then he pulled her onto his lap for a resounding kiss.

If anyone tried that with Mattie, even someone she was joined with in matrimony, she'd slap them round the face, but Posy clutched onto the lapels of Sebastian's very expensive, bespoke suit jacket and swooned a little. Though the swoon could have been her high blood pressure reinstating itself.

'Technically, you're meant to buy the book *before* the kissing,' Posy said once the kiss was over, taking the book from Sebastian's hand so she could have a cursory look at the cover before bopping him over the head with it. 'I didn't know you were a big fan of George Eliot.'

'I've read all of his books and also I have hidden depths,' Sebastian said gravely.

'George Eliot was a woman, you fool,' Posy said and she kissed him again and even the interviewer, who'd looked quite peeved about Sebastian's interruption, went misty-eyed. But as the kissing went on and on and on, the misty-eyedness turned to irritation.

'You're ruining everything!' announced Nina, standing behind the camera crew with her hands on her hips and as furious as Mattie had ever seen her. 'God, I haven't even had a chance to test drive it myself yet!'

'This is all just too awful to contemplate and yet here we are, contemplating it,' said Tom's voice from behind Mattie. Very close behind. Close enough that she could feel his warmth against her back. She wanted to step forward with a warning about respecting her personal space boundaries, but they'd been snappy with each other enough over the last thirty-six hours.

Also, in this rare instance, she and Tom were united in their horror of the scene before them. 'Too many awful things to contemplate,' Mattie said sorrowfully. 'That horrible booth, which I still say brings up some serious consent issues.' (Though Posy and Sebastian were once again consensually kissing each other while the cameras rolled.)

'And public displays of affection,' Tom said with real loathing.

'And let's not forget all this Christmas nonsense.' Mattie reached up so she could give the *Joyeux Noel* banner a vicious flick.

'You're right, it is all nonsense,' Tom agreed. He sighed, his breath ruffling her hair, which actually was a bit annoying. 'We could sue, you know. For being forced to work in a hostile environment.'

'We could, except technically I'm self-employed and I don't think either of us want to upset Posy at the moment,' Mattie said.

'Because she's pregnant . . .'

'And because she doesn't expect either of us to pay rent for the flat.'

Mattie turned her head so she could smile at Tom, who smiled back at her and shook his head with exaggerated regret, and Mattie was just about to—

'Did you make these?'

The BBC London producer was suddenly in front of Mattie with a half-eaten pig-in-blanket roll in her hand.

'I did,' Mattie replied a little uncertainly, because the woman was looking at her with narrowed eyes. Was the sausage not cooked all the way through? Worse! Was there a *hair* nestling between the puff pastry and the bacon?

'This is the best thing I've ever *ever* tasted,' the producer said, eyes still narrowed. 'You have a great face for television, has anyone ever told you that?'

'No, I can't say they have,' Mattie said, and behind her Tom sniffed slightly and took a step away so his body no longer blocked her from the draught that always whistled through the shop when someone had left the door open.

'Every day, I have to find an item for a light-hearted, Christmas-related clip to end the show. It's the bane of my bloody life. Now, I've got that stupid Mistletoe Booth and we could do a second piece on your pig-in-blanket rolls. I mean, there is a queue out the door for them.'

'There is? Oh my goodness!' All this time Mattie had been standing there and watching the Mistletoe Booth shenanigans, and poor Cuthbert had been left to cope with a sudden run on her pig-in-blanket rolls. 'I'd better go.'

'I'll just need you to sign a release form,' the producer said, following her. 'Can you think of something snappier to call them, because "pig-in-blanket rolls" doesn't exactly roll off the tongue, does it?'

Alas, nobody could think of anything snappier, but the TV crew still filmed the queue for pig-in-blanket rolls, which was starting to snake across the mews. Then they shot a quick interview with Mattie, who claimed that the pig-in-blanket rolls were an old family recipe (which sounded better than admitting inspiration had struck her when she was having a wee at three in the morning), and several sound-bites of happy punters extolling the delights of puff pastry and two different kinds of pork.

'And if sweet is your thing, then these red velvet cake-balls disguised as mini Christmas puddings should be top of your festive wish list,' concluded the reporter, a pale young man who, despite scoffing five pig-in-blanket rolls 'in the name of research', looked like he was in dire need of a good, square meal. Then he took an enthusiastic bite of a mini Christmas pudding and, even though it was bad manners to finish a broadcast with your mouth full, said, 'Mmmm mmmm! Christmas never tasted so good.'

'I hope you're about to take on extra staff,' was the producer's parting shot as her crew were loading up their equipment. 'When we did a piece on the first place in London to serve cronuts, they had two thousand customers the next day. Had to set up a wait list.'

'Two thousand customers?' Mattie echoed, not in glee but horror. She could manage about two hundred pig-in-blanket rolls by herself if she didn't have any other bakes, but two thousand?

'It's all right,' said the producer, as she hoisted herself into the equipment van. 'No need to thank me. In fact, you've done me a favour because I had nothing to fill tomorrow's slot after my Santa Zumba instructor tore his meniscus.'

19 days until Christmas

Thankfully, the only place in London where the tide of Yule wasn't happening was the flat above the shop. Neither Mattie nor Tom (who was still keeping the lowest of profiles) had so much as stuck a Christmas card on the mantelpiece in the living room or hung a stray strand of tinsel around the butler's bell in the hall.

Even once she'd finished her evening prep, there was no respite for Mattie this evening. If her pig-in-blanket rolls were about to take London by storm, then she had to be prepared. And so, although Pippa had wanted to try a new pop-up ice bar in Notting Hill, Mattie begged off and, after waving goodbye to Tom, she dragged one of the stools from the tearooms up to the flat so she'd be comfortable as she made industrial amounts of puff pastry.

In between batches, she put an order in to her butcher

for a frightening amount of sausage-meat and home-cured bacon and wondered if she had the money and space for another fridge.

As evenings went, Mattie had had much better ones. And as she was on her fifth batch of puff pastry, her mother rang.

'*Mathilde, ma cherie! C'est Maman!*' Sandrine had a voice that could carry roughly the same decibel level as a foghorn, so Mattie barely needed to put her on speaker. 'How is my favourite daughter?'

'Up to my elbows in rough puff pastry,' Mattie said mournfully. 'I haven't even got time to make proper puff pastry.'

She quickly filled Sandrine in on the funny, festive, light-hearted clip on the six o'clock local news, which would feature her favourite daughter.

'But that's wonderful! You'll light up the TV screens,' Sandrine declared as Mattie chopped butter into small squares. 'And you have the perfect face for television. Those big doe eyes! That button nose! Not to mention those lips. A perfect cupid's bow. Ian! *Ma petite Mathilde* is going to be on the news! Everyone at the BBC is in love with her sausage rolls!'

There was a cough and then a gruff, 'Bloody well done, Mattie!' from Ian in the background.

Mattie pressed her perfect cupid's bow tight so she wouldn't smile. She might have put in a sausage and bacon order that would bankrupt her if her TV slot was bumped, but after that ringing endorsement from her mother, surely everything would be all right. Sandrine was her biggest fan and she certainly wasn't shy about letting the world know that she had the most beautiful, most talented, most amazing daughter that any mother was blessed with.

'Well, nice to chat, Mattie, love, but the hot-water pipes aren't going to lag themselves,' Ian said, although he and Mattie hadn't chatted at all.

'He doesn't have a poet's soul,' Sandrine whispered as Ian no doubt shuffled out of the room she was in. 'But he has the heart of a lion.'

'Very true,' Mattie agreed. 'He is the best of men, you do know that, don't you, Mum?'

'I do,' Sandrine said softly and without any of her usual flourishes. 'The very best, and I should know, because I've experienced the very worst.'

Like mother, like daughter, Mattie thought, and she had to hold herself very still so she didn't shudder, but then she heard a familiar tread on the stairs to the flat, taking them two at a time, and she did shudder as the front door opened.

'Only me,' Tom said loud enough that Sandrine on speaker in the kitchen would easily be able to hear him. 'Forgot I left my phone charging. Are you staying up *all* night to make pastry?' he added as he peered down the corridor to the kitchen where Mattie had bowls of rough puff pastry in various stages of development resting on the table and both chairs.

'Not *all* night,' Mattie tried to say lightly, though she had a sneaking suspicion that she wouldn't get to bed until very, very late.

'Well, I'll try not to wake you when I come in,' Tom promised with an easy smile and a nod of his head, as if they were proper flatmates and not just two people who were sharing the same living space.

The easy smile was so transformative, making Tom seem a hundred per cent more friendly and approachable and a hundred per cent less tweedy, that Mattie smiled back.

'Have a nice time,' she said automatically, as Tom headed out again. 'Don't do anything I wouldn't do.'

Tom shot her a surprised look (probably because Mattie currently lived like a nun and the list of things she didn't do was pages long) and then, instead of leaving, he stood in the hall taking for ever to wrap a hideous dark-green scarf around his neck.

'That must be Tom,' Sandrine breathed down the phone, each word practically coming to the boil. 'When I met him at the opening of the tearooms, I thought he was so handsome. *Très magnifique!* Mathilde, you naughty girl, not to tell your *chere maman* that the two of you are shacked up.'

Mattie couldn't look at Tom, for fear that the inevitably appalled look on his face might turn her to stone, and all she could hear was a rushing in her ears. The shame! The utter shame!

'Not shacked up,' she managed to say in a strangulated voice. 'Definitely not shacked up.'

'Sharing a living space with a very firm set of rules and boundaries in place,' Tom enunciated from the hall, each word as clipped and precise as a bullet, while Mattie's expression froze on the 'horrified' setting.

'Whatever you say,' Sandrine cooed, as if she didn't believe a word either of them had said. 'Guy did mention something, but you know how he likes to tease. So, it's just the two of you? So cosy! So romantic!'

'It's the furthest from romantic that it's possible to get,' Mattie said. Tom had a pinched look as if he was holding his breath. 'Anyway, Tom is on his way out now, as we lead very separate lives.'

'The most separate of lives,' Tom clarified as he finally opened the front door, his phone clutched in his hand as if it were a protective talisman to ward off any of Sandrine's most fervent hopes and dreams for her beloved daughter. 'See you, then.' He raised his voice: 'Bye, Mattie's mum.'

'The pleasure was all mine. I cannot wait to see you again,' Sandrine called out, but Tom was gone, the door slamming shut behind him.

Mattie put a pastry-encrusted hand to her chest, where her heart was racing like she'd recently run a marathon.

'Even Guy said he was very good looking,' Sandrine recalled gleefully. 'And he has very high standards. Now tell me how love first blossomed.'

Tom's footsteps as he thundered down the stairs grew fainter, then there was the slam of the door that led to the shop, so that Mattie could finally relax. She slumped against the fridge. 'Nothing to tell because there is no love. He's very dull. The absolute dullest,' she said firmly. 'The most interesting thing about him is that he's thinking of becoming a Jesuit priest and they have to take a vow of celibacy.'

'How boring,' Sandrine said. 'Talking of vows of celibacy, does that mean your love life is still non-existent?'

Mattie pulled a face at the nearest bowl of pastry. 'Yes and I'm very happy about that. Next question!'

'Couldn't you get one of those friends with benefits, *ma petite ange*?'

'Change. The. Subject,' Mattie demanded.

'Fine, we'll talk about Christmas instead,' Sandrine said, a firm tone creeping into her voice. 'Now, I've spoken to Ian and Guy and we're all in complete agreement that there can't be a repeat of last year.'

The mention of Christmas made Mattie's shoulders slump, and the thought of last year's Christmas made the rest of her droop: it was a wonder that she didn't fall to the floor.

'It's not like I was any bother last Christmas,' she reminded her mother in a small voice as she began to put the bowls of pastry in the fridge.

'You took to your bed on Christmas Eve and you didn't emerge until late on Boxing Day,' Sandrine recalled sadly. 'You wouldn't even accept any presents, though I'd got you a lovely gift set from Jo Malone.'

'And I loved that gift set, I even wrote a thank you note,' Mattie said as she rested her hot head against a cool bottle of mayonnaise.

'Yes, when you finally let me give it to you for your birthday in March.' Sandrine sounded concerned now, even troubled. 'Darling, it's been two years. Time to put it all behind you and let your heart find another song.'

Had it really been two years? It felt like only yesterday and at the same time, it seemed as if it had happened to someone else several lifetimes ago. 'Honestly, Mum, both me and my heart are fine,' Mattie said, as she always did when Sandrine steeled herself to bring up this unwelcome topic of conversation. 'And as for Christmas, I'll probably stay here. I mean, we're open every day from now until Christmas, longer opening hours and more customers means more bakes, so I'll probably be exhausted and—'

'*Mon Dieu!* You still hate Christmas and you're planning to take to your bed again!' Sandrine exclaimed, and though Mattie hadn't planned any such thing, it did sound tempting. Pulling the covers over her head and not coming out until the last cracker had been well and truly pulled, all the cold turkey had been eaten and all the festive specials had disappeared from the TV schedule.

Until Mattie was safe from anything Christmas-related.

'Let's talk about this some other time,' she decided.

'But Christmas is less than three weeks away, *ma petite*!'

'We'll talk about it at a later date. That means not now.'

'But I need to know how many we'll be for Christmas dinner,' Sandrine protested. She did like to menu plan well in advance.

'I said not now,' Mattie insisted. She could just about cope with Christmas in a work environment, though she was fed up with getting poked in the face by pink and silver stars every time she walked through to the shop. But the thought of actual Christmas, the memories of a past Christmas, the enquiries about how she'd be spending

Christmas Day, sent panic leapfrogging through her. And after she'd inhaled and exhaled for a count of three, as all of Pippa's books on mindfulness advised, Mattie was calm again. 'Give it a rest, Mum. Christmas is *ages* away.'

But it wasn't *ages* away. It was less than twenty days away and as it crept nearer, Mattie could feel that grey cloud settle over her like a fine mist of foul-smelling perfume.

CHAPTER

15

18 days until Christmas

The grey cloud was still hovering above her head the next day as she rolled out pastry for her mince tarts. It was a dull, relentlessly rainy morning that had put off even the most determined Christmas shoppers or regulars from nipping out for coffee. Both shop and tearooms were uncharacteristically quiet and, apart from the faint accompaniment of the Phil Spector Christmas album that Cuthbert was playing, Mattie was alone with her thoughts.

These thoughts were not happy ones. Her tiny kitchen smelt of all things festive; of clementines and brandy and cinnamon, as she expertly cut out her clementine-infused pastry and placed each disc in a greased tart tray, all ready to have her own special blend of mincemeat spooned in. Oh, just the scent of Christmas was enough to roll back the years . . .

There had been a time, not that long ago, two years to be precise, when Mattie had loved Christmas. As soon as Halloween was over and the last November 5th firework had spluttered and died, she'd have the champagne fizz-tingle of anticipation in her veins that soon, but not soon enough, it would be Christmas!

She'd count the days off on her calendar, willing 25th December to arrive just that little bit quicker. Mattie would throw herself into buying the perfect presents for everyone in her life, haunting Pinterest for new things to do with wrapping paper and ribbon, then arranging the gifts around the tree that went up no later than the first week in December.

And then she'd moved to Paris. Paris at Christmas time was a magical place. There were the *Manèges de Noël*, the Christmas carousels that would pop up in every neighbourhood, and walking the length of the Champs Élysées felt a lot like walking through a magical forest of twinkling lights. The Eiffel Tower all dressed up for the occasion would shimmer in the distance.

Then there was the shopping. Stopping at Strohers, the oldest patisserie in Paris, for a *bûche de Noël*, or Yule log. Picking out baubles for the tree at La Colomberie in Saint Germain and choosing gifts from the little Christmas market in Montmartre . . .

Mattie stared, unseeing, out of the tiny window of her tiny kitchen, with its unpicturesque view of the grubby backyard and the outdoor privy. In her mind, she was standing in another tiny kitchen, maybe even tinier than the one she currently stood in, with a tiny window that looked out onto a view that never failed to stir her soul.

The higgledy-piggledy rooftops and chimney-pots and crooked skyline of Paris.

If Mattie clambered up onto her postage-stamp-sized draining board and stuck her head out of the circular window, she could just make out the Eiffel Tower.

Sometimes Mattie thought that the last time she'd been truly happy was in that kitchen in her tiny Paris flat, which consisted of one small room to live and sleep in, an alcove to cook in and a bathroom that had toilet and shower but no room for a washbasin, on the sixth floor of an apartment building.

She'd spent her days at her classes at L'Institut de Patisserie, her evenings waitressing at a bistro in Les Marais and her nights creating cakes of the lightest sponge, the richest buttercream, the stiffest, perfectly peaked meringues, ganache as smooth and as glossy as a frozen lake. Road-testing recipes again and again until they were perfect, scribbling ingredients and instructions and notes in her recipe book. Perfect enough to even meet with the approval of Madame Belmont, who ruled Mattie's class at L'Institut de Patisserie with a snowy-white toque and a whisk of steel.

And then there were the other nights, when the only thing that Mattie was making was sweet, sweet love with Steven, the man she'd met on her first day at L'Institut, when they'd been assigned adjoining work benches in a crowded test kitchen.

The last time she'd seen Steven was two years ago, three

days before Christmas, when she should have been thinking of nothing except the holidays and spending time with the people she loved. Instead Mattie's world had been torn into pieces because in Steven's hands was *her own* recipe book that he'd stolen from her.

'How could you do this to me?' she'd asked, and he'd winced as if the sound of her voice, the sight of her standing there with a stricken look on her face, her eyes glassy with tears that she was trying to hold back, offended him.

'Loving is sharing, isn't it? That's what you always say.'

As if somehow this were all her fault, in the same way that everything always ended up being her fault.

'Matilda . . .'

'Mattie! Mattie! MATTIE!'

Mattie was pulled abruptly from the painful past into a present where Steven was replaced by Cuthbert, who was standing in the kitchen doorway with an aggrieved expression on his usually cheerful face and a trayful of empty cups and plates.

'What?' Mattie asked defensively, her eyes dropping to her half-assembled mince pies, which should have been in the oven by now.

'Queue's almost out the door. It's fast approaching a code red. Your assistance is urgently required.' Cuthbert didn't even wait for a yay or nay but hurried back to the tearooms.

With a sigh and a shake of her head to clear the unwelcome thoughts away, Mattie rinsed her hands and stepped through the curtain to find that the tearooms were heaving with customers. The windows were steamed up but people were shaking off umbrellas and hanging damp coats and jackets on the backs of chairs so it was obviously still raining.

Mattie took a deep breath, pulled out a smile from somewhere and raised her head so she could look the person at the head of the queue in the eye.

'Just my usual coffee,' said Tom, with a pointed look at his stupid old-fashioned wristwatch. 'I've been waiting ages. Posy must be about to send out a search party.'

Mattie had sworn that she would never let another man take advantage of her, and yet she'd been letting Tom do exactly that for months, without even a please or thank you! Longer than months!

The grey storm cloud above her head changed to pink, deepening and darkening until it was a scarlet mist so that Mattie could hardly see as she gave Tom a tight, teeth-baring smile and snatched the mug that he was proffering.

She shoved the mug under one of Jezebel's spouts and yanked at a lever in a way that had Cuthbert clucking anxiously.

'Be gentle with my favourite lady,' he admonished, giving the hissing machine an affectionate pat.

By way of reply, Mattie yanked the lever the other way and slammed Tom's mug down in front of him, slopping coffee over the rim.

'That'll be one pound, twenty-five pence, please,' Mattie gritted, the 'please' almost killing her.

Tom blinked owlishly from behind his glasses. 'I beg your pardon.'

'Black coffee is one pound and twenty-five pence,' Mattie repeated. She gave Tom another teeth-baring smile, which made him take a step back. 'You get fifty pence off for bringing in your own cup. We're all about caring for the environment.'

'You want me to *pay* for my coffee?' Tom asked incredulously. 'Is this a joke?'

'Do I look like I'm joking?' Mattie's smile, by now, was all teeth. In fact, it was pretty close to a snarl and the long queue of people behind Tom were suddenly silent, ears straining not to miss one word of what sounded like it was about to become the mother of all rows. 'And do I look like I'm running some kind of charitable organisation where I give out free coffee to someone who I know for a fact is in regular employment and doesn't even have to pay any rent?'

Mattie did give out free coffee (and food, for that matter) to anyone who came in and looked as if they really needed it, but Tom didn't come under that category.

He pulled out a handful of change from his trouser pocket, his lips so thin that they'd all but disappeared, as he sorted through the coins. 'I was under the impression that Happy Ever After staff got free tea and coffee,' he bit out.

'Generally they do, but then ALL the Happy Ever After staff apart from you actually buy food from me . . .'

'You're always sending over cakes and buns to the shop free of charge,' Tom protested, which was true, but that was neither here nor there.

'That's at *my* discretion. None of the other shop staff bring food into *my* tearooms that they've purchased from another establishment.' Mattie gestured at the paper bag that Tom was holding. 'Every morning you come in with your bloody breakfast panini and expect me to provide free coffee to wash it down. Well, no longer. You have to pay for your coffee now.'

'Fine.' Tom's thin face was pink with emotion, though whether it was anger or shame, Mattie couldn't tell. 'You only had to say. And as my presence and my breakfast panini is such a burden to you, then I'll make my own coffee from now on.'

'Fine,' Mattie snapped. This was exactly what she wanted. Except . . . she didn't feel fine about it. She felt distinctly unfine. Like she was the one being unreasonable. She knew that she was right to *finally* take a stance on his free coffees, but her delivery left a lot to be desired. She'd let her anger take over and so her harsh tone had completely negated all the very good points she'd raised.

Tom left, taking a couple of customers with him who'd obviously decided that their need for coffee and a bite to eat wasn't that great after all. Especially if they were going to be harangued when they tried to order.

'You know what? I can handle these fine people on my own,' Cuthbert said, taking Mattie's arm and pulling her away from the counter. 'Why don't you go back to the kitchen?'

'But we're very busy,' Mattie said, staring at the line of punters waiting to order who all immediately looked elsewhere as if they were frightened to make eye contact with her.

'I'll call if I can't manage. You obviously need some alone time, happens to all of us,' Cuthbert added, as Mattie let herself be gently but firmly guided behind the teapot-patterned curtain so she could get back to her mince pies and think about what she'd just done.

She hadn't done anything wrong though. It was Tom who'd taken shameless advantage of Mattie's good nature and the complex goodwill system that existed between the tearooms and the bookshop. Anyone else would have done the same thing in Mattie's position . . .

CHAPTER 16

18 days until Christmas

'I'm not taking sides, I'm neutral like Switzerland, but how could you have been so harsh with Tom?' Posy lamented. Mattie had steeled herself to take a couple of invoices through to the shop, along with a plate of leftover breakfast pastries, because it was now after lunch. 'He's been having the same panini every morning for the last four years. Is that a crime?'

'It's not a crime,' Mattie said evenly, though it was a carb-laden, grease-soaked two fingers up at all her freshly baked, organic breakfast savouries. 'But he doesn't have to rub my nose in it every morning. Now, these invoices . . . they're actually for the ingredients I used to make those cakes for the author signing last month. Remember? They wanted their book cover on a cake.'

'Verity can deal with that,' Posy decided and Mattie,

grateful not to have to talk to Posy a moment longer, because she definitely wasn't being as neutral as Switzerland, hurried across the shop floor to find Verity.

There was a muffled 'Ooof!' behind her as Posy struggled up from the depths of the sofa. 'We really do need to sort this out.'

Tom was serving behind the counter as Mattie approached. 'Excellent book selection,' he said, handing over a Happy Ever After tote bag to a tired-looking woman. Then he smiled at her, a kind, warm smile that made his face look kind and warm too. The woman smiled back and in that instant, she was no longer tired-looking but had a light in her eyes and a spring in her step as she walked away.

Then Tom saw Mattie slipping past the counter to reach Verity in the back office and his kind, warm smile disappeared as quickly as if someone had taken an eraser to it. He pointedly picked up the mug next to him that was half full of black coffee that he certainly hadn't got for free or even for one pound and twenty-five pence from the tearooms. He took a sip, eyes on Mattie, then sighed appreciatively, as if it was the best sip of coffee he'd ever had, though Mattie would have bet her entire collection of vintage cookery books that it had started life as freeze-dried granules from a jar.

Mattie glared at Tom who gazed innocently back at her, and she longed to give his elbow a quick nudge as she walked past, to spill instant coffee down his disgusting knitted waistcoat.

She didn't though, just walked through to the office

where Verity was frowning at a spreadsheet on her computer screen. 'Invoices,' Mattie announced, placing them down on Verity's desk. 'And some flaky pastries to sweeten the experience of dealing with invoices. I had some leftover caramel so I experimented with a pain au caramel instead of a pain au . . .'

'No!' Verity said rather forcefully. 'We can't accept any more baked goods from you, gratis.'

'We really can't,' added Posy sadly, who'd followed Mattie in and was now collapsing onto the nearest chair. 'In fact, Verity's calculated the amount of free food the shop staff have had from you since the tearooms have been open—'

'Oh, this is ridiculous,' Mattie exclaimed, putting down the plate of pastries because her hands really needed to be on her hips for this conversation.

'It's a very rough estimate,' Verity continued. 'Even so, it appears that we owe you hundreds of pounds.'

The thought of supplying hundreds of pounds' worth of free cake to Verity, Posy and Nina left Mattie feeling quite unmoved and not at all like the feeling of teeth-grinding irritation of Tom coming in every morning to demand his free coffee while *flaunting* his breakfast panini.

'And obviously you'll want to stop the free tea and coffee,' Posy said, rubbing her bump. She had bags under her eyes as if she wasn't sleeping that well. Mattie felt like the worst person in the world for adding to Posy's stress.

'But this isn't about you,' she said, hands very firmly on her hips now and chin tilted, eyes flashing. 'This is about Tom taking advantage of the system. I am *happy* to supply free tea and coffee but you always buy something from me in the morning. It's like an unspoken rule. Tom, on the other hand, doesn't buy anything, he just demands. Sometimes he doesn't even say please!'

'I'm pretty sure that I do say please every time,' Tom called out because he was listening in like some kind of flappy-eared eavesdropper.

'Pretty sure you don't,' Mattie snapped and she longed to slam the door shut but this wasn't her house, so these weren't her rules. 'Anyway, I refuse to accept any money for free food that I willingly gave and I'm offended, *mortally* offended, that you would even suggest paying. Like you think I'm some tight-fisted skinflint who's been secretly resenting every last piece of cake you've eaten.'

'Oh dear,' Posy moaned softly and her bump-rubbing speeded up.

Meanwhile, Verity's head had sunk so low that she no longer looked as if she had a neck. She hated confrontations and could hardly meet Mattie's gaze. Once again, Mattie was having a horrible flashback to those times with Steven, of which there'd been many, when she had always ended up being the villain when she'd been convinced that she was the victim. 'We obviously need to establish some ground rules,' Verity said with a pained grimace. 'I'd hate to think that *you* thought we were taking advantage of you.'

'But you're not!' Mattie wrung her hands like one of the heroines in the romantic novels that all the Happy Ever After staff were obsessed with. Even Tom. Ha! Especially Tom! 'The only person taking advantage of me is Tom, and he can either buy his breakfast from me and get a free coffee or he can pay for his coffee, and if he doesn't want to do that, then he's free to drink that instant swill that passes for coffee. I don't actually think that this is an unreasonable request.'

Was she saying this wrong somehow? Judging from their matching incredulous expressions, she was.

'I see your point about Tom not buying things, absolutely. And we all really need to stop taking advantage of your good nature. But the coffee thing aside, I don't know why you always have it in for poor Tom,' Posy said reproachfully. 'He's actually really rather lovely when you get to know him, not at all stuffy.'

'Thanks for the validation, Posy,' Tom called out. 'No, sorry, I wasn't talking to you. That'll be twenty-seven pounds and thirty-five pence, cash or card?' he added to the customer who he was obviously meant to be serving, instead of listening to a conversation that had nothing to do with him, even if it was about him.

'Yes, Tom's great,' Verity added, jumping on the Tom train. 'You've been living with him for a couple of weeks now, so surely you can see that underneath the stern, tweedy exterior, Tom's a teddy bear.'

'Not a teddy bear,' Posy said, shaking her head. 'More like a cat that pretends to be stand-offish but actually goes all purry and headbutty when you're stroking him.'

'Not that we've ever stroked him,' Verity said quickly. 'But Tom is kind and thoughtful, he's our friend as well as our colleague and . . . and . . .'

'You and Tom really need to sort things out. Neither of you can live like this; snapping and snarling all the time. And also it's very hard for the rest of us because if you and Tom have a problem with each other, then it affects everyone else and becomes our problem too,' Posy said with a sad little sigh. 'And I don't want to have problems. Problems are not good. Problems play havoc with my heartburn and my blood pressure.'

Could all these so-called problems be resolved if Mattie agreed to let Tom have a free cup of black coffee each morning? Quite frankly, she'd rather have her nails detached slowly from her nail-beds with a pair of rusty pliers.

Besides, her terms were not actually unreasonable. Posy had even admitted that Tom shouldn't have been shamelessly freeloading off her. So Mattie wasn't the problem. Tom was the problem because Tom wasn't a lovely, tweedy teddy bear, he was a . . . 'Tom's not a stand-offish cat, he's a no-good Lothario!' Mattie heard herself blurt out as if her mouth was acting independently of her brain. 'He's a shameless seducer of women!'

'What?'

'No!'

Posy and Verity both had their hands to their mouths, eyes wide.

'Yes! And what's more, he's been lying to you all this time because he's an expert on romantic novels. In fact, he wrote his bloody thesis about them!'

'Oh. My. God!' Posy said gleefully, clasping her hands over her bump. 'No! It can't be true.'

'But even if it is true, it's Tom's business,' Verity said, and now she had no trouble looking Mattie straight in the eye with an unwavering and yes, slightly condemning stare. 'If he'd wanted us to know then he'd have told us.'

'Yes, you're right,' Posy agreed somewhat unwillingly, eyes flitting from Mattie to Verity and to the open door that led to the counter where Tom was serving – he was strangely and unnervingly silent, now that his dastardly secrets had finally been revealed.

And Mattie, far from feeling triumphant, felt the same way as she had when she was a small child and had been caught shoplifting pick'n'mix from Woolworths by Sandrine, who'd promptly marched her over to the nearest assistant and demanded to see the manager so that she could report her own daughter for stealing. The white-hot and yet cold and clammy feeling, which now enveloped Mattie was strangely and yet horribly familiar.

'I was just pointing out that Tom isn't as perfect as you think he is.' Mattie wished that she could stop talking because every time she opened her mouth, she just made things a hundred times worse than they'd been a minute before when they'd already been pretty bad. Although to be fair, both Posy and Verity had asked for any intel Mattie could give them on Tom, so it was very hypocritical of them to now act as if Mattie had betrayed the Official Secrets Act.

She managed not to tell them that, though. 'You should probably get back to the tearooms,' Verity said coolly, picking up the plate of pastries. 'And we really can't accept these.'

'No, we really can't,' Posy chimed in, staring at the plate hungrily. Then she turned her head towards Mattie, but couldn't quite look her in the eye. 'Maybe it's time to put things with the tearooms on a more formal basis.'

That sounded ominous. Currently, Mattie paid rent to Posy and the tearooms were very much her own domain, but it was a very relaxed, loosey-goosey arrangement. Verity helped out on the admin side, arranging permits with the council for all sorts of things, from serving alcohol at shop events to Mattie having tables and chairs outside in the summer months. Mattie supplied the catering for all the Happy Ever After events and had happily provided free misshapen baked goods that she couldn't sell in the tearooms or were early prototypes, plus tea and coffee when people were buying something else.

Not to mention the fact that Mattie lived rent-free and at Posy's pleasure in the flat above the shop. Although that might all change. Posy would be well within her rights to chuck Mattie out, as she wasn't the sort of person who could be trusted. Not to mention that the rent Mattie paid on the tearooms was very competitive for central London. Very competitive indeed.

What a stupid idiot she was. She'd had right on her side, Posy and Verity had admitted as much. But Mattie couldn't just quit while she was ahead. Oh no! She'd opened her big mouth and made everything worse. Turned Tom into the victim and she'd whacked her own moral compass off its stand while she was at it. Nobody liked a telltale, which was why Mattie didn't like herself very much at this precise moment.

She picked up the plate of flaky pasties, smiled so feebly that trying to lift up the corners of her mouth was as hard as bench pressing her own weight, and backed out of the office, only to be confronted by Nina, who was standing behind the counter with her eyes blazing.

'How dare you betray Tom's trust like that?'

Mattie felt herself bristle: like the others, Nina had been quite beside herself when Mattie had the opportunity to dig some dirt on Tom, but now that dirt had been well and truly dug, she wanted nothing to do with it. But then Mattie's bristles subsided – she'd said from the start that she wouldn't dish anything, and now look what she'd gone and done.

'Sorry,' she whispered and whether the apology was aimed at Nina or Tom, she didn't really know. She simply wanted to escape the shop for the sanctuary of the tearooms and the inner sanctum of her kitchen.

'Sorry!' Nina snorted. 'Sorry doesn't even begin to cover it.'

Mattie risked a sideways look at Tom but he was resolutely tackling a pile of customer orders as if the future of the world depended on him successfully completing the task.

This was dredging up a painfully familiar deja ewww. As she scurried back to the tearooms she was reminded of how every time she and Steven rowed, by the time she arrived in class at L'Institut de Patisserie the next morning, Steven would have got there first. Even if he'd been the one in the wrong, he would always paint Mattie as a vengeful, hysterical, over-reacting harpy that made his life utter hell.

No wonder she hadn't made many friends at L'Institut. But then Steven had always said that she didn't need friends because she had him. But when Steven was angry with her, which happened more and more often, she felt like the loneliest girl in the world.

'You don't hate me, do you?' she demanded of Cuthbert as soon as she was safely back behind her own counter. 'Over the whole coffee thing with Tom?'

Cuthbert paused from steaming organic milk to look at Mattie as if she'd just turned turquoise.

'Of course I don't hate you. "Hate" is a very strong word. I don't think I hate anyone,' he mused, which wasn't the answer Mattie had hoped for.

'What about "dislike"? Do you dislike me?' she persisted.

'I like you very much,' Cuthbert said, turning his attention back to the steamer. 'And I would even if you didn't pay my wages. Do I think the situation with young Thomas could have been handled better? Yes, but as my Cynthia says, it will all come out in the wash.'

Mattie sighed. It probably would have, except for the fact that she had somehow managed to turn the situation with young Thomas into a major incident.

And that was that. Except, Tom didn't come home that night. Mattie listened out for the slow, scrapey turn of his key in the lock, but all was silent until she fell into a fitful doze at gone two in the morning.

He didn't come home the next night either, or the one

after that, which was fine. Mattie was done poking her nose into Tom's business. If he wanted to stay out all night, shagging his way around London and the Home Counties, being a Casanova, inveigling his way into women's beds and hearts with his shameless flirting and trickery, then that was absolutely his business.

It wasn't anything to do with Mattie, which was exactly how she liked it.

15 days until Christmas

As the damp drizzly days gave way to frost-bitten, freezing days, a skin-scouring crispness that Mattie always associated with Christmas clung to the air, and both Happy Ever After and the tearooms were busy from the moment that Verity and Mattie respectively flipped their door signs from 'closed' to 'open'.

Mattie liked to think, especially given recent Tom-related events, that the tearooms would be busy even if they weren't attached to a successful romantic fiction bookshop. They had their own loyal customer base and thanks to glowing write-ups in *Time Out*, the *Evening Standard* and countless food blogs, and the fact that their cakes were extremely Instagrammable (Cuthbert had painstakingly taught himself to stencil designs with chocolate powder on their cappuccinos), they were a viable business in their own right.

Still, it didn't hurt that the TV news segment on Nina's Mistletoe Booth had captured the imagination of every romantic in London, and that was in addition to the increased numbers of book buyers as Christmas crept ever closer. Then it was Mattie's own turn in the TV spotlight. Clearly, lovers of pork encased in pastry outnumbered even hopeless romantics, so the daily lunchtime queue for pig-in-blanket rolls stretched now around the mews and out into Rochester Street.

Mattie was happy to be busy. She was even happier when Little Sophie and Sam broke up early from their fancy academy school for the Christmas holidays and Sophie was available to serve in the tearooms full time so that Mattie could stay in the kitchen. Not just because she was still keeping a low profile but because she needed to spend most of the day prepping, mixing, baking and cooling. It was against all sorts of food-safety regulations but she was even using the oven in the flat upstairs. It felt as if all her waking hours were punctuated by the beeping of one of three different timers to let her know that she had something to take out of an oven.

But when she wasn't being beeped at, then she had her own unhappy thoughts for company. Posy, Nina and Verity were cordially polite when their paths crossed, which wasn't that often, as they no longer came into the tearooms for a coffee or tea each morning. Even worse than getting their coffee and tea from a rival establishment, Mattie had seen them making their own coffee and tea in the sliver of space in the back office which could laughably be described as a kitchen. It was like a knife to the heart that they'd rather drink instant coffee and substandard, non-organic tea than Mattie's own bespoke blends. And as for coming in for their lunch, which they all used to do? No. Not any more.

Although Mattie had briefly tortured herself with visions of the four of them, all sitting around in the Italian café eating paninis and bitching about her, the truth was a lot more tragic than that. Rather than partaking of Mattie's delicious lunchtime savouries, Verity and Posy were bringing lunch from home. Tired-looking leftovers; floppy pasta from the night before. Ready meals cooked in the microwave that had languished unused in the back office and stank out the shop. Once Mattie had popped through to the office with some invoices for Verity and had caught her eating the most depressing sandwich in the world: some droopy ham and a bit of wilted lettuce between two slices of stale-looking white bread.

Mattie was also spending a considerable amount of time tormenting herself about Tom, who apparently was kipping on the sofa at a friend's house. Tom had mentioned the sofa surfing to Nina who'd told Sam, who told Sophie, who discussed it with Cuthbert as they wondered aloud at how rumpled Tom was looking lately.

Mattie hadn't noticed Tom's rumpledom, because she was avoiding Tom at all costs. But when she overheard Sophie and Cuthbert talking about Tom's bad back from sleeping on an ancient sofa and how cross Posy was with him because he said that he couldn't be expected to hump boxes of books about for the foreseeable future, Mattie decided that enough was enough.

Though she'd had a valid point about Tom's cavalier coffee consumption ('Oh my God, let it go,' Sophie had groaned when Mattie had brought the subject up yet again), she shouldn't have outed Tom as a closet Casanova and expert in romantic fiction, so she had to make things right. She wasn't brave enough to face Tom (and anyway, he did a swift about turn any time Mattie was near) and though they'd shared a living space, they'd never shared mobile numbers so she had no option but to message him on his Happy Ever After email address:

To: Tom@HappyEverAfter.co.uk
From: Mattie@TheTearoomsHappyEverAfter.co.uk

Tom,

I feel absolutely wretched about EVERYTHING. I'm sorry that I reacted so badly (though it was incredibly thoughtless of you to bring your breakfast panini from the Italian café into the tearooms every day but whatever, I'm over it) and I am so sorry, quite sick with shame, that I told Posy and Verity about your thesis. And that I called you a Lothario. Although I did see you in action at the Banter Boys' bonfire party and you were coming across as quite Lothario-ish – just saying.

Anyway, it's silly for you to be sleeping on a

sofa in zone four, when you have a perfectly comfortable bed upstairs and a ten-second commute. Please come back to the flat and things can go back to how they were before. I'll stay out of your way. Honestly, I'm quite happy to sit in my room and only come out when you tell me I can.

Again, I really am sorry.

Mattie

All day Mattie was on tenterhooks, staring at her phone and listening out for the ping that told her she had new mail, and not listening out for the beep that told her she had something that needed to come out of the oven. She even burned a batch of sponges.

Finally, as Mattie was staring disconsolately at the back of a customer who'd ordered two of her mince pies and had decimated both of them between his fingers and was now eating them crumb by crumb, the phone in her apron pocket pinged:

To: Mattie@TheTearoomsHappyEverAfter.co.uk
From: Tom@HappyEverAfter.co.uk

This whole living arrangement thing will only work if we agree not to talk to each other.

Regards,

Tom

It was harsh. Almost as harsh as the look on Tom's face when he caught sight of Mattie an hour later as she was directing a tearoom customer to the Regency shelves in the bookshop. He looked at her in the exact same way he'd look if he'd trodden in something disgusting and it was all Mattie's fault.

Filled with regret, Mattie messaged back:

To: Tom@HappyEverAfter.co.uk
From: Mattie@TheTearoomsHappyEverAfter.co.uk

Fine.

Considering that she was exhausted, sleep should have come as a blessed, sweet relief but that night it eluded her. Instead she thought about her current situation and how it was very similar to the situation she'd found herself in two years before. Memories of Steven were never pleasant; they turned up like gatecrashers at a party who just wouldn't leave, but when Mattie wasn't thinking about Steven, she was thinking about Tom and what she could do to finally bring their cold war to a swift and warm end.

CHAPTER
18

14 days until Christmas

Desperate times called for desperate measures – bright and early the next morning a temporary kitchen assistant started. Mattie had already had to limit her pig-in-blanket rolls to two per customer and had a 5 p.m. cut-off time, otherwise she'd never get anything done that wasn't making pig-in-blanket rolls.

Meena was in her second year at catering college and, judging from the exquisite-looking cakes she posted on her Instagram, she knew her way round a mixing bowl and a pallet knife.

Mattie had been worried about sharing a kitchen made only for one person with another human being, but not only was Meena adept at making flaky pastry, she was also very small and didn't talk much. She also had quite the work ethic. So, by three o'clock that afternoon, everything was under control and Mattie felt like they wouldn't run out of baked goods, if she popped out for an hour to make a start on her Christmas shopping.

Armed with her list, she headed straight to the beauty shop on Rochester Street to buy Sandrine's favourite perfume *and* a scented candle. While she was there, she went off-list to buy Ian a male-grooming starter-kit because Sandrine had mentioned that he had become quite fixated on the fact that the fine lines around his eyes were starting to upgrade to crow's feet.

In the very hipster gentleman's outfitter, she bought Guy some four-leaf clover cufflinks because he was the most superstitious person Mattie had ever met. He wouldn't even set foot in a park in case he happened across a single magpie.

Then she paused by a glass display case of bow-ties, which made her think of Tom, though she was trying really hard not to. Tom wasn't on her Christmas present list because even though they shared a living space, even before their current hostilities, they certainly weren't friendly enough to exchange gifts.

Anyway, if Mattie were to get Tom a present, it wouldn't be anything brand new and box fresh. He'd want something old. Maybe a leather-bound book of literary criticism that stank of mildew, or a tweedy jacket that had been briefly fashionable sometime between the wars, with leather trim around the cuffs and pockets. A fountain pen, unused and unwanted for many years, waiting to be brought back to life with ink and a firm but light touch.

Yes, Tom would want something pre-loved. And as Mattie

gazed at a young couple, the woman slowly tugging on the end of her boyfriend's scarf to pull him nearer for a kiss, Mattie's eyes prickled. Then, unbelievably, she felt a tear suddenly begin a slow descent down her cheek.

She was pre-loved too. She'd tried love and it had chewed her up and spat her back out. If that happened again (and judging by her mother's track record of three husbands and four near misses until she'd met Ian, good love genes didn't run in the family), Mattie knew that there'd be nothing left of her. She didn't like to think of herself as a quitter, but she'd had to give up on love.

Mattie stepped outside onto Rochester Street. It was like a scene out of a Dickens novel, with its cobblestones and old-fashioned-looking shops with the bay windows, all strung with fairy lights and Christmas decorations. The little street thronged with couples, all arm in arm as they shopped together, trying to find the perfect gift, which represented what they meant to each other.

Come Boxing Day, Mattie would be perfectly all right with her single status. But there was something about Christmas and especially the run-up to Christmas, which brought out the melancholy in her now. Not just because it was the anniversary of her own particular heartbreak but because Christmas was a time of togetherness and family. Not just the family that you were born into but the family you made with someone else.

By swearing off love, Mattie was giving up on being someone else's family too.

She bit her lip and tried not to blink as she made her

way back to the mews. Tried to be pleased that she'd made a major inroad into her Christmas shopping, which she'd bought with money earned from doing what she loved. And how many people could say that they loved their jobs? That they'd found their calling in life? In lots of ways Mattie was very lucky. But as she opened the door to the tearooms and was enveloped in a welcoming smell of freshly ground coffee and the sweet, aromatic fragrance of mince pies out of the oven and heard the lively hum of chatter, the hissing chugga–chugga of Jezebel in full throttle and Cuthbert loudly singing along to Mariah Carey's 'All I Want For Christmas', which was playing on his ancient tape deck, she took no pleasure in this world that she'd created.

'Mattie! Can you take over for a minute? I'm dying for a wee!' Little Sophie was fidgeting from one foot to the other, and Mattie lifted her hand in acknowledgment and quickly hurried over to the counter.

For the next half an hour she was caught up in the afternoon tea rush. Darting into the kitchen to put things in and take things out of the oven, trying to sort out a problem with the red velvet cake batter, which had separated. Then it was back to the tearooms to sort out a belligerent man who wanted to buy out their entire stock of pig-in-blanket rolls. She took drinks orders, cleared tables and said brightly, 'Yes, Merry Christmas to you too,' to departing customers.

It was a bravura performance for which Mattie definitely deserved some kind of acting award. The customers began to thin out but she knew there'd only be a brief lull before the late-night shopping crowd descended.

She very nearly did cry when she went back into the kitchen to find that Meena had several batches of puff pastry for tomorrow's pig-in-blanket rolls already in the fridge.

'You have literally changed my life,' she said as Meena swapped her apron for coat and scarf and hat. 'You will be back tomorrow, won't you? We haven't scared you off?'

'This is so much more fun than catering college,' Meena declared. 'I always end up getting stuck sous-cheffing for some boy who can't cook half as well as I can but thinks he's the next Gordon Ramsey. I'll see you at eight tomorrow.'

As soon as she was gone, Mattie drooped against the fridge. Maybe Mercury was in retrograde and that was why she was feeling so blue, she thought as she peeled herself off the fridge, opened the door and took out eggs, butter and cream.

If she was going to mope in here, then at least she could mope productively. And she wasn't going to cry because there really was nothing to cry about – she was unloved by choice. And she especially wasn't going to cry while she was creaming butter and sugar. Her French grandmother had always said that when you were cooking, you put your mood into the bowl along with your ingredients and nothing tasted good with a splash of tears.

She would bake Tom a cake. Cake made everything better. In the past, she'd baked cakes for birthdays, anniversaries, weddings, once even a funeral. There'd been a cake in the shape of the Sydney Opera House for a friend about to go travelling. When Ian had retired after forty years in property management, Mattie had baked him a cake in the shape of an open toolbox. She'd even made tiny screws out of fondant.

Whatever the occasion, Mattie could make a cake for it, though she didn't think she'd ever baked an 'I'm sorry for betraying your deepest, darkest secrets to your workmates' cake before. Still, she'd give it the old college try.

Now she was thinking about Tom more than ever. Mentally scrolling back to all the treats she'd made for bookshop events or just because it was a miserable Monday morning and everyone needed a little cheering up, and Tom's reaction to each one.

He wasn't like Nina or Posy who were effusive in their praise for a profiterole or a pecan and butterscotch doughnut. Even Verity would give an appreciative hum when she bit into her favourite apple and cinnamon crumb cake.

But Tom was never effusive or hummed appreciatively. Mattie clenched her fists as irritation rose up in her again like a prickly heat rash. It wasn't just the coffee – over the last eighteen months, he'd eaten countless cakes and tarts and savouries all made by Mattie, and he'd barely grunted out a thank you.

Yet here she was: having to make amends to him through the medium of cake. She was half inclined to make Tom a coffee cake, but she could already hear Guy's voice in her head saying, 'Have I mentioned lately that you're the most passive-aggressive person I've ever shared a womb with?'

Mattie decided that gingerbread was a less contentious option and as gingerbread was a staple of her festive menu, she had to make some for tomorrow anyway. She'd make gingerbread kisses because Nina had brought back more bags of Hershey's Kisses from the States than any one person could eat. Before relations between tearooms and bookshop had become so frosty, she'd asked Mattie if she wanted some of the kisses to incorporate into her baking. 'I'd much rather have the real thing than the chocolate substitute,' Nina had said, her eyes holding that faraway look which meant that she was thinking about Noah. 'I really think kissing is my favourite thing ever. It's even better than leopard print.'

As Mattie shoved Hershey's Kisses into the scored squares of her just-out-of-the-oven gingerbread, all she could think about were kisses. She'd probably never kiss anyone ever again. Or be kissed. Or be held in someone's arms.

'And I'm absolutely fine with that,' Mattie muttered the words out loud so they'd have more meaning, then cut out five gingerbread squares, arranged them on a plate and left the kitchen.

'Just taking these into the shop,' she said to Cuthbert as she passed. It was nearly eight, almost closing time, and only the last stragglers were left in the tearooms, resting aching feet, shopping bags stashed under the tables as they chased the last crumb of a restorative snack, drained the last drop of a reviving coffee.

The bookshop was also almost empty of customers: a couple of browsers, someone paying at the till, someone else paying Sam *in situ* as he perched on the sofa with an iPad. Even the Mistletoe Booth was empty, but as Mattie came through the arch, her eyes found Tom, who was halfway up the rolling ladder, while a middle-aged man stood underneath with a spreadsheet.

'No, she's definitely got that one,' he said in a despairing voice. 'Are you sure that Jilly Cooper hasn't written any more books?'

'I could look on the computer, but I'm ninety-nine per cent sure that she hasn't,' Tom said in an equally despairing voice as if the man and his spreadsheet had been there for quite some time. 'What about a writer who's similar to Jilly Cooper?'

'They have to have horses in them,' the man said. 'My mother will only read books about romance and horses.'

Tom's jaw looked particularly tense. Mattie knew him well enough now to be able to tell when he was stifling a sigh or, more likely, a sarcastic retort. He looked behind him for a kindred spirit he could roll his eyes at, but unfortunately for him Nina was back in the Erotica section where she'd been talking about *ménage* fiction with two young women. 'One man is hard enough work,' Nina had been explaining. 'Having to cope with two of them would just be exhausting because you know that neither of them would remember to put the loo seat down.'

Tom had to settle for Mattie, who tried to smile to show that she was here to make amends. He was too overwrought to do anything but grimace back and slant his eyes in the direction of his customer who was staring down at his spreadsheet.

This would be the perfect time for Mattie to hold up her plate and say in a jaunty tone, 'Fancy a kiss?' Except it would be a gingerbread kiss, which was the only kind of kiss that Tom could expect from her. Even as she lifted the plate, the shop door opened, the bell jangled.

Mattie glanced over at the new arrival, only for the colour to drain from her face as her blood rushed through her veins and down to the floor, leaving her cold and trembling.

The plate left Mattie's nerveless fingers and crashed to the floor, gingerbread scattering to the four corners.

'Mattie? Are you all right?' she heard Posy say from somewhere behind her – but she only had eyes for the man at the door.

'Matilda,' he said, in that silky voice that she'd once loved until it had been used as a weapon against her. 'It's been too long. How the devil are you, my darling?'

CHAPTER

19

14 days until Christmas

Steven was as beautiful as Mattie remembered him. More beautiful because she'd let her anger and grief dim the sheen of his dark hair, dull the light of his warm, brown eyes, blunt the angles of his quite extraordinary cheekbones and the strong line of his jaw.

Her memory had played tricks on her and made Steven less – less beautiful, less charismatic, less everything. When Mattie had thought about him, wondered how she could ever have loved him, the Steven she'd seen in her mind's eye hadn't been as tall, or as finely put together.

Now, as he came closer, Mattie was too shocked to shrink back but stood there, still and pale and cold, as he took her frozen hands so he could brush his lips against each cheek. She'd even forgotten that he always smelled good, of figs and exotic spices.

But she hadn't forgotten how Steven could fill a room with the sheer force of his presence so no one else seemed to exist.

'Matilda,' he said reproachfully, teasingly. 'You look like you've seen a ghost. No welcome for your old friend?'

'What are you doing here?' Mattie was amazed that she could make words come out of her mouth. Was astounded that her legs still worked and that she could take the unsteady steps she needed to sink down on the sofa.

'I'm in town for a few days,' he said easily, although all eyes were on him. Posy and Verity behind the counter unabashedly staring at him, Nina had come out from the Erotica section and was running an appraising eye over Steven's lithe, lean form as if she was about to put a bid on him. 'I couldn't be in London without looking you up, could I?'

Only Tom seemed disinterested. He shot Steven one cold, dismissive look from his eyrie halfway up the rolling ladder then turned back to the man with the spreadsheet. 'I've got a couple of novels by Fiona Walker. They're very horsey. Your mother might like them.'

'You could have,' Mattie said, wishing suddenly that Tom wasn't up the rolling ladder but on terra firma, tutting loudly and complaining about people bringing their personal lives into the shop, as he did whenever Posy or Nina were oversharing about their husbands. Tom could kill a mood quicker than boiling hot water could kill a swarm of ants, but he was of no help in this instance. That was all right though. Mattie could deal with Steven's sudden and very unwelcome appearance, all by herself. She lifted her chin, the way she faced every challenge. 'Why on earth would you think I'd ever want to see you again?'

Steven smiled sadly. 'That's rather unfair, isn't it?' Then he turned his face away from her and ran his hand through his glossy brown hair, temporarily ruffling it the better to display his exquisite bone structure. It was a move that used to make Mattie come quite undone in the early days when she still couldn't believe that she'd bagged herself such a hottie. Now she realised she was immune to it.

'Mattie? You're not going to introduce us?' Posy asked in a rather breathless voice. Despite her handsome husband, she obviously wasn't immune to the charms of a man who looked like he modelled for Calvin Klein in his spare time.

'Steven,' Mattie said flatly. 'He was in my patisserie class in Paris.'

'We were a little more than classmates,' Steven admonished. 'A *lot* more.'

'I'm Posy, this is my shop and Mattie runs the tearooms attached to it,' Posy said in a friendly voice because she was at the mercy of her hormones and completely off her game. Whereas Nina and Verity had now picked up on Mattie's distress: the stiff line of her spine, the raspy tone of her voice, the stricken, desperate look in her wide eyes.

'It's one minute past eight,' Nina announced in an unnecessarily loud voice. 'This is your five-minute warning, people! Please make your way to a pay point, some of us have got homes to go to!'

'Don't be so rude, Nina!' Posy scolded.

'But she has a point,' Verity hissed, with a pointed look at Steven, because Verity wasn't the type to be taken in with an easy smile and a killer pair of cheekbones. 'We don't want any last-minute lingerers.'

'These tearooms sound charming,' Steven said to Mattie, as if the five-minute warning and Verity's absolute lack of a welcome didn't apply to him. 'I'm so proud of you.'

'I don't need you to be proud of me,' Mattie said, beginning to thaw out. The feeling was coming back to her frozen limbs so that her fingers and toes were twitching and she was irritated and getting angrier as she stared at Steven, at the pleasant smile on his face, his even tone.

'Well, I am proud of you. I haven't seen you in two years and you're already running an empire.'

It was as if they hadn't parted on the worst possible terms after he'd done the worst possible things to her. Had she somehow imagined everything that had happened between them? Had the time apart made her embellish the truth of not just that final fight but all the fights that led up to it? All the times that Steven had made her feel small, humiliated her, stormed out leaving Mattie to sob for hours?

No, it had all happened.

She stood up on feet that still felt shaky. 'What a mess,' she said loudly. She wasn't just talking about Steven turning up out of the blue and all the conflicted thoughts that were tugging at her, but the actual literal mess of broken china and smashed gingerbread kisses. 'I'll get the broom.'

'It's all right,' Nina said breezily. 'I need to sweep up

anyway. And I bet you've got a mountain of prep to do for tomorrow.'

Mattie seized the excuse that Nina had given her with both hands. 'Yes! Yes I have!' She forced herself to turn to Steven with some semblance of a smile. 'Well, it was nice of you to drop in, but I really have to go . . .'

'And do your prep? I'll help,' Steven offered, though to Mattie's ears it sounded more like a command. 'It'll be like old times. Flaky pastry for tomorrow's viennoiserie?'

'Yes, but . . .'

'Croissant or brioche dough?'

'Both, but . . .'

'I should have known. It's not like you to cut corners,' Steven said warmly as if they really were old friends, and he even had his hand in the small of her back to guide Mattie as she walked through the arch into Classics, though she knew the way without help. 'I can't wait to see these tearooms of yours.'

'Well, I just rent them,' Mattie said stiffly. She wanted him to leave more than she'd ever wanted anything and was all set to tell him that as soon as they were away from an audience, but as they came through the glass set of doors into the tearooms, she felt a fierce burst of pride.

Mattie had escaped from Paris with nothing. She had left her broken heart and all her old dreams behind and yet, somehow she'd put herself back together, piece by piece, and through sheer bloody hard work, she'd created the tearooms. Not just a place that sold hot drinks and cakes, but a sanctuary from the bustling world outside.

Somewhere that her customers could rest their aching feet and souls and lose themselves in the best coffee in Central London (according to the *Evening Standard*), then treat themselves to the finest cakes and savouries that Mattie knew how to make (and again the *Evening Standard* and *Time Out* plus the *Guardian* and countless food blogs and Instagram influencers would back her up on this).

The tearooms were her greatest glory and no one could take that away from her.

'Well, this is *charming*,' Steven said from behind Mattie and she swivelled around to see his eyes taking it all in. In the few minutes since she'd left the tearooms and her whole world had tilted on its axis, her last customers had left. All the tables had been cleared and wiped, the counter was free of clutter, and Cuthbert had buffed up Jezebel so that she gleamed.

Now Steven's smile was less easy, the quirk of his lips could be classed as a smirk. 'Of course, you always used to say that you wanted to do the really high-end patisserie but, this is . . . *sweet*. Well done, you.'

Mattie wasn't going to let Steven tread all over her hard work and her happy place. 'There were a lot of things I used to say,' she said with heavy meaning that was lost on Steven. He advanced on the counter where Cuthbert was just putting on his hat and coat.

'I'll be off then,' Cuthbert said with a curious look at Steven, who was studying the chalkboard menu on the wall. 'Cynthia says that she'll have dinner on the table in ten minutes. Shepherd's pie, my favourite.'

'I wish I had a Cynthia,' Mattie said, because it was what she always said when Cuthbert mentioned one of the many, many ways that Cynthia doted on him, and Mattie just wanted to feel normal. 'Another two weeks and we're back to closing at six o'clock.'

'Hallelujah,' Sophie said, coming through from the kitchen with mop and bucket. 'Although the extra money is nice. See you tomorrow, Gramps. Love to Nanna.'

Cuthbert was gone with a wave of his hand, the door shutting firmly behind him.

'What's a "croque missus" and a "croque guvnor"?' Steven suddenly asked, and Mattie was sure that his eyes were beadier than they had been before.

'Never you mi—'

'Mattie loves to do an English twist on French classics,' Sophie piped up as she upended a chair and placed it on a table. 'So, we make our croque . . .'

'Trade secret!' Mattie snapped out with a smile that was all teeth. 'I'm not giving away my prized recipes. Not again.'

'Silly Mathilde,' Steven scoffed gently, actually daring to cuff her gently on the chin, though she jerked away from his touch. 'Not still banging that old drum? I'm just here to catch up with a dear old friend and to lend a hand.' He was already peeling off his coat. 'Where shall I put this?'

'You can put it straight back on,' Mattie said, with a desperate look at Sophie, but she was intent on mopping the floor. When she turned her head, Mattie saw that she had her ear buds in, which explained why she was mopping in a four/four rhythm.

'Now, where's the kitchen?' Steven said, as if Mattie hadn't even spoken. 'Ah! Here! And I can hang my coat on the hook on the back of the door. So, this is where the magic happens. God, it's poky . . .'

Mattie hadn't imagined it. Not any of it. This was what Steven did. Rode roughshod over everybody else in the guise of doing them a favour, of helping out so they'd feel beholden to him. And he did much worse things than that . . .

She all but ran into the kitchen to squeeze past Steven, yank open the drawer of the cupboard to the left of the cooker and pull out her recipe book. Surely she wasn't imagining the gleam in Steven's eyes as he saw what Mattie was holding.

'If *you must* help, then the butter's in the fridge. Use the unsalted. Flour and dry ingredients in here.' She gestured to a cupboard. 'You do remember how to make a laminated dough, don't you?'

Steven smiled as he opened the fridge door, making himself at home. 'I'm insulted that you'd think otherwise,' he said.

'Right, well I'll be back in a minute,' Mattie said, grabbing a couple of sheets of paper from the worktop, new recipes she was fine-tuning, and heading back to the bookshop.

She was just in time. Posy was waddling out of the door with Nina, and Verity was bringing up the rear.

'I'm fit for nothing but a takeaway curry and maybe one episode of *Queer Eye*,' Posy was saying as Mattie burst through the arch.

'Wait! Don't leave!' she cried out. All three of them turned to look at her.

'Everything all right?' Verity asked with a concerned look on her face. 'Is this going to take long?'

'Two minutes,' Mattie promised. 'I just need you to lock my recipe book in the safe.'

'Okaaaay,' Verity said with a frown because as requests went, it was pretty weird. 'I can do that. Any particular reason why?'

'So that no one can steal it,' Mattie said – it sounded ridiculous but she didn't care. All she cared about was not losing another two years' worth of recipes that she'd painstakingly created and finessed and tweaked over and over again.

'Who would do that?' Posy asked, leaning against the door jamb. 'Can I wait until tomorrow to find out? Sebastian's just pulling up outside.'

'Go! I'll explain everything tomorrow,' Mattie said and with a grateful smile, Posy left and Mattie could follow Verity through to the office, Nina bringing up the rear.

'Is that bloke still here?' she demanded. 'An ex-boyfriend, obviously.'

'How can you tell?' Mattie asked, watching intently as Verity turned the dial on the old-fashioned safe. It was where they kept the day's takings when they hadn't had a chance to get to the bank, the till float and, most importantly and the reason it was a fire-retardant safe, a first edition of Noel Streatfeild's *Ballet Shoes*, which was Posy's most prized possession.

'If I ever went on *Mastermind* then ex-boyfriends would be my specialist subject,' Nina said, pulling on hat and gloves. 'And I could *smell* the badness coming off him in waves. A right wrong 'un, yeah?'

'The wrongest 'un,' Mattie said and her shoulders slumped in relief as Verity placed her recipe book and worksheets in the safe, then slammed the door.

'Do you want me to get rid of him for you?' Nina asked, her tone all seriousness. It was a tempting offer. Mattie didn't doubt that Nina could see Steven off in a spectacular fashion. She wouldn't put up with any of his clever power-plays. No, Nina would probably yawn in his handsome face and drawl, 'Why are you still here?'

Alas, Mattie had to face down her own demons. 'No, but thank you for the offer. I think I need to deal with him myself. I have some things I need to say to him.'

'Don't forget, Tom's upstairs if you need him,' Nina called after her. But Mattie didn't need Tom. She certainly didn't want the man who'd ruined her for all other men to meet the man who thought she hated *all* men.

The thought of all the love that she'd never be either giving or receiving because of Steven put a spring in Mattie's step, and as she marched through the darkened anterooms back to her domain, she steeled herself to confront him.

CHAPTER

20

14 days until Christmas

'There you are! I wasn't sure of quantities so I reckoned starting with about five hundred grams of flour would give you about twenty-five pastries,' Steven said. He was already slowly mixing the dough with Mattie's beloved KitchenAid mixer, which had belonged to her grand-mother.

'Hmm. I usually double up,' Mattie said, opening the fridge to take out some dough that she'd made earlier, plus a packet of her favourite Normandy unsalted butter. 'Look, I'm perfectly capable of doing this by myself. I don't know why you're here and actually, I don't even want you here so—'

'I missed you, Matilda,' Steven said softly. 'I miss everything about you.'

'Really?' Mattie asked, raising an eyebrow and starting

219

her dough. 'Because, according to you, there wasn't one good thing about me.'

'That's not fair,' Steven said, shaking his head, and he was doing that thing that he did with his eyes. Furrowing his brow and gazing downwards as if he was in deep, existential pain, like he was the innocent victim in all this. 'You know I loved you, even though there were times when you made it very difficult to love you.'

Fortunately, Mattie had reached the part of pastry making that required her to place her unwrapped butter between two pieces of greaseproof paper, then bash seven shades of hell out of it with her rolling pin.

It was something she always enjoyed doing. It relieved the stresses of the day just as effectively as Pippa's Boxfit classes and wasn't such a strain on her upper arms. But never before in the history of flaky pastry had one woman gone to town as hard on the butter as Mattie was doing.

'I. Didn't. Used. To. Be. Difficult,' she said between blows, each one making Steven blink. 'You're. The. One. Who. Made. Me. Difficult.'

'No, no, Mattie,' Steven said firmly. 'That's not the way I remember it. You're mistaken.'

'I. Am. Not. Mistaken.'

'You know that you become quite irrational when you get too emotional. Calm down, sweetie.'

'If. You. Don't. Like. The. Way. I. Am. Then. You. Can. Leave.' Mattie gestured with her rolling pin. 'Door's over there.'

'Don't be silly. I said I'd help you with your prep and

that's what I'm going to do,' Steven said calmly, trying to take a step back as Mattie picked up a knife to cut her flattened butter into small squares. 'You know, I would cut much larger squares, if I were you.'

'Yeah, well, you're not me,' Mattie growled. 'And forgive me for not following your culinary advice when *you* were the one who stole my recipes . . .'

'You've got absolutely no proof,' Steven said with a shrug. 'And you're getting hysterical.'

'I am not hysterical,' Mattie said because she wasn't even close. She remembered, from her skim read of Tom's dissertation, that there was a certain kind of man who was quick to label women as hysterical whenever they stood up for themselves.

'You're shouting,' Steven said in a quieter voice so that Mattie gave a guilty start even though she hadn't been shouting. Or . . . she was pretty sure that she hadn't been shouting, she couldn't say for certain.

'Sorry,' leaked out of her mouth, a dirty old habit, before she could stop it.

'Apology accepted,' Steven said magnanimously and they worked in silence after that, apart from when Steven asked for instructions then insisted that his way was better. Mattie had a good mind to throw out every single gram of pastry that Steven had worked on, but it would just be cutting her nose off to spite her face, not to mention shocking food waste.

By the time the prep was done forty-five minutes later, Mattie was exhausted. Not just the physical exhaustion of

a day spent mostly on her feet, but mentally and emotionally exhausted from dealing with Steven and his constant
undermining and deflection.

'I'll see you home,' he said, although Mattie was desperate
for him to leave. She no longer had the energy to have
things out with him and couldn't face the thought of
launching into the impassioned, scathing speech that she'd
been working on for the last two years. She just wanted
him gone.

'No need. I live above the shop,' she said, peeling off her
apron. At least he would leave now. 'Well, it was ni—'

'Poor Matilda, you look so tired,' Steven interrupted. 'I'll
come up with you.'

'Please don't.' She froze, horrified.

'That's very ungrateful. You obviously needed my help
with all this prep and you haven't even said thank you,'
Steven said. It was funny the things you forgot – now
Mattie remembered his hurt voice only too well. It sent
shivers down her spine. 'The least you could do is offer me
a cup of tea.'

'No. I'm not making you tea,' Mattie said, folding her
arms. 'Thank you for your help with the prep. There, I've
said thank you, now you can go.'

Steven ignored her and stepped away, out of the kitchen
– maybe he'd had a change of heart?

'Above the shop, is it, Mattie? So back the way I came
in?'

How could she have forgotten that Steven didn't have
a heart?

By the time Mattie caught up with him, he was already in the main room of the shop and slipping behind the counter. 'This door marked private?' he asked.

'Stop, Steven. It's marked private for a reason.' But arguing with Steven was always as much use as howling at the moon. He was waiting for her at the foot of the stairs. 'Please. Will you just go?'

It was as if she hadn't even spoken. He gestured at the stairs. 'Ladies first.'

'I've asked you to go . . .'

'And I've asked you for one cup of tea and you begrudge me that?' Steven shook his head. 'You never used to be so selfish.'

Whereas Steven had always done what he damn well wanted. 'OK, one cup of tea and then you have to leave. I mean it, Steven.'

He nodded his assent, eyes a shade cooler than before. Mattie could feel his eyes on her, like daggers, as she climbed the stairs up to the flat. She'd worked so hard to eradicate him from her life, to build a life without him, and now he was invading all the spaces where she most felt herself: her tearooms, her work kitchen and now her home.

There was light spilling under the door as she unlocked it, opened it, then came to a halt because she suddenly couldn't bear to have Steven come any further.

Mattie turned round. 'Really, Steven, why are you here?' she asked, her voice absolutely devoid of expression or emotion so she couldn't be accused of being too emotional, too hysterical, just too bloody much.

He put a hand to his chest, eyes wide as if to imply it was an unjust question bordering on an accusation. 'I already told you: to catch up.'

'We're caught up,' Mattie said flatly. 'I have my tearooms—'

'Not *your* tearooms. You only rent it, isn't that what the pregnant woman said?'

'—and I don't really care what you're doing—'

'A word of advice, Matilda. Nobody likes a bitter woman. It's a very unattractive quality,' Steven said. 'But actually, I'm doing very well.' He paused expectantly, for what?

For Mattie to say that she was pleased for him? Well, he was going to have a long wait.

'Good for you,' she said in the same flat voice. 'Now that we're properly caught up—'

'Yes, it's actually very exciting,' Steven said, preening a little. 'I've got a cookbook and a TV show in the works. The commissioning editor reckons I could be the male Nigella. Quite flattering, I suppose, though I'd prefer to be known for my baking rather than for my good looks. Perhaps I could tell you about it over that cup of tea . . . ?'

Mattie had dreamed, still dreamed, of her own cookbooks, her own TV show, but the expected knife-twist pang of jealousy never came. Steven was many things, not *all* of them bad, but above all he wasn't a grafter. Mattie knew only too well, that he preferred to get someone else to do the heavy lifting and then take all the credit. If and when she was in a position to have her own cookbooks published, her own TV show, a chain of tearooms, it would be because she'd earned them through her own hard work.

So she was pleased, and proud of herself that she could smile and say, 'Congratulations, you must be thrilled,' in a voice that didn't waver.

'Thank you, Matilda. That means a lot, coming from you,' Steven said and he looked past Mattie to the door that was still ajar. Mattie stood firm.

'So, was there anything else? Because I really am tired, far too tired to make a cuppa for you,' she said, folding her arms.

Steven smiled and Mattie had to catch her breath. When Steven smiled his face creased in the most beautiful way, teeth gleaming, eyes so bright as if he was the sun and everyone else was just a lonely planet revolving around him.

It was dazzling but Mattie had learned the hard way not to be blinded by that smile but instead to shield herself from its damaging rays.

'Now, I know things ended badly between us, and I really am sorry for any distress I *may* have caused you,' Steven said, which was the closest he'd ever come to an apology. Then his tone hardened. 'But I need to know that you're not going to cause trouble for me.'

'Cause trouble for you? Why would I do that?' Mattie asked, stung. Her revenge fantasies about Steven were never about inflicting hurt on him; they were more about Mattie living well and fabulously, then bumping into Steven one day only to discover that he was so down on his luck that he was selling dodgy batteries out of a suitcase on Oxford Street. 'If you think that's my style, then you never really knew me.'

'Well, I'm glad to hear that,' Steven said and before Mattie realised what he was doing, he grabbed her hand so he could squeeze her fingers in a tender gesture. 'I'm so relieved that you wouldn't go around saying, for example, that my recipes are yours.'

This – *this* – was the real reason for Steven rocking up. She could finally launch into her speech, even if she had to start somewhere in the middle.

'But Steven, those recipes *are* mine, aren't they? Because you stole them from me when you took—'

'You can't copyright a recipe, Matilda.' He spoke over her, just as he always had done. 'Any reasonable person would agree that you need a set quantity of flour, sugar, butter and eggs to make a sponge.' His hold on her hand tightened, so if she hadn't been spluttering in disbelief, she might have cried out.

'You . . . You . . .'

'Honestly, can you two keep it down?' The door, which had been merely ajar, was now wrenched open by a furious Tom. 'I've had a long day at the coalface of bookselling and I just want some peace and quiet.' He glared at Mattie. 'Anyway, I thought we agreed that we weren't going to have dates round.'

'He's not my date!' Mattie said just as furiously, yanking her hand free from Steven's crushing grip.

'Well, in that case, apologies,' Tom said stiffly. 'But please have your conversation at a more considerate volume.'

He nodded, then leaving the door open, he strode down the corridor towards the kitchen. Mattie had never been so sorry to see him go. She turned back to Steven, who'd dropped the smile and thinned his lips.

'As I was saying, you can't copyright a recipe, so if you sign a non-disclosure agreement that says that the recipes aren't yours, then it would be in both our interests,' he said. 'I'll make it worth your while.'

'You'll pay me for the recipes you stole?' Mattie clarified. That didn't make things right, but at least she'd get something back for all that time she'd spent on them, not to mention the cost of her ingredients.

Steven wagged a finger at her. 'I didn't steal them. Christ, you're like a dog with a bone. Poor Mattie, I'm sure I could get you some work on my show.' He put the finger to his chin as if he was trying to think of a solution that would benefit them both.

It was a gesture that he'd always employ when he was coming up with a way to repair the damage after they'd fought. Usually after he'd done something to humiliate Mattie, whether it was flirting with another woman in front of her or passing off her madeleines as his. Then after Mattie had cried and shouted and said that she was leaving him, Steven would give her the silent treatment so she felt as if everything in her, everything she touched, had turned to frost. As if their fight had all been her fault.

'I hate this atmosphere,' he'd say. 'There must be a way that we can make things better.' Then he'd put his finger to his chin in the same way that he was doing now. 'I know, you could apologise to me.'

But in the two years since Steven had broken her, Mattie

hadn't just put herself back together, she'd made herself stronger, tougher. She was never going to let another person make her feel less when she was so much more.

'I don't want to work on your show,' she said slowly.

'I knew you'd be jealous about it,' Steven said with a knowing little grin – if only her rolling pin was still in close proximity. 'But I'm offering you a great opportunity here. You could be my research assistant. It would be your job to come up with new recipes! You'd like that, wouldn't you?'

She actually gasped. 'Are you for real?!'

'I know it's a lot to take in. Don't say yes straight away just because you're excited, sleep on it,' Steven advised her kindly. Then he sighed. The sigh was never a good sign. 'Although . . . how do I put this, without upsetting you?'

How did I ever fall in love with you? Because I was twenty-four and had never been in love before. Mattie had mistaken her attraction to Steven's beauty and the glory of him noticing her as love, when it hadn't even come close. She'd been so sure that Steven wouldn't deliberately set out to hurt her and manipulate her, because they were in love and you didn't do things like that to the person you loved. But Steven's final act of treachery and the two years that had passed since then had made the scales fall from Mattie's eyes. God, he wasn't even trying to make it convincing!

Mattie rolled her shoulders, ready for the fight. 'Oh, I'm pretty sure that you couldn't upset me any more,' she said, and now that she knew that Steven no longer had any power over her, she felt free. Liberated. At last! She wanted to laugh, but she settled for a calm smile.

'Well, I wanted to say: this isn't about you and me getting back together. I'm sorry to disappoint you, you're a cracking girl, but I'm with someone else now. She's a model,' he added with a faux-embarrassed chuckle. 'Not sure what she sees in my ugly mug.'

'Mmm. Me neither,' Mattie said.

'But I wouldn't want things to be awkward if we're going to work together,' Steven said. He made another grab for Mattie's hand, but she was ready for him and with the same serene smile, she held her hands up so it was very clear that she wasn't there to be touched. Steven's own smile dimmed. 'Anyway, I can't wait to hear some new recipe ideas from you. That girl who was mopping the floor – and by the way, I would have someone much more attractive front of house – said that you make these mini red velvet cakes that look like little Christmas puddings. Sounds inter-esting!'

'Yes, it is,' Mattie agreed.

'So how exactly do they work . . . ?'

She knew then that Steven was never going to go. He was going to stay on her doorstep with his tired old tricks and his mean little jibes, unless Mattie made him go. 'It's probably better if I show rather than tell. Stay there!'

'I can't come in?' Steven asked.

'You've seen what my flatmate's like.' Mattie grimaced and nodded down the hall to the kitchen where Tom was stiff-backed and doing something that no doubt involved one of Mattie's non-stick pans and metal cutlery. 'He has a temper on him and a black belt in karate. You'd better stay there.'

She backed away, down the hall, smile fixed on her face. It was eight paces at most and Steven, peering round the door, could see what Mattie was doing.

'Now I'll need flour and sugar,' she said loudly, reaching for them as Tom turned to stare at Mattie as if her head was spinning around in a full 360-degree *Exorcist* twist. Actually, she did feel like she'd been demonically possessed as she tipped flour and sugar into the bowl. 'Of course you'll probably need to measure them out,' she called to Steven who was still peering around the door and – the rat – making notes on his phone. 'I don't need to, because I'm a seasoned professional. Let's say two hundred grams of flour, two hundred of sugar.'

'Are you sure you don't need a lie-down?' Tom murmured, but Mattie was too busy rooting around in the fridge to pay him any attention. 'You seem a bit . . . manic.'

'Butter. Milk,' she said, pulling out the items in question. 'Eggs. Where are the eggs?'

'They're on the counter because I'm about to fry two of them,' Tom said. 'Really, do I need to stage some kind of intervention?'

'I'm so sorry for what about I'm about to do,' Mattie said, snatching up the last two eggs that were left, and cracking them one-handed into the bowl. 'But my need is far greater,' she added as she sloshed in some milk, then grabbed a lump of butter with her bare hands. 'Then you take a wooden spoon and you mix all the ingredients together.'

'You don't cream the butter and sugar together first?' Steven asked as Tom handed Mattie a wooden spoon with a resigned sigh.

'No, it's a one-bowl, chuck-it-all-in method,' she said. 'It's so easy, even you could do it.'

'I didn't quite catch that,' Steven called out as Tom murmured, 'Why are you giving *him* one of your recipes?'

Mattie smiled another teeth-baring smile. 'Because he really, really deserves it,' she said, and even to her own ears she was sounding pretty manic. 'Are you watching this, Steven?' Still mixing, she walked down the hall towards him.

'Did you just add cinnamon?'

'No, I added a generous pinch of go fuck yourself,' Mattie said, as she tipped the bowl, or rather its gloopy contents (she really had put in too much milk), over Steven's head. 'Now get out and don't ever, *ever* come back.'

Cake batter dripped from Steven's formerly glossy brown hair onto his expensive leather coat. Lumps of flour and sugar sat on his shoulders; strands of egg white hung from his nose.

'How – how *dare* you? You mad bitch! You always did have a screw loose. You need therapy!'

Sticks and stones may break my bones but words will never harm me. Steven's words had lost their power to paralyse Mattie.

'Believe me, emptying a bowl of batter over your head

has proved to be very therapeutic,' Mattie said with a bright smile.

'You're not normal.' Steven gave a snarl of pure rage. Mattie took a step back and trod hard on Tom's foot, which he responded to with a muffled 'Ooof!'

'Really, Mattie, we've already spoken about this.' It was Tom's most annoyed voice, the one she'd only ever heard once, when Nina was trying to persuade him to pose for the shop's Instagram with just one of Posy's beloved tote bags to hide his modesty. 'Why isn't he leaving?'

'I don't know,' she said a little desperately. She'd thought the batter would be enough to send Steven fleeing, but he was still there, dripping all over the carpet of the hallway. It was comforting, though, to have Tom right behind her, supporting her with what felt like a wall of solid muscle.

'Going to get your new boyfriend to fight your battles for you? Does he know what a pathetic waste of space you are? God, Mathilde, everyone knows you were nothing before you met me and now you're nothing again.' It wasn't anything Steven hadn't said before but Mattie knew her worth now. She wasn't nothing. She was something. She was somebody.

Before Mattie could defend herself, Tom leaned over her shoulder: 'Actually, I'm not Mattie's boyfriend, and actually, she's not nothing, as you so unimaginatively put it. She's a strong, intelligent woman who certainly doesn't need me or anyone else to rescue her, but I cannot stand to listen to you gaslighting her for another second. So go on, shove off!'

Tom stepped around Mattie so he could take a hold of Steven's arm and begin to walk him down the stairs.

'Get your hands off me!' Steven bellowed, struggling to free himself. Tom held firm.

'Or we could just call the police and have you arrested for public affray, verbal assault . . .'

'Verbal assault isn't even a thing, and she *threw cake batter* over me!'

'It's a public disorder offence and Mattie accidentally slipping and chucking batter over you would never stand up in a court of law,' Tom said. 'I should know because I have a law degree. Now start moving before I make you.'

'You deserve each other,' Steven muttered. 'And I've never gaslighted her.' He paused to navigate the first step. 'What is gaslighting?'

'It's from a play, *Gas Light*, later made into a very good film starring Ingrid Bergman, but I digress. In *Gas Light*, a husband tries to convince his wife that she's imagining things and going insane. In this particular instance, she thinks the gas lights are flickering and he says they're not, when in reality, he's been sneaking into an upstairs flat and turning on the gas lights there, which causes the gas lights in their flat to dim. Come on, sunshine, pick your feet up!'

'Yeah, let's keep it moving,' Mattie said, poking Steven between his shoulder blades with the wooden spoon that she was still clutching in her batter-splattered hand.

'In common parlance, gaslighting is the completely despicable and coercive tactic used by men, who don't even deserve to be called men, to control their partners. They'll convince them that they're suffering from all sorts of person-ality defects when in reality, they've been goaded into displaying these sorts of behaviours.'

'Oh my God!' Mattie gasped. 'That's exactly what you did! I never even knew that it was a thing, that there was a name for it. I thought that I had all these things wrong with me. You made me think I was lucky to have you put up with me.'

He'd had Mattie doubting herself so much that if Steven had said that it was day when it was very clearly night, she'd have gone along with it.

Of course, Steven wasn't going down without a fight. 'I never gaslighted you. Let's not forget that you *were* lucky to have me, it wasn't like you had any other friends . . . Ow! That hurt!'

Mattie continued to viciously jab the wooden spoon into Steven's back, as Tom walked him down the last two steps. 'You're the reason why I didn't have any friends at L'Institut, you turned everyone in our class against me with all your stories about how impossible I was . . .'

'Textbook gaslighting,' Tom said with a sniff. 'And I bet he'd tell you that any other friends that you had weren't really your friends and that only he really loved you.'

'How do you *know* this?'

'Because it's classic emotional abuse,' Tom said and he sounded genuinely angry now. 'To isolate someone, convince them that they're worthless and that the only person who really loves them is their abuser. It's the worst kind of toxic, controlling behaviour.'

'I'm not an abuser,' Steven said as Tom frogmarched him through the empty shop. 'I never laid a finger on you.'

Mattie flexed the fingers that Steven had had in a crushing grasp only minutes before. He'd never hit her. But there had been so many instances when he'd taken her hand forcefully enough to hurt, had pinched her hard enough to leave a bruise when they were out with friends because she'd done something, said something, to displease him.

'Thank you,' she said and she wasn't speaking to Tom, though she owed him a debt of gratitude that she'd still be working off when she was ninety. She was talking to Steven as he stood, arms hanging limply at his sides, as Tom unlocked the shop door. 'Thank you for breaking my heart and stealing my recipe book and all the other terrible things that you did to me, because if you hadn't, then I might never have found the courage to leave you.'

'Actually, Mathilde, I think you'll find that I left you,' Steven snapped, but Tom pushed him through the now-open door. 'And believe me, I have no intentions of coming back this time.'

'Oh good. Can I have that in writing, please?' Mattie snapped as she followed Tom and Steven, Tom's hand wedged into the other man's armpit, out of the shop and across the yard. It was freezing outside, frost already glistening on the cobblestones, but even though Mattie only had a thin jumper on, she didn't feel the cold at all. Not when she was boiling with righteous fury. 'I feel sorry for the poor girl that you're seeing now. You should come with a government health warning.'

'She's ten times the woman that you were,' Steven growled.

They were at the electronic gate now, which opened on the shop side with just the press of a button. Mattie hit it and Tom gave Steven a gigantic shove through the gap.

'Time to crawl back under your rock,' he said, slamming the gate in Steven's incredulous face.

Steven's mouth twisted into an ugly shape as he hurled insults at them; Mattie didn't know how she'd ever thought him attractive.

She waited until he finally ran out of steam in the face of their indifference.

'Do you think he's finished?' Tom asked her.

'I don't know and I don't care,' Mattie said. 'Also, I owe you two eggs, if you still fancy a fried-egg sandwich.'

'Yes, please, I'm famished,' Tom said, holding out his arm so Mattie could tuck her own through it. 'Shall we?'

'We shall,' Mattie agreed.

'Don't you dare walk away from me!' Steven shouted. But Mattie proceeded to do just that and yet . . . she couldn't bear to let him have the final word.

She glanced over her shoulder. 'Merry Christmas, Steven,' she called out brightly. 'And I hope you have a really crappy new year!'

14 days until Christmas

After stopping off in the tearooms so Mattie could pinch a box of eggs, they worked their way through the shop with damp sponges to clear up errant blobs of cake batter.

The top of their stairs had come off worst but Tom said that he didn't mind doing the mop-up if Mattie did something more exciting with the eggs than fry them sunny side up. 'Maybe one of your famous four-cheeses omelettes?' he suggested.

She rejuvenated the stale end of a loaf of sourdough by dousing it in water then sticking it in the oven as she whipped eggs and grated cheese. Once Tom had finished cleaning up, he sat down at the little kitchen table so Mattie could present him with a three-cheeses omelette on refreshed sourdough toast with a parsley garnish. Then she promptly burst into tears.

'Oh, Mattie,' Tom said unhappily. 'I really am starving but I can hardly eat if you're crying.'

'I didn't mean to cry,' Mattie sobbed. 'I don't even know why I am crying.'

'Maybe if you splash your face with cold water. That's what Posy does when she's tearful,' he mumbled through a mouthful of omelette because it turned out he could manage to eat while in the company of a weeping woman. 'And she should know, because she cries on average about five times a day at the moment.'

'And I don't even have pregnancy hormones,' Mattie hiccupped, but she got up from her chair and her own omelette to splash cold water on her hot, tear-streaked face, and she did feel a little better.

'I've got a bottle of Malbec, quite a decent one, on the one shelf in the one kitchen cupboard which I've been able to claim as my own,' Tom said. 'If you fancy a glass. And if you're having a glass, then it would be rude to make you drink alone.'

Mattie didn't need to be told twice and actually she did feel much better after she and Tom had eaten their supper and finished a glass of wine. Maybe it was because Tom hadn't bombarded her with questions, but was happy to sit in silence. And not the awkward silence that they usually found them-selves in. This silence was warmer, maybe even companionable.

'Thank you,' Mattie said when Tom poured them both a second glass. 'Not for the wine. Well, yes, thank you for the wine but also thank you for what you did back there. For getting rid of him.'

'It did look as if you had things under control,' Tom said, though they both knew that was a lie. 'And I meant what I said about you being a strong, intelligent woman who didn't need to be rescued, but I couldn't just stand there and let him talk to you like that. It made me very angry,' he added in a quiet but dark voice.

'All this time, these last two years, I've hated him for ruining my life,' Mattie said, 'but now I realise that he's not worth even my hate. It takes a lot of effort and energy to hate someone, and I'd be much better off using that time to work on new recipes.'

Tom took a long, meditative sip of wine. 'Did he really steal your recipes?'

'He really did. I had a big notebook that I'd written everything in,' Mattie said with a sigh and she waited for that fiery hit of rage to punch her in the stomach – now it felt like more of a gentle prod. 'Sometimes it can take months to get a recipe just right. Adding in a little more of one thing, taking out a little bit of something else, experimenting with flavours and textures. It was my life's work. I was only twenty-four, but I'd been writing my recipes in that book since I was ten, and he stole it.'

'Did you confront him about it?' Tom asked.

'Not at first. At first, he convinced me that I'd lost the book. And that I only had myself to blame for being so careless.'

Mattie wasn't looking at Tom or even at their little kitchen. She was two years, and a world away. In another tiny little flat that looked out over the rooftops of Paris.

It had been two weeks before Christmas and she'd strung garlands of fairy lights across the ceiling and found the smallest Christmas tree in all of Paris, and decorated it with miniature baubles, placing it on the windowsill.

Their miniature home had looked homely, cosy and festive until Mattie had pulled the place apart looking for her recipe book, which wasn't where it always lived in a drawer in the kitchen.

By the time Mattie had finished it looked as if a tornado had torn through. 'Maybe you left it at L'Institut,' Steven suggested in a bored voice.

'But I never take it to L'Institut. You know that I don't,' Mattie insisted, as she lay on the floor and swatted a hand under the sofabed, though there was no earthly reason why the recipe book would have migrated from the kitchen drawer to under the sofabed, as Steven pointed out.

'You're being completely irrational. You took it to L'Institut and either it's in your locker or maybe it fell out of your bag on the Métro.'

'No,' Mattie said firmly.

'But are you sure? Like one hundred per cent sure? Because there was that time that you thought you'd lost your keys . . .'

'*You* lost your keys and took mine without telling me.'

'I did tell you. Several times,' Steven said and he clenched his jaw and pinched the bridge of his nose. 'Can you tidy up in here? I can't think in this mess. I do have finals coming up.'

'Yes, I have finals coming up too and that's why it's absolutely vital that I find my recipe book!' Mattie swiped her hand under the sofa again, but her fingers touched nothing but dust bunnies.

'I don't appreciate your tone,' Steven said. 'We've talked about you being shrill before. Nagging. Hysterical.'

Mattie winced in her prone position. Had she been shrill? Probably. Steven hated it when she became shrill. 'I'm very sorry, Steven,' she said contritely. 'I didn't realise that I was getting so high-pitched. I'm just panicking.'

Steven said nothing. Mattie sat up to see him standing there with his arms folded, the forbidding look on his face that always set her nerves on edge.

'I'm very, very sorry,' she said again, trying to make each word as sincere as she possibly could. There was a tiny space heater in the little flat that didn't heat much of anything, so Mattie could see her breath curl in front of her face as she spoke. 'I shouldn't take my frustration out on you. Will you forgive me?'

Steven nodded curtly. 'Apology accepted. And if you have lost your recipe book, it's your own fault for being so careless, isn't it?'

Mattie had a perfect memory of shutting her recipe book in the kitchen drawer the morning before, after copying out a recipe in progress for an almond and blackberry financier. It was a thick book with a faded hardboard cover and an 'I heart Paris' sticker on it. She'd put it in the drawer, patted it fondly as she always did and then closed the drawer.

She knew she had.

'I said, it's your own fault for being so careless, isn't it?' Steven repeated his question in a louder, colder voice.

Mattie flushed. 'Yes, it's my own fault,' she parroted back. 'I have no one to blame but myself.'

'That's better.' Steven grinned. Mattie was so relieved that the grim set of his face had relaxed that she grinned back. 'Were all the recipes you were working on for your finals in that book?'

It was no grinning matter but Mattie tried to be flippant about it, light-hearted, so that she didn't become shrill again. 'Yup! And the ingredients and the bake times were so precise that I'm not sure I can replicate them. Might have to start again from scratch.'

'Sucks to be you!' Steven drawled, flopping onto the sofa. 'Going to make me dinner then? It's the least you can do after putting me through this horrible scene.'

Mattie had agreed that it wasn't nice for Steven to come home after a day at L'Institut to one of her scenes and even though she only had half an hour before her waitress shift started at the bistro fifteen minutes' walk away, she leapt at the chance to make it up to him.

'I didn't mention the recipe book again after that,' Mattie told Tom, who was listening intently to her sorry tale, his chin resting on his hand. 'And I had to try and work up my finals recipes as best as I could remember them, but it had taken me months and the finals were only a week away. The Great Parisian Bake-Off, we called them.'

To graduate from L'Institut de Patisserie, all students had

to individually make three different cakes in front of a panel of instructors: incorporating such techniques as meringue, ganache, piping and sugar work.

They didn't have to be Christmas-themed, but Mattie was such a big fan of the most wonderful time of the year, that her three exam pieces had been given the full festive treatment, albeit in an exquisitely tasting, beautifully constructed, high-end way. Mattie had made an apricot and brandy cream millefeuille topped with miniscule marzipan fruits; a croquembouche, choux balls filled with a delicate chestnut puree and exquisitely decorated with spun-sugar Christmas decorations; and a humble cupcake. Except there was nothing humble about a cupcake, which featured the lightest Christmas-pudding flavoured sponge, frosted with sparkling champagne buttercream.

She'd spent over a year perfecting the three cakes and considering she'd lost all her detailed notes, she didn't think she'd done too badly. But her instructors were stony-faced. Monsieur Brel wouldn't even taste Mattie's creations but gave an impassioned rant about her being '*une petite voleuse*'. A little thief.

It was all Mattie could do not to burst into tears, although when Madame La Directrice swept into the test kitchen, pointed her finger at Mattie and said, '*Vous êtes malhonnête!*' it was also very hard not to pee her pants a little.

It turned out that another student had turned in three identical bakes of a far superior standard to Mattie's. This student had spent months fine-tuning them, adjusting ingredients and writing up meticulous notes, whereas Mattie had just three scrappy pieces of A4 paper to prove the provenance of her patisserie.

'But someone stole my recipe book!' Mattie kept insisting, her face getting redder, her voice growing squeakier and squeakier and higher and higher, so that every dog in Paris must have been able to hear her.

It had been a long day. Mattie was told to cool her heels outside Madame La Directrice's office while the other student was called in so they could get to the bottom of it.

Mattie sat on a hard-backed chair in the corridor for what felt like hours. News of the scandal had whipped round L'Institut like sprinkles on a cupcake and it seemed as if every student felt the need to detour past where she sat, with condemning stares. As if Mattie was already guilty. She wasn't exactly popular, unlike Steven, who everyone adored and sympathised with because he had to put up with Mattie and, as he was constantly telling their classmates, 'Mathilde is very difficult to love – but someone's got to.'

Mattie tried to ignore the hostile faces and instead thought about what she'd say to the other student, who'd obviously stolen her recipe book. By the time she'd finished with them, they'd rue the day they were ever born. She'd demand that their locker was searched, that she'd be allowed to scrutinise their notes . . .

'Mathilde!' Her revenge fantasies were interrupted by Steven beetling down the corridor with Madame La Directrice.

She'd never been so relieved to see him. He knew she'd

spent months on her recipes and he'd stand up for her, defend her – he'd tasted endless variations on each creation and had complained bitterly every time . . .

'You'll never guess what's happened!' she cried, jumping to her feet and running to him.

She tried to put her arms around Steven so he could comfort her, tell her that he was here to set the record straight.

But he didn't put his arms around her, rather he thrust Mattie away, his thumbs digging into her collar bones with a painful pressure. 'Oh, Mathilde, how could you?' he demanded in a broken sort of voice. 'I told you so many times that you needed to knuckle down and do some work, and instead you decided to take the easy route and steal my recipes!'

'*What?*' Mattie was so shocked that she giggled. The giggle became a laugh because this was a joke, right? And then the laughing finally became the tears that had been threatening for the last couple of hours. 'That's not true. You know that's not true!'

It had been Mattie who'd told Steven that he needed to put the work in when he'd mock her for coming home each day and practising at least one bake before she went off to do her waitressing. Although she'd soon stopped telling him that, because it would just lead to a fight about how she was nagging him, trying to control him.

'You know that it is,' Steven said solemnly, turning his head away. 'God, I can't even look at you!'

Oh, he was good. Very, very good.

'He produced a recipe book that hadn't existed even a week before,' Mattie said bitterly to Tom. Just remembering it all over again, made her feel cold and dirty. 'I lived with him for two years. You'd have thought at some stage it might have made an appearance. He'd copied out all my recipes, not just the finals recipes. Copied every last correction and crossing-out. He'd even made sure to splatter them with butter and batter and God knows what else so they'd look properly authentic.'

Mattie had even started to doubt herself. Steven was so convincing as the innocent victim, so hurt that he'd been taken in once again by his notoriously volatile girlfriend, so indignant that his own marks might be in jeopardy. Had her recipe book really existed or had she made it up?

'It sounds ridiculous when I say it out loud, but that's how good he was at manipulating not just me, but everyone else around him.' Mattie put her head in her hands.

'I did get a brief insight. Nasty piece of work,' Tom said. 'I wish I could tell you that he'll get what's coming to him, but life doesn't always work that way, does it?'

'Nah. Karma's never as much of a bitch as you want her to be,' Mattie said.

'So what did you do?' Tom asked, pouring the last of the Malbec into their glasses.

'Well, I wasn't going to back down. I insisted that I hadn't stolen his recipes and because I'd had pretty much top marks in all my classes and coursework, they said I could graduate. Just a pass though, when I'd been set to get a distinction. Maybe even the Pupil d'Honneur, which

was awarded to the most talented person in each year,'
Mattie recalled with a sigh. She'd only got a pass because
one of the instructors, the elderly and usually terrifying
Mademoiselle Belmont, had stuck up for Mattie, pointing
out that not only had she been an exemplary student over
the last two years but that she herself had been witness to
an early prototype of two of Mattie's finals pastries.

'And Steven may be charming,' Mademoiselle had spat
the word, 'but in two years he has never proved himself to
be anything other than decidedly average.'

This was entirely true and Steven was always at his most
savage on the days when Mattie excelled in one of their
classes.

So Mattie was allowed to graduate, although she'd been
cold-shouldered at the graduation ceremony two days before
Christmas Eve. Her class had gone off to celebrate but it
had been made clear that Mattie wasn't welcome.

Steven hadn't come home since the day of Mattie's final
but he turned up after the party, drunk and not at all
contrite.

Mattie was a dry-eyed husk, without even the energy
to shout at him and then be accused of being shrill. She
had had the energy to pack all of Steven's belongings in
bin liners, though, and get Edouard, their landlord, to change
the locks. It helped that Steven's rent cheques invariably
bounced and that Mattie kept Edouard and his family
supplied with cake on a weekly basis.

'We're over,' Mattie said through the gap in the door,
security chain firmly on, when Steven demanded entry.

'But you must have known that's what would happen when you took my recipe book.'

'You mean this recipe book?' Steven asked, holding it up, breathing stale alcohol fumes in her direction. 'Loving is sharing, isn't it? That's what you always say. Besides, you got to graduate, so why are you bitching about it?'

'How could you do this to me? To someone you love? If you'd needed help with your finals prep, you know that you only needed to ask me and . . .'

'Who says I love you?' Steven had sneered. 'Who could ever love *you*?'

'And that was the last time I saw him until today,' Mattie concluded. 'Pippa brought me home two days before Christmas, and then six months after that I took on the tearooms and began to rebuild my life.'

Tom rubbed the tips of his fingers against his forehead as if he were struggling to take in everything that Mattie had told him. It wasn't a story that she shared. Ever. She was so ashamed of how utterly she'd been taken in, made to look like a fool, betrayed by someone who'd claimed to love her. Even her mother and Guy only knew the edited highlights; that things had ended badly with Steven, so badly that all mentions of his name were banned. When they'd met Steven, he'd been charm personified, so they were at a loss to understand what could have happened to make Mattie so distraught.

'But why would he take your recipe book? Only a complete bastard would do that,' Guy had said. 'And Steven wasn't a complete bastard. I mean, he kept telling us how much he loved you. Said he was the luckiest man in the world.'

Having to tell them that Steven had said she was unlov-able? Mattie couldn't do that for the very simple reason that she was afraid that it was true. That she possessed every one of the character flaws Steven had described and that secretly everyone else thought so too.

Mattie had only confessed to Pippa because Pippa was the least judgemental person to walk the earth. When Mattie had poured what was left of her heart out on the journey out of Paris and back to London, not once had Pippa trotted out any one of her personal mantras. Not even, 'Someone else's opinion of you is none of your business.' She'd just said, 'If I ever meet Steven, I'm going to separate him from all of his vital organs with my bare hands, my tweezers and my eyelash curlers.'

So Tom was only the second person she'd told and he hadn't made a single Tom-esque, acidic quip. He stood up to get another bottle of Malbec from the one measly shelf that Mattie hadn't requisitioned (neither of them were going to be in any fit state to cope with the Christmas shopping crowds the next morning) and said, 'Well, no wonder you hate all men.'

His head was obscured by the cupboard door so Mattie had no way of knowing if Tom was joking; his voice, whether he was cracking a funny or lecturing on the evils of capitalism, rarely changed tone.

'I don't hate *all* men,' Mattie said. 'For instance, I don't hate you. I think that I might even owe you cake on a weekly basis too, like I do Pippa.'

'Never one to pass up free cake, but you don't have

to do that,' Tom said with a slow, sweet smile that Mattie had never seen before. It kind of made her want to cry because it was that good a smile. Also, it had been a long day capped off with an emotionally exhausting confrontation and she'd had three glasses of wine and was now heading for her fourth. 'I meant what I said about you not needing rescuing. You were doing a fine job of standing up for yourself and I was proud to sacrifice two eggs just to see you upend a bowl of batter over his smug head.'

'But if you hadn't been here . . .' Mattie shook her head. 'In the end, I might even have agreed to hand over even more recipes just to get rid of him.'

'You'd have thought of something,' Tom said. 'Still, it's just as well I wasn't out Lothario-ing my way round London and seducing impressionable young women.'

Mattie's cheeks had been wine-flushed but now they burned with something a lot closer to shame. 'Have I apologised for that? I tried, but that email I sent was a bit passive-aggressive.'

'Just a bit,' Tom agreed with another one of those ten-out-of-ten smiles.

'That gingerbread that I dropped was actually meant to be a peace offering . . .'

'I think we're at peace now. Nothing like coming together to defeat an evil villain,' Tom said with a grin, pulling the cork out of the bottle with an emphatic 'pop'. 'Though can I state for the record that I'm not some callous Casanova and I'm not interested in impressionable young women. I like my women to be at least twenty-five and to have their wits very much about them.'

'OK. I'm glad to hear that,' Mattie said, as Tom sat back down. If she lived to be a hundred, then she still didn't think she'd ever be able to figure him out. 'You're quite the man of mystery.'

'I have to be, for the sake of my own sanity and my own private life,' Tom said and then he pulled loose his tie (a mustard-coloured, knitted affair that was only fit for burning) and unbuttoned the top two buttons of his shirt. The shock of Tom kicking back, *relaxing* in her company, was so great that Mattie had to hold on to the edge of the table for support. 'I know I sound a bit like your pal, Pippa, but I do think a work–life balance is important.'

'Pippa is evangelical about work–life balance. She's always telling me that I shouldn't work so many hours and do I want to borrow one of her favourite business self-help books, *How to Delegate*?'

'I mean, look at the three of them.' Tom pointed at the floor. 'Verity isn't so bad but Posy and Nina are always bringing their personal lives into work. In fact, there is no distinction between the two.'

'Well, Posy did end up marrying your Lavinia's grandson so I can see how work and home have blended together . . .'

'Always with the public displays of affection.' Tom was really warming to his theme and leaned closer to Mattie. 'Nina has absolutely no boundaries. Once she even made me go out and buy her two litres of cranberry juice.'

'That doesn't seem so bad in the general scheme of

things,' Mattie said. Compared to Nina's usual conversation and demands, it sounded quite tame.

Tom leaned even closer so that Mattie could see that behind his specs, his eyes weren't simply brown, but had flecks of amber in them. Another glass of wine and she might even challenge him to prove that he even needed to wear them, but not now – not when he was being so sweet to her that she could have him for pudding.

'She insisted loudly, in a shop full of customers, that I go out and buy her cranberry juice because she had *cystitis*, and I quote, "I can hardly bloody walk."'

'Oh, Tom.' At one stage this evening, Mattie thought she'd never laugh ever again, but now the thought of Nina demanding medicinal cranberry juice and Tom's current outraged expression, complete with flared nostrils, made her snort with laughter. 'That's not really a stretch to imagine Nina doing that.'

'So, you can see then why I try very hard not to reveal any personal details because the three of them, but especially Nina, would never let it go,' Tom said with a shudder. 'She's teased me mercilessly ever since she found out about the topic of my dissertation.'

Mattie put her head in her hands. 'Again, I'm really, really sorry about that.'

'Well, you should be,' Tom said with no sweet smile to take the sting away. Then he sighed. 'Though it was on the bookshelves in a communal room, so it's my own fault really.'

'Is Nina being very mean?'

'She's started calling me Doctor Love.' The corners of his mouth lifted slightly.

'Doctor Lurve,' Mattie echoed in a breathy voice as if she was providing backing vocals for a steamy R'n'B track. 'Though technically, I suppose you did get your doctorate in love.'

'Well, actually I got my doctorate in literature . . .'

'Why did you decide to study romantic fiction anyway?' Mattie asked, resting her elbows on the table and her chin in her hands so she could gaze intently at Tom as if this time she might finally work out what made him tick.

Tom stared back at her, still with that slight smile. 'That's a story for another day.'

'Spoilsport,' Mattie said and she stuck her tongue out at him – she really had had quite a lot to drink – and it might have been a trick of the light but behind his glasses, Tom's eyes seemed to darken.

Suddenly the atmosphere in their cosy little kitchen felt thick and charged. Mattie couldn't tear her eyes away from Tom and he was staring straight back at her. She swallowed hard, sure that the sound of her nervous gulping was deafening as Tom leaned towards her. They were sitting at right angles from each other at the tiny little table and as he moved, their knees brushed against each other and set off a chain reaction in Mattie. From that one spot on her right knee, it felt as if the tiniest of electrical charges were zapping all her nerve endings.

Tom must have felt it too because he lurched back, still

gazing at Mattie as if she was one of the seven wonders of the ancient world.

'I'm wondering what it would be like to kiss you,' he said. *What?* She must have heard him wrong.

Why would Tom want to kiss her? Why would she *want* Tom to kiss her? Because she did. She really did. She felt quite breathless, as though someone had squeezed all the air out of the room.

'Do you think that would be a good idea?' she gasped.

'I think it's probably a very bad idea,' Tom said gravely and Mattie felt everything in her deflate as if someone had stuck a pin in her.

'Oh,' she said. 'Oh. OK, then.'

'Though I still want to,' Tom said, but he looked away, shifted his long legs so they couldn't brush against Mattie's poor, defenceless knees, and the moment was gone. If the moment had ever happened, that is. She must have imagined it. 'But, sadly, yes, it's a very bad idea.'

She took a deep breath, then with one hand braced on the edge of the table, she managed to get to her feet, which felt as wobbly as a new-born foal's. 'We need a new house rule!'

'We've got so many house rules that I'm losing track of them all,' Tom complained, with a weary look at the ceiling. 'We'll have to print them out and get them lanimated. Animated. Lantimated.'

'You mean laminated.' The only reason that Mattie could pronounce the word was because she made laminated dough on a daily basis. 'Anyway, new house rule: anything that happens in this flat, stays in this flat. Flatmate solidarity and all that. Sound good to you?'

'Sounds amazing,' Tom agreed. He shot out his arm. 'Shake on it!'

Mattie's hands were hot and sweaty. 'Do we have to?'

'Shall we seal it with a kiss then?'

'You are unhealthily obsessed with the idea of kissing me,' she said, breathless once more, because he really was being so *nice*. Better than nice. It was quite validating that a man wanted to kiss her. Especially Tom, who she'd been so mean to. Still, Tom had been quite mean to her too and, despite his protestations to the contrary, he still might prove to be a Lothario. 'No, look! We'll shake.'

Hot hand collided with hot hand, fingers entwined, skin ablaze. It wasn't so much a handshake as a clasp.

Both Mattie and Tom stared down at their joined hands. His thumb gently rubbed the soft and suddenly very sensitive scar from a burn where Mattie had once dropped a just-out-of-the-frying-pan beignet.

'Bed,' she said desperately.

'Oh, yes. Our own beds? Is that still the plan?'

'*Yes!*' Mattie slowly pulled her hand from his grasp. 'How could you think otherwise?' She took a very definite step away from him. And another one. And another, until she was at the kitchen doorway. 'It's *always* going to be the plan.'

'That's a pity,' Tom murmured, so quietly that Mattie wasn't sure if she'd heard him correctly, before she fled for the safety of her bedroom.

CHAPTER

22

13 days until Christmas

Mattie had barely placed her muggy, fuggy head on her pillow, quite convinced that she wouldn't be able to go to sleep, when a few seconds later, her alarm was blaring out.

A quick glance at the time showed that it wasn't a few seconds. She'd actually slept for a not-great-but-doable five hours. She'd done a whole day on five hours sleep before, but not when she'd had a bruising confrontation with the former love of her life and then sunk two bottles of red wine while having an emotionally exhausting heart to heart with the man that she shared a living space with.

Who was she even kidding? She and Tom lived together. They were flatmates. After last night, they were probably friends. Tom had made it perfectly clear that kissing her

256

was something he'd thought about, which had made Mattie wonder what it might be like to kiss him . . .

Mattie rushed to the bathroom to splash icy cold water on her face. The shock of it was enough to make her come to her senses, though not enough to lose the pounding head or the furry, sour taste in her mouth.

A bracing lukewarm shower and a vigorous teeth-cleaning session afterwards didn't make Mattie feel any more human. And as she left her room, trying to walk and tie the laces on her sneakers at the same time, she cast a longing look at Tom's door, behind which he was sleeping peacefully because Happy Ever After didn't open until ten.

In fact, it wasn't until ten thirty that Tom appeared in the tearooms. His face was grey, his hair looked as if it had lost an argument with a force-ten gale and the buttons on his cursed cardigan were done up crooked. Mattie paused from picking up a croissant to scrutinise Tom's midsection – she was finding that cake tongs and shaking hands were not a great combination. Then she blushed.

Fortunately, Tom was in no fit state to realise where Mattie's eyes had been lingering. 'You're well?' Tom asked in the same manner that he might enquire about the health of an elderly aunt. 'Because I'm not. I feel like I've been trampled on by elephants.'

Cuthbert peered at Tom from his perch behind the counter. He'd taken to wearing a tie with little Christmas trees on it. Sophie was convinced that by Christmas week he'd have upgraded to a full Santa suit. 'Young man, this is what we call the wages of gin.'

'Gin had nothing to do with it,' Mattie muttered because she'd already had a lecture from Cuthbert that morning on the dangers of excessive drinking. 'It was all the fault of the red wine and I feel horrible too,' she added in a low voice because she didn't want the couple who were waiting to hear and start a wild rumour that she was infecting her baked goods with a flu virus. 'Having to handle sausage meat when you have a hangover? I wouldn't wish that on my worst enemy.'

'Talking of which . . .' Tom said, 'are you still upset about what happened with Steven?'

'I think I'm all right,' Mattie said slowly. What with feeling so rotten, physically rotten rather than metaphysically rotten, and not having a moment to call her own since she'd entered the tearooms, she hadn't had time to do an emotional stocktake. 'It all seems like a bit of a bad dream, to be honest. I'm surprised you can remember much of last night. We were both quite tipsy.'

'I wasn't quite tipsy, I was quite drunk,' Tom said. Then he blinked, his mouth twisting. 'Although . . . well, I have a total recall of last night. One of the reasons why I feel so wretched today. This isn't just a hangover, it's mortification too.'

'What have you got to be mortified about?' Mattie asked and Tom went from grey to pink. Her own cheeks flamed in response: just as Mattie hadn't had much time to perform a post-mortem on the ugly scene with Steven, she also hadn't even begun to really analyse the long, long soul-bearing session with Tom afterwards.

She scrolled forward to the talking about kissing and Tom wondering whether they might sleep in the same bed. And how could she have forgotten the handholding-slash-caressing?

Her face went even redder.

'I am so sorry,' Tom said, but Mattie held up her hand to cut him off.

'If you have total recall of what happened last night, then you remember our new house rule?'

'What happens in the flat, stays in the flat,' Tom said gravely.

'What exactly does happen in the flat?' Sophie wanted to know, relieving Mattie of the tongs so she could get some misshapen pastries for the table she was serving. She had her hair tied up in a scarf decorated with jaunty robins.

'Nothing happens,' Mattie said, the pink of her cheeks deepening a few shades.

'Absolutely nothing,' Tom confirmed. 'The pair of us lead very boring lives.'

'Well, I'm glad that we've sorted that out and we're cool now—'

'Totally cool,' Tom assured her in a strained voice. 'Anyway, I've also come to purchase one of your delicious pastries.'

'Oh, you don't have to do that!'

Tom leaned against the counter in a conspiratorial manner. 'Look, the only reason that I get a panini from the Italian café is that I feel sorry for Chiro,' he admitted sheepishly. 'His rent's gone up, his rates have gone up and he does have quite an unfortunate manner.'

Chiro was indeed very temperamental. Mattie didn't have occasion to go into the café but she walked past it often enough to see that some days Chiro would be all smiles, singing along to 'That's Amore' and even dancing with his customers. But just as frequently, he'd have a scowl on his face and would shout at his customers for smothering his food in ketchup, lingering in the run-up to closing time, which was five on the dot, or asking for a glass of tap water.

As Nina had once said, 'You don't get to call yourself a proper Londoner until you've been shouted at by Chiro at least once.'

'Well, that's very public-spirited of you,' Mattie said, thoughts of Chiro's unreasonableness making her feel much better about her own occasional bouts of pettiness.

'And he does make a damn good panini, but I fancy something a little different this morning,' Tom insisted.

'But Chiro has his rent increases to deal with and I don't want to deprive you of your favourite breakfast,' she said, because this morning was a do-over.

Tom was already running his eyes along her temptingly displayed croissants and pains au chocolat and pains aux raisins. This morning a lot of them were misshapen, victims to Mattie's trembling hands and the headache that two Nurofen and a pot of tea couldn't cure. Her croissants would have got her kicked out of every culinary institute in Europe and her pains aux raisins would not be adorning anyone's Instagram grid. Mattie couldn't help but feel that some of their unfortunate appearance was due to the bad energy that Steven had given off when he was helping her with her flaky pastry prep.

'It's so hard to decide,' he said. 'In my fragile state, I feel as if I need complex carbohydrates.'

'Maybe you'd like something savoury?' Mattie suggested. 'I could knock you up a croque guvnor.'

'Is that like a croque monsieur?' Tom asked doubtfully.

'A British take on a croque monsieur. Sourdough, butter, cheddar cheese, Old Spot ham, béchamel sauce with extra cheese and some mustard.' Mattie leaned over the counter. 'I add in a little nutmeg,' she said in a whisper because she didn't want all and sundry hearing about her secret ingredients.

'Sounds great!'

Mattie would bet every penny she had that it would completely crush Chiro's panini. But just to seal the deal . . .

'Tell you what, I'll turn your croque guvnor into a croque missus and put a fried egg on top,' Mattie said graciously. 'I'll bring it through to the shop when it's ready. Do you want coffee too?'

'Ah yes, coffee,' he rasped, holding up his mug with a not-very-steady hand. 'Dear Lord, I need more coffee than the human body can normally withstand.'

'That'll be £4.95 for the croque and coffee's on the house,' Mattie said, as Tom got out his wallet.

'It says £6.95 on the chalkboard,' he pointed out.

'Shop staff get mates' rates,' Cuthbert said, whisking away Tom's mug.

Mattie didn't feel the need to point out that if Tom had ever bothered to actually buy something from the tearooms he'd already know this. She was, after all, reasonable. And Tom had obviously decided to be reasonable too for he dropped a shiny pound coin in the tips jar. 'For my coffee,' he said. 'A compromise,' and only once he'd left, did Mattie allow a small, satisfied smile to break through.

When Mattie took Tom's breakfast through, the shop was already busy with customers browsing the tinsel-bedecked shelves while trying really hard to avoid any low-flying pink and silver stars. Mattie was never going to get used to finding a massive, pimped-out Christmas tree standing in the middle of the shop where two of the sofas usually sat.

She'd also forgotten just how much space the Mistletoe Booth took up. Despite the TV slot and the initial flurry of interest, there was just one couple loitering by the booth waiting for a photo of their recent smooch to come sliding out of the appropriate slot. The booth really did completely obscure the new-releases shelves.

Tom was sitting behind the counter, whacking Bertha, the Happy Ever After till, with a copy of *War And Peace*, while Nina scolded him.

'Don't be so rough with her. She needs a much more gentle touch,' she said. 'Honestly, Doctor Love, thought you'd have more respect for romantic fiction. Bet you had a whole chapter on boring Russian novels in your thesis, didn't you?'

'Stop calling me that stupid name and may I remind you

that the other day you thumped Bertha with your shoe,' Tom pointed out then paused, his nose twitching for his breakfast.

'One croque missus,' Mattie said brightly, setting down plate and cutlery folded in a napkin. 'Bring back the plate and knife and fork when you get a chance.'

Tom was staring down at the plate hungrily. 'This looks amazing. Thank you,' he said. He looked up to stare at Mattie, the hungry expression still on his face. 'Thank you.'

'You've already said thank you,' Nina said, with a curious look at Tom, then at Mattie, who looked back at Nina with one eyebrow slightly raised as if there was absolutely nothing odd about her bringing breakfast in to Tom and for Tom to be abjectly grateful about it.

'I have a lot of "thank yous" to make up for,' Tom muttered, unwrapping the napkin then pausing. 'Oh, Mattie! Why are there holly sprigs on this napkin? Have you gone dark side and embraced Christmas?'

'I have not!' Mattie said. 'I sent Sophie out to get plain napkins from the pound shop and this is what she came back with. We're still united in our loathing of Christmas.'

'Good,' Tom said and then, unbelievably, he offered Mattie his fist, which she bumped while Nina stared at both of them as if she'd recently suffered a blow to the head. Then he picked up his croque missus but paused with it halfway to his mouth. 'I hope you're not both planning to stand there and watch me eat?'

That was Mattie's cue to leave. She and Tom were fine now, after the events of last night. As soon as she thought about the strange way the night before had ended, that moment when she thought that Tom might kiss her, her face heated up and her lips began to tingle.

'I need to get started on my lunch bakes,' she said and backed away, resisting the temptation to put a finger to her mouth. '*Bon appetit!*'

Mattie was almost through the Classics arch, when Nina called her name.

'Yes?' Mattie hesitated in the doorway: she really should have been up to her elbows in puff pastry by now.

'It's just . . . could you put a couple of pig-in-blanket rolls by for me? I'm not allowed to take lunch until three,' Nina said plaintively. 'I'm sure they'll all be gone by then.'

'I can do that,' Mattie agreed.

'Now that you and Tom have got over yourselves, do we still get mates' rates and free tea or coffee?'

'You give new meaning to the word "shameless",' Tom said, his croque missus gratifyingly almost half gone by now. 'And I made a point of putting one pound in the tip jar for my coffee. Mattie still has to buy the coffee and milk, plus electricity, rent . . .'

'OK, OK. Sounds fair,' Nina decided. 'God knows you've ruined me for that instant sludge, and do you know how much Chiro in the Italian café charges for coffee? Three pounds! And I got a lecture about how much the council had put the business rates up when I asked for steamed milk.'

Where Tom and Nina trailblazed, Posy and Verity followed. Both of them tried to come into the tearooms to buy their lunch, but the queue for pig-in-blanket rolls was so long that Mattie had had to lock the glass doors that led to the shop to discourage any queue-jumpers.

Posy was forced to come out of Happy Ever After by the front door and fight her way through the queue and into the tearooms by shouting, 'Coming through! I own this building and I'm very heavily pregnant!'

'I'm so glad you and Tom have sorted out all this silliness,' Posy said, once Sophie came around the counter with a stool so that Posy didn't have to stand a second longer than necessary. 'How did you sort it out?'

Mattie's cheeks were already bright red, as she'd just been redeploying her afternoon tray bakes in the oven, but she fancied they now became even brighter. 'We've come to an understanding and Tom did me a massive favour last night when my ex-boyfriend got a bit *difficult*,' she said. 'In fact, I'd go so far as to say that Tom and I are friends now.'

She really needed to stop thinking about the kissing.

'I'm so glad,' Posy said fervently. 'I tried to be neutral but it turned out to be much harder than I thought. I mean, I've known Tom for *years* and I'm a pretty good judge of character. Though I did think your ex-boyfriend seemed charming. He's very handsome.'

'But he has a very ugly personality. Anyway, Tom and I are fine now. Better than fine, and you don't need to worry about us any more.'

'Well, I'm very grateful because these days I'm a slave to my blood pressure. Now, can I have two pig-in-blanket rolls and a mince pie for afters?'

'One pound in the tip jar for hot drinks is such a

sensible solution,' Verity said, after she'd finished queuing for almost half an hour so she could purchase a turkey and cranberry Scotch egg. 'But honestly, Mattie, I've been running the numbers and you have to be out of pocket when you provide the catering for our events. Ingredients-only doesn't cover the cost of your time or equipment and then there's all the other times that you bring us buns and cakes for free. We're going to have to come up with some kind of formal, financial agreement.'

'You're not going to toss me out on my ear when the lease is up for renewal?'

Verity looked at her in some concern. 'No! Why on earth would we do that?'

'Because I betrayed Tom's secrets,' Mattie reminded her in a small voice.

'You did, and he's been annoyingly tight-lipped about it ever since,' Verity said, as she accepted the plate that Sophie passed across the counter to her. 'I'm not one to pry but now the cat's out of the bag, the least Tom could do is be a bit forthcoming about the cat. Lothario-ing? Our Tom? It doesn't seem possible. Could you be a bit more specific?'

'I'm not saying a word.' Mattie assumed a virtuous expression. 'All I will say that it's exactly two weeks until Christmas and I have a queue out of the door and round the block, and you're holding up that queue.'

CHAPTER

23

11 days until Christmas

Christmas was rushing closer at an alarming rate.
Each morning Posy very helpfully provided
everyone with a text message to let them know how close
they were to the big 25, the number of exclamation marks
growing exponentially.

Mattie was now dreaming of pig-in-blanket rolls in her
sleep. Never-ending sheets of puff pastry coming at her
from all angles, which she had to bat away with her rolling
pin.

Now she knew what people meant what they talked
about being a victim of their own success. The pig-in-
blanket rolls queue started forming each morning long
before the tearooms opened. Meena had drafted in her
most reliable friend, Geoffrey, from catering college to join
the assembly line that Mattie had going in the upstairs

kitchen, though Verity was still having conniptions about the environmental health implications.

It left Mattie free to use the tearoom kitchens for the hundreds and hundreds of mince pies, red velvet Christmas puddings and festive flavoured shortbreads, not to mention all the other items that she had to prepare.

Christmas shopping really gave people an appetite. They'd come into the tearooms frazzled and frustrated and by the time they left, their energy and good humour was restored.

'Merry Christmas!' they'd say as they left and Mattie, if she wasn't slaving away in the kitchen, found that she was saying, 'Merry Christmas!' in reply.

She'd also noticed that the tearooms were looking a little more festive every day. At first she suspected that Nina had been sneaking in under cover of darkness to add to the veritable solar system of pink and silver stars hanging from the ceiling. But she also knew Nina would never do anything that involved overtime and Mattie couldn't say for definite that the stars had multiplied.

'Do you notice anything different about this place?' she asked Tom when he came in for his coffee and croque missus, which had completely replaced the panini in his affections.

Tom glanced around the tearooms. Although it was only thirteen minutes past ten, every table was full and the queue was already out of the door. Even with the door open, the windows were steamed up with condensation from all the people.

'It's very busy in here for this early,' he remarked. 'We're not this busy in the bookshop, and Posy *is* ruing the day she agreed to the Mistletoe Booth. People are queuing around the shop to use it and we have to check their proof of purchase. Then after they've mauled each other under the mistletoe, they loiter about waiting for their photo to print out. Of course, Nina won't have a word said against it.' He glanced around the tearooms again. 'Why do you have tiny Christmas trees on each table?'

'I don't!' Mattie peered past Tom to see that on every table was a Christmas tree no bigger than a bottle of ketchup, twinkling with LED lights. 'I do! How did they get there?'

'How could you have forsaken me?' Tom asked, a hand to his heart as if he were mortally wounded. 'You're a closet Christmas groupie.'

'I still loathe Christmas,' Mattie said with enough volume that several people in the queue looked at her in horror. 'I have no idea where those Christmas trees appeared from.'

'Pound shop,' Sophie said, as she squeezed past Mattie so she could start stacking the dishwasher under the counter. 'Grandpa said I could take the money out of the petty cash.'

'That I did,' Cuthbert agreed cheerfully as Mattie turned to stare at him in open-mouthed dismay.

'Cuthbert! You know my feelings about Christmas,' she hissed quietly so she wouldn't alienate any more of her paying customers.

'She's not angry with you, she's just very disappointed,' Tom chimed in, fixing Cuthbert with a stern look. 'As am I.'

'I can live with your disappointment,' Cuthbert said,

leaning back so he could press play on his tape deck and fill the tearooms with the sound of Noddy Holder screaming, 'It's CHHHRRRRIIIIISSSTTTMMMMAAA-ASSSSSSS!'

'And you haven't even noticed *this*,' Sophie said, gesturing at the wall behind where one of Nina's infernal *Joyeux Noel* banners was pinned above the menu chalkboard. 'We didn't think you'd mind, what with it being in French and all.'

'I do mind!' Mattie protested but Cuthbert and Sophie shared a grin – they weren't remotely bothered. Not only had they gone against Mattie's express wishes but having a sparkly banner behind the counter was sure to be a breeding ground for all sorts of bacteria and germs.

'I have to go,' Tom said, looking at his old-fashioned watch instead of checking the time on his phone like a normal person. He held out his fist towards Mattie. 'Stay strong. Keep the anti-Christmas faith.'

Mattie obligingly bumped Tom's fist. 'I'll bring your croque missus through when it's done.'

Tom was already fighting his way back down the queue. 'Thank you,' he called over his shoulder. 'And I'd much prefer a plain napkin without any Christmas nonsense on it.'

Yes, Christmas was coming and there was nothing that Mattie could do to stop it. Although this year, she didn't seem to be quite so adversely affected by the Christmas spirit.

Maybe it was something to do with finally facing all her Steven-related demons. Ever since she'd emptied a bowl of cake batter over his head and told him exactly what she thought of him, Mattie had felt different. There was a lightness to her as if she'd been buckled under the heavy weight of the load she'd been carrying for the last two years, and now it was gone. Instead of looking back, she was looking to the future and the future was looking good.

As she came downstairs each morning, unlocked the front door and stepped outside to wait for her deliveries, Mattie delighted in the crispness in the air. How her breath crystallised in front of her. She'd feel a little anticipatory tug in her belly that she used to get at the thought of Christmas, even though she still wasn't on board with the idea of actually *celebrating* Christmas.

'I still haven't decided what my plans are,' Mattie told her mother, phone clamped tightly between shoulder and chin as she opened the oven door in the tearooms kitchen so she could move her mince pies down a shelf to make room for a fresh batch of shortbread. 'So I don't really have an opinion on whether you should do turkey or goose.'

'Yes, but is it worth making bread sauce when only Ian likes it?' Sandrine demanded as if Mattie's Christmas plans involved spending a lot of time on December 25th helping her mother make dinner. 'And those sprouts? *Ils sont horribles!* Maybe we could strip them down and sauté them with bacon. Also, none of us really like Christmas pudding, so can you make *une bûche de Noel?*'

It was stuffy and hot in the little kitchen. Mattie shut the oven and asked, 'If I make you a Yule log, that doesn't mean I'm coming to you on Christmas Day.'

'But you said that you'd seen Steven. That you'd finally settled the dust on him . . .'

'Well, it was actually cake batter and you mean that the dust has settled . . .'

'So, there's no need for you take to your bed on Christmas Day,' Sandrine triumphantly pointed out and now Mattie's sweaty brow was nothing to do with opening the oven door and everything to do with her mother and her extensive Christmas to-do list being quite trying.

Mattie opened the back door so she could get another hit of that crisp, Christmassy air, only to surprise Sophie and Sam who appeared to be eating each other's faces off. They jumped apart as the door swung back on its hinges with a loud crash.

'I have to go now, Mum,' she said.

'But is there anything we can add to that infernal bread sauce to make it . . .'

'Really have to go,' Mattie insisted and she terminated the call as Sophie and Sam, now a respectable half a metre apart, looked everywhere but at Mattie and at each other.

Little Sophie and Sam? K.I.S.S.I.N.G.?

Of course, she knew that Sam had a crush on Sophie. Pretty much everyone in Bloomsbury knew that, because he wasn't subtle about it; always gazing adoringly at her when he thought she wasn't looking; asphyxiating them all with his aftershave on Saturdays when he knew that Sophie was going to be working in close proximity.

And Sophie had always humoured Sam but somehow it seemed there'd been a major upgrade from quite fond to proper full-on fancying.

Did Posy know? Did Cuthbert know? Was it Mattie's place to tell them?

She realised she'd been standing, slack-jawed, for a good two minutes. 'Um, is this something we need to talk about?'

'Oh my God, nooooooo!' Sam whined in alarm, daring a glance at Sophie, whose pretty face was distorted by a horrified grimace.

'We don't ever have to talk about it,' Sophie said firmly. 'Especially not to my grandpa. He says I'm not allowed to have a boyfriend until I'm at least thirty. Please don't tell him, please Mattie. Will you promise?'

It wasn't Mattie's place to tell anyone. Or stand in the way of young love.

'Your secret's safe with me,' Mattie said with a smile. Then she remembered that all this young love was happening in work hours. 'Now, can you go and do what I'm paying you to do?'

'Yes! Of course,' Sophie agreed, scurrying up the yard to rush past Mattie, still avoiding making eye contact.

Sam slunk towards Mattie like a dog that had been caught with its head in the treat jar, though when he did make eye contact with her, he flinched slightly. 'We are entitled to take a break,' he muttered out of the corner of his mouth, just to show that he wasn't completely cowed, but when

Mattie fixed him with her most frosty look, he bolted past her like the hounds of hell were after him.

Sam still wouldn't look Mattie in the eye when she popped into the shop later with a plate of mince pies that were too oozy to be sold. Really, it was a flimsy excuse to take a five-minute breather and have a sit down, although she was hampered in this quest by the fact that two of the three sofas had been put into storage to make way for the gigantic Christmas tree and the one that was left had been colonised by truculent-looking men who'd been reluctantly dragged into the shop by their partners. Mattie had to make do with sitting on the second rung of the rolling ladder.

'So, you're quite busy then?'

'Yes, it's horrible,' said Nina, as she scanned a customer's books with her iPad and dumped them in a tote bag. 'You get a free tote bag if you buy more than three books, which you have. Happy Christmas, please don't come back until the new year! Joke!'

'I just have to go and buy some novelty pants for my husband and then I'm done,' the woman said with great feeling.

The shop was as rammed full as Mattie had ever seen it, though it didn't help that the Christmas tree, the life-sized baby reindeer and the Mistletoe Booth took up so much space. And despite the fact that all the staff could take payment on their shop iPads, there was a huge snaking queue to pay at the counter, where Posy was perched on a stool in front of Bertha, the temperamental and ancient shop till, who had a mechanical hissy fit at least once every day.

There was now also a massive queue for the Mistletoe Booth, which was out of the shop door and into the mews. It was a pretty cheerful queue, unlike the queue for pig-in-blanket rolls, which was getting quite hangry. Next year Mattie had plans to set up a pop-up pigs-in-blankets stall in front of the tearooms so they wouldn't disturb her regular customers. Maybe they could also serve hot chocolate and buns. As it was, Sophie, keen to stay in Mattie's good books ever since she'd been caught snogging Sam, was working her way down both queues with a laminated menu and taking orders.

Tom was manning the Mistletoe Booth because 'He's the only one who's stern enough to check proof of purchase and instigate a strict two-minute time limit,' Nina said, which explained his beleaguered expression and the stopwatch in his hand. He caught Mattie's eye and made an agonised face as if he were being attacked by some invisible foe.

'You and Tom are pretty pally these days,' Nina noted, her eyes narrowed as she shifted her gaze from Mattie to Tom, who immediately stopped with the theatrics and went back to looking stern.

'Are we? I suppose we are. Guess that's what comes of being flatmates,' Mattie said, though she didn't think of Tom as a pal. He was something other than that. Could he be . . . more than a friend?

'It's pretty forgiving of Tom after you spilled all his secrets,' Nina decided. She narrowed her eyes again, in a way that made Mattie squirm. 'We never did have a talk about Tom's thesis or all the women he's . . .'

'Less chatting, Nina, more serving, please!'

Mattie was saved from spilling any more of Tom's secrets by Verity as she walked past with a pile of books and three women trailing after her like a family of ducks.

'Verity's actually serving on the shop floor?' Mattie asked, keen to distract Nina, though it was a genuinely shocked observation. Verity hated coming into contact with the general public and would much rather hide in the back office and wrestle with Excel spreadsheets.

'Did I mention how busy we are?' Nina moaned, as she turned her attention to two twenty-something women who were hovering. 'Can I help you with something?'

There was a lot of giggling. 'What's the rudest book you've got?'

'For under ten pounds. It's for our work Secret Santa.'

Nina straightened up. This was just the sort of customer enquiry she loved. 'Depends. Do you want tasteful smut or absolute filth?'

The two women looked at each other, giggled again, then said as one, 'Absolute filth, please.'

'Then follow me to the deepest depths of our Erotica section,' Nina said and she offered each woman an arm so they could barrel through the crowded shop together. 'Talking of Secret Santas, I hope you got me, Mattie, and I hope you've made me something chocolate-based. I'll see you later this evening.'

10 days until Christmas

Because it was Sunday and due to Sunday trading laws, they had to close at a very respectable five o'clock, they were having their works Christmas party at The Midnight Bell. Or rather, Posy had made it pretty clear that attendance was mandatory at the pub's legendary Christmas quiz.

Every Thursday, The Midnight Bell held a quiz. The Happy Ever After team attended regularly but had only won once, when Nina's Noah had turned out to be a walking, talking version of Ask Jeeves. Alas, Noah was in Denmark working on a holistic HR strategy for a lifestyle company, so Mattie expected that they'd probably end up where they usually did, somewhere near the very bottom of the leader board.

Not that Mattie minded. As they closed at five, she was done with her next-day prep by an unprecedented six, and by six fifteen, she was sat on a velvet banquette in their usual corner of The Midnight Bell, with a laden plateful of food that someone else had cooked.

Carol and Clive, landlady and landlord, were having no truck with thematic and tasteful Christmas decorations. Tinsel of every sparkly hue was hung from every possible place you could hang tinsel. It was even lovingly entwined around Clive's collection of horse brasses above the bar.

There was a fake Christmas tree ('We bought it from Woolies in 1985, the year that we got married, and it's still going strong') hung with so many twinkling lights that it had to be a major fire hazard, and an alarming nativity tableau in a glass display case.

'Joseph and Mary are terrifying,' Mattie commented to Tom, as she tried not to stare at them. 'Like those creepy-faced Victorian dolls that come to life in the dead of night and kill people.'

'And the shepherds look as if they've got a bad case of mange.' Tom watched Mattie take an enthusiastic bite of a doorstep sandwich, which was basically half a turkey liberally smeared in cranberry sauce and stuffed between two slices of crusty bread.

'I'm so hungry,' Mattie mumbled unapologetically as she held the huge sandwich aloft. 'When you spend all day making food, you never feel like eating it.'

'That's probably why you're so trim,' he remarked, eyes on Mattie's legs. In honour of the occasion, she'd changed out of her work uniform of black jumper and trousers into a grey and navy blue striped dress, which she was wearing with black tights and Converse. No one had seen Mattie's legs in months, but, judging from the way that Tom was still looking at them, they were quite the spectacle. 'God, sorry,' he muttered, though Mattie wasn't sure if he was sorry for commenting on her figure or for staring at her legs.

'Trim?' Mattie queried, face inevitably going hot as she remembered that Tom had seen her in much less than a jersey cotton dress from Uniqlo.

'Very trim,' Tom murmured huskily. It was the same tone he'd deployed while getting the phone numbers of defenceless young ladies at parties.

He had to be winding her up. There could be no other reason for Tom to remark on her figure while using his Lothario voice. Some light-hearted banter because they were friends now, in which case, two could play at that game.

'You're quite trim yourself,' Mattie remarked. 'Despite your love of a complex carbohydrate. I guess that's the advantage of being on your feet all day. Or is it the football?'

Tom was steadfastly *not* looking at Mattie's legs now. 'What football?'

'The football you allegedly play with your friends. Phil mentioned it,' Mattie stared at Tom over the edge of her mammoth turkey sandwich. He was looking quite discomfited now. 'We haven't talked about that yet, have we?'

'And we never will,' Tom said firmly.

'Do you wear full kit?' Mattie's voice was a little husky now – Tom, *Tom!*, in football strip and shorts. It was also her turn to stare at his legs, though they were covered in a light woollen tweed so there wasn't much to look at.

'You really do have quite a cruel streak,' Tom told her, though there was a half smile playing around his mouth just before he took a sip of his pint. 'I expected better from you.'

'Ha! Don't dish it, if you can't take it!'

'Oh God, get a room,' scoffed Sam, who was sitting on Tom's other side and had been listening to their exchange with an expression of growing incredulity.

Mattie and Tom both turned to look at Sam, who wilted slightly under their collective gaze.

'We don't need to get a room because we're just two friends having a joke,' Tom said a little stiffly. 'What's the harm in that?'

'Quite frankly, Sam, you're the last person to tell someone else to get a room,' Mattie said quietly and Sophie, who was sitting opposite them, gave a little squeak of alarm, glancing across at her grandfather who was debating quiz team names with Verity and Nina.

'Have I missed something?' Tom asked idly with an amused glance at Sam, who looked ashen.

'Please, Mattie . . .' Sam moaned.

Mattie had made a promise so she shook her head. 'It's between me and Sam but we're not going to be hearing any more salty remarks. Right?'

'Right,' Sam agreed and by the time his face had returned to its normal hue, Clive, the landlord, had passed around the Christmas quiz question sheets and was going through the very, very long list of rules that accompanied the regular quiz at The Midnight Bell. And because it was the special Christmas quiz, he'd thrown in a few new ones.

'All team names must be Christmas-related but not blasphemous. I will be deducting marks for any ungodliness,' Clive droned on.

Mattie rolled her eyes. 'How did we get stuck doing a Christmas quiz?' she asked Tom. 'When we hate Christmas.'

'We just won't participate,' Tom said as Clive moved on to discuss the special glitter pens he was distributing but how he wanted them returned at the end of the quiz and to put the tops back on in between answers so the glitter wouldn't dry up.

'It's not as if we're going to know any of the answers,' Mattie said. 'So, we might just as well sit the whole thing out and it's not like we're going to come close to winning anyway.' She jerked her head in the direction of a table across the pub where The Battering RAMS, from the computer repair centre around the corner, the reigning champions of The Midnight Bell quiz, were discussing tactics.

'Pair of scrooges,' Nina complained when the quiz started and Mattie and Tom carried on their own little conversation about going halves on some IKEA shelves for the spare room.

Mattie was dimly aware of the quiz happening going on

without them. There was a round on Christmas carols that got very heated with Verity snapping, 'The cattle are lowing, not mooing. Honestly, what is wrong with you people?'

The round on Christmas films passed with Cuthbert and Sophie carrying the rest of their team, as it turned out there wasn't a single Christmas film they hadn't seen. 'Grandpa knows all the dialogue to *It's a Wonderful Life* and *The Muppet Christmas Carol*,' Sophie proudly explained, but then they got on to Christmas literature, which should have been a slam dunk but apparently wasn't.

'Tom! Tom!' Posy hissed urgently from across the table. 'What is the last line of *A Christmas Carol*?'

'Why are you asking me?' Tom complained. 'You own a bookshop.'

'A romantic fiction bookshop,' Posy pointed out. 'I can't get on with Dickens. He's just too Dickensy, but I bet you've read all his greatest hits. Come on, take one for the team. What's the last line?'

Tom sighed, then with an apologetic glance at Mattie, whispered, 'It's "God bless us, every one."'

It didn't end there. Tom was also called upon to answer questions about Christmas-related stories from J. R. R. Tolkien, Mark Twain and Hans Christian Andersen.

'Traitor,' Mattie whispered at him. 'I thought we were sitting this one out.'

'I don't want Posy withholding my Christmas bonus,' Tom whispered back but when they got onto the Christmas food round, it was his turn to sit there with a disapproving expression as Mattie was forced to field questions such as

'Name three ingredients in bread sauce that aren't bread', 'What date is stir-up Sunday?' and 'What's the German name for stollen?'

In the end, Team A Happy Ever After Christmas won the quiz by one extra point because there were *two* German names for stollen and Mattie knew both of them.

'For two people who hate Christmas, you know a hell of a lot about it,' Nina said as The Battering RAMS (renamed The Battering HAMS for this special Christmas quiz) complained bitterly about the outcome and demanded a recount. 'I bet if I sneaked into the flat while you were both working, it would be dripping in Christmas baubles.'

'Then you'd be disappointed,' Tom said, returning from the bar with a tray of drinks. 'And also trespassing.'

Posy patted her bump, which was more bump-like than ever, though she had a good month to go until her due-date. Carol had made Clive drag over a plump maroon wingback chair and matching footstool especially for Posy and she seemed very content with her lot in life. Or maybe it was just the sheer bliss of closing the shop at a civilised hour and putting her feet up. 'No arguing,' she said. 'This is a time for celebration and joy and giving, so let's do Secret Santa now.'

Everyone pulled out rectangular-shaped gifts from various bags and coat pockets. Despite Nina's wish for handmade chocolate treats, it was tradition that the Happy Ever After Secret Santa presents had to be books.

'You'd think they'd all be sick of the sight of books by

now,' Sophie had muttered when the email was sent round the staff. She was a big reader herself but the Secret Santa had made her sour, because she'd been assigned Posy, who'd pretty much read everything. Luckily, in a moment of inspiration she'd realised that Posy was cooking a baby who hadn't read a single book and had bought her a beautiful collection of feminist fairy stories.

Mattie had been assigned Verity who was delighted with the 1960s edition of *Pride and Prejudice* (her favourite book) with a lurid cover typical of that era. Mattie didn't think there was a single cookbook that she didn't already own but when she opened her present, wrapped in plain brown paper, she was amazed to see that Secret Santa had managed to find her one: a 1953 edition of the legendary cookery writer, Elizabeth Craig's *Court Favourites: Recipes from the Royal Kitchens*, in its original dust jacket.

'This is the best Secret Santa present ever,' Mattie said, holding the book up to blank faces all round. 'Elizabeth Craig. She was the Mary Berry of her day. My mincemeat for my mince pies is actually a variation on the mincemeat in her 1932 book, *Cooking with Elizabeth Craig*.' The blank faces now had glazed-over eyes.

Except . . . Cuthbert, who was far too polite to look bored unless . . .

'Are you my Secret Santa?' Mattie asked him but he shook his head and Nina held up her own Secret Santa book, a collection of vintage saucy postcards, which Cuthbert had already confessed to buying (with Cynthia's blessing).

'Guess again,' Verity suggested.

It wasn't Sophie, who'd had Posy, nor Sam because Mattie doubted he even knew who Delia Smith was, much less Elizabeth Craig. Posy had got Tom and, hilariously, depending on your point of view, had bought him a copy of *The Complete Memoirs of Casanova*. Nina had got Sam and had bought him a book of hacks for the latest computer game he was obsessed with.

'I give up then,' Mattie said.

'It was me!'

'It's Tom!'

Mattie and Tom turned to each other, which was a bit of a squeeze on the three-seater banquette, especially when Sam was quite the seat hogger.

'Thank you!' Mattie beamed at Tom, who blinked, then smiled back. 'How did you know?'

'If you will put your books in communal areas of our shared living space, then you'll have to face the consequences,' he said, oh so very loftily. Ah! Mattie was finally and genuinely forgiven for coming across his bound thesis, then blurting out the contents to all and sundry.

'I love it. I'll have to make you dinner from one of the recipes,' Mattie said, as she started to flick through it, but Tom put his hand over hers to stop her progress.

'Please don't,' he said. 'I had a quick look before I wrapped it and all the recipes involve disgusting things like aspic. Do you hate me that much?'

'You know, I hardly hate you at all these days.'

His hand was still resting on hers, his touch warm rather than hot and sweaty this time. His fingers twitched so it felt a little like a caress, and when he took his hand away, it felt a lot like a loss.

'Wow, you two obviously don't hate each other any more,' Nina said. 'I'd say get a room, but you have several rooms all to yourselves, and who even knows what you get up to in them?'

'I said the same thing,' Sam dared to point out because he obviously had a deathwish.

'Oh, do shut up, the pair of you,' Tom drawled but it lacked his usual acidity and Mattie, with all eyes upon her, could feel herself heating up.

'It's Christmas,' she muttered. 'We decided it was traditional to have a break in our hostilities. Like the British and German soldiers playing football in no-man's land on Christmas Day during the First World War.'

'Although that's a touching story, it's actually a bit of an urban myth,' Tom began but he was shouted down and, eager to change the subject, Posy asked everyone what they were doing for Christmas.

'Sebastian, Sam and I will be spending a peaceful Christmas together, our last as a trio, before the baby arrives,' she said with a contented little sigh.

'She lies,' Sam added. 'She actually expects Sebastian and I to get the nursery ready. He's at IKEA now. She won't even get someone in to do the painting!'

'It's more personal if you and Sebastian do it,' Posy said. 'When the baby comes, it will sleep in a room which has been lovingly decorated by its father and uncle. It's very good energy, I read it in one of my baby books.'

'The baby's going to be barely sentient for *months*,' Sam argued rashly. His callous utterance was enough to have Posy's eyes filling up with unshed tears.

'So unkind,' she said in a voice thick and throaty. 'Talking about my child like it's an alien from one of your sci-fi shows.'

Anyone else would have apologised. But Sam was a sixteen-year-old boy so he doubled down.

'It can't even see properly for the first three months,' he insisted and Posy was sobbing now and everyone else was looking around at each other helplessly as they racked their brains for something to say that would make Posy stop crying and let the good times roll once more.

Mattie nudged Tom. 'Can you think of anything to cheer her up?' she mouthed but Tom pressed his lips together and shook his head.

Even Nina, usually ready with an overshare about her sex life or someone else's, was looking as panicked as the rest of them.

'I think it's bad luck to cry at a Christmas party, Posy,' she said. 'It means that you'll cry at every Christmas party from now on.'

'That's birthdays,' Posy sobbed and Mattie wondered how soon it would be before she could make her excuses and leave.

'Oh God, Posy, stop crying!' Verity demanded. 'You have to stop crying all the time. Think of something nice.'

'I'm giving birth to a barely sentient creature. That's not nice!'

'Way to overreact, Pose,' Sam said, which earned him a withering look from Sophie. It was left to Verity to provide the diversion by jumping to her feet and announcing to the assembled company, 'I'm engaged!'

Nina turned her head so quickly, it was a wonder she didn't get whiplash. 'You're *what*?'

'Johnny asked me to marry him last Thursday night after we had an argument about Strumpet's litter tray – we're still not letting him out after the gate incident,' Verity explained like anyone even cared about Strumpet's litter tray at that particular moment. 'Anyway, I said yes and now we're engaged and you absolutely can't tell anyone. Posy, why are you still crying?'

'They're happy tears,' Posy insisted snottily, as everyone got to their feet to congratulate Verity and hug her, though she backed away, hands in front of her.

'You know how I feel about hugging. This isn't an occasion that merits hugging,' she said.

Tom settled for patting her on the arm, while looking quite unsettled. 'Another one of you getting married? Is there something in the water supply at the shop? I'm going to have to start drinking the bottled stuff.'

Sophie smirked. 'Are you sure you're not already married, Tom?'

'No, I'm not secretly married with five children and neither am I a Russian sleeper agent waiting to be activated by my handler,' he sniffed, sitting back down. 'I know exactly what you all say about me behind my back.'

'You don't know the half of it. Now, come here, Very,

and prepare to be hugged,' Nina said fondly, smooshing Verity to her bosoms. 'How exciting! I barely got to plan my wedding, what with us being in Vegas. Oh! You can get married in Happy Ever After. We could apply for a special license. We'd be bound to go viral.'

Posy clasped her hands together in rapture. She was no longer crying, but sporting an ear-to-ear grin. 'That would be perfect!'

'Or I can get married in the village church that my father happens to be vicar of,' Verity said tartly, accepting Cuthbert's congratulatory handshake. 'Can we all sit down and stop making a fuss? You know how I feel about fusses.'

Yet for someone so newly engaged, Verity didn't look very happy. If Mattie had found someone that she wanted to spend the rest of her life with, she'd be quite chipper about it. She waited for that horrible scalding, panicking feeling that she always got when she thought about being in another relationship, but it never came. Instead she felt the faintest pinprick of excitement at the possibility that there might be someone out there for her.

'You've had the soppiest smile on your face,' Tom whispered in her ear. 'Don't say you're going to be next and I'll have to go to all the trouble of finding a new flatmate.'

That wiped the allegedly soppy smile off Mattie's face immediately. 'Highly unlikely,' she whispered back. 'Don't forget, I hate all men.'

'Not *all* men,' Tom quoted back at her with a sly little smile, which made Mattie want to smile too while she dug him in the ribs.

'Also, as you pointed out when you were trying to do me out of the flat, you've worked in the shop longest so it will definitely be you who gets married first,' Mattie informed Tom. 'It's obvious that working in a romantic fiction bookshop addles the brain.'

Mattie could tell that he was working up to saying something particularly crushing from the way his eyes narrowed and his nostrils flared, but Verity provided another diversion. She'd only just sat down again and had Nina on one side and Posy on the other, both of them yammering in her ears, so who could blame her for jumping to her feet again and shouting, 'Stop! Just stop it! All of you! I never meant to tell you that I was getting engaged. I only did it to stop Posy crying and now you all have to swear to keep it secret! No one must know. Even Merry doesn't know!'

Verity was the middle one of five sisters, all four of them garrulous and completely lacking in personal boundaries. Much like Nina, and Mattie's own mother. But despite the fact that Verity was the complete opposite, she was very close to all her sisters, particularly Merry (or Mercy as she'd been christened), so it was quite the surprise that she hadn't told her the good news.

'We want to do things properly,' Verity explained, sitting back down. 'Johnny is planning to ask Dad for his blessing. In person. Over pints in the local pub, as is traditional.'

Nina pulled a face. 'So old-fashioned and kind of sexist.'

'He's not asking for permission, I'm not a piece of property, but I am a vicar's daughter and Johnny says that as he only plans to marry once, he wants to do things by the book.' Verity smiled happily. Then the corners of the smile drooped. 'It's just that we already promised that we'd spend Christmas with Johnny's dad and his girlfriend, Celia, and we're booked to go away after Christmas, so we won't be able to go up to Lincolnshire until the new year. And I can't tell my sisters in the meantime.'

'They wouldn't mean to but all four of them would end up telling your parents in a matter of minutes,' Tom said because they'd all met the Love sisters and while they were good company, they couldn't keep a secret if their lives depended on it.

'Exactly,' Verity said rather unhappily. 'I have this lovely news, the best news, and I have to sit on it for weeks when I want to shout it from the rooftops.' She pulled a face. 'Not that I ever shout but I would like to tell my parents . . .'

'You're having next weekend off and that's an order!' Posy shrieked. 'It will be my engagement present to you!'

'Do we have to buy engagement presents now?' Nina asked. 'As well as a wedding present and shelling out for the hen do . . .'

'I am absolutely not having a hen do,' Verity said firmly. She took Posy's hand. 'And I am not taking next weekend off. It's the last weekend before Christmas.'

'So? I bet everyone will have done all their Christmas shopping by then,' Posy said blithely, as if she hadn't worked in retail for the last eight years and knew nothing of the frantic hysteria that gripped people on the last weekend before Christmas.

'Anyway, this is also the busiest time of year for Dad,' Verity said.

'Really? Is it? Why?' Nina asked.

'I don't know,' Sam said with all the scorn a sixteen-year-old boy could muster. 'It might have something to do with it being the birth of Jesus Christ.'

'Well, take two days off this week. Say, Wednesday and Thursday,' Posy was undeterred. Nothing was going to stop her from giving Verity her perfect engagement, Christmas trading hours be damned. 'Love is more important than Christmas and this way you'll be back before the weekend.'

'I don't know, Pose.' Verity twisted her hands anxiously. 'Johnny might not be able to take the time off.'

'But he's his own boss,' Nina pointed out. 'He can take time off anytime he wants, the lucky sod.'

'You're having Wednesday and Thursday off and that's an order,' Posy said, settling her hands over her bump once more. 'Otherwise I'll have to fire you and don't think I won't. You probably haven't noticed but my pregnancy hormones are making me quite crazy and irrational.'

9 days until Christmas

Although he hadn't said anything at the time, Tom was quite furious about the prospect of Verity swanning off to Lincolnshire and leaving the shop one man down.

'I know that she mostly just lurks in the back office, but now we're expected to cover all the website orders ourselves on top of everything else, including manning the Mistletoe Booth,' Tom complained the next morning.

Mattie was in the tearoom kitchen doing her inevitable prep and knocking up a quick croque missus for Tom, with the back door wide open because the kitchen was steamy hot and she didn't want her dough to get too warm.

'Isn't Posy getting cover in?' Mattie asked as she happily battered flat a stick of butter.

'She says we'll manage,' Tom said. He was perched on a stool in the no-man's land between tearooms and kitchen.

'I beg to differ, but then I get accused of being a complete curmudgeon who'd begrudge Verity her newly engaged happiness.'

'Her pregnancy hormones are getting worse by the hour, but don't tell Posy I said that . . .'

'Don't tell me what?' Posy had managed to waddle up behind Tom without either of them noticing. 'What's happened? What's wrong? Have we been done by the council for using the oven upstairs? I knew this would happen! Have you given people food poisoning by using out of date bacon in the pigs in blankets?'

'I'm insulted that you would even think that,' Mattie sniffed and before she could cast imploring eyes at Tom, the traitor used her to further his own agenda.

'Mattie doesn't know how we're going to cope with Verity gone either,' Tom informed Posy with a put-upon sigh. 'I just dread to think how many website orders we're going to get while Verity's away during the final posting dates.'

'Oh dear! Why didn't I think of that?' Posy put a hand to her forehead. Without being asked, Tom vacated the stool and took Posy's arm so he could help her onto it. 'I'm a fool for love, that's my problem.'

'You were just trying to do something nice for Verity,' Mattie said, thankful that she was now onto folding and kneading her dough, the familiar movements soothing in such anxious moments. Posy was eight months pregnant but she looked like she was about to pop and shouldn't she be on maternity leave by now? 'I'm sure it will all be fine.'

'You're stressing me out. I'm not meant to get stressed,' Posy said, now looking like she was one more disaster away from a complete nervous breakdown. Then, as was so often the case with Posy and her mercurial mood swings, her attention shifted and focused first on Tom now leaning against the door jamb, and then on Mattie who was cling-filming one of her bowls of dough. 'What were you two doing in here together, all cosy? Are you *friends* now?'

She made being friends sound like a quite unsavoury pastime. 'Friends!' Tom snorted, which hurt Mattie's feelings a little. 'We're almost colleagues who just happen to share a living space.'

'I do think that we could describe ourselves as flatmates by now and no one would be surprised,' Mattie said tartly. 'I mean, we've eaten dinner together twice, so we're not just sharing a living space. We are living . . . like . . . communally.'

'You've had dinner together twice?' Posy asked.

'Soon it might even be three times. Mattie's having to work later and later on her never-ending flaky pastry prep, so I was thinking that tonight we could get fish and chips from No Plaice Like Home.'

Mattie allowed herself a small, grateful smile. She and Tom had moved so far on in their evolving friendship that he wanted to spend the evening with her. 'Sounds like a plan. I'm too tired to even think about doing any more cooking,' Mattie said, putting the last bowl in the fridge.

'And I'm not going out tonight because you're working

me to the bone, Posy, and I refuse to cook because this one provides a running commentary on everything I'm doing wrong,' Tom said with a weary gesture at Mattie who stuck her tongue out at him. 'Harsh things have been said about my misuse of her non-stick saucepans.'

'He won't use a wooden spoon and ends up scraping the bottom of my pans with metal utensils,' Mattie said, as she untied her apron. 'I can only take so much.'

'Right. OK, then,' Posy muttered, her eyes fixed on the pair of them. 'I probably would say that you are flatmates verging on friends verging on I don't even know what.' She shook her head. 'Anyway, entertaining as this is, I came to get something for my mid-morning bun break.'

'It's not even half past ten, I still haven't had breakfast,' Tom said, his eyes intent on Mattie as she took his beloved croque missus out from under the grill and placed it on a plate. 'That looks good and just an extra dash of . . .'

'Yes, I know, Worcester sauce,' Mattie said, opening the bottle and giving the piping-hot open sandwich a sprinkle. 'Before you ask, we don't have any non-Christmassy napkins.'

'Appalling,' Tom said good-naturedly, taking the plate. 'I don't know why I honour this establishment with my custom. I hope Cuthbert's got my coffee ready.'

And he was gone with a cheery wave, which caused Posy to stare at him in some consternation before extricating her bleeping phone from the back pocket of her maternity jeans with some difficulty. 'Mattie and Tom? Who'd have thought it?' she muttered.

'Mid-morning bun break is a bit early today, isn't it? Let's go and have a look for something to turn that frown upside down,' Mattie said, hoping to distract Posy away from any more disturbing thoughts about her and Tom. But Posy's attention was on her iPhone where the Met Office and the BBC and the weather app had all sent simultaneous weather alerts predicting heavy snow for later in the week – what would this do to their footfall?

'We have to take a lot of money over Christmas to make up for the times in the year when we take much less,' she fretted, as she followed Mattie out of the kitchen and into the tearooms. 'Also, I've eaten every cake that you do several times over and now I'm craving something else and I don't even know what it is.' Mattie was sympathetic but Posy had pushed to the front of the sizeable queue without even an 'Excuse me.'

'When my Cynthia was pregnant with our Shane, the poor woman had such a taste for cheese on toast that she had it for breakfast, lunch and dinner,' Cuthbert helpfully reported.

Posy pondered. 'No, I don't want cheese on toast. I want something else and I want it not to snow and I want to feel like I'm not gestating a pair of elephant babies. I just want to feel like me again, you know?'

Mattie had never been pregnant but she knew quite a lot about not feeling like herself. In the two years she was with Steven, she tried hard to mould herself into the kind of woman he wanted because he seemed to have so many objections to the woman she actually was. And in the two years since she'd left Steven, she'd moulded herself into the woman she thought she should be: one who didn't need love because she wasn't worthy of love.

Now, Mattie was starting to wonder if maybe, just maybe she was as deserving of love as the old Mattie had been. The one who'd loved Paris and Christmas and cupcakes . . .

'I do know what you mean,' she told Posy slowly. 'Not the bit about gestating elephants, but it can be very easy to lose sight of yourself. To only see yourself as other people see you.'

'Wow! That's very deep,' Posy said as Cuthbert gently harrumphed.

'Young ladies, this is all very philosophical but you're coming between these good people and their hot beverages,' he said, and Mattie and Posy both looked round to see that the queue hadn't got any shorter. On the contrary, it had grown much longer and was full of people staring daggers at them.

Later, in a tiny lull when nothing needed to go into or come out of an oven and Meena and Geoffrey were doing sterling work in the upstairs kitchen, Mattie thought once more of the old Mattie and the new Posy, who seemed utterly miserable at the moment. Not to mention stressed. Posy shouldn't be so stressed when she was so very pregnant and there had to be something that Mattie could do to make her less stressed. To put a smile on her face.

Mattie stared around the tiny kitchen. At the purple and green tiles that never failed to lift her spirits and make her think of Lady Agatha, then sing a couple of lines of 'Sister

Suffragette' from *Mary Poppins*. At her jars and bottles and tins full of ingredients and her pots and pans; all ready for her to make magic, or at least some delicious and highly calorific treats, with her own hands.

And actually, making Posy happy was easy. She hadn't made them in two years, but Mattie didn't need to look at a recipe; she simply began pulling down jars to get the ingredients she needed. There had been a time when she made them once, twice, three times a week and, as soon as she started measuring out her dry ingredients, a sort of culinary muscle memory kicked in.

Ninety minutes later, including a wait for them to cool down before she could decorate them and an absolutely frantic half hour in the tearooms, Mattie tracked Posy down to the back office where she presented her with a laden cake stand.

'Twelve gingerbread cupcakes with cinnamon frosting,' Mattie said, putting down her precious cargo with a little flourish. 'For you, because I'm very fond of you and also very worried about you.'

Posy, who was very red of face as if she'd been crying, looked at the cupcakes then at Mattie, who was wearing a smile like a game-show hostess standing in front of the star prize, then back again.

And then, inevitably, she burst into tears.

'Are they happy tears?' Mattie asked aghast. 'Please say they're happy tears.'

'I can't even tell at this point,' Posy sobbed. 'But this is the nicest thing anyone has ever done for me.'

'Not strictly true.' Tom stuck his head around the door. 'When you were living upstairs, I once had to rescue you from the attentions of the world's smallest spider. She'd been standing on the kitchen table for half an hour apparently,' he added to Mattie.

'That spider was *huge*,' Posy hiccupped, holding a tentative hand out towards the nearest cupcake as if she was afraid it was just an illusion. 'How did you know that I *need* a cupcake?'

Mattie shrugged modestly. 'It was just a hunch.'

'I thought you said that cupcakes were a patriarchal plot to suppress female power,' Tom recalled.

'Posy's need was greater than the patriarchy's need to keep women down,' Mattie said vaguely as she watched Posy take her first bite of the first cupcake that Mattie had made in two years.

'Oh!' Posy sighed around a mouthful of moist gingerbread and delicately flavoured cinnamon buttercream. Then Posy's eyes closed as she experienced a moment of sheer bliss when woman and cupcake became one. 'Oh!'

'Good?' Mattie asked a little anxiously.

'Very good. Very, very good,' Posy said, holding up her hand for silence so she could take another massive bite.

'Could I get in on the cupcake action?' Tom asked, leaning his whole torso around the office door. Posy snatched the plate out of reach.

'Mine,' she snapped. 'Mattie made them for me and they taste so good that for fifteen seconds there I even managed to forget that I was pregnant so no, I'm not sharing.'

'Well, next time you can deal with your own spiders.' Tom removed himself from the door, as Posy took another bite.

Two more bites and it was gone.

'Have another one,' Mattie urged Posy. 'You are eating for two, after all.'

Posy pulled a face even as she selected another cupcake. 'Sadly, that's a myth, even though my appetite is off the charts. My GP says that in reality I should only be eating an extra three hundred calories a day.'

'I would think it took more extra calories than that to grow a human being,' Mattie said, watching again as Posy brought the cupcake to her mouth like a satellite docking.

'Oh! Damn it!' Posy exclaimed, plonking the cupcake back down on the plate with some force. 'These things are evil!'

'They have a bad aftertaste?' Mattie asked in disbelief, having to cling to the edge of the nearest desk for support.

'Oh! Ooh!' Posy groaned and for a second Mattie hoped she was having a delayed reaction to how yummy the cupcake had been. 'Oooh. Oh goodness. Oh no.'

Suddenly it was Posy clinging to the edge of her desk for dear life, her face drained of colour.

'Are you all right, Posy?' Mattie asked anxiously and Posy shook her head briefly as if she was so far from all right that she couldn't speak. 'Are you . . . are you *having the baby*?'

Posy groaned again and Mattie, panic rising in her like

dough proving, did a full 360-degree turn where she stood. They'd need towels! And hot water! And . . .

'Not having the baby. Just feel a bit peculiar,' Posy managed to say and the colour was returning to her pretty face, which was still a bit squinched up.

'Enough, Posy,' Mattie said as firmly as she could. 'I think you should go home. Put your feet up. Or even better, go to bed.'

'No, I'm fine now,' Posy said, releasing her death grip on the desk. 'It was just a funny turn.' She smiled at Mattie, a forced smile which didn't quite meet her eyes. 'Better get back to the bookselling, and don't you have tearooms to run?'

'Yes, but . . .'

'Well, then.' Posy hoisted herself up and walked slowly and laboriously out of the office, leaving Mattie with no option but to follow her into the shop, which was hot and stuffy, despite the cold of the day.

Nina had obviously been inspired by Cuthbert and his never-ending supply of festive tunes because instead of the sound of excited chatter from book-buyers, the Phil Spector Christmas album was blaring out. It was quite hard to make oneself heard over The Crystals inviting everyone to take a walk through a winter wonderland.

'Posy! I really think you should be resting,' Mattie called out but she wasn't sure if Posy had heard her because she didn't turn round. Instead she barrelled through a couple of customers who were waiting to use the Mistletoe Booth and then crashed into the Christmas tree, which wobbled alarmingly, pine needles raining down like confetti, baubles crashing to the floor, a few panicked yelps from shoppers. Miraculously the tree stayed upright, unlike Posy who swayed on her feet and seemed on the verge of crumpling to the floor, before Tom was suddenly there, a strong arm around her.

'What is going on in here?' Nina asked sharply from the archway that led to the Regency room. 'I'm trying to sell some books! Why is no one manning the Mistletoe Booth?'

'What's all the commotion?' Verity appeared from the archway that led to the Classics room. 'I can hardly hear myself think with this music on.'

Then their eyes alighted on Posy at the same moment, who had one hand clutching her bump, her face ashen as Tom slowly guided her to the sofa, which was instantly vacated by the two sullen-looking men who'd been sitting on it.

'Posy!' Nina and Verity cried in unison.

'I'm fine,' Posy said in a high-pitched, decidedly unfine voice. 'Just a bit dizzy.'

Nina and Verity took charge. The music was turned off, Nina dealt briskly with any customers waiting to pay, Tom handled any Mistletoe Booth stragglers and Verity patted Posy's forehead with a damp cloth. Then the shop was temporarily closed.

'My profit margins,' Posy faintly moaned but she didn't put up any real protest. 'I'm not about to go into labour, I just need to lie here for ten minutes.'

Mattie felt quite helpless. 'I'll make you a cup of tea. Sweet, strong tea.'

She hurried blindly for the tearooms, surprising Sophie and Sam, locked in an embrace in a quiet corner of the Non-fiction and Foreign Language room.

'Oh, really!' Mattie exclaimed as they sprang apart. 'For two people who want to keep this a secret, you could be a bit more discreet.'

Sophie wrung her hands. 'It's hard to ignore *feelings* . . .'

'Well, try harder,' Mattie snapped and she didn't mean to be unsympathetic but their timing was terrible. 'Sam, Posy's not well! She says she's not in labour but . . .'

She was already talking to their backs.

'I'm calling Sebastian,' Sam shouted as he disappeared through the anterooms back to the main room.

'I'm calling my nanna!' Sophie shouted as she headed towards the tearooms. 'She'll know what to do!'

The tearooms were in an *uproar*. With both Sophie and Mattie missing in action, Cuthbert had been left to manage on his own and when the displaced shop customers had arrived, he'd been forced to call Meena down from the upstairs kitchen to lend a hand.

'I'm so sorry,' Mattie kept gasping, as she darted between tables with orders and empty plates, or replenished the baked goods, or took people's money.

It was a good forty minutes before Mattie was able to head back to the shop with a strong, sweet tea for Posy who was still prostrate on the sofa, while Sebastian, his face pinched with worry, stood over her.

'Honestly, Morland, I *told* you to stay at home today, preferably horizontal, but I let myself be bamboozled, browbeaten, blackmailed . . .' Sebastian ran out of words beginning with 'b' to describe how Posy had run roughshod over his attempts to take care of her.

It was all very troubling but Mattie only had eyes for a tall woman in her late sixties, who was as elegant as her husband.

Normally, it would have been thrilling to finally meet Cynthia, Cuthbert's 'queen', because he had very strict ideas about not mixing business with pleasure. She'd been an A&E nurse before she retired and she'd come ten minutes after Sophie had called her.

She was now examining Posy with thorough but gentle hands and ignoring the garbled explanations that were coming at her from all sides.

'Your pulse is very fast and I'm not happy with your blood pressure either,' she said mildly.

'She cries,' Sam told Cynthia, who was still casting an expert and rather worried eye over Posy. 'And we know that she's not meant to get stressed because she has high blood pressure, so we end up letting her do things that end up stressing her even more.'

'I'm pregnant, not an invalid,' Posy protested, struggling to swing her legs round and sit up.

Sebastian dropped to his knees, with no thought for his expensive suit or how tight his trousers were, so he could bodily prevent her from getting to her feet. 'Morland, I know in the past that I've been guilty of doing what I think is best for both of us without discussing it with you first, and I'm genuinely sorry for that—'

'Finally! An apology,' Posy panted as she tried to manoeuvre past the immovable block of Sebastian Thorndyke in her way.

'—but you are staying put on that sofa even if I have to tie you to it.'

Mattie exchanged a horrified look with Tom who was hovering by the door, occasionally making shooing motions at any would-be customers trying to get in. Nobody wanted to witness yet another blazing domestic from Posy and Sebastian or hear about what they might get up to in the privacy of their own home.

'How about some more tea, Posy?' Mattie offered. 'Cynthia, tea? Nina, tea? Anyone, tea?'

'It's been an hour, should we move Posy upstairs so we can open the shop again?' Tom asked. They all looked over to the door, where there was a small, shivering group of shoppers waiting for admittance.

'Ugh! Stop talking about me like I'm not even here,' Posy complained.

'I'd love a cup of tea, milk, two sugars,' Cynthia said, standing over Posy with a determined expression, which made Posy, who'd clearly been about to start protesting again, close her mouth with an audible snap.

Cynthia picked up Posy's hand so she could place her fingers around her wrist while looking at her own watch to check Posy's blood pressure again.

'I really am fine,' Posy insisted. 'Look! We have customers! They need me!'

'Hmmm mmmm.' Cynthia didn't seem convinced and

placed her other hand on Posy's shoulder to hold her in place. 'The only thing that needs you, young lady, is your bed. How many weeks until your due date?'

'I'm only eight months pregnant . . . !'

'Three weeks,' Sebastian said as Posy cast him a furious look. Mattie decided it was time that she got on with making more tea and checking Cuthbert and Sophie were all right.

She was pleased to see that the tearooms still had a respectable amount of customers and that a fresh batch of pig-in-blanket rolls were out of the oven and attractively displayed on a wooden board on the counter.

She gave Cuthbert and Sophie a quick update on Posy, who was 'being quite difficult'.

'Cynthia's very good with difficult patients,' Cuthbert said fondly, as he made his wife her tea – apparently only he knew exactly the precise colour she preferred it. 'She'll have Posy minding her p's and q's in no time.'

And when Mattie returned with tea and mince pies, Cynthia was in mid-lecture, with a visibly chastened Posy prostrate once more on the sofa.

' . . . the last thing anyone needs on a day when the A&Es are full to overflowing because it's the middle of flu season is you taking up a bed because you wouldn't listen to the advice of your GP, your midwife, your obstetrician and a woman who worked as an A&E nurse for forty years. Have you worked as an A&E nurse for forty years?'

Posy, eyes wide, shook her head.

'So, this handsome husband of yours and young Sam are

going to walk you to your car and when you get home, you're going to go to bed and you're going to stay there for the duration of your pregnancy, do you hear me?'

Posy nodded.

'I'm going to need a verbal answer,' Cynthia said.

'Yes!' Posy flung her head back in frustration. 'But it's only nine days until Christmas! Who will manage the shop without Verity here?'

'You are ridiculous,' Verity told her crossly. 'As if I'm going to take two days off now. I'll tell my parents about the you-know-what after Christmas. It can wait.'

'But love shouldn't wait!' Posy said tearfully. 'I won't stand for it.'

'Of course you won't because you're going to be on bed rest,' Verity said in a quiet but resolute tone of voice that ordinarily brooked no denial.

'You're not the boss of me, I'm the boss of me,' Posy insisted, her face getting redder as she once again struggled to her feet. 'I'm the boss and I say that you're taking those two days off from tomorrow and oooh! Oh! Goodness.' Posy sank back down on the sofa with a little gasp, hands clutched round her bump. 'It's all right. Just another funny turn.'

Sebastian dropped to his knees again, his hands in the prayer position. 'Vicar's daughter,' he began, his eyes fixed imploringly on Verity who sniffed.

'I have a name, you know.'

'Verity,' Sebastian amended. 'Dear, sweet Verity. Will you please take the agreed two days off from this shop during the busiest time of the year so I can get my beloved wife and unborn child safely home? Please? Will you do that for me?'

'But who will look after the shop?' Verity asked with a desperate look around at the assembled company as if she doubted that there was a designated adult among them.

'Me! I will!' Nina's hand shot up. 'I can do it. I'll *ace* it. I'm always keen to take on new responsibility.'

Verity looked doubtful. 'Are you?'

'Unfair and also unkind,' Nina admonished, wagging her finger at her colleague. 'Look at how I've revolutionised the marketing and social media side of the business.'

'I do the Twitter,' Tom reminded everyone. 'My Twelve Days of Christmas tweets are going down a storm.'

'Well done you,' Nina said in a very patronising tone. 'Look Very, I am ready and able to assume the reins of power.'

Mattie shot Tom a sympathetic smile but luckily she had no skin in this fight.

'Well, if you're sure,' Verity said.

'Tattoo Girl will be fine,' Sebastian said. 'And Tom has several degrees – that has to count for something, and Sam has bookselling in his blood. What can go wrong?'

'Well, when you put it like that . . .' Posy considered what would be left of her motley workforce. 'You will keep an eye on them, won't you, Mattie? I mean, from one successful businesswoman to another, I'm counting on you.'

As if Mattie didn't have enough to do! 'I'm happy to check in but I'm sure they won't need me.'

'Too right we won't,' Nina agreed rather crushingly.

'I'm going to leave you with a very detailed trouble-shooting guide,' Verity told Nina grimly, as if she wished that she'd never become engaged to the love of her life and was now forced to take two days off work. 'And you're to call me if you need to.'

'But we won't,' Nina said with an airy little flap of her hands as if she was already waving them off. 'Right, Tom?'

'Right,' Tom agreed with a beleaguered sigh. 'I have worked here for the last five years. Longer than Nina, in case you've forgotten, and I'm certain that whatever curve-balls fate might throw at us, we'll be able to catch them.'

'If you say so.' Posy didn't sound convinced but her face was its normal colour once more. 'Very well. Sebastian, you can take me home now.'

'I love the way you make it seem like you had a choice, Morland,' Sebastian noted, but his expression was tender as he helped Posy up from the sofa.

CHAPTER 26

8 days until Christmas

They should have known, after the whole Christmas decorations debacle, that the power of being in charge would go to Nina's head.

Although it was freezing, with frost glittering on the cobblestones and a bitter wind wrapping around them, they gathered in the mews the next morning to wave off a suitably embarrassed Verity (who'd insisted on coming in so she could go through the website orders protocol with Tom and Sam one last time) and Johnny as if they were going off to war, rather than taking the A1 to Lincolnshire. As Johnny's car turned the corner in Rochester Street, Nina clapped her hands.

'Right, you lot,' she said rather belligerently. 'I'm not paying you to stand around doing nothing. Back to work!'

'Whatever!' Sam shrugged this off while Tom looked

down his nose (which was pink with cold) at his power-mad colleague.

'Actually, Nina, I think you'll find that *you* don't pay me at all,' he pointed out.

'I pay myself because I'm my own boss,' Mattie said, which earned her a furious glare from Nina, but Mattie was already hurrying back to the tearooms. It was too cold to stay out there simply for the joy of annoying Nina.

Besides, it was toasty warm in the tearooms, the air thick with the scent of freshly brewing coffee and the cinnamon and gingerbread cupcakes that Mattie was baking. Because, yes, it seemed as if the ban on cupcakes was well and truly over – why should she deprive the world of her cupcakes because they reminded her of Steven's perfidy? Mattie made great cupcakes and the world was a better place for them.

Also, at £4 per cupcake (which was not expensive for London) the mark-up on them was spectacular. No wonder Mattie was in such a good mood that she even pretended not to notice that Sophie and Cuthbert were wearing matching light-up Santa hats. 'From the pound shop,' Mattie heard Sophie tell a customer proudly.

Although Mattie had promised to check in on Happy Ever After, it was a promise that was hard to keep. The tearooms were frantic and when she'd popped in mid-morning with a plate of spiced buns, telling Nina they were free because she'd forgotten to add mixed peel to them, Nina had said, with a straight face, 'Don't bring me problems, Mattie. Bring me solutions.'

'I'll bring her a flea in her ear,' Mattie had muttered to Tom as she left the shop.

'It's a hundred times worse for Sam and I than it is for you,' Tom had whispered from his sentry duty at the Mistletoe Booth.

Mattie had fled through the anterooms to the sound of Nina shouting, 'You're not getting paid to chat, Tom!'

But by four o'clock, the tearooms were frantic in a more manageable way, and Mattie thought she should probably make sure that Tom and Sam hadn't gone on strike over their impossible working conditions.

They hadn't. Though Sam was mostly obscured by the large stack of books he was carrying. 'Can't stop. Post Office van is coming to collect the website orders in thirty minutes.' Mattie lunged forward to steer him away from the baby reindeer, which he was about to fall over.

Nina was policing the Mistletoe Booth *and* taking payment for books on her iPad *and* wasn't looking quite so happy any more. Heavy was the head that wore the crown, or in this case a tinsel tiara.

'Mattie!' she cried forlornly. 'Be a love and grab a handful of bookmarks, carrier bags and tote bags from the display unit nearest to the counter. They're in the bottom drawer.'

For the next five minutes, Mattie bagged and bookmarked for a chastened and grateful Nina. 'I thought being in charge would be fun. But it turns out that it's the complete opposite of fun,' she said. Then she banged on the booth. 'Come on, you've been in there two minutes! Time's up!'

Now wasn't the time to point out that the Mistletoe

Booth wasn't really such a great idea. Mattie settled for a less controversial, 'Where's Tom?'

Nina groaned. 'He's in one of the anterooms, helping a customer. Been ages actually. Could you go and hurry him along?'

The bagging and bookmarking had died down so Mattie went through the Regency room into Historical, past Non-fiction and Foreign Language and in the tiny room that housed Happy Ever After's sizeable stock of Erotica she found a man and woman, and Tom halfway up an ancient and rather rickety ladder, reaching books down from the top shelf.

Mattie didn't want to startle Tom as he was perched so precariously with his hands full. Not just with several volumes of Erotica (why was Posy even selling the very unromantic *Collected Works of the Marquis de Sade*?) but with the woman who was ordering him about in a very high-handed manner.

'No, dear,' she drawled. 'I don't want a condensed version of *My Secret Life*. I want all seven volumes.' She turned to her companion and arched one thin, impeccably shaped brow. 'God, you just can't get the staff these days.'

How rude, Mattie thought, glaring at the woman's back. She was very striking. Tall and slim, all the better to show-case the tight black leather trousers and black leather jacket she was wearing, accessorised with a pair of heels so high that they'd even give Nina pause for thought. Her face was in profile, framed by a sleek, glossy, razor-sharp black bob.

She was actually much older than Mattie had thought. About the same age as Sandrine, who was in her late fifties and equally well preserved so that she could be early forties on a good day and in flattering light. Though Sandrine wasn't one for skin-tight leather. Not that Mattie was judging.

'Darling, I'm sorry this is such a bore,' the woman cooed at her companion, who was tall and what Sophie would call 'a fittie'. He was also head to toe in leather and when he turned to nuzzle the woman's neck, Mattie could see that he was much younger than his girlfriend. He appeared younger than Mattie and she was going to be twenty-nine next birthday. But still, she wasn't judging. Age was just a number and love didn't ask for a date of birth before making its presence felt.

'It is very boring,' the young man agreed in a voice of studied disdain, as if showing any genuine emotion was too uncool for words. 'What a dreary, sad little shop. All these romance novels.' He shuddered and made it sound as if romance novels were somewhere between bin juice and flying ants on the scale of horrible things.

'I suppose sad old spinsters and housewives have to get their jollies from somewhere.' The woman barked out a laugh (and yes, now Mattie was judging her and finding her sadly wanting) then turned her attention back to Tom when he coughed nervously.

'Um, well. Let me just . . . I could count . . .' Tom didn't seem able to speak in full sentences.

'Come on! Spit it out. Some of us have proper jobs to get back to,' the woman said.

'We . . . we have got all seven volumes of *My Secret Life*,' Tom said, his knuckles white as they clutched a pile of books. 'Shall I get them down for you?'

'Hmmm, let me think.' The woman rested one long, red talon on her chin. 'A bit too vanilla for me. What else have you got, Tommy? I know it's not really your forte, but you could at least *try* to think outside the box.'

This hide-clad harpy knew Tom? *Tommy*? This woman who was now resting her hand proprietorially on the bottom of the young man that she was with.

Mattie thought her brain might short circuit. What was going on?

For one split second Tom rested his forehead against the top rung of the ladder. His shoulders rose and fell as he took a deep breath. 'I suppose if you wanted to go outside the box, then you could try werewolf erotica. Mermen are quite popular with our more adventurous readers,' Tom said in a very polite voice.

'Bor-ing!' the woman declared. 'Though I can't imagine why I'd expect anything else from you, Tommy.'

That was enough! No one was going to talk to Tom like that on Mattie's watch, or treat him so appallingly. The only person who was allowed to treat Tom appallingly was Mattie, but that was in the past and they were friends now, and friends didn't let their friends get spoken to like that.

Mattie took a step back only so she could step forward, as if she was coming into the little room for the first time. 'Tom! There you are!' she cried in quite a breathy voice. All three of them turned to look at her. The woman flicked her eyes over Mattie, standing there in her apron with her name embroidered on it, then looked away with little interest, as did her manchild a second later. Tom's expression verged on horrified, even though Mattie was there to rescue him, so by rights he should look a lot more relieved.

'Here I am,' he confirmed. 'Did you need me for something?'

'Well, the shop's really busy. And there's an Italian man who no one can understand, but I know you talk Latin so I thought you might be able to get the general gist of what he wants,' she said, fluttering her lashes for all that they were worth.

'Well, yes, I suppose ancient Latin and modern Italian do share some similar ethnography,' Tom agreed gravely and Mattie would have done anything for him to crack a little conspiratorial smile at her. Hell, she'd even settle for a smirk, though usually when Tom smirked it annoyed her beyond all measure.

'And there's this other woman who wants to know what order to read Jane Austen's novels in, and we all decided that you'd be the best person to answer that, and something very complicated and technical has gone wrong with one of the iPads, again you're the only one who knows how to do complicated and technical stuff and . . . and . . .' Mattie paused because she was running out of breath, and also for dramatic effect.

'And?' Tom prompted.

Mattie giggled girlishly and ducked her head. 'And I missed you!'

'You . . . did?' Tom asked uncertainly because he might have several degrees but he certainly didn't have a clue.

'Of course I did,' Mattie assured him with another outrageous flutter of her eyelashes as he finally climbed down from the ladder. 'I'd hurry if I were you. The Italian man was becoming quite agitated.'

Head down, Tom brushed past the leather twins and when he got to Mattie, he patted her arm in what might have been a silent 'thank you' or just a 'you're blocking my exit and I need to get the hell out of here'.

Either way, Tom was gone so Mattie could look the other woman dead in the eye, her expression as icy as her voice: 'Can I help you with something?'

The woman returned Mattie's frosty look with amusement. 'No, dear. I'll wait for darling Tommy to come back.'

Mattie folded her arms and she could feel her features harden, was pretty sure she had a warning glint in her eye because manchild took a hasty step back. '*Tom* won't be coming back. As manager of our bookshop—'

'*Romantic fiction* bookshop,' the woman said like romantic fiction hardly counted as reading.

'As manager of our bookshop,' Mattie repeated as if she hadn't been rudely interrupted, 'the week before Christmas he's rather busy, so if you want to buy a book, I can help you. And if you just want to waste our time, I can show you where the door is. What's it to be?'

The woman pursed her rather thin but blood-red lips together so tightly that they all but disappeared and shot Mattie a positively malevolent look.

There was a moment of silence so tense and thick that Mattie could have chopped it into thin slices with her sharpest knives, then Miss Leather 2018 dropped her gaze first, because Mattie had right and reason on her side.

'Don't worry, dear, we're going,' she said. 'Come on, Ally.'

She clicked her fingers at her companion as if he was a little dog. He quickly came to heel. 'It's Alex,' he said in a stage whisper. 'And I still need to buy a Christmas present for my sister. It's why we came here in the first place.'

'We're leaving,' his lady friend said in a quiet and furious voice, sweeping away through the anterooms in a cloud of black leather and Dior's Poison until she got to the main room and was forced to stop sweeping and inch her way through the crowds. She even had to say, 'Excuse me,' through gritted teeth to two young couples who were blocking the door as they waited for their Mistletoe Booth pictures to come tumbling out of the slot.

'I'm really sorry,' Ally/Alex mouthed at Mattie, though he didn't have anything to be sorry about other than his questionable taste in girlfriends.

Then they were gone.

Mattie breathed a deep sigh of relief and looked around the shop for Tom. He was currently doing something to Bertha with a Philips screwdriver while Nina stood over him. 'Be gentle with her,' Nina admonished. 'Don't think much of your bedside manner, Doctor Love.'

'Oh for God's sake, stop calling me that ridiculous name,' Tom snapped. He wasn't being sarcastic or weary or even lofty but snapping like a man who was at the very end of his very last nerve.

Then he looked up from his ministrations and caught Mattie's eye, but only for a second. Not even a second. A nanosecond, then he looked away, his gaze stricken as if he couldn't bear for her to see him.

CHAPTER 27

8 days until Christmas

I f memory served Mattie right, whenever she made her chilli chocolate brownies for shop events, Tom would haunt the refreshments table, snatching up yet another brownie when he thought no one was looking. So, that night, after her prep session, she set to work in the tearoom kitchen; tripling her quantities so she'd have enough brownies left over to sell the next day.

It was gone ten o'clock when Mattie finally left the kitchen carrying a plate with twenty-four chilli chocolate brownies piled high. She was pretty sure that she hadn't seen Tom leave the shop at all and as she climbed the stairs, her heart quickened with every step, until it became a pounding as she opened the door to see Tom in the kitchen standing over the stove.

He looked up, glanced her way long enough that Mattie

could see he still looked mortified, and then turned back to the oven.

'I come bearing gifts,' she announced in a perky voice, which didn't suit her. 'Chocolate is the universal panacea, isn't it?'

'I don't have much of a sweet tooth and I don't have anything that needs panacea-ing,' Tom said tightly: he could hardly look at her.

Mattie could feel herself start to bristle. She hadn't done anything wrong! On the contrary, she'd rescued Tom from . . . Oh! Then she got it. Or at least she understood why Tom was looking so unhappy and kept avoiding her gaze. She couldn't know what history there was between Tom and that horrible woman in leather but she'd been witness to her attempts to humiliate him. In much the same way that Tom had seen Steven gaslighting her.

Nobody in their right mind wanted an audience when they were exposed and at their most vulnerable. Mattie certainly hadn't, but in the end she'd been glad that Tom had been there to help her when she couldn't quite help herself.

'Tom,' she said softly, coming into the kitchen and placing the plate of brownies down on the table. 'I know you're a strong, intelligent man who doesn't need rescuing, but just like when Steven was here and you stepped in, I couldn't bear to see that horrible woman treating you like that. Please don't be cross with me for having your back. Who even was she?'

He didn't reply but carried on stirring whatever he was

cooking, which made an awful scrapey sound that had Mattie wincing.

A dreadful thought occurred to Mattie.

'Oh my God, is she . . . is she your *mum*?'

'No! God, no!' Tom whirled around from the stove. 'A world of no. How could you even think that?'

Mattie held up her hands in despair. 'You never talk about your family! You're not giving me a lot to work with here, are you?' She came close enough to Tom that she could place her hand ever so lightly on his arm, so he'd hardly be able to feel her touch through the cotton of his shirt and the wool of his hideous cardigan. 'We have a house rule . . .'

'We have more house rules that I can remember,' Tom conceded in a more Tom-like way than he'd sounded for hours.

'We have a house rule that states that what happens up here stays up here, so anything you want to tell me, any confidences you might want to share, I'll take them to the grave,' Mattie promised. And then she couldn't bear it any longer: she took the fork, the non-stick saucepan-destroying fork out of Tom's hand, and tossed it lightly in the sink. 'I have a bottle of vodka in the freezer. Christmas gift from Stefan from the Swedish deli for helping him out with sourcing—'

'It's against my principles to accept Christmas gifts, you know how I feel about Christmas . . .'

'Oh, shut up. It's bad manners to turn down free premium vodka,' Mattie said, steering Tom into a chair. 'Just the thing to counteract the chilli heat from my brownies.'

She got two shot glasses and two side-plates down from the cupboard and let Tom have half a brownie and a couple of generous sips of vodka, before she tried again.

'So that woman . . . Not your mother, then?'

Tom had just taken another generous sip of vodka, which might have been the reason why he shuddered.

'God, no, please stop saying that,' Tom begged. His expression grew serious and he put down his glass so he could knit his fingers together, as he always did when he was anxious. 'She was my PhD supervisor, for a brief period, and she was my girlfriend for a little bit longer than that.'

Not spitting out a mouthful of vodka took all of Mattie's powers of restraint, as it was she choked as it went down her throat, eyes watering, as Tom gave her a slightly exasperated look.

'Girlfriend?' she spluttered, frantically searching for some way to process what she'd just heard. Her gaze settled on the frayed cuff of Tom's woolly cardigan. 'You don't seem her type.'

'Oh, I was *exactly* her type,' Tom said a little bitterly. 'I was young, hopelessly naïve, easily flattered, just how Candace likes her men. But, ironically, when I decided that I was going to write my dissertation on the effects feminism has had on romantic fiction, she went right off me.'

Again, so much to process. 'She what? Can you rewind?' Mattie asked.

So, Tom rewound to when he arrived in London to do his PhD, with a first-class honours degree from Durham University and very little experience with women apart from a few short-term relationships and six months with a girl called Lizzie, who'd cheated on him with her landlord.

'I was dazzled by Candace. She'd written three books, was a leading expert in the semantics of erotica and had gone down in university legend for throwing a copy of Freud's *Group Analysis of the Ego* at a boy who'd had the audacity to fall asleep in one of her lectures. I was besotted. I had no idea that I was just the latest in a long line of wet-behind-the-ears postgraduates that she seduced and then recreated in her own image.'

They were two shot glasses of vodka down so Mattie felt brave enough to ask the question that had been haunting her for the last fifteen minutes. 'Did she . . . did she . . . get you up in leather too?'

Tom shut his eyes. 'Yes.' It was barely a whisper. 'It gets worse than that. I was going to write my dissertation on recurring themes of sadomasochism in romantic novels. Her mother was a very successful romantic novelist in the eighties and Candace hates both romantic novels and her mother. Now, of course, I realise that it's a classic anti-Oedipus complex—'

'Eh?'

'It's not important,' he assured her. 'Suffice to say that my dissertation was going to be a savage takedown of the romance genre and its readers, who were all desperate to be dominated by an alpha male so they could abrogate all responsibility for their sad little lives.'

'Oh, Tom,' Mattie couldn't keep the disappointment out of her voice. She was no expert but she'd read enough romance novels about women setting up their own successful cafés and cake shops to know that 'romance novels are *nothing* like that.'

'Well, yes. I arrived at the same conclusion as soon as I began reading a cross-section of them. I'd realised that romance novels, which were largely written by women for women, were social history documents about the way that gender roles had evolved over the last fifty years. I'd argue the case, as I did when I defended my dissertation, that more than anything, romance novels are also unclaimed feminist texts.'

'But surely Candace must have been pleased about your feminist awakening.' Mattie frowned. Candace had looked very much like a woman who had no truck with any man who thought he was better.

'She was furious. Didn't like dissent in the ranks or anything that interfered with her own rigid academic agenda.' Tom sighed unhappily. Then he poured out another measure of vodka into his shot glass and downed it in one, wincing as the liquid fire hit his belly. 'She humiliated me in front of the undergraduate class I was teaching. Called me a milksop and said the reason I couldn't wrap my puny and quite unremarkable mind around the concept of the alpha male was because I was as far from an alpha male as it was possible to get.'

It was Mattie's turn to wince. 'Ouch. That's brutal.'

'Especially as I was standing there all trussed up in the leather trousers she'd bought me,' Tom said with a full-on shudder this time. 'It all but destroyed me. Everything I believed about myself, I suddenly doubted.'

'But she didn't destroy you,' Mattie pointed out. 'You're still here. You're still in one piece and you *did* write your dissertation about feminism and alpha males and romance novels, and now you're an *actual* doctor.'

'All of that is down to Lavinia,' Tom said and just saying her name made his face light up and his voice grow warm and tender. 'I came to Bookends to buy some reading material. Solely because it was guaranteed that I wouldn't see anybody I knew while I was stocking up on bodice rippers.'

The Bookends that Mattie vaguely remembered from the two occasions that she'd visited it to talk to Posy about taking on the tearooms had been a run-down shop full of dark wood and dark corners. It was amazing the difference that Posy's grey-with-clover-pink-accents paint job and some strategically placed spotlights had made to the interior. Not to mention the whole rebranding as a 'one-stop shop for all your romantic fiction needs'.

'It's just as well that Posy or Verity or Nina didn't serve you,' she mused, grinning at the thought.

Tom pulled an anguished face. 'I go hot and cold just thinking about it. But it was before Verity and Nina's time, thank God, and Lavinia got to me before Posy did. I kept coming back. Not just to buy books but because I looked forward to our conversations about them and, being Lavinia, she encouraged me to trust my instincts and my intellect instead of trying to mould them to fit into the narrow box where Candace wanted to put them.'

'I would have loved to have met Lavinia,' Mattie said

because everything she'd heard about the former owner was delightful; a kind, caring, mischievous woman who didn't suffer fools, though Mattie couldn't help but think of herself as foolish. While Tom had been confessing how he'd been naïve enough to fall prey to Candace, Mattie couldn't help but think of the wide-eyed, impulsive girl she used to be. A silly foolish girl who'd wasted two years of her life loving Steven.

'Lavinia would have liked you.' Tom splashed more vodka into their glasses, his hands now a little unsteady. 'She'd have been thrilled to have the tearooms open again. Lavinia loved cake.'

'She definitely sounds like my kind of woman.'

'On Fridays, she'd go on what she'd call a bun run,' Tom recalled, with a faraway look. 'She'd take a taxi to Patisserie Valerie in Soho and get us all our favourite cakes. Lavinia loved a good Bakewell tart. For her eightieth birthday we had a gigantic one with her name iced on it sent all the way from the actual town of Bakewell.'

Mattie was quite partial to a Bakewell tart herself and immediately her mind was racing with things that she could do with frangipane as a tribute to Lavinia. Maybe a play on a Bakewell tart with fresh raspberries and . . .

'. . . anyway, when Candace tried to get my PhD funding stopped, Lavinia saved the day. It helped that she was particularly pally with the Dean of the English Department, so I was assigned another, far more simpatico supervisor and Lavinia offered me a part-time job so I could jack in delivering pizzas.'

The shocks just kept on coming. '*You* can drive a moped?'

Tom grinned, which wiped away all the strain that this trip down his own memory lane had caused him. 'That's the part that surprises you?'

Mattie grinned back. 'Well, yeah. I mean, *you* on a moped!' She gave Tom a thoughtful look. 'Why didn't you tell Posy and Verity any of this? I'm sure they'd have been nothing but supportive.'

'Yes, the two women who have had a four-year running gag about writing me up in the mythical sexual harassment book,' Tom said dryly.

'I thought Nina had invented the sexual harassment book.'

'Verity,' Tom confirmed.

'No!'

'Yes!' Tom put his glasses back on, though Mattie preferred him without them. Not because he was more attractive without his glasses (and where had that little idea come from?) but because he looked more unguarded, approachable.

'How funny though, that Bookends then became a specialist romantic fiction bookshop,' Mattie mused.

'Yes, hilarious. I tried to persuade Posy it was a bad idea but she was having none of it,' Tom said with a sniff.

'And all this time you pretended that you *hated* romantic fiction.'

'See, I never actually said that I *hated* romantic fiction. People just assumed. When people assume, they make an ass out of you and me.'

'You are so full of it,' Mattie said, staring at him. Tom stared right back at her so she was suddenly self-conscious about her face. Not what it looked like, there wasn't much she could do about that, but that she still couldn't tear her eyes away from him and she wasn't sure what to do with her mouth. Licking her lips or catching the bottom one between her teeth, or even letting her mouth hang open slightly, all felt odd. And the more she contorted her mouth, the more Tom stared. Who could blame him?

And yet the Tom she was staring at was very different from the Tom he'd been describing. 'So . . . is that why you wear all these old clothes? The bow-ties, the cardigans? Because it's about as far away from wearing black leather as you can get?'

'Can we never mention the black leather thing ever again?' Tom asked, then he looked down at his clothes. 'I suppose they are quite the antithesis of my former wardrobe, but also I was a very poor PhD student on part-time bookseller wages so I could only afford second-hand clothes. And I did find it rather amusing to affect the look of what one imagines an academic or a bookseller might wear . . .'

'Yeah, if they were born a hundred years ago.' Mattie held her hands up. 'Not that I'm judging.'

'Though funnily enough, you sound very judgemental,' Tom tried to narrow his eyes but only succeeded in squinting. 'And as you're someone who wears the same outfit every day, I don't really think you're in a position to pass judgement on my sartorial choices.'

'Not the *same* outfit. I have multiple copies,' Mattie

protested. 'Like a uniform. Saves me from having to plan an outfit every day and anyway, what I wear is mostly hidden by an apron.'

'I did wonder if the all-black ensembles were meant to make you look unattractive—'

'I *beg* your pardon?' That stung almost as much as the quick shot of vodka that Mattie gulped down.

'Yes, because you hate *all* men. Apart from your brother and Cuthbert . . .' Tom paused, not because of Mattie's furious intake of breath but because he was pouring himself another shot of vodka. 'Who else? Maybe Sam – by the way, I caught him and Little Sophie snogging in the Foreign Language section, which was beyond awkward, but I digress – you also don't hate the guy who supplies your fruit and veg, and I think that's it.'

Mattie scraped her chair back so she could stand over Tom and glare at him.

'I don't dress in black to make myself look unattractive to men. What a ridiculous thing to say. You're ridiculous!'

Tom glared back and then he was getting to his feet too.

'You're more ridiculous!' he insisted and they were nose to nose now, or they would have been if Tom weren't a good eight inches taller than Mattie.

She had to tilt her head. 'No! I think you'll find that you're much more ridiculous than I am.'

It was funny peculiar rather than funny haha, but looking up at Tom should have ensured that Mattie caught him at his most unflattering angle, but he was looking down at her and his face was all tight and prissy, which actually did wonderful things to his cheekbones. Tom had cheek-bones?

'You are the most ridiculous person since records began,' Tom countered, and this was the most pointless, most stupid, yes, most *ridiculous* argument that Mattie had ever had.

'You . . . you're much more ridiculous than I am. In your ridiculous glasses that you don't even need.' And Mattie couldn't believe that she was doing this, reaching up quickly to pluck the glasses from Tom's face before he realised what she was doing.

He didn't blink owlishly at her, which he would have done if he'd needed to wear them. Instead his eyes, which were practically all pupil, narrowed.

'You shouldn't have done that,' he said in a low voice, which made something in Mattie quiver in a very good, very unexpected way.

'Why not?' Mattie tilted her chin in a way that her family and close friends knew only too well. It meant that she was spoiling for a fight; that she wasn't going to back down from a challenge. 'What are you going to do about it?'

There was a moment's pause, both of them breathing hard, so that Mattie imagined that she could hear the beat of her own frantically pounding heart.

She locked eyes with Tom, lifted her chin again . . .

'I'm going to do *this*.' And before Mattie could ask what *this* was, Tom was kissing her.

Tom was kissing her!

Mattie was kissing Tom!

His mouth moving on hers insistently, passionately and with considerable expertise, and Mattie's kissing skills might have been rusty and all but forgotten these last two years, but it was all coming back to her now.

How lovely it was to be held in someone's arms, his hands splayed on her hips as her hands wound through his hair so that he couldn't escape even if he wanted to.

Though he didn't seem to want to. In fact, he seemed quite happy to be kissing her, one hand sliding up her body in a slow, unhurried and entirely pleasurable way to cradle her cheek.

Tom's mouth became more insistent, more demanding, and he twisted them both round so that he could bump her up on to the edge of the table, not that Mattie minded, as she wrapped her legs around his waist. She gave in to the insistence, the demand and opened up to him so she could taste vodka and chocolate and chilli heat that was no match for the sudden fire in her blood, in her belly; as if she'd spent the last two years encased in ice and Tom had turned up with a blowtorch . . .

But hang on! She didn't want to be set free. She was perfectly fine in her ice prison, not cold at all, but safe. Prisons didn't just keep people in, they kept other people out. Mattie pulled herself from Tom's arms, and put a hand to her tingling lips.

'Wow, what was *that* about?' Mattie asked slowly because she really wanted to know. 'Did you kiss me or did I kiss you?'

Tom shook his head and held up a hand to his own lips,

which looked twice the size that they had done before. His face was flushed and his eyes were dark. It was as if Mattie was seeing him for the very first time. Not the sort of man that you'd ever be embarrassed to kiss even if he was wearing that awful cardigan with the leather patches on the elbows.

He snatched up his glasses from the table, put them on and Superman was back to being Clark Kent. He stepped back and detangled himself from her legs, leaning back against the fridge as though he couldn't hold himself up.

She'd been kissing Tom! Not even being kissed by Tom, but mutual kissing.

'What just happened?' Mattie asked again.

She waited for Tom to say something sneering about how she was still ridiculous and what's more, she kissed ridiculously. He cleared his throat and Mattie steeled herself for Tom at his most cutting.

'Oh God, Mattie, I'm so sorry. So sorry. Oh dear. What ever must you think of me?' Tom took his glasses off again so he could polish them on the end of his shirt, which had come untucked. Mainly because Mattie had untucked it. Now she could see smooth skin, taut muscles and she had a sudden memory of how they'd felt under her hand, and it was her turn to flush . . .

'Really, I can't apologise enough,' Tom said quickly, mistaking Mattie's pink cheeks as a sign of maidenly outrage. 'I don't know what came over me. Forcing myself on you . . .'

'No!' Mattie had to stop him right there. 'You didn't

force yourself on me. I was a willing kissee. Not even a kissee. I was a kisser. *I was kissing you*. Why did we do that?'

'I don't know.'

They looked at each other, confusion writ large on their faces.

'I absolutely don't fancy you,' Mattie said because she wanted Tom, and herself, to be very clear about that.

'Believe me, I don't fancy you either.' Tom frowned.

'It must never happen again,' Mattie said with grim finality.

'Too right.' Tom took a step and collapsed into the chair he'd been sitting on, as if his legs really could no longer support him. 'Look, you don't have to worry . . . I'll . . . I'll move out.'

'Really, you don't have to move out,' she said with feeling. 'I'm sure it was just a heat-of-the-moment thing.'

'Well, if you're sure.' Tom could hardly keep the relief out of his voice. 'And you don't have to worry that I'm going to make a habit of kissing you.'

'I should think not!' Mattie had to tear her eyes away from Tom sitting there, with his shirt still untucked, his lips all kiss-bitten, long legs stretched out. She quickly gathered their glasses and their brownie plates, so she could hurry to the sink and not have to look at him because looking at him was making her come undone. 'New house rule: No kissing! Agreed?'

'Agreed!' Tom said quickly. 'So we're good then, you and I?'

They were far from good. They'd only recently formed

a fragile friendship, which now seemed in jeopardy and, to make cohabiting even more complicated, they'd just kissed like kissing was about to be rationed.

'Of course we're good!' Mattie assured him, turning around to flash Tom a bright and insincere smile.

'So that's all sorted then,' Tom said. 'Everything's great.'

'Never been better,' Mattie chirped, turning back to the sink so she could pull an agonised face at the glass she was rinsing.

CHAPTER 28

7 days until Christmas

Mattie hardly slept that night. Every time she closed her eyes, she was assaulted by a sense memory of being kissed by Tom. An HD, 3D, surround-sound playback of Tom kissing her and Mattie clinging to him like he was about to go off to war. Then she'd have to fling the covers back to cool down.

But she must have fallen asleep at some point because she was rudely awakened by the persistent buzz of her phone.

'I'm down here with all your fruit and veg and a traffic warden who's circling the block,' said Charlie when Mattie answered it, and she realised that she'd overslept and had to fly downstairs in her pyjamas to sort out the delivery. There had been a thick ground frost overnight and her fingers were blue by the time she waved Charlie off.

The rude awakening set the tone for the rest of the day. Mattie never managed to catch up with herself and was still in her pyjamas trying to frantically get her breakfast bakes done in time, when Meena, Cuthbert and finally Sophie arrived.

And it was just as well that Mattie didn't have a spare moment because when her brain wasn't busy enough, it was devoted to Tom. Tom's lips. Tom's hands on her hips. Tom . . . coming into the tearooms at exactly thirteen minutes past ten, as he did every morning. As if last night, *the kiss*, had never happened.

Of course, he arrived during the two minutes when Mattie had left the kitchen so she could arrange her second batch of morning pastries, still warm from the oven, on the counter.

'Hello,' Tom said, swallowing hard.

'Hello,' Mattie said, clutching onto her pastry tongs as if they were the last lifebelt on the *Titanic*. 'I've got a bit of a sore head this morning. Have had to ban Cuthbert from playing any of his awful Christmas carols until after lunch.'

'That's verging on blasphemy,' Cuthbert said mildly. Then he went back to whistling 'Once in Royal David's City', which was annoying at the best of times (both whistling and song choice) but especially when Mattie was mildly hungover, sleep-deprived and kiss-sore. Because she'd kissed Tom last night. And Tom had kissed her back.

'Anyway, last night is a bit of a blur,' Mattie lied. 'There was a lot of vodka.'

Tom nodded gratefully. 'So much vodka. I have complete

amnesia. By the way, I'm out tonight,' he added with what seemed to Mattie heavy emphasis, as if he was worried that she might be getting ideas that they'd have another cosy night in and end up kissing each other again. Not that he could remember that they'd already kissed, or so he claimed, even though it had been some pretty stellar kissing.

'I have plans too,' Mattie said, though the plans mostly involved a pizza delivery and lights out before ten.

'Great,' Tom said.

'Great,' Mattie echoed. She brandished her tongs. 'Are you going to order something, then?'

Tom's croque missus had become something of a daily habit, but this morning he said that Meena had already made him a bacon sandwich when she was frying bacon for the pig-in-blanket rolls in the upstairs kitchen. 'Just a maximum-strength black coffee, though I am still quite peckish. Maybe a couple of croissants to keep me going until lunchtime.'

After that, Mattie would have been quite happy to avoid Tom for the foreseeable future, but she had promised Posy to check in at the shop. And Posy wasn't to know that last night Mattie had known the touch of Tom's lips. Oh God! She had to stop thinking about the kissing, the really good kissing, especially as Tom had no memory of it.

Thankfully, checking in at the shop didn't require much more than poking her head around the Classics arch and shouting over the heads of the heaving throng of customers, 'You all right, Nina?'

'I suppose,' Nina called back rather plaintively – but if she really needed help, then she'd have asked for it. Nina was hardly a shy, retiring wallflower incapable of expressing her needs and desires. Ha!

It wasn't until after the lunchtime rush that Mattie even had a chance to look at her phone to see that she had five missed calls from Posy and numerous text messages demanding to know why Mattie was screening her calls.

'About time!' Posy squawked, answering Mattie's call on first ring. 'Put me on speaker and take me through to the shop!'

'Everything all right, Pose?' Mattie asked, though she didn't appreciate Posy's peremptory tone. 'Is there something preventing you from calling Nina or Tom yourself?'

Posy gave a growl of pure annoyance. 'They won't take my calls.'

The tearooms were busy but not horribly so and Sophie, who'd gone AWOL for ten minutes, had now returned with suspiciously tousled hair and noticeably reddened lips, so Mattie was free to do Posy's bidding.

'You've been calling them a lot?' she guessed as she walked through the anterooms.

'I wouldn't say a lot. I don't think calling every half hour is excessive,' Posy mused.

'Kind of is. So, how's the bed rest working out for you?'

'I'm horizontal as we speak,' Posy said. 'I even have my feet propped up. I'm very calm. Goodness, how long does it take to walk a few metres to the shop?'

'You don't sound very calm, Posy,' Mattie said, stepping

into the main room of the shop and grabbing a passing Nina by the arm. 'Got Nina here for you.'

Nina was already trying to make a run for it while making slashing motions with her hand.

'AM I ON SPEAKER?'

'Yes, and no need to shout,' Nina said with a dramatic rolling of her eyes. She wriggled free of Mattie's grip and pulled a book off the shelf she was standing by. 'You've all but perforated my eardrum!' Then she turned to the customer she had in tow. 'This one is very good. It's a contemporary version of *Vanity Fair* that saves you the bother of actually reading *Vanity Fair*.'

The customer nodded and Nina took her over to the counter to pay, with Mattie following like a little dog, while Posy complained non-stop about Nina's inability to answer a phone.

'I'm perfectly able to answer a phone,' Nina said. 'I just didn't want to talk to you for, like, the twentieth time in one hour.'

'That's a total exaggeration!'

'You wouldn't be checking up on Verity like this.'

Posy growled again – it couldn't be good for her blood pressure. 'That's why I'm calling. I've spoken to Very and she says that she's not coming back tomorrow!'

'Why ever not?' Tom popped his head around the Regency arch – Posy's voice was so loud, they could probably hear her all the way down Rochester Street. 'She'd better have a good reason. Tomorrow is the last Friday before Christmas!'

341

'Snow!' Posy all but shrieked. 'There's heavy snow in Lincolnshire and Verity says that the roads are completely impassable. Nobody can get in or out of the village.'

'Snow up north is different to snow down south,' Tom said knowledgeably as he took a customer's credit card and scanned it on his iPad. 'It's much more deep and crisp and even.'

'I'm on the BBC website right now,' Posy reported. 'A yellow warning isn't anything good, is it? No, it isn't. It's very, very bad.'

'Well, no wonder Very's snowed in, but we can manage without her,' Nina said with great confidence but a slightly crazed look in her eyes.

'But the BBC says that heavy snowfall is also going to blanket the south-east overnight,' Posy moaned. 'We're in the south-east! Why would it snow this close to Christmas? What is it going to do to my profit margins? Especially when I have a baby on the way.'

'We're not really the south-east,' Mattie said as Tom snorted in disbelief. 'I mean, we are, but we're London. Central London. They'll be gritting all the roads and the tube is mostly underground, so that's going to be running. It's nothing to worry about.'

'Are you sure?' Posy asked her as if Mattie was suddenly the fount of all meteorological knowledge.

'Pretty sure,' Mattie decided, even as she felt a spike of panic shoot into her. 'Though to be on the safe side, I'm going to phone my suppliers and see if they can do a delivery this evening with whatever they've got left over.'

'That's not the vote of confidence I was looking for,' Posy grumbled, but Mattie was already speedwalking back to the tearooms and trying to calculate exactly how much butter, eggs and milk she might need if blizzard conditions were on the way.

CHAPTER 29

6 days until Christmas

When Mattie went to bed that night not one single snowflake had fallen, even though she'd watched the weather forecast after the ten o'clock news and they were chucking around phrases like 'The Big Freeze' and 'Eight inches of snow predicted overnight.'

'I bet it will be a tiny amount of snow and it won't even settle,' she'd said to herself as she cleaned her teeth. 'But it will be just enough snow for all the trains to stop running because it's the wrong kind of snow.'

But when Mattie woke up that morning, something felt different. She lay there in the dark for a moment trying to think what it was, and then she realised – it was the silence.

She'd grown used to the hum of the city. The distant throb of traffic, the unloading of the early morning deliveries, the particular rattling sound of the dustcart, which always did its rounds as Mattie was waking up.

But this morning, someone had muted the outside world. Already shivering in anticipation, Mattie threw off her duvet and top quilt, swung her legs over the side and groped for her slippers. Wrapping herself in the quilt, she tiptoed to the window, sent up a silent prayer and then pulled back the curtain. For one awful second, she thought she might have gone suddenly blind because she couldn't see a thing.

Then she used a corner of the quilt to wipe the condensation off the window and she still couldn't see a thing because all there was to see was white.

It *had* snowed in the night. And it was still snowing now. These were the blizzard conditions they'd been promised. A complete whiteout. Mattie doubted that there was enough grit in the Greater London area to get the city to work today, never mind getting on with their Christmas shopping.

But still she showered (thanking every available deity that the pipes hadn't frozen . . . yet) and dressed and hurried downstairs.

They never left the lights on in the tearooms overnight so the place was in darkness as Mattie came in through the shop. No wonder, when the snow was swirling so heavily about the windows.

She snapped on the lights and went about her morning routine; heating up the oven, switching on Jezebel so she could drink coffee and plan the timings for her bakes. But was there any point baking if no one could get into Central London, never mind the tiny mews, to eat them?

Mattie put the radio on but the news was hardly encouraging. There were no trains running in and out of London. Buses had been abandoned at the foot of steep hills, huge tracts of the underground weren't working, schools were closed and people were being told not to make any journeys unless they were absolutely necessary.

She definitely wasn't going to make double her usual quantities of breakfast pastries, as she had been doing. Her phone rang, Sandrine's picture flashing up on the screen.

'*C'est abominable!* I was going to go into town today to finish my Christmas shopping but I can't even get out of Hackney,' Sandrine said by way of a greeting. 'What a country! One bit of snow and everything stops working.'

'To be fair, it is quite a lot of snow,' Mattie said, tucking the phone under her ear, as she began to take last night's laminated dough out of the fridge. Once Sandrine started railing against her adopted country, where she'd happily lived for thirty-five years, she was likely to be some time.

As it was, Mattie had shaped her first batch of croissants and had them in the oven before Sandrine rang off, and Mattie had another call waiting. It was Meena, full of apologies but snowed in on Muswell Hill.

'None of the buses are running because you can't get in or out of Muzzy without having to go up or down one of two really steep hills. We're so high up here, we have our own micro-climate,' she said before promising to check in a couple of hours later if the bus situation improved.

Two ladies down, Mattie thought, as she started on her

pains aux raisins, though she wondered why she was both-ering. Were they going to have any customers or, indeed, staff today?

'It's been snowing,' said a voice from the kitchen doorway and Mattie almost dropped her laden baking tray in fright.

'God, you nearly gave me a heart attack!' she told Tom. 'It's only just eight, what are you doing up so early?'

'It's been snowing,' Tom repeated.

'Yes, I'm all caught up with the weather,' Mattie said, crouching down to open the oven. Then she transferred her croissants to the bottom shelf so she could put the pains aux raisins on the middle shelf. 'Again, what are you doing out of bed before nine?'

'The silence woke me up,' Tom said, scratching his head. Obviously he hadn't had time to brush his hair, which was standing up in all directions. Much like it had been the other night when Mattie had been running her fingers through it. She gulped and looked away. 'It was too quiet to sleep. I'm used to a certain amount of ambient traffic noise.'

'Not much chance of that,' Mattie said, straightening up and getting her first proper look at Tom. She thought she'd seen all of his interesting and outdated sartorial choices but somehow the ancient navy-blue duffel coat he was currently wearing had escaped her attention. 'Nice coat.'

'Sarcasm doesn't become you,' Tom said with a sniff, which turned into a little shiver, probably because they were still being frosty with each other. 'I have no idea why I'm being so public spirited but I seem to remember that there's a shovel in the coal hole outside and so I should probably clear a path through the mews.'

'That is very public spirited of you,' Mattie agreed. She was fed up with the awkward atmosphere between them. So, they'd kissed? It was no big deal unless they made it into one. 'Do you want coffee first?'

He did and Mattie yanked a croissant out of the oven for him, then they walked through the shop, stopping to retrieve the coal hole key en route, peering out at the winter wonderland. The snow was still coming down, but maybe not as hard as it had been, so Tom unlocked the door and stepped outside. Mattie quickly shut the door, before he could let too much cold air in, and waved encouragingly at him through the glass.

He was already covered in a fine coating of snow as he lumbered, like an astronaut walking on the moon for the first time, to the coal hole, which was directly in front of the shop and accessed through a hatch. It was used to store all manner of old junk, rather than coal, though Posy had had the bad fortune to be locked in it twice. Once by Sebastian when they were both kids, and more recently by an evil property developer, though that time she'd been rescued by Sebastian.

Now Tom unlocked the hatch door and disappeared from view. He was gone quite a while, long enough for Mattie to go back to the kitchen to take out her trays and put in two new ones and then return to her vantage point, with still no sighting of him.

With a sigh, she stuck her head out of the door and

over the swirl of snowflakes and the roar of the wind, called out: 'Tom! Are you all right?'

'Can't get out,' came the muffled reply. 'Normally I'd hoist myself out, but my coat and boots are getting in the way and if I take them off to jump out, then I'll have to leave them down here.'

Mattie looked up to the heavens and was almost blinded by snow. 'Not sure I'd be any help,' she shouted doubtfully. 'I have no upper-body strength.'

'Liar! I've seen you beating sticks of cold butter and whisking stuff so fast it's a blur,' Tom called back. 'Can you go and get the kick-steps from the shop?'

'I can do that.' Mattie retrieved the little stool they used to fetch books down from the shelves not served by the rolling ladder. With an unhappy sigh, she stepped out into the mews and instantly regretted the fact that she was wearing her Converse, which were instantly soaked through, and no coat. She peered down into the coal hole where Tom stood, his head almost level with the hatch. 'You could easily jump out of there.'

'Not helping,' Tom gritted, as he held up a shovel. 'Swap you.'

With some difficulty – it was quite hard to get purchase on the ground in slippery trainers and while all her extremities were in danger of freezing – Mattie handed down the kick-steps in return for a spade.

'There's also two sacks of gritting salt down here,' Tom reported. 'Shall we heft them out?'

'If we must,' Mattie agreed, though she was glad that

Tom did most of the heavy lifting and she only needed to drag them the final few inches.

Then, despite his bulky coat and cumbersome boots, Tom managed to heft himself out with the aid of the kick-steps, which he stared at thoughtfully, then back at Mattie.

'If I dangled you down, you could just about grab hold of the steps and get them out,' he ventured.

'You are not dangling me, no way. It's absolutely against Health and Safety.' Mattie plucked at her black jumper, which was thoroughly damp. 'I'm going inside to put on non-soggy clothes but I'm super grateful that you're going to clear and grit the mews.'

'So much for gender equality,' Tom muttered, but Mattie ignored him and hurried back inside.

She'd barely had time to change and put in the next lot of breakfast pastries, when the tearoom door opened and Cuthbert announced himself.

'All this snow,' he said, taking off his trilby hat.

'I noticed,' Mattie said with a grin. She had to resist the urge to hug her barista. 'I'm so pleased to see you.'

'My five-minute commute was a ten-minute commute this morning,' Cuthbert said, pointing at his feet where old-fashioned black rubber galoshes were covering the natty brown lace-ups he preferred to wear. 'Now, young Tom looks like he's in need of sustenance.'

Mattie went over to the window to see that Tom had cut a path through the snow and was now sprinkling gritting salt in his wake. She rapped on the glass, to get his attention. He turned and raised a gloved hand in greeting.

It was quite hard to mime, 'Do you want a croque missus for when you're done? Yes, the one with the fried egg on top,' but Tom seemed to get the general idea because he gave her a thumbs up and went back to work.

When he came to claim his prize, he was accompanied by Little Sophie.

'Mum said that I could easily walk to work and she didn't raise me to give up at the first sign of trouble,' she said rather mournfully. 'Apparently no one likes a quitter.'

'Well, I'd like you no matter what, but I am glad you're here,' Mattie said, but it was past nine now, with not a customer in sight, and even as she pulled two tables together so they could all eat a communal breakfast, she wondered whether she should give it another hour then send everyone home.

'Should we phone Posy?' she asked Tom, who was face-deep into his croque missus and just shrugged. 'Do I start on the pig-in-blanket rolls? Are there any signs of life outside the mews, Sophie?'

Sophie said that the gritters had been out on Grays Inn Road and Theobald Street and as she'd continued her 'perilous journey', there had been quite a few people grimly trudging the streets.

'It's quite fun, this, isn't it?' Cuthbert said cheerfully. 'Blitz spirit and all that. I'm sure a bit of snow won't stop people from getting on with their Christmas shopping.'

'Nothing stands in the way of rampant capitalism,' said Tom, who'd finished his breakfast. 'Though I'm not looking forward to running Happy Ever After single-handed. Mind you, Sam should be all right to come in. He only lives round the corner. I'm going to WhatsUpp him now and then I'd better do a tweet to let people know we're open.' He eyed his shiny shop iPad with some distaste – he much preferred his trusty but ancient Nokia. 'Sometimes I feel like Schubert.'

Sophie looked at Mattie and mouthed, 'What the hell is he on about?' Mattie shook her head.

'Schubert?' she echoed.

'When he got to heaven the angels gave him a laurel wreath because no one had appreciated his gifts when he was alive,' Tom said sadly because he was a ridiculous drama queen.

'I did make you a croque missus,' Mattie reminded him, then jumped to her feet as the door opened and two of her regulars came in, stomping the snow off their feet as they did so. 'Good morning!'

'Cold enough for you?' asked Gerald, who owned the sweetshop on Rochester Street.

'Quite balmy, I thought,' Mattie said, walking towards the counter. 'Your usual, Gerry?'

They weren't run off their feet like they were most mornings, but there was a steady enough stream of regulars and non-regulars grateful that they were open and serving hot coffee, that Mattie decided that she'd better get cracking with her lunch bakes and make as many pig-in-blanket rolls as she could manage single-handed.

By ten o'clock, there still wasn't a single member of the Happy Ever After staff to be seen, apart from Tom, who kept popping into the tearooms with a martyred expression so he could fill them all in on the onerous duties he was expected to perform all by himself.

'It's a pity that the internet hasn't been snowed in,' he noted sourly on his latest excursion. 'All these people with their last-minute website orders because it's almost the final posting day before Christmas. They should have been more organised.'

Rather than being annoying, Tom's put-upon airs were actually quite endearing, Mattie decided as she sent him packing with yet another flaky pastry to keep his strength up. By rights, he should be the size of a house.

She walked over to the tearoom door to look out on the mews. It had almost stopped snowing. There were just the laziest of flakes drifting down and coming through the mews was a familiar figure who, predictably, laughed in the face of appropriate cold-weather gear.

Nina was wearing one of her trusty leopard-print fake-fur coats, a black beret perched at a jaunty angle on her plat-inum-blonde hair and on her feet were her beloved motorcycle boots. Though Mattie wouldn't have been surprised if Nina had been wearing her four-inch day heels because she really believed in committing to a look.

Nina looked up and waved when she saw Mattie standing in the window. Then she did a little shimmy and when Mattie smiled, Nina couldn't resist turning that shimmy into an extravagant slide like she was Tom Cruise skidding along a highly polished floor in *Risky Business*.

Except, there was no highly polished floor but cobblestones, which Tom had tried his best to clear of snow and then grit, but were still very slippery in the bits that hadn't been gritted.

And Nina kept on sliding, her grin transforming into a panicked scream as she frantically pin-wheeled her arms and tried to keep her balance. She hit one of the benches in the middle of the mews with such force that she went flying over the top of it, landing in a heap.

Mattie yanked open the door, expecting Nina to be sitting up and swearing profusely but she was motionless, just a heap of leopard print and platinum hair against a backdrop of snowy white.

Mattie was out of the door in an instant but Tom had beaten her to it, flying out of the shop door to reach Nina's side while Mattie was still gingerly taking her first steps.

By the time Mattie had picked her way over, Nina had her eyes open and was moaning wordlessly.

'Where does it hurt?' Tom asked her gently, taking her hand in his. He didn't seem to realise or care that he was kneeling in the snow as he cradled Nina's head in his lap.

'Everywhere,' Nina said faintly. 'Everywhere.'

'Nina! Oh my God, Nina!' Mattie turned to see Sam plodding steadily towards them, both arms held out for balance. 'Is she all right?'

'She's bleeding. Head wound,' Tom hissed at Mattie, who tore her eyes away from Nina to see the little patch of bright red staining the snow. 'Go and call an ambulance. I'm pretty sure she's got a couple of broken bones.'

'I'll never dance again,' Nina said in a tiny, wheezy voice.

'They'll have to find another ballerina to go on in my place.'

'Also possible concussion,' Tom added.

There was a long wait for an ambulance. Apparently people, a lot of them much older and needier than Nina, were dropping like nine-pins, so once again they had to call on the services of Cynthia, who got there as quickly as she could after Cuthbert's urgent summons.

Cynthia, wearing a spectacular orange wool coat and matching hat, quickly assessed both the situation and Nina.

'Well, you've definitely broken a couple of ribs and possibly your collarbone,' she announced. 'Not to mention a mild concussion. I don't like head wounds. They can be tricky things. Now, normally I'd say you weren't to be moved, but you can't lie here and get hypothermia, on top of everything else.' She gazed around at the little group of concerned colleagues and bug-eyed bystanders. She pointed at Tom and Sam. 'What I really need is a couple of strapping young lads, but you two will have to do.'

Very slowly and very carefully, Nina, with much gasping and biting her bottom lip, was transferred to the sofa while Mattie raced upstairs to fetch a quilt.

But by the time Mattie came back downstairs, Nina was shaking with shock and cold. 'Let's get this around you,' Cynthia said to her, taking the quilt from Mattie. 'The rest of you aren't needed if you're just going to stand around gawping.'

'I never had a chance to sort out the till float and now there's a queue of people outside,' Tom said, and they all looked over to the door, which they'd locked when they'd brought Nina in, where a small group of shivering shoppers were waiting for admittance.

Mattie felt utterly helpless and knew of only one thing she could do to offer more assistance. 'Anyone want a nice cup of tea?'

'Milk and two sugars, please,' Cynthia said, giving the uncharacteristically silent Nina one last tuck-in. 'No tea for this one in case she needs to have an operation once she gets to hospital.'

When Mattie returned with Cynthia's tea, made by her doting husband, Nina was still motionless on the sofa and Posy was on speakerphone.

'It's less than a week to Christmas! Who will manage the shop without Verity here and Nina with a gaping head wound?'

Posy's distress shocked Nina out of her inertia. 'Nobody said it was gaping.'

'It isn't gaping,' Tom called out from behind the counter where he was serving the only customer in the shop who wasn't rubbernecking the makeshift field hospital that had been set up on the sofa. 'Posy's exaggerating for dramatic effect and I will manage the shop. I have worked here for five years, you know,' he added with genuine annoyance.

'And I can do the website orders,' Sam offered. Usually he didn't offer to do anything but had to be cajoled, bribed and finally threatened in order to perform the duties he was being paid for. 'Especially if we're quiet because of the snow, I can easily get them done.'

'You can have Little Sophie too,' Mattie said.

'That's all very well, but it's meant to stop snowing tomorrow,' Posy complained. 'Then we'll be busy again and I need a grown-up in charge. No offence, Tom.'

'So much offence taken,' Tom said, flaring his nostrils. 'I am a grown-up. I'm actually a doctor . . .'

'Yeah, but a doctor of boring academic stuff, not a proper doctor,' Nina reminded him: she was obviously feeling better by the second. 'Besides, you've never once cashed up.'

'Only because Verity won't let me,' Tom pointed out. 'I'm confident that I could cash up. I could absolutely crush cashing up.'

'Posy Morland-Thorndyke, what did I tell you about your blood pressure only a couple of days ago?' Cynthia demanded of Posy.

'My blood pressure is *fine*! I'm lying down!'

If the snow was going to cease its infernal falling, that meant that the tearooms would be packed to capacity again and Mattie had enough to do as it was, but for the sake of Posy's blood pressure and the health of her unborn child . . .

'I can do the cashing up,' Mattie offered. 'And I will help Tom, who really is a perfectly capable grown-up, if and when he needs it.'

'I'm more than perfectly capable,' Tom said. 'I think you'll find that I'm an exemplary grown-up.'

'A genuine grown-up wouldn't keep banging on about what a great grown-up they were,' Posy hissed but she sounded happier. 'Very well. Mattie, I'm counting on you. And Nina, get better soon. Very soon.'

Posy rung off just as they heard an ambulance siren in the distance. 'I hope they give me something for the pain because this all hurts even worse than getting tattooed,' Nina said sadly from underneath Mattie's quilt. 'And when I'm not in huge amounts of agony, I'm going to be really cross with Posy for taking the attention away from me and making it all about her and her profit margins.'

5 days until Christmas

It stopped snowing at lunchtime the next day and by three o'clock, it was elbow room only in both Happy Ever After and the tearooms.

Lulled into a fugue state by the snow, people had suddenly realised that they'd lost serious Christmas-shopping time and it felt like half of Greater London had descended on Rochester Mews in a blind panic.

Now that Mattie had volunteered to be the designated adult in the shop, she was grateful that the tearooms were a well-oiled machine. Cuthbert could be relied upon to maintain law and order. When Sophie wasn't covering in the shop she was perfectly able to wait and clear tables and take orders all in one perimeter sweep, and Meena and her friend Geoffrey were on a generous hourly rate that made them happy to flit between tearoom kitchen and upstairs kitchen with a minimum of grumbling. Mattie didn't even care that every day there seemed to be yet more Christmas decorations in the tearooms. If a few strands of tinsel and some Christmas-pudding fairy lights (which at least were on brand) were what it took for her staff to be happy, then so be it.

Yes, Mattie liked to think that she ran a tight ship in the tearooms but the shop, without Verity, was not a tight ship. It was absolute chaos.

When Tom had claimed to be an exemplary grown-up, what he really meant was that he was as slow and as method-ical as an OAP counting out their daily pills. Five years he'd worked in the shop, yet he still stabbed uncertainly at Bertha's keys as if he was seeing them for the first time, in a way that made Mattie grit her teeth and want to scream.

Sam, on the other hand, was so quick and slapdash that someone (Tom) had to doublecheck the website orders after he'd done them, while Sam had a mid-level hissy fit that he was being treated like a child.

Only Little Sophie was a time-efficient, effective member of staff, when she wasn't needed in the tearooms and when she wasn't sloping off to smooch Sam. Mattie had caught them at it again in the back office, only to discover that Tom had already caught them at it in the corridor by the stairs.

To make matters worse, Sebastian had given in to Posy's demands to set up a webcam in the shop, so even though she was meant to be resting and not getting stressed, she was spying on them.

'She's not even stealthy about it,' Tom complained as his

shop iPad beeped with one of Posy's interminable text messages. 'It's an infringement of our civil liberties.'

So far Posy had complained about how long it was taking them to process the never-ending queue for the Mistletoe Booth and to serve each customer. She was also very cross about them eating and drinking in the shop (though Posy had never had any complaints when she was the one frequently eating and drinking in the shop). Finally Tom had tossed a tote bag over the webcam so she couldn't see what they were getting up to.

But nothing united a malcontent workforce like bonding over a common foe, and so the Happy Ever After-and-tearoom staff were quite content as long as they were bitching about Posy. Even Sam. In fact, especially Sam, as he said that they only had to cope with Posy over webcam and text message, and that he was the one who had to go home and have her complaining in real time and in the flesh every evening.

The only thing that kept Mattie sane was the hope that soon Verity would be back to instil some discipline and decorum into the Happy Ever After staff. For someone who was an introvert and refused to do any kind of inter-facing with a customer, Verity could still quell an uppity colleague with a withering look.

But it was not to be. Verity sent word that the snow was still at blizzard-like proportions in Lincolnshire and that they'd had to call out the army to bring in supplies. If it had been anyone else – say, Nina – Mattie would have suspected that they were on a massive skive, but the news was full of footage of the white world north of the Watford Gap. Cue, lots of rosy-cheeked children sledding down hills, cars abandoned on the side of a snow-banked desolate motorway, sheep being dug out of snowdrifts.

'Makes me glad to be a poncey Southerner,' Tom remarked as he and Mattie slumped on the sofa in their living room on their first full non-snow day, Friday. Five days before Christmas. With the weekend still to go.

No wonder Mattie had her feet in a bucket of warm water with a generous helping of Epsom salts in it. And no wonder that instead of Mattie rustling up some culinary delight, they'd tossed a coin to choose who'd go to No Plaice Like Home to get one cod and chips, one haddock and chips and two mushy peas. Once again, they'd used one of Tom's coins and once again Mattie had lost the coin toss. Next time she'd insist that they use one of her pound coins, because although she and Tom were firm friends now, she still wouldn't put it past him to nobble the democratic process of calling heads or tails.

'Well, Verity grew up in Hull and she didn't seem to be coping very well when she phoned,' Mattie said tiredly. They were sitting so close together on the sofa, which dipped in the middle, that they were almost, but not quite leaning against each other. The temptation to give in to the lean, maybe even rest her head on Tom's shoulder, was strong. And Mattie felt weak. Oh, so weak. 'She said that she was looking into the cost of being airlifted out because the central heating in the vicarage has broken and she'd never been so cold in her life.'

'Whereas the central heating in this place is turned all the way up to eleven and it's still freezing,' Tom said, which explained why he was wearing not just one of his knitted waistcoats but also his infamous cardigan with the leather patches. 'Can you stop leaning on me?'

Mattie shot into a vertical, non-leaning position as if she'd been shot. 'Oh God! Sorry!' Tom probably thought that she was angling for another kissing session, except Mattie wasn't. She absolutely wasn't and anyway, Tom had claimed that he couldn't remember anything about any kissing, due to all the vodka they'd drunk. Whereas Mattie had total recall and once again, she was reliving the memory of Tom's mouth on hers, his hands . . .

'There's no need to look as if you're about to cry.' Tom shook his arm. 'It's just that my arm was going to sleep.'

It just got worse. Mattie was, literally, a dead weight. With some difficulty, given that her feet were still submerged, she managed to manoeuvre herself to the furthest end of her half of the sofa.

'Better?' she asked as frostily as the little particles of ice that had become a permanent fixture at the corners of the badly fitting windows.

Tom stretched out luxuriantly then tucked his arms behind his head and propped his feet up on the coffee table. 'Much better, thanks.' He cast a sideways look at Mattie, as she commandeered the smallest patch of sofa possible. 'My arm's wide awake again, if you want to lean on me.'

'I wasn't leaning on you.'

'Well, it's the dip in the middle, isn't it? It's hard not to lean on each other, like two magnets,' Tom said diffidently, as if the leaning was neither here nor there. He gestured at her bucket. 'Isn't that water getting cold?'

'Definitely verging on lukewarm,' Mattie said, though she was too tired to move until the water was verging on cold, but Tom was already levering himself to his feet with a groan.

'As you lost the coin toss,' he said, picking up their discarded fish and chip wrappers (like savages, they hadn't even used plates), 'feet up!'

Mattie used every last ounce of strength to lift her legs so Tom could take away the bucket. He was back a minute later with two bottles of fancy imported lager and Mattie somehow found herself back in the middle of the sofa with a blanket tucked around her legs.

There was a moment or two of fidgeting after Tom had sat down, but finally they were settled. Tom had his feet back on the coffee table, one arm over the back of the sofa so it wouldn't go to sleep, and gently, very gently, Mattie leaned against him. It was because there was that dip in the middle of the sofa and she was tired and also Tom was very comfortable to lean against and also despite a long, hard day of bookselling, he smelt nice. Not musty at all as Mattie had always imagined that he smelled, but Tom-like: new books and coffee and the surprisingly posh aftershave that smelt of sea salt and citrus from an old-fashioned barber's in Piccadilly with a royal seal. Not that Mattie was snooping through Tom's personal things, but the bathroom cabinet was a communal space.

'So, you didn't fancy going out tonight?' Mattie asked. The episode of *Extreme Cakes* they were watching wasn't very gripping and also it was still quite a rarity for Tom to stay in. Either he was out with the Banter Boys or . . . 'Didn't have a hot date with one of those women from the party or . . . some other woman? I mean, you were pretty successful at scoring those phone numbers.'

If Tom really couldn't remember the kiss, even though it had been an amazing kiss, then he was free to have hot dates with anyone he liked . . .

'I like women. I like working with women, hanging out with women, and yes, dating women. It's not my fault that my friends become such a bunch of drooling idiots in the presence of a woman, that I end up looking pretty damn suave in comparison.' He smirked. 'Even Donald Duck would appear suave next to Phil.'

'Oh, Phil's all right! I have a lot of time for him, but he really needs to realise that women are part of the human race too and not some rare species that he has to hunt down and stun with his rather overpowering aftershave.'

'Just be thankful that you didn't know him in the days when he first discovered Lynx,' Tom said sourly and as Mattie snorted, he added quietly, 'I used to be just like them.'

'Just like who? Oh!' Mattie's eyes widened, her mouth a perfect 'O' of surprise. 'No! You were a Banter Boy? Say it isn't so!'

'If I did I'd only be lying,' Tom admitted sorrowfully. 'They call me the Professor now, but back in the day, I was

Saint Banter of Banthood. I completely outranked the Archbishop.'

'Oh my God.' Mattie shifted away from Tom because she was laughing too hard to lean on him any more.

'I invented our war cry. Do you want to hear it?'

'That's the most rhetorical question since records began . . .'

'Smoke some fags, drink some beer, shag some birds 'cause the Banter Boys are here!' It wasn't just the shocking content of the war cry but the Mockney accent that Tom had assumed while he chanted it that made Mattie slide off the sofa onto the floor so she could roll from side to side, her arms clutched around her aching ribs.

'I. Can't. Breathe,' she wheezed. 'No more.' Then she managed to sit up. 'Do it again!'

'Do what again?' Tom asked in his usual voice. 'I'm sure I don't know what you mean.' Then he smiled wickedly. 'Needless to say, none of us actually smoked and we were eighteen, all newly arrived at university, and none of us had so much as held hands with a girl, let alone shagged any.' He peered down at her. 'You can't be comfortable down there, Mattie.'

'I kind of am actually,' Mattie said because she could stretch out her arms and legs, which were aching after a long day, and also she didn't have the energy to haul herself back onto the sofa. She waved a hand at Tom. 'How did you go from Saint Banter to . . . to . . . you know, how you are now?'

'You mean a prim and proper doctor of Philosophy and Literature who walks about with a face like a slapped arse?'

Tom asked her drily, and though Mattie had never described him using those *exact* words, they were close enough.

'You said it, not me. I meant the change from Banter Boy to . . . um . . . not Banter Boy?' Mattie asked.

'It was a gradual process,' Tom said, holding up his lager to see how much was left. 'I'd gone to an all-boys school but once I got to Durham and actually started to meet girls – and there were a *lot* of them studying English Literature – I realised to my surprise, that they were autonomous beings in their own right, with their own thoughts and feelings and opinions. That they didn't simply exist in order for idiotic boys to try and shag them. But my bantering companions were studying far less female-friendly subjects so they never had the same epiphany as me. It really was quite the revelation.'

'I'm sure it was,' Mattie said, struggling to sit up and swivel around so her back was supported by the sofa. 'Must have been a real learning curve.'

'Yeah, got my face slapped a couple of times, which I very much deserved,' Tom said, rubbing his chin. 'Anyway, I had a couple of short-lived relationships, then I moved to London to study for my MA and I met Candace and well, you know what happened next.'

Mattie knew some of what had happened next. But some of it was still a mystery. 'But Candace didn't put you off dating and relationships?'

Tom's face was grave as he considered Mattie's question. 'Well, relationships aren't my favourite thing. Maybe that's why I prefer to be a Lothario.'

'You're never going to let me forget that, are you?' Mattie groaned, tipping her head back to pout at Tom who raised his eyebrows at her.

'It shouldn't matter, not after all this time, but every time I get a woman's phone number, it proves Candace wrong when she said that I was a poor excuse for a man,' Tom said and Mattie's heart ached for him a little. 'Though there is something to be said for the thrill of the chase.'

'And do you catch them once you've chased them?' she asked because if he did, then he certainly didn't introduce them to his colleagues.

'A few,' Tom conceded with a wry grin. 'Quite hard to let anyone get close once you've had your heart ripped out for someone else's amusement, if you know what I mean.'

Mattie sighed. 'I know exactly what you mean.'

'Yes, I think you probably do,' said Tom and then neither of them spoke. Mattie imagined that he was thinking of Candace but she was hardly thinking of Steven at all. Since their showdown, he'd become less of a demon who haunted her at every turn and more of a minor irritant, like a cut or burn that was itching while it healed. And soon even that pain would be gone and she'd have the smallest of scars to show for it.

She wanted to tell Tom that maybe he'd have the same kind of closure after his recent encounter with Candace, but before that she had one pressing question to ask him.

'Um, Tom, are you stroking my hair?' Mattie mumbled then wished she hadn't because the hair stroking, which had actually felt wonderful, immediately stopped.

Mattie was still sitting with her back to the sofa but Tom had shifted position so that he was sprawled out on his side with Mattie's head resting against his chest, which made the most perfect pillow, being firm with just enough give, as if he was someone more active than his bookish exterior suggested. For example, someone who could leap over a six-foot-high electronic gate without breaking a sweat.

The same someone who'd been propped up on one elbow while his other hand had been absent-mindedly running his fingers through Mattie's hair.

'No,' Tom said shortly, straightening up so that Mattie was forced to sit up too. 'You know, you're tired. You should go to bed.'

'I should,' Mattie said, making no move to get up from the floor.

'Long day tomorrow,' Tom said in a slightly robotic voice, his eyes fixed on the extreme bakers who were creating a nativity scene through the medium of sugarcraft. 'The last Saturday before Christmas. Didn't you say you were planning to get up at six to get a jump start on all your baking stuff?'

'I did,' Mattie said without much enthusiasm and if she just slumped slightly to her right, she'd be leaning against Tom again.

Tom stiffened and pushed Mattie upright again. 'Go on,' he ordered in a very peremptory tone. 'It's gone eleven now. Off to bed with you.'

'All right, all right. I'm not a child, I'm quite capable of deciding when I'll go to bed.' Although it was nearly half eleven and yes, she had foolishly decided to set her alarm for six. Mattie stood up with a laboured grunt. Tom tapped her on the leg with an impatient hand.

'Sorry, you're blocking the TV,' he said, as if the hair stroking, the leaning, had been the work of someone else. 'It's just this programme is riveting. Who even knew you could use vodka to wipe fingerprints off fondant icing?'

Unusually, Mattie had zero opinions on fondant icing but she had quite a few opinions about Tom and right now, they weren't good ones. Trailing her blanket behind her, she left the room with what she liked to think was a quiet dignity.

CHAPTER 31

3 days until Christmas

'I'm not an idiot! You! You're the idiot!' Mattie shouted at Tom, approximately thirty-six hours later.

'No, the only idiot here is *you*,' Tom decreed in damning tones. 'I told you that customers only got a free tote bag with purchases over twenty pounds, and it turns out you've been giving away free tote bags to everyone. Even if they just buy a bookmark.'

'You didn't tell me,' Mattie insisted, because he hadn't. 'And anyway, how am I expected to remember all the strange and completely arbitrary ways this bookshop is run? They defy all laws of logic.'

They were in the back office, sent there by Little Sophie, of all people, after Tom had made the unhappy discovery that they'd completely run out of 'Reader, I Married Him' tote bags and had said some very unkind things to Mattie when he'd realised that she was the culprit.

And yes, she'd shouted at him on a crowded shop floor, but she'd had very little sleep (which was all Tom's fault because he'd gone out the night before without even telling her where he was going and she hadn't been able to sleep until he was safely home – on his own) and also she was doing the work of two people. No, three people. Three very busy people.

'Yes, I'm sure Posy would be delighted to hear you running down the business she's put her heart and soul into,' Tom snapped, because if Mattie was in a filthy mood today then his mood was a perfect match for it. 'About as delighted as she'll be when she hears that you've left us with none of our bestselling tote bags with only three days to go until Christmas.'

'I bet you've got boxes of them stashed away in the coal hole or in here somewhere.' There were boxes everywhere and apparently Verity had a system and knew where everything was, but Verity was still snowed in. 'This isn't a business. This is chaos and not even organised chaos—'

'Bookselling is about passion and—'

'Well, you could look more passionate when you serve people, instead of looking bored,' Mattie said with a stabby finger at Tom who was standing there, arms folded and looking incredibly bored in that moment, which just made her crosser. 'Posy left me in charge and the very least you could do—'

'You're not in charge,' Tom said quickly, a look of pure

annoyance flashing across his face. 'You're absolutely not the boss of me.'

'Oh, if I was the boss of you, you'd be fired so fast you wouldn't know what had hit you,' Mattie promised in a low, murderous voice. She employed her stabby finger again. 'And Posy *did* leave me in charge, so I'd watch it if I were you.'

Tom caught her hand and used it to tug her closer. 'You wouldn't dare,' he breathed and of course Mattie wouldn't, not when she was trapped between Tom and a filing cabinet so she couldn't escape, not that she wanted to – and, oh God, she had to get out of there. She liked Tom. Liked him a lot. Maybe even more than a lot, but Tom had been so damaged by the vile Candace that he wasn't ready to like a woman more than a lot. And also at this precise moment in time, Mattie didn't like him at all. Even if being in such close proximity to him was giving her what Posy would call stirrings.

There was a pause as they scowled at each other, Tom's hand pressing Mattie's hand to his chest, where she could feel the thud of his heart. Then the alarm on her mobile phone began to beep, breaking the moment.

'Don't push me then,' she warned, pulling her hand away as Tom stepped aside. 'And you'll have do without me for a bit, my cupcakes need me.'

'Your cupcakes are welcome to you,' Tom muttered as Mattie left the office. The shop was heaving: the queue for the Mistletoe Booth was extremely restless and a gang of teenagers were taking it in turns to ride the baby reindeer like they were the odds-on favourite to win the Grand National.

But the tearooms were busy too so if Tom seemed to think that he had superior bookselling skills, then let him get on with it. Mattie surveyed her crowded domain where everything had a place and there was a place for everything. Not like the bookshop . . .

It took forty-five minutes for Tom to cave. Or rather he sent Sam to do his dirty work for him.

'You have to come back to the shop,' Sam groaned, slumping over the counter, unhygienically. 'People are taking liberties with the kissing booth. One couple were in there for five minutes doing things that we really didn't want automatically posted on the Happy Ever After Instagram. And Sophie has to keep going up the rolling ladder, but Sophie shouldn't have to because she has an inner-ear thing, and also there's a problem with tomorrow's order from one of the book suppliers and no one knows what to do about it.'

'And . . . ?' Mattie prompted, folding her arms because she knew what was coming and she wanted to savour it.

Sam tossed back his fringe so that the extravagant rolling of his eyes wouldn't go unnoticed. 'And Tom says he's sorry and can you *please* come back and help in the shop?'

'*Help?*'

'Be in charge of the shop.'

'Tom said that?' Mattie clarified. 'Can I have it in writing, please?'

'He *knew* you were going to say that,' Sam grumbled,

producing a crumpled piece of till roll with something scribbled on it:

Dearest Mattie

I am wicked and ungrateful. Please come and be in charge of us all before the customers cause a civil disturbance.

As well as my undying gratitude, I will go and get dinner tonight.

Yours ever so truly,

Tom

'I'm going to have your note framed,' Mattie said to Tom when she returned to the shop five minutes later. 'Or screen-printed onto a T-shirt, I haven't decided which.'

'Nobody likes a gloater,' Tom said, from where he was hemmed in by the baby reindeer with customers coming at him from all sides. 'People, please! Can we form a queue?'

It was all very well having the shop staff roaming about with iPads in a freeform, organic kind of way, but not when there were only two shopping days left before Christmas. It was time for drastic action.

Mattie waded her way through the book-buying public until she reached the counter where absolutely no one was serving even though a huge, malcontent queue had formed. Mattie hoped that Posy wasn't watching all of the badly organised retail madness on webcam, because if she was, then she was definitely going into early labour.

Mattie didn't have the agility or the upper-body strength

of Tom, but somehow she managed to climb up on the counter and clap her hands.

'Enough!' she said, and when no one paid her any attention, she increased her volume. 'ENOUGH!'

Now, all eyes were on Mattie, which was what she wanted and yet, at the same time, how she longed to be back in her dear, familiar tearooms whose clientele were much more civilised than book buyers. Who'd have thought it?

Then she caught Tom's gaze, not difficult when he was the tallest person in the shop, and he gave her a nod and an encouraging smile. And she was back to liking him. A lot. Maybe even more than a lot.

'Right,' Mattie called out decisively. 'Tom and Sam, I want you behind the counter serving on your iPads. I will man the Mistletoe Booth and, ladies and gentlemen, there is now a ninety-second time limit on getting your picture taken. Sophie, you're on the door. We're at capacity. You don't let anyone in, until you've let some people out.

'So, if you'd like to pay, then please make your way to the counter. If you have paid and you have proof of purchase and you want to use the Mistletoe Booth, then please queue along this wall on the right, your right, not mine. We'd also like to thank you for your patience at this time and wish you all a very Merry Christmas,' Mattie finished. Miracle of miracles, the seething mass of people shifted, with quite a bit of grumbling, into one long queue to pay and a not-so-long queue to avail themselves of the Mistletoe Booth.

Now, all she had to do was somehow get down from

the counter and go and phone Verity to beg her to call the book distribution people and get to the bottom of whatever their beef was.

It had been much easier to get up than to get down, but then Tom was there, holding out his hand, which Mattie gratefully took. 'I would jump, but it's quite a tight squeeze behind the counter,' she said.

'You'll be fine,' Tom said gravely. Then his other hand took a firm grasp of Mattie's waist and she sort of jumped as he sort of *lifted* her off the counter so she came to land so close to him that not even a Happy Ever After bookmark could come between them. 'Great crowd-wrangling skills, by the way.'

'As a teenager I worked weekends in a burger van at Wembley Stadium for all the major sporting events,' Mattie said, glancing up at Tom who looked predictably horrified at the mention of a burger van. 'Gave me nerves of steel.'

'I worked in a garden centre. It gave me an in-depth knowledge of when best to plant hardy perennials that I've never been able to shake,' he said, smiling down at Mattie, his eyes twinkling behind his glasses, though admittedly that could have been the reflection of the fairy lights . . .

'Oi! Romeo and Juliet! Can you save the lovey-dovey stuff for when you've knocked off?' Mattie and Tom turned towards a red-faced man at the front of the queue who was waving a twenty-pound note and a copy of *The Viscount Who Loved Me* at them. 'Some of us have still got to get to the bleeding Apple Store and Footlocker before the shops close.'

They sprang apart, Tom to serve Mr Buzzkill and Mattie so she could restore order to the Mistletoe Booth *and* phone Verity to ask her if there was literally a snowball in hell's chance of her making it back to London for tomorrow. Unlike certain other people, Mattie was a champion at multi-tasking.

3 days until Christmas

That evening, though technically it was past evening and actually very late, Tom and Mattie were back on the sofa, argument forgotten, as they leant against each other and shovelled pizza straight out of the takeaway box and into their mouths.

'I hate Christmas,' Tom sniped, as he tore off another slice of sourdough pizza with extra capers and no anchovies. 'There was very little peace on earth and goodwill to all men in the shop today.'

'Well, it was the Sunday before Christmas,' Mattie pointed out. 'And Christmas is on Wednesday – it was bound to get a bit hairy in places, but we're still alive and mostly sane . . .'

'No, Mattie, this is the bit where you say that you hate Christmas too,' Tom said plaintively. 'It's our thing. That we both hate Christmas.'

'Oh, yes! I do hate Christmas, don't I?' How had Mattie forgotten that she hated Christmas? 'Well, working in a customer-facing environment over Christmas isn't much fun, is it?'

'Can't you do any better than that?' Tom asked. 'Come on, Mattie! Brutal commercialisation of what was once a pagan festival. Knowing you're going to get some really crappy presents and, no matter what you do to it, the turkey is always dry.'

'Actually Sandrine is the best gift-giver,' Mattie said apologetically. 'And we're not having turkey this year. We're doing a goose and a ham and some Yotam Ottolenghi thing for Guy and his boyfriend Didier as they're having another crack at being vegetarians. I mean, I haven't said for definite that I'm going to Hackney for Christmas but, well, I'm thinking about it.'

'You're really letting the side down,' Tom grumbled, sinking lower on the sofa so that they were shoulder to shoulder, thigh to thigh. 'My mother always gives me socks and her turkey is so dry that it leeches all the moisture from your body as you're eating it. Why are you suddenly Christmas's biggest fan?'

Mattie wasn't Christmas's biggest fan but she now had Christmas gingerbread cupcakes decorated with tiny fondant holly leaves on the tearoom cake rotation, and had even arranged the Christmas cards given to her by her regular customers on sparkly ribbon, and pinned them to the wall behind the counter.

'The times they are a-changing. Before Steven, I loved

Christmas.' Mattie smiled slyly at Tom who shook his head in protest at her statement. 'I used to start wearing novelty jumpers in November. I'd campaign to get the tree up by December the first and I loved Christmas shopping. Finding the perfect present for someone, picking out their card . . .'

'You mean you got people individual cards instead of buying a charity selection box?' Each new Yuletide-related revelation from Mattie had been greeted with a shudder but Tom had reached his tipping point.

'Well, yeah! I mean, it's fun. It *was* fun, and a way of showing my friends and the people I loved what they meant to me. It's the thought that counts . . .'

'No! Not another trite and sentimental word!' Tom clapped his hands over his ears. 'I can't believe you're abandoning me at a time like this.'

Mattie nudged him with her arm. 'I'm afraid you might have to bah humbug all by yourself.' Then she sighed and her expression grew more serious 'Why should I let one bad man ruin all the things I love? It's not Christmas's fault that Steven reached the full peak of his evil powers at Christmas time. For too long, I've been depriving myself of things that give me pleasure, just because they reminded me of him, but I'm done with that now.'

'So, you're over him?' Tom sat motionless with a slice of pizza poised in mid-air.

'So over him and my God, I wish I'd never, ever been under him,' Mattie said with great feeling and Tom, who'd finally taken a bite of his pizza slice, spluttered so hard that Mattie had to whack him on the back.

'Sorry, it went down the wrong way,' he said, pulling out a handkerchief from somewhere so he could mop his streaming eyes. 'Well, I'm glad you've got your Christmas spirit back, really I am, but you've gone down in my estimation.'

'I didn't realise I'd ever gone *up* in your estimation,' Mattie said teasingly because there was nothing she could take offence to in Tom's tone of voice; it was warm, friendly, even *affectionate*.

'Oh, you have been up in my estimation for quite a while,' Tom said, but his eyes were now fixed on the TV and the episode of *Gogglebox* that they'd barely been watching. 'You must have realised that.'

'Well, yes, when we're not shouting at each other about tote bags . . .'

'I think you'll find that the only person who was actually shouting was you.' It was Tom's turn to nudge Mattie. 'I was saying things in a perfectly modulated tone.'

'It was lofty, Tom. Very lofty and also unbelievably annoying.' It felt good to get that off her chest. Did she want another slice of pizza? No, she didn't. 'Anyway, it's a shame you haven't had a change of heart about Christmas, but at least it's one less person to buy a present for.'

'You would have bought me a present?'

'Well, we'll never know now, will we?' Mattie said, turning to Tom so he'd see the especially sad smile she'd put on.

'I'm sure that somehow I'll get over the disappointment,' Tom said, but for a nanosecond he looked quite disconsolate.

Maybe if she had fifteen minutes spare between now

and after work on Christmas Eve, when both she and Tom planned to depart the flat for their respective parental homes, she'd knock him up another batch of chilli chocolate brownies to take with him to . . .

'Where exactly are you spending Christmas again?' she asked Tom, who was setting about the last slice of pizza, albeit unenthusiastically.

'With my parents,' he all but grunted. 'We've been through this.'

'Tom, we are flatmates. We've shared some of our deepest, darkest secrets,' Mattie reminded him, and as she did she thought of the other things they'd shared. Or one other thing, the kiss, which she'd tried to forget about but the memory of it still caught her unawares. She'd be whisking batter and suddenly recall Tom holding her. Or first thing in the morning, as she was waiting for Jezebel to come to life, she'd remember the feel and taste and heat of Tom's mouth on hers and she'd have to take a bottle of milk out of the fridge to press against her heated cheeks until she'd banished the memory away. So, yeah, they were far from strangers. 'Just blooming well tell me where your parents live and where you grew up and stop acting like it's some great mystery! Unless they were in the witness protection scheme.'

'Yes, how ironic that Verity's running gag was that I was a Russian sleeper agent, when actually it was my parents who were high-ranking KGB officials who defected at the height of the Cold War,' Tom said flatly so that for the life of her Mattie couldn't tell if it were a joke or not.

'You're kidding . . . right?'

Tom sighed. 'My father has a landscaping business and my mother does the books for him.'

'This would be Jerry and Margot, I saw their name in your dissertation acknowledgements . . . and where do they live? Where did young Tom spend his formative years?' It was like trying to clean congealed grease off the back of the oven. 'Come on! What's the big secret? Unless you grew up somewhere with a comedy name like Staines or Basingstoke.'

'I've been to Basingstoke and there is nothing remotely amusing about it,' Tom said and he was exasperating enough that Mattie picked up the empty pizza box and biffed him over the head with it.

'Tell me!'

'Why?'

'Because the not knowing is killing me!' Mattie burst out, but it was more than that. It certainly wasn't because Tom was a puzzle that she couldn't figure out (though he was still that in a lot of ways), but more because she wanted to know everything about him. What made him laugh? When was the last time he cried? What was his favourite food when he was little? And what was his favourite food now? (It had better not be the breakfast panini from the Italian café.)

Tom took the pizza box out of her hands before she could do any more damage with it – his quiff was quite flattened – and put it down on the coffee table. Then he took Mattie's slightly greasy, pizza-y hand in his, which was equally the worse for wear. Mattie's heart quickened.

'I'll make a deal with you,' he said in a quiet, solemn voice as if they were about to make a sacred vow, and the mood shifted from light-hearted and playful to something more tense, more charged.

'What kind of deal?' Mattie asked in a voice that suddenly sounded quite sultry.

Was Tom stroking the back of her hand?

'If we manage not to kill each other in the shop tomorrow, by which I mean if you manage not to scream at me, I will give you a guided tour of Tom Greer, the early years. Deal?'

For a moment, Mattie felt disappointed, cheated, even, after the anticipatory promise of Tom's quiet voice and the hand-holding. But then curiosity won out.

'OK, and if you manage not to do the lofty voice, I will whip up a batch of chilli chocolate brownies for you to take back to . . . now, where was it again?'

'Lofty voice? I'm sure I don't know what you mean,' Tom said in a voice that was pretty bloody lofty, but before Mattie could call him on it, he took her hand again and her heart did the quickstep all over again. 'Deal!'

Mattie had never been so disappointed with a handshake before.

CHAPTER

33

2 days until Christmas

Sadly, there was to be no trip down memory lane featuring a prepubescent Tom because within ten minutes of Happy Ever After opening on Monday morning, the last but one shopping day before Christmas, Bertha had a meltdown.

Tom was the only person, apart from Nina who was currently convalescing in Bermondsey, who knew how to calm her down and change her till roll and Tom was nowhere to be found.

Mattie eventually tracked him down in the furthest reaches of the erotica/Paranormal anteroom where he was furtively stuffing his face with a breakfast panini.

Mattie couldn't remember the last time she'd been so disappointed in someone.

'Chiro texted me to say that he hadn't seen me in a

while and I thought that it wouldn't do any harm to have one for old times' sake,' he explained, a little defensively.

Mattie tried to be the bigger person. Especially as everyone knew that her croque guvnor and croque missus were much better.

'Bertha needs a new till roll,' she said and what she thought would be a neutral tone of voice came out rather huffy. 'Apparently, you're the only one who knows how to put one in.'

'Fine,' Tom said rather huffily back and it set the mood for the rest of the day, which culminated in another shouting match at just gone three when Tom decided to interrupt the only break that Mattie had had since seven that morning.

She'd been on speakerphone to Sandrine for ten minutes – just ten minutes! – to finalise the Christmas food shopping list while she also went through a last-minute delivery that had come in from one of their book suppliers. Her mother planned to be at the supermarket at crazy o'clock in the morning to do a full food-shop and then start cooking for the Christmas Eve party she hosted for her friends and neighbours every year.

'I'll just have to trust Ian to put all the food away, but it's been ten years and still he doesn't understand my fridge system,' Sandrine said.

'He puts *eggs* in the fridge, what kind of monster does that? Shall we get an extra jar of goose fat, just in case?' Mattie looked up to see Tom positively glowering at her from the door of the back office, where she was hiding.

'Matilda,' he bit out. 'If you can bear to tear yourself

away from this pressing business, I have a queue to pay and a queue for the Mistletoe Booth and they've got tangled, so can you come and untangle them? Sometime before Christmas would be great.'

'Tom! It's Sandrine, *la mère de Mathilde*,' Sandrine said with a tinkling laugh. 'Now don't be cross. You'll get lines on that handsome face of yours. Although, then you'll look handsome *and* distinguished. You men are so lucky! Anyway, my Mattie will be with you presently. *Dans un minute.*'

Sandrine believed that you caught more flies with honey than vinegar, while Mattie wished that Tom would buzz off with his unreasonable demands and all-round, all-purpose loftiness. Also, if they didn't have enough goose fat, then Christmas would *literally* be ruined.

'The job that I get paid for is to run the tearooms,' she began furiously as she terminated the call. 'And . . .'

'Well, it doesn't look like you're doing that job either!'

That was when Mattie stomped off, bodychecking Tom with her hip on the way, and they'd sniped at each other for the rest of the day. Maybe it might have resolved itself if they'd had another tired night on the sofa, eating takeaway and leaning against each other, but they both had other plans.

After the shop had closed and everyone but Mattie – who was furiously kneading dough – had gone home, Tom was collected by a brace of Banter Boys.

'We always go out the night before Christmas Eve to drink London dry. The Met have already put out an APB warning people to lock up their daughters,' Phil explained, when Mattie, hearing a chant of 'Oi! Oi! Oi!', had gone outside to investigate.

'Somehow I doubt that very much,' Mattie said, with a bowl tucked under her arm as she kneaded her dough like her life depended on it, and they all guffawed, except for Tom who came out of the shop door looking pinch-faced and peeved as he shrugged into a coat as frayed and tweedy as his jackets.

'You can come if you want,' Phil said, which made a mockery of their claim on the capital's daughters. Tom went from pinch-faced to looking as if he was sucking on a whole bag of lemons, so Mattie was tempted to accept the offer.

But winding Tom up wasn't the fun that it used to be. In fact, it made her sad and anyway she had her own hot date for the evening.

'It's a tempting offer, but I have other plans,' she said just as Pippa turned into the mews, her stride confident and her hair bouncy. She was the only person Mattie knew who could wear a white wool winter coat and keep it spotless.

'Mattie! Tom! Phil! Mikey! Costa! Daquon!' One of Pippa's many superpowers was being able to remember people's names, which left all the Banters Boys' mouths hanging open as they looked at Pippa with shock and awe. 'Haven't seen you since your Christmas party. Happy Holidays one and all!'

'We could stay . . .' Phil began to say . . .

'But we won't,' Tom said firmly, marching across the

mews as his comrades in arms lingered in front of Pippa who was quite oblivious to the love in their hearts. 'Come on! This beer isn't going to drink itself.'

The Banter Boys stumbled after him, Daquon dragging his heels long enough to say to Pippa, 'You on HookUpp? 'Cause we should totally hook up.'

'That's very sweet, but I don't think so,' Pippa said. Then she beamed at him, because she knew how to let a man down gently. 'But have a great Christmas. And I would say have a happy new year but I believe that you either make a conscious decision to be happy or you don't. Right?'

Judging from the suddenly gormless expression on Daquon's face as he tried to process Pippa's positivity philosophy, he was going to have to get back to her on that one. 'Um, right, OK. I hope you choose to have a happy new year,' he garbled at last and then hurried after his friends who were being ushered through the gate by Tom, like a mother hen counting her chickens home.

Just before he followed Daquon through the gate, Tom paused and looked back to where Pippa and Mattie were standing in the mews. It was too dark and Tom was too far away for Mattie to see his face, though she imagined that his expression still resembled a bulldog chewing on a wasp. He lifted his hand in a salute, but before Mattie could return the gesture, he was gone.

Then Mattie looked down at her bowl. 'Oh. I think I've overworked my dough.'

'Yes, you probably have,' Pippa said, looking over at the spot where Tom had been standing. Then she glanced down at Mattie's bowl. 'Are you really talking about your dough or are you using your dough as a metaphor for your relationship with Tom?'

Mattie tried to stare Pippa down, but it didn't work. Pippa was also great at returning eye contact. 'You know, sometimes dough is just dough.'

'Of course it is,' Pippa said as if she were merely humouring her friend. 'Now, put that dough in the fridge. Table's booked for nine – I've just done a Boxfit class and I'm starving.'

When Mattie didn't need to be rescued from Paris, she and Pippa had a Christmas Eve eve tradition of curry and presents. Then Pippa would drive all the way to her parents' stone cottage on the outskirts of Halifax. She said she'd rather drive through the night and beat the traffic. The only downside was it meant that Pippa refused all alcohol and had one eye on the time, exhorting Mattie to 'eat up, I want to get going before ten thirty,' resulting in Mattie choking down her king prawn chilli so fast that her eyes watered and she had to chug her bottle of Cobra beer in record time. She felt distinctly unwell as she walked Pippa to Sebastian's offices in Clerkenwell where Pippa's car was parked, the fierce wind scouring their faces.

In every shop window, Christmas lights twinkled back at them. There were even flashing fairy lights entwined around the top of each lamp-post, courtesy of Camden Council. How festive, Mattie thought to herself, like some kind of Christmas-loving loon.

'Thank you for my new boxing gloves,' Pippa enthused

as Mattie tried not to burp. 'And I'm so glad that you're choosing to have a merry Christmas this year.'

'I wouldn't say that I was particularly merry at this precise moment,' Mattie said: she was pretty sure that the roof of her mouth was minus a couple of layers of skin.

'Well, you just need to make some more dough and not overwork it this time,' Pippa said sagely but with a glint in her eye. Once she got an idea into her head . . .

'Pips, when I said I'd overworked my dough, I had an actual bowl of dough in my arms that I'd just overworked. It wasn't a metaphor and it didn't have anything to do with Tom . . .'

'I never said it had anything to do with Tom and yet here you are, bringing up Tom's name,' Pippa said, taking out her car keys. 'Interesting. Very interesting.'

'Annoying. You're being very annoying.'

But Pippa simply smiled obliquely. 'Well, to be completely transparent, Posy told Sebastian, who can't keep a secret so he told me, that she's glued to the webcam,' Pippa said as she beeped her key at her car, which obligingly beeped back.

'That's hardly news. She doesn't stop texting to complain about our queue wrangling techniques and to ask how much we've taken every half hour,' Mattie said wearily.

'Sebastian said that she's much more interested in watching you and Tom flirting than your queue wrangling. Although I did read a study where an ice-cream parlour in Venice Beach gave out free water to the people queuing . . .'

'Never mind that. Rewind!' Mattie demanded, physically blocking Pippa from getting into her car. 'Flirting? Tom and I don't *flirt* in the shop.' (Though Mattie was still undecided if they flirted out of work hours when they were leaning against each other on the sofa.) 'Mostly we fight in the shop. About Posy's precious tote bags, among other things. She should have been complaining about that instead of gossiping and making up stuff.'

With her superior strength from her Boxfit classes, Pippa moved Mattie out of the way. 'Posy thinks the fighting is just the snapping of courtship,' she cheerfully reported as she got in her car. 'Says she and Sebastian were exactly the same and that going by all the recent romantic activity in the shop, you and Tom will be engaged before Valentine's Day.'

'*What?*' This was typical of Posy. Typical of someone who'd read so many romantic novels that she had difficulty in telling the difference between fiction and real life. Not to mention all those pregnancy hormones.

Also, Posy had no way of knowing about the kiss that Mattie absolutely wasn't going to think about. Anyway, Tom didn't feel that way about her. If he did, then he'd be clear with his intentions, wouldn't he? And he couldn't even remember that they had kissed.

'Then Posy told Sebastian that you and Tom would have to plan your wedding for after she's lost the baby weight,' Pippa said with a grin. 'This is such a breakthrough on your personal development, Mattie! You said that you thought it was time you gave Paris another chance but you never said that you were going to give love another chance too. And with Tom!'

'That's because I'm not,' Mattie said, now bodily preventing Pippa from closing the car door. 'I mean, I'm not violently opposed to love any more. In fact, I think that I deserve to be loved.'

'I'm so proud of you,' Pippa said, grin gone, and with great sincerity. 'You are absolutely deserving of love. Now, please, let go of the door, I want to be in Halifax by three at the latest.'

Mattie stepped aside. 'Let's get one thing straight, though. This love, it's not going to be with Tom,' she said but Pippa had shut the door and from her little wave then a jaunty thumbs-up, Mattie wasn't sure that she'd heard her.

CHAPTER 34

1 day until Christmas

Mattie was woken on Christmas Eve not by her alarm clock, but by the unmistakable sounds of someone throwing up at the exact same time that her mobile started ringing.

The early caller – and if it was someone who wanted to know if she'd been mis-sold PPI, then God help them – took precedence over the early vomiter. Especially as it turned out to be Sandrine.

'*Mon ange!* We've been queuing to get *into* the supermarket for two hours,' she lamented without even a *Good morning, sorry to be calling before six*. 'What will we do if there are no pigs in blankets left?'

'I thought we weren't having pigs in blankets on account of the fact that I never want to see another pig in a blanket until at least next November?' Mattie asked, her mother's panicked tones waking her up just as effectively as a very large cup of black coffee.

'Well, everyone else likes them,' Sandrine replied implacably. Mattie heard Ian swear in the background and wish a long and painful death to the driver that had just cut in front of them. 'So, you are coming home for Christmas then, instead of spending the day in bed? *Très bien!* Do you want to come over after work or shall Ian come and pick you up tomorrow?'

They were closing at four today, then re-opening on the twenty-eighth. Mattie couldn't remember the last time she'd had a day off and though she was pretty sure she wasn't going to take to her bed again to avoid Christmas, she did quite fancy taking to her bed to sleep three days straight due to extreme exhaustion.

Across the landing the sound of someone throwing up grew louder and though they'd parted on bad terms, Mattie felt a twinge of sympathy for Tom. Then she thought of the three days when she wouldn't see him and even though those three days would be spent feasting and presenting and watching back-to-back musicals, they suddenly seemed like quite a dull three days.

'Yes, I've decided that I will be an active participant in your Christmas celebrations,' Mattie said. 'But I'm very tired and if I come over this afternoon you'll just stick me with all your Christmas Eve party cooking. I know you.'

'As if I would do such a wicked thing?' Then Sandrine gave a sudden shriek. 'Oh! Ian! *La!* That white car's just pulling out.'

Mattie's services were no longer required and Tom was *still* being sick. Squinching up her face in anticipation of the smell and sight that awaited her, Mattie opened her bedroom door and stepped out into the hall. The bathroom door was ajar and on his knees hugging the toilet was . . . the Archbishop of Banterbury.

'You all right, Phil?' Mattie asked gently.

There was a groan in reply and Mattie retreated. Five minutes later, when the puking sounds had stopped, she ventured back out and met a sheepish and pale-looking Phil loitering in the hall.

'I'd give it a few minutes if I were you,' he said. 'I cracked open the window but even so . . .'

'I'll use the er, facilities downstairs,' Mattie decided. 'I have to get my croissants on and start on my pigs in blankets . . . Sorry!'

At the mere mention of food, Phil retched, one hand out in front of him to ward Mattie off, not that she had any intention of going near him. She took several steps back but it turned out to be a false alarm.

'Never drinking again,' he said sadly. 'It's all Tom's fault.'

'Tom enabled you to get very drunk?' Mattie asked in disbelief. Had he reverted back to Saint Banter of Banthood? 'My Tom?'

Phil's brow crinkled in confusion. 'Your Tom? Our Tom! Said he was going to drown his sorrows and I said I'd match him drink for drink because that's what brothers from another mother do, but I forgot that Tom's bigger than me.'

That was putting it mildly. Phil was literally half Tom's size. 'Did he say why he was drowning his sorrows?'

'Something about women. Was it having to work with a bunch of women? There was a whole rant about tote bags but really, the whole night's a bit patchy. Though I definitely remember Tom shouting that he was done with women and their cupcakes.'

'Cupcakes?' Her faintest hope gave way to fury at the news that Tom was done with her. They'd barely even started anything and so he didn't get to say that it was over without any discussion with her. 'I'll give him cupcakes!'

'Oh no!' This time the retching wasn't a rehearsal but the real deal. Phil dived for the bathroom again, thankfully slamming the door shut behind him.

'You'll feel much better if you clean your teeth afterwards,' Mattie called out. 'Use the blue toothbrush, I'm sure Tom won't mind!'

Just once, it would be nice to make laminated dough and not have to work out her demons while she kneaded, but today was not that day.

Today was also not going to be a quiet day. By the time Cuthbert arrived, resplendent in a suit covered in tiny Father Christmases, swiftly followed by Sophie, who'd come as a very cute elf, and Sam who'd come as a much less cute elf (such were Sophie's powers of persuasion), there was already a sizeable queue outside the tearooms.

'Wow!' Mattie said, taking in the sight of the three of them. The sight of Sam in an elf onesie would stay with her until her dying day. And as for Cuthbert . . . 'That is a whole lot of look!'

'It's Christmas,' Sophie said, digging into her bag for something and pulling out a pair of reindeer antlers that lit up when she flicked a switch. 'These are for you. I got them in—'

'The pound shop, yes. Somebody should ban you from that place,' Mattie said, folding her arms and pressing her lips together to keep back the smile that was tugging at the corners of her mouth. 'And I'm not putting those *things* on my head.'

'Scrooge.' Sophie advanced towards Mattie, who took a little step back.

'The same Scrooge who was planning on giving you a very generous Christmas bonus?' Mattie asked.

'The lady doth protest too much,' Cuthbert decreed, plucking the antlers from Sophie's hand and plonking them on Mattie's head. 'That's better!'

There was no point in arguing, Mattie decided. Just like she'd long since stopped complaining about Sophie and Cuthbert's stealth Christmas bombing of the tearooms. There was now so much tinsel, bunting and paperchains, not to mention miniature Christmas trees and a whole heap of festive-themed table ornaments, that it was hard to tell where the Christmas decorations ended and the tearooms began.

The festive spirit was contagious: as they got busy with their pre-opening chores, Mattie even found herself duetting with Cuthbert on 'Baby, It's Cold Outside' even though it was basically a song about date rape.

The prep was soon done and the first coffees and pastries were being served but there was still an impatient queue outside, waiting for Happy Ever After to open. Yet there was no sign of Tom, who was no doubt stewing in his own hungover juices.

'Oh God, we need more people than this,' Mattie exclaimed. She could feel her blood pressure rising and stopping somewhere in her left eyelid, which was twitching wildly. 'Sam, I want you to go upstairs and haul Tom out of bed.'

'I don't feel comfortable doing that,' Sam said, as he tried to hide behind the baby reindeer, which was looking decidedly the worse for wear. They were never going to get the deposit back. There was a sudden commotion at the door and Mattie, fearing that the queue was about to turn nasty, hurried over to tell them to pipe down. That was when she saw Nina standing there.

She had to be hallucinating because Nina should have been at home, convalescing after breaking pretty much every bone in her body – not standing outside the shop on crutches, sporting a fetching neck brace, and generally being held up by Noah.

Mattie quickly unlocked the door to let them in.

'It's so good to see you!' Mattie cried, moving in to hug Nina, but she was body blocked by Noah.

'Mind the ribs!' he said as Nina began to make her very slow and very laborious way to the sofa.

'Sophie, I need you to deploy cushions,' Nina ordered, as Mattie quickly shut the door and held up her hands to the queue to indicate that they might be open in another five minutes. Possibly.

'I can't believe you've come to help us in our hour of need,' Mattie exclaimed. 'Nina, this is really going above and beyond.'

'I know,' Nina agreed, wincing a little as she sat up so that Sophie could stick a couple of cushions behind her back. 'But I've just been so bored at home. I did a whole binge watch of *Sex and the City*, which, by the way, hasn't aged well, and if I had to spend one more day cooped up in our flat, I was going to scream.'

'Oh dear. But . . . you can work though, can't you?' Mattie asked urgently.

'No,' Noah said firmly.

'Yes,' Nina said equally firmly. 'I can operate an iPad so people can pay me and I can direct them from here to any book in the shop. In fact, I'm amazed that you managed without me for even these last few days.'

'Great!' Mattie said, rubbing her hands in agitation. 'I'm going to open up now. Sam! Why haven't you gone upstairs and dragged Tom out of his bed?'

'Because I'm already up.' Tom staggered through the door that led to the flat. 'Evidently.'

He was barely up, clinging to the counter with a white-knuckled hand, and his face was grey. Mattie had zero sympathy.

'Well, you should have been down here ready to start work ten minutes ago.' She turned round sharply so she wouldn't have to look at the man who was apparently done with her. 'I'm going to open the shop now and you'll have to manage without me for fifteen minutes because I do have tearooms to run as well, you know.'

'Why has Mattie got a massive stick up her arse?' Mattie heard Nina ask as she flicked the shop sign to 'Open' and unlocked the door. Mattie was quite tempted to tell Nina exactly why, but there was no time.

Meanwhile, the tearooms were in chaos. There was a large and grumbling queue snaking back from the counter where Jezebel was making a series of angry hissing noises like she was about to blow at any second. Mattie could empathise.

'What's going on?' she asked Cuthbert who was not looking his usual unflappable self but very frazzled. He was down to his shirtsleeves as he prodded at his beloved coffee machine.

'Jezebel is very unhappy today,' Cuthbert explained. 'She doesn't want anything to do with steaming milk.'

Mattie tugged on her fringe in frustration. 'Bloody Jezebel!'

'It's that sort of attitude that's made her so ornery,' Cuthbert said sadly. 'I've called the engineer, but he can't come out until the new year.'

'Typical!' Mattie groaned. 'Well, it's black coffee, then, or nothing.' There came a frantic beeping from the depths of her apron pocket. 'Oh God, that's my alarm, I need to take stuff out of the oven.'

It was a morning from hell. Even though Mattie had written an apologetic note and pinned it to both tearoom door and the recalcitrant Jezebel, she had to explain countless times (at least one hundred and forty-seven, at a conservative estimate) to furious customers what the hot-drink situation was.

Added to that, she kept being called to the shop to help out because of all the thoughtless people who'd left their present buying to the very last minute. Sophie was trying to man the Mistletoe Booth queue but no one was respecting her authority. Nina was reclining on the sofa like an elderly monarch and serving people in a very languid, not-at-all speedy way. Sam and Tom were behind the counter and being monosyllabic with their customers.

'I haven't seen them mouth "Merry Christmas" to a single customer,' Posy complained on her fifth phone call of the morning. 'Tell them off! Do it now!'

'I would love to but I don't actually have time to tell anyone off,' Mattie said, as one of the timers in her apron pocket started beeping. 'In fact, I'm going back to the tearooms now.'

'Before you do that, can you angle the webcam so that I can get a better view of the counter?' Posy asked. Mattie had never been more tempted to throw her phone in the nearest body of water. 'Also, you and Tom haven't had a single row this morning, which is quite disappointing.'

'The day is young and Posy, spying on your employees and then reporting the spying back to your husband, who then tells *his* employees, such as my best friend, Pippa, has to be breaking several laws,' Mattie panted as she shouldered some customers out of the way on her journey back to the tearooms.

'I'm pretty sure it isn't,' Posy said cheerfully; enforced bed rest was obviously agreeing with her.

'I haven't got time for this,' Mattie said, hanging up on Posy and vowing that, unless the shop was on fire (and given how today was panning out, that was a distinct possibility), she wasn't going to answer any more of Posy's calls. She felt very good about this decision.

There was very little to feel good about until five minutes to twelve when Mattie came barrelling into the shop to make sure everyone was working at full capacity and saw Happy Ever After's erstwhile manager walk through the door.

'Verity! Is it really you or am I having a stress-induced hallucination?' Mattie cried.

'Don't hug me!' Verity said, inching away from Mattie, who was trying to do just that. 'This isn't a hugging situation. The snow turned to slush and we'd promised to spend Christmas with Johnny's dad in London so, here I am. You don't need me to serve *actual* customers, though, right? I should probably get on top of the website orders.'

'Verity Love, it's Christmas Eve, if you don't get behind this counter and serve *actual* customers, then I will never speak to you again,' Tom snapped from where he was dealing with Bertha, who was almost as frazzled as Jezebel. 'Worse, I'll sign you up to a find-a-friend service and tons of randoms will get in touch with you, wanting to chat.'

'You wouldn't dare,' Verity breathed.

It was Tom at his narrow-eyed worst. 'Just try me.'

Considering she was the most responsible grown-up on

staff, Verity stomped behind the counter with all the bad grace of a surly teenager and, though they were down a Posy, Mattie could let them get on with it.

She went upstairs to the flat to start bringing down the pig-in-blanket rolls that Meena had been making while Phil had languished on the sofa complaining that the smell of bacon was making him feel sick. Eventually the smell of bacon had revived him and he'd wolfed down five pig-in-blanket rolls that were meant for paying customers.

'Four more hours,' Mattie muttered under her breath, as she raced back down the stairs with a laden cooling tray in each hand. 'Four more hours and then it will be over for three days and you'll never have to look at another pig-in-blanket roll or a mince pie or a red velvet cake masquerading as a miniature Christmas pudding, for eleven whole months.'

'Excuse me, but why aren't you serving cappuccino?' As Mattie stepped into the tearooms, a woman in a bright-yellow faux-fur coat popped out of nowhere, giving Mattie such a fright that pig-in-blanket rolls went flying in all directions.

'Oh, damn it all to hell!' Mattie tipped her head back, blinked her eyes frantically and willed herself not to burst into tears.

'No use in crying over spilt pig-in-blanket rolls,' Sophie said sympathetically as she came over to clear up the porcine-and-pastry carnage. 'By the way, did you know that Chiro has heard that Jezebel's had a meltdown? One of his sons is standing at the entrance to the mews and telling all our potential customers to turn back if they want a hot drink made with steamed milk.'

'I can't,' Mattie said, sinking down heavily on the nearest chair and disturbing a young couple who were feeding each other cupcakes. 'I just can't any more. I've nothing left to give.'

'Oh dear.' Sophie shepherded Mattie back into the kitchen and delivered in short order a double espresso and a pain au chocolat, which did wonders for Mattie's energy levels, so that when Sam summoned her back to the shop an hour later, she was nearly fully revived.

'It's just Nina's dying for a wee and also it's against the law not to let us have a fifteen-minute break after we've worked for five hours.'

'Nearer to four hours, as we opened at nine. But of course, go for it.'

'Then me and Sophie are going to Burger King to get chicken nuggz,' Sam insisted. 'That's non-negotiable.'

Mattie didn't dare argue, but took over from Verity who needed to accompany Nina to the lavatory, which meant that she and Tom were the last two members of shop staff standing.

Tom looked a lot less grey than he had done earlier, but he was still very tight of lip as he served customers from behind the counter in a very mechanical way, while Mattie took up position at the Mistletoe Booth.

Instead of explaining about the lack of steamed milk to people who were quite capable of reading a sign, she now had to explain that you could only use the booth on proof of purchase, to people who were equally capable of reading a sign.

No wonder the queue was always so long, the couple currently in there went way over their allotted ninety seconds.

'I look so chinny,' the girl kept exclaiming, until Mattie could bear it no longer and pulled back the curtain.

'Thirty more seconds and I'm cutting you off,' she told them. 'It's a bloody selfie, you're not shooting the cover of *Vogue*.'

'What a bitch!' the girl muttered as Mattie pulled the curtain closed again.

'One minute,' she announced to the people still waiting. 'You have one minute in the booth. Sixty seconds and that's it.'

There was a general, discontented mumbling, which Mattie silenced with her best bitch face.

'I don't think that's reasonable,' Tom called out from behind the counter. 'A minute isn't long enough.'

'A minute is plenty of time and I don't remember asking for your opinion,' Mattie called back.

'Fine. Good. Glad we've cleared that up.' Tom glared at Mattie over the top of his current customer's head and she glared back, and how long did it take people to have a wee, get chicken nuggets and no doubt snog each other's faces off?

By the time Nina and Verity were back from the loo, Sophie and Sam had returned with their chicken nuggets spoils and Cuthbert had popped in to say Cynthia had asked him to go to Boots to get some Rennies and a shower cap, Tom and Mattie were nose to nose in the middle of the shop.

Shouting at each other.

Again.

'When someone asks you if we provide a gift-wrapping service, you don't say to them, "You've got to be kidding me,"' Mattie told Tom in no uncertain terms, her hands on her hips. 'Honestly, you shouldn't be allowed near the general public.'

'And you shouldn't be allowed to boss me about when I've worked here longer and I have a doctorate!'

'But it's in books, it's not in anything *useful*!'

'So says the woman who has a diploma in cake!'

'It's patisserie!'

'Cupcakes. A certificate in cupcakery,' Tom snorted.

'That's not even a word, Tom.'

They were circling each other now, like two wild animals ready to spot a weakness in their opponent and pounce. The Christmas Eve crowd and their colleagues had all melted away and all Mattie could see was Tom and his infuriating, lofty face.

'When I first met you, I thought you were cool and laid back with your Audrey Hepburn vibe and the witty French twist on classic English bakes,' Tom said thoughtfully. 'But it soon turned out that you were completely uptight and controlling, and Audrey Hepburn must be turning in her grave over the fact that you stole her look.'

Mattie opened and shut her mouth a few times. How

dare he? How very dare he? 'Well . . . well . . .' she blustered, absolutely unable to use her words. 'My opinion on you hasn't changed because I thought you were a dull, dusty academic with a cardigan that should be burned, and even if you did turn out to be charming and handsome with hidden depths, you've ruined several of my non-stick pans by scraping at them with metal utensils. So there!'

'Why are you so obsessed with my cardigans?'

'Because they're an affront to my eyes! That one with the leather patches on the elbows – what were you thinking when you bought it?'

'That it would be both warm in a draughty shop and practical because I tend to wear out the elbows on my other cardigans from leaning on them when I'm reading. Charming and handsome, eh?' Tom stepped closer to her and she could hardly breathe.

'I didn't say that,' she denied in a throaty little voice.

'You did. You definitely did,' Nina called out and Mattie and Tom looked around and realised that they had an audience of not just their colleagues but an entire shop of book buyers.

'That's quite enough,' Tom decided and in one of those smooth, deceptively strong moves of his, he pulled Mattie into the just vacated Mistletoe Booth, sitting down on the stool and pulling her into his lap.

'I don't know why you're going all Alpha Male when you're obviously not interested in me. Phil said that you were done with women and their tote bags and their cupcakes, so you obviously meant me!'

'I never said that,' Tom protested, putting his arms around Mattie, which made her precarious position on his lap much more comfortable. 'Phil's unintelligible recalls of last night's activities would never stand up in a court of law.'

'You can't be done with me: we're not even doing anything for it to be done with,' Mattie said.

'You're done with me! You can't even remember kissing me, when that kiss was one of the greatest moments of my life,' Tom said in a hurt voice.

'But you said that *you* couldn't remember the kiss!'

'Only because you said that *you* couldn't remember it first. I didn't want to be accused of kissing you when you were incapacitated, though I genuinely didn't think you were incapacitated at the time.' Tom frowned.

'I wasn't incapacitated but I am confused. You're the king of mixed messages,' Mattie said, placing her hand flat on his chest so she could feel his heart positively thundering away. 'One day you're shouting at me about tote bags, then the next day, you're *stroking* my hair. Don't even try to deny the hair stroking this time.'

'I denied it because you clearly don't feel the same way about me as I feel about you. I mean, you said you were ready to start seeing other men now that you're over your evil ex-boyfriend.'

'I don't want to see other men,' Mattie said and Tom's face fell and even though his arms were still around her, she felt him withdraw, shuttering his charming and handsome features so he became a pinch-faced stranger again.

'So, you still hate *all* men,' he confirmed sadly.

'Not *all* men . . .' Mattie began but stopped when Tom rested his forehead on her shoulder as if he was in despair.

'I really didn't want to take advantage, Mattie,' he said, swallowing hard. 'I felt so guilty about kissing you. It's a very fine line to walk when you're attracted to someone who's been hurt before by a man who blurred all the boundaries. If my attentions were unwelcome . . .'

'Goodness me! I kissed you back! With bells on! For someone who has a PhD in romantic fiction, you really are clueless when it comes to picking up signals,' Mattie said, gently tugging on Tom's hair so he had to raise his head and see the tenderness that had softened her features. 'I don't hate *all* men but I don't want to see other men when the only man I want to see is you.'

There was a moment's silence and Mattie couldn't look at Tom any more so she stared down at the floor, at his feet in his old-fashioned brown lace-ups, until he cleared his throat. 'Oh, I see. Well, that rather changes things, doesn't it?'

Mattie's heart was beating just as fast as Tom's, even as it unfurled like a flower, when before it had been tucked away out of harm's reach. 'I hope it does.'

'I do know that I'm punching above my weight with you and that if you did decide to see other men, then there's no way I can compare, with my cardigans and my dull academic books,' Tom said and Mattie put a finger to his lips so he couldn't say any more because he was talking utter rubbish.

'Underneath the cardigans is some pretty fine muscula-ture,' she said. 'The way you leapt over the gate when we were trying to free Strumpet . . . I hardly even noticed the hunky firemen after that display of impressive upper-body strength.'

Tom met her eyes. 'You've been perving on me *all* this time?' he asked. 'While I was compartmentalising. Separating work from life, business from pleasure.' He all but purred the last word and his eyes were fixed on Mattie, darkening when she nervously licked her lips.

'Not *all* the time. There's also quite a lot of time that I'm genuinely cross with you.' Mattie put her arms around Tom's neck, so they were nose to nose again. 'You're not punching above your weight with me. Not at all. Apart from my certificate in – what did you call it? – *cupcakery*, I left school with two GCSEs and the only books I read are cookbooks.'

'Well, nobody's perfect,' Tom said. 'But perfection is kind of boring.'

'So boring,' Mattie agreed and like the one angry kiss that they'd shared weeks before, she couldn't say who kissed who first, only that they were kissing.

Four years ago, she'd run away to Paris. Two years ago, she'd run away from Paris. And over the last two years, even as she carved out a life for herself in London, striving for and achieving her dreams, it had still always felt as if something was missing.

Now, as she sat in a glorified photo booth in the arms of a man who was a leading expert on romantic fiction, his mouth on hers, his thumb doing something quite delicious to the pulse point behind her left ear, Mattie was no longer running. There was no longer something missing. She was where she wanted to be with someone that she wanted to be with.

'So much nicer kissing each other when we're not in the middle of a fight,' she murmured when they came up for air.

'I think we can do much better than nice,' Tom declared, taking her mouth again. Mattie didn't know how long they kissed under the solitary sprig of quite bedraggled mistletoe, but suddenly the curtain was pulled back by Sophie, who was clutching something in her hand. Something that looked a lot like a webcam, while in her other hand, she had a mobile phone on speaker so they could hear Posy squawking, 'Can you two do that *after* we shut up shop? There's still two hours left of shopping time.'

'Yeah, get a room,' Nina called out from the sofa where her neck was craned so she didn't miss out on any of the action.

'And to think that you tell me and Sophie off when we're kissing,' Sam piped up, then turned pillar-box red as Nina and Verity looked at him with great interest. 'Not that we were actually kissing and anyway, this is about Tom and Mattie. Who were definitely kissing. Look at them!'

Both blushing furiously, Tom and Mattie peered out at the shop floor and the people peering in at them. Mostly customers, most of them smiling indulgently, who broke out into a round of spontaneous applause.

'We don't need an audience, thank you very much,' Mattie said, pulling the curtain shut again.

'Couldn't agree more,' Tom said. 'Though I have to say, maybe Christmas isn't so bad after all.'

'Christmas has been severely underrated,' Mattie said, pulling his head down so their lips were on a level. 'Now why aren't you kissing me?'

CHAPTER

35

Christmas Day

'Merry Christmas, Tom,' Mattie said, nudging him with her elbow so he'd wake.

They'd spent all night on the sofa, dozing in between the snuggling, stroking and so much kissing that Mattie thought that her lips might be about to go on strike.

Tom struggled to alertness, his hair rumpled in fifty directions, his eyes bleary but focused. He'd sworn last night that he absolutely needed his glasses but when Mattie tried to take them off so she could try them on, he'd batted her hands away, which had just led to more kissing. A lot more kissing.

'Did you just wish me Merry Christmas?' he mumbled. 'You know I don't do Christmas.'

'You're going to have to do Christmas this year,' Mattie said, settling back in his arms, which Tom obligingly wrapped round her. 'Ian's coming round to pick us up in an hour. My mother's told him not to come back empty-handed. Unless . . .' A thought occurred, which made her frown, which made Tom instantly kiss her furrowed brow.

'Unless . . .?' he prompted.

'Unless, you think it's far, far too soon to meet my family,' Mattie blurted out.

'Technically I have already met your family,' Tom pointed out. 'And I would say you could come to mine for Christmas but I was meant to be on the six o'clock train out of Euston bound for Wolverhampton last night, and I'm pretty sure that my failure to catch said train has led to me being excommunicated.'

Another piece of the puzzle slotted into place. 'You're from Wolverhampton?'

Tom smiled and tugged at a lock of Mattie's hair. 'That's not really important right now. What's important is that all we have foodwise is several pig-in-blanket rolls and a few cupcakes left over from yesterday, so I'm more than happy to spend the twenty-fifth of December with you . . .'

'Christmas Day! Just say it, Tom,' Mattie said, rolling her eyes.

'Never!'

Mattie's phone beeped.

'That will be my mum again, demanding to know if I have a spare roll of tinfoil or if I can bring my second-best rolling pin with me.' Mattie rolled her eyes.

'I love that you have a second-best rolling pin,' Tom

said, as Mattie retrieved her phone from beneath a cushion.

But the text message was from Posy with a picture attachment of . . .

'Oh! Oh my days! Oh my goodness, you're never going to believe this,' Mattie exclaimed, handing over her phone so Tom could read the message too.

You'll be pleased to know that you and Tom and your shenanigans made me go into early labour. Lavinia Angharad Lady Agatha Morland-Thorndyke (Lala for short) was born at half past seven this morning, weighing in at a very respectable seven pounds. Mother and baby doing blissfully well. Love, Posy xxx

And there was a beaming Posy sitting on her kitchen floor, propped up against the stove (obviously there hadn't been time to get to the hospital), cradling a tiny, swaddled baby in her arms.

'I said that she was very pregnant,' Tom said, although he'd said no such thing. But Mattie let him off because he was furiously scrubbing away the tear that had begun to trickle down his left cheek. She could feel the prickle of happy tears herself. 'Still, it's nice to know that Lavinia lives on.'

'It is,' Mattie said softly. Their eyes met and as their lips found each other again, he whispered, 'Merry Christmas.'

Less than three miles away, Verity and Johnny were sitting down to a Christmas brunch of eggs benedict and champagne. As they held their glasses up in a toast, the diamonds on Verity's engagement ring caught the lights twinkling on the Christmas tree, which were a perfect match for the sparkle in her eyes.

A few miles to the south-east, Nina and Noah were snuggled on their own sofa. Well, partially snuggled as Nina's injuries didn't allow for full snuggling. And also owing to Nina's injuries (which hardly hurt at all now), they'd cried off going to their respective families. Now they could stay in their own cosy flat to drink all the cocktails and eat all the food, as they spent their first Christmas together.

At the same moment, in Bloomsbury, Sebastian Thorndyke wrestled a huge turkey into the oven as Posy Morland-Thorndyke supervised, while her three-hour-old daughter slept in her arms.

Outside in Bloomsbury Square, Sam and Sophie (who'd told their respective caregivers that they were just popping out for some fresh air, though their respective caregivers knew exactly why they were really popping out) sat huddled together on a bench and kissed, while around them the first few fat flakes of snow began to fall.

And so it was that all the staff of the Happy Ever After bookshop and tearooms really did live happily ever after.

Acknowledgements

Thank you to my agent Rebecca Ritchie for getting me through the difficult business of writing a Christmas novel in the middle of a flaming heatwave!

Huge thanks also to my editor Martha Ashby who, when my Christmas spirit was flagging, encouraged me to listen to some carols and eat some mince pies as the temperature edged into the nineties. I'm sure my neighbours secretly loved listening to the Phil Spector Christmas album on repeat. Thanks are also due to Jaime Frost, Emma Pickard, Eloisa Clegg and all the team at HarperCollins.

An extra special, perfectly punctuated thank you to Simon Fox, the best copy editor in the business.

Finally, I want to thank all the readers, bloggers, reviewers and lovers of romance novels who have browsed the shelves of Happy Ever After with me. It's been an absolute pleasure to write these books for you.